AFTER THE WEDDING

BOOKS BY LAURA ELLIOT

Fragile Lies

Stolen Child

The Prodigal Sister

The Betrayal

Sleep Sister

Guilty

The Wife Before Me

The Thorn Girl

The Silent House

AFTER THE WEDDING

LAURA ELLIOT

bookouture

Published by Bookouture in 2022

An imprint of Storyfire Ltd.
Carmelite House
50 Victoria Embankment
London EC4Y 0DZ

www.bookouture.com

Paperback ISBN: 978-1-80314-102-2
eBook ISBN: 978-1-80314-101-5

After the Wedding is dedicated to my circle of family and friends. To those who enrich my life with love, laughter, music, song, food and good conversation, thank you one and all.

PROLOGUE

Everyone said Christine was the prettiest flower girl, ever. More beautiful even than the bride but, *shush*, that was a secret, a finger to their lips when they told her. She looked like a princess, with sparkly shoes and a lacy, purple dress with petticoats. Now, her flower-girl dress lies on the floor. It's wet and torn, and her shoes are lost.

'Tell us – what happened to you?' They keep asking her the same question over and over. They don't say cross words about her dress, even though it's ruined from the river. Instead, they tell her: 'You fell into the river, Christine, darling, but you're safe now with Mammy and Daddy.'

The doctor gives her an injection. It hurts but not for long. He says she now has the cleanest lungs in all of Dorset. He puts ointment on the big cut on her forehead and tells her to stay away from rivers in future.

'Where did you go?' Daddy asks her again. *Tell us... tell us... tell us.* His forehead is wrinkly and there's red all around his eyes. Mammy's cheeks are black from the mascara and she's no longer wearing her floppy wedding hat.

Sharon comes into the bedroom and says, 'Oh, my lambkin,

what a fright you gave us.' She has taken off her wedding dress and is wearing a yellow one with ruffles that flounce. She doesn't look happy anymore. Not the way she did when Christine was scattering petals all along the aisle to make a carpet of love for her to walk over.

Tell us... tell us... They won't stop asking about the river. When she falls asleep, Christine sees it leaping and roaring. But that's okay because she's wrapped tight in Mammy's arms and the dream is gone when she awakens.

She remembers running through the rose garden. Red roses everywhere, not like the petals she scattered for Sharon – they were antique-gold petals, like her wedding dress. Christine scattered them all along the aisle of the church. Everyone turned to look at her. They were all adults because Sharon didn't want children at her wedding. 'Only you, my little flower girl,' she'd said. 'You have the most important task of all to do.'

No one noticed her anymore when they reached the hotel. It was just like a really posh castle with suits of armour standing inside the entrance and swords criss-crossed on the walls. Everyone went out into the rose garden and held glasses with long stems. They talked... talked... *talked*. The sun dazzled her eyes. It would dance in the sky if she stared at it for too long. Then she would go blind. The grown-ups didn't notice when she pulled one of the roses apart. She watched the petals fly away on the breeze. She pulled the petals from another rose, then another. Grumpy, old Great-uncle Ned frowned so hard she ran away.

That's all... that's all... She tries hard to please Mammy and Daddy but she can't think of anything else except the hole in the wall at the end of the rose garden. Two steps up and two steps down into the meadow. It was filled with buttercups that reached up to her knees. She could see a real castle on a hill. It was old and scary, just walls with holes that looked like eyes watching her. She turned the other way and the long grass swished against her flower-girl dress as she ran... and ran.

But that's a memory that comes like a dream and flies away from her again.

All she can see are the roses. Big, thorny roses with their droopy heads and the red petals spilling like drops of blood to the ground.

PART 1

ONE
CHRISTINE

She has a feeling about Jessica from the beginning. *Unsettling* – that is the only word Christine can use to define the sensation that affects her whenever she leaves her office and enters Foundation Stone's central hub with its circle of work stations and small, private alcoves, its bucket armchairs, coffee bar, storyboards and flat screens. Jessica is usually on her laptop, fingers flying over the keyboard, her attention on the screen. She wears her hair loose, streaks of red highlighting the sleek brown strands. Sometimes she ties it in a ponytail, which accentuates her cheekbones. She is beautiful but Christine, who has been working in advertising for ten years, is accustomed to beauty and its allure. However, she is not immune to its impact. Like a perfect painting or the streaks of a flame-hued sunset, beauty will always quicken her heartbeat and it is this same sensation, only sharper, and almost disconcerting, that she experiences when her gaze settles on Jessica.

Christine shakes herself, as if awakening from a reverie, and hurries back to the quietness of her own office.

Jessica looks younger than she remembers from the interview: more like a teenager than a woman in her mid-twenties.

Her hair was in a chignon then, a sophisticated style that she wore with confidence as she sat upright but relaxed on a high-backed chair, her legs together, her hands cupped primly on her lap as she faced Christine and her husband, Richard Stone. Jessica's reference from the editor of the celebrity magazine *Zing* was excellent, and her knowledge of digital marketing, especially her awareness of the reach of social media, was impressive enough for Richard to nudge Christine discreetly with his elbow to signal his approval. Had she been aware of her uneasiness then? She and Richard had been interviewing all day and Jessica came to them in the late afternoon. If she had experienced any disquiet, it was forgotten when she agreed with Richard that Jessica Newman was the most suitable candidate for the position of copywriter. Since then, she has become part of the competitive, argumentative and flamboyant team that has made Foundation Stone one of the most successful advertising agencies in Dublin.

Christine tries to analyse her reaction to their newest employee. Is she afraid Richard will be attracted to her? Is it something as simple as jealousy? Christine shakes this thought off and wonders if, at the age of thirty-five, she is becoming attracted to women or, in particular, to one woman? This possibility is also dismissed. She is as confident in her sexuality as she is in her marriage. One possibility is that Jessica reminds her of someone. She has no idea who that could be yet there is something transfixing about her – tantalising, even. Christine feels as if she is on the verge of making this connection yet it continues to elude her.

She must stop watching her. It seems voyeuristic, unworthy of her, but denying her fixation only adds to her awareness of the younger woman's presence. This constant preoccupation could become irritating: an itch that can't be scratched, which is an unpleasant comparison to make but that is what it is beginning to feel like as the first month of Jessica's presence at the agency draws to a close.

Christine considers firing her. A performance assessment will be coming up at the end of the second month. Richard will carry it out but a few hints from Christine could shape the result. But what hints, what reasons can she possibly give him to justify firing Jessica? How can she explain to him that Jessica Newman is no longer a suitable employee because she causes Christine's heart to tremble?

TWO

The tide is high on the Liffey as Christine crosses over the Ha'penny Bridge and a gusting October wind forces her to hold onto the brim of her hat. She has booked a table for two at Mira's Restaurant in the Italian quarter and is the first to arrive.

Seated by the window, she watches Amy hurrying as fast as it is possible to do with a three-month-old baby in a sling. Making time for Amy is important. Christine's friendships have dwindled in recent years as more of her friends marry and become mothers. Apart from Amy, she has let them go. She is too busy with her career to pretend to be interested in the merits of breastfeeding or the agonies of that first tooth forcing its way through tender gums.

Amy arrives with a breathless explanation about a delay at the Rotunda Hospital where Daniel was undergoing a test for something or other. Christine's ignorance about baby matters is profound. Daniel remains undisturbed as his mother unwraps various straps from around her body, and then holds him out to be admired.

Christine coos and gurgles at him, a procedure that fixes her face in a rictus-like smile. She doesn't dislike babies. She enjoys them when they belong to other people, and is convinced that they must abhor the nonsensical sounds and expressions adults force upon them until they are old enough to be treated normally.

'How's life with New Girl?' Amy asks, after the waitress has departed with their orders. 'Do you like her any better?'

'I never said I disliked her.'

'Sounds like it, from what you've told me over the phone.'

'She disturbs me, but it's hard to dislike her. I can't put my finger on it. Just when I think I've become used to having her around she triggers this uneasy feeling in me again. It's as if I've seen her before but can't remember where.'

'What does she look like?'

'She's... oh... I guess she's beautiful.'

'Beauty is nothing new in the great dream factory.'

'True enough.' Christine often wonders how she gravitated towards an industry that is based on illusion. If she hadn't met Richard and been introduced to a world where imagination has the ability to conjure a different reality, she would never have appreciated the creativity necessary to lift a product from the mundane into a must-buy brand. Richard's vision and her hard-headed financial acumen, they are the perfect business partnership.

'You were saying...' Amy is waiting for a response.

There is nothing illusionary about Jessica, yet Christine finds it hard to describe her. Eyes, green, framed by dark, sweeping eyelashes; a perfect nose; and lips that are full yet not excessive enough to take from the symmetry of her face. Her skin is flawless, her legs long and shapely, her figure in proportion. She is like a self-assembly kit with no screws left over at the end of construction.

Amy laughs at this description and when their food arrives, she returns to the subject of Jessica. 'It's unlike you to be insecure. Are you sure that feeling is not related to Richard?'

'I'm *not* insecure. And if you're suggesting I've something to worry about with Richard—'

'No... no,' – Amy backtracks quickly – 'I know you've nothing to worry about there. But could *she* be attracted to him?'

'They work closely together but it's professional. I'd know immediately if it was otherwise.'

'How can you tell?'

'Antennae alert. I always trust it.'

Amy sighs. 'I'm so busy wiping off dribble that Jonathan could be keeping a harem and I wouldn't know a thing about it.' She says it cheerfully and draws her scarf around her shoulders as Daniel stirs, his lips puckering.

Christine looks away as her friend unbuttons her blouse. She should be used to it by now. Daniel is Amy's third baby in four years and her friend has been breastfeeding for what seems to Christine like an eternity. 'I feel as if I know her, which isn't possible because we never met until I interviewed her.'

'Maybe you knew her in another lifetime?'

'Other lifetimes don't exist.'

'So you keep saying. But what do we really know about the dimensions beyond this one? I read a book recently. I'll email the title to you. You really should read it and broaden your horizons.' Amy insists there is more to life than the mortal coil they occupy. She reads tarot cards, studies the energy of chakras and has an angel who comforts her during night feeds. She will email the title of the book to Christine, who will promise to buy it then forget to do so.

They part amicably. For once, Amy has not warned Christine about the tick-tock of her biological clock. For that reason, she is hugged tightly before she straps her baby in front of her and transforms him into a contented joey.

. . .

The restaurants and sandwich bars on Temple Bar are quieter after the lunchtime rush when Christine returns to the agency. She loves this part of the city with its cobbled streets and old buildings. Foundation Stone sits between an art gallery and a bar that specialises in craft beers. No matter how often she studies the brass plate on the exterior wall with *Foundation Stone Advertising Agency* engraved on it, she feels a swell of pride when she thinks about everything that she and Richard have achieved since they met.

Eleven years previously, Christine had been travelling home from work when the train stopped shortly after leaving Connolly station. Passengers had muttered and checked their watches when ten minutes passed and no announcement had been made to explain the delay. Christine shrugged resignedly at the man sitting opposite her when a crackling explanation was finally heard.

'Did you understand one word he said?' she asked.

'I've learned to interpret "tannoy".' He grinned back at her. 'It happens if you travel regularly on the 5.30 to Glencone. We should be moving again in another five minutes.'

'You must be quite a linguist, then.'

'A modest one,' he replied. 'You're a new learner. You'll pick it up soon enough.'

'What makes you think I'm a new learner?'

'I recognise you from the station in the mornings. The 7.35 express to Connelly but only recently. You're a newbie to Glencone. Am I right?'

She nodded and laughed with him. To be observed yet be unaware of someone else's scrutiny could be unnerving, but on that occasion, she found it flattering.

By the time the train was moving again they were talking animatedly. He was an only child whose mother had died two years previously. Glencone seed and breed, he said, unlike Christine, who had only recently moved there. Its distance from the centre of the city had made her apartment affordable, but she was still trying to adjust to the quietness of the small, coastal village.

How had she not noticed him among the commuters in the morning? He was tall and handsome enough to stand out from the crowd, and when she arrived at Glencone station the following morning, it was Richard Stone who filled her eyes. She was twenty-five and bored with her job in finance. Richard, two years older, was an advertising executive with plans to open his own agency. She lacked the innovative spark that was driving him forward but she could see the potential for him to expand rapidly if the clients he hoped to attract followed him from his current position.

Over the following months, she helped him to formulate a proposal to present to his bank manager. Somehow, they managed to do so in tandem with falling in love; heady, dizzy days, when all they needed was a look, a word, a gesture, to wind up in each other's arms. She re-mortgaged her apartment when his proposal was accepted, and became his business partner. A year after that first meeting, they were married and living at High Spires, an apartment complex within walking distance to their new agency.

Despite the struggle to make a success of Foundation Stone, it had seemed as if nothing could go wrong until three years ago, when Tom, Richard's father, was diagnosed with progressive supranuclear palsy, a rare brain disorder that was beginning to affect his balance. When it became clear that Tom was unable to manage by himself, they rented their apartment and she moved with Richard into Redstone, his family home. Tom was easy to love. His noisy, enthusiastic personality dominated the house where he had lived both as a boy and a married man. But as his illness became more advanced, Richard and Christine found it difficult to give him the care he needed. Some months previously, aware that his condition was deteriorating, he had informed them that he intended moving into a nursing home.

Tonight, after they have eaten, they will visit him. He will advise them to have children and fill Redstone with their laughter. No sense telling him that they have no interest in children. They have each other, and Foundation Stone is their own unique creation.

The familiar rhythm of the agency greets Christine when she enters the main office. Lorraine, the graphic designer, is working on her laptop and Rory from research interrupts a phone call to wriggle his fingers at her. Richard, unaware that she has returned, is checking his mobile on the coffee deck.

The door to Christine's office is open and Jessica is standing in front of her desk. She is in profile, the light from the window highlighting the russet streaks in her hair. Christine is uncomfortably aware that she has spent a sizable chunk of her lunch hour talking to Amy about her. The fluttering feeling in her chest strengthens as she focuses on the line of Jessica's shoulders, the curve of her chin. Unlike Richard's office, hers is a private space and the unwritten rule is to knock before entering.

Jessica smiles when she sees her but her face is strained, as if Christine's arrival is an unwelcome intrusion into her thoughts. 'It's beautiful.' She gestures towards the billboard-sized Kava poster that has pride of place behind Christine's desk. 'Richard's decision to film on Cullain was brilliant. Kava was one of his finest campaigns. I'm not surprised it won him the Elora Award.'

The poster is only one of many on the office walls but it is the largest and most eye-catching. The island of Cullain swells beyond the rocks like a bloated stomach. A model, bare-footed and wearing a white dress that clings to her body yet allows the diaphanous material to play with the wind, is balanced on the edge of a foreboding plateau. As she stretches out her hand to catch a bottle of Kava perfume, she seems as airborne and as ephemeral as the swirl of sea birds and wispy clouds floating overhead.

'What made Richard choose such an unusual location?' Jessica asks.

Christine controls a sudden swell of annoyance. Filming on the island of Cullain had been her decision: Richard only agreed, reluctantly, after much discussion; yet he ended up being fascinated by Cullain's wildly beautiful isolation. But to correct Jessica and say it was her choice seems to Christine to be petulant and childish. 'The magic,' she replies, instead. 'Cullain is foreboding yet beautiful. No soft edges, just primitive, wild and unspoiled. Like Kava. Is there anything I can help you with, Jessica?'

'Are you satisfied with my performance?' The younger woman's smile is hesitant, her face suddenly flushed.

Christine looks at her. 'Yes, of course I am. What makes you think otherwise?'

'Your opinion matters to me. If anything about my work is not to your satisfaction, it would help enormously if you'd tell me what it is. I'd rather know now than later on, when I'm having my performance assessment.'

'I can assure you, if something was bothering me, you'd know about it immediately,' Christine replies crisply. 'However, your performance assessment is Richard's responsibility. I can't speak for him, apart from telling you that everything he has said about you has been positive.'

'Thank you, Christine. I appreciate your feedback. Everyone thinks the creative department is where it all happens but I understand how business operates. Every decision that's made here must have your stamp of approval. My father works in finance. Like you, he's aware of everything that goes on in the companies he runs.'

She doesn't sound gushy yet Christine can feel the furrows on her forehead deepening, a slight tension pulling at her hairline. She notes the plural in 'companies' and wonders why his daughter is not working for one of them. Jessica's comment about the financial management of the agency is true: Christine is the only one who has an awareness of how close Foundation Stone has come to closure on a number of occasions. Richard is useless with figures, or so he claims. They disrupt the imaginative flow of his thoughts. All he wants to see is the bottom line, and he has no interest in how that is achieved. Each to their own, he says, but in an agency filled with diverse talents, Christine often feels like an eagle-eyed mother trying to control her extravagant family.

Considering that she has no intention of ever having a family, the irony does not escape her.

'Isn't that the night Richard won the Elora Award?' Jessica glances at a photograph on Christine's desk.

'Yes, it is.'

'Do you mind?' She waits until Christine nods before lifting a photograph that shows Richard smiling broadly as he accepts the award for the Kava campaign. Christine is standing behind him, her image blurred by the spotlights, and Richard is the dominant image.

When she checks her watch, Jessica replaces the photograph with a muttered apology and leaves the office.

'I found Jessica in my office today after I returned from lunch,' she says, after she and Richard find seats on the train to Glencone that evening. 'She claims to be worried about her performance assessment.'

'Really? She doesn't strike me as the worrying type.'

'Me neither. That's why I'm suspicious—'

'Suspicious?' He sounds surprised. 'What do you mean?'

'Well, she had no reason to be there. And her behaviour was a little bit off.'

'How so?'

'It's hard to explain. She disturbs me.' Christine hesitates, unable to explain her reaction when Jessica turned around and saw her... kitten claws scrabbling furiously at her chest... *that* was what it felt like. She has been experiencing that same sensation since she was a child. It hits suddenly for reasons she never understands, and is so familiar that it is usually forgotten as soon as it fades.

'In what way does she disturb you?' Richard asks.

'I don't know, and that's my problem. I'm sure it will sort itself out one way or the other.'

He shrugs, obviously puzzled, but makes no further comment. They check their phones to catch up on the news of the day.

The train stops shortly after it pulls out from Connolly station. When a voice over the public address system apologises for the delay, Richard lifts an eyebrow and smiles to remind her, as he always does whenever this happens, that if it wasn't for the unreliable nature of trains, they might never have met.

THREE

Four months have passed since Jessica joined Foundation Stone and she now follows the unwritten rule to knock before entering Christine's office.

'You need to see this, Christine.' She sets her laptop down on the desk and taps into the company's Twitter account. 'Something very strange and disturbing is going on here.'

The hashtag *#foundationstoneforsale* seems to rise from the screen and blast Christine between her eyes. The hash tag has already gone viral.

'I've been responding ever since I saw the first tweet this morning,' Jessica says. 'But it's impossible to stop the speculation.'

Even as they watch the screen, new tweets appear and are retweeted, shared, liked. It seems to Christine as if the hashtag is becoming a malicious contagion, as toxic as it is infectious. 'Have you shown this to Richard?' she asks.

'Yes. He can't believe what's happening. He's on the phone right now with a client but he wants to see you in his office.'

'Foundation Stone has weathered worse than this in the

past.' Christine hopes she sounds reassuring. 'Our reputation is strong enough to cope with such ridiculous misinformation.'

Her phone rings as she is about to leave her office. The first call of the day is direct and brutal. She has known Edward Norris, the marketing director of Kava, for eight years; long enough to be aware that he never pulls his punches, yet his decision is so unexpected that she is unable to respond with anything like her usual vigour. She asks him for an explanation but he is short on words, determined not to engage in a discussion with her. His mind is made up. Already, Christine and Foundation Stone are in the past tense, and he is moving towards the next meeting on his morning schedule. Before he ends the call, he has the grace to sound mildly apologetic, but that is all he is prepared to give her: a mealy-mouthed apology that takes account of a business relationship that, until today, was based on mutual respect and a professional yet warm friendship.

'I can't believe Edward Morris would do that to you.' Jessica looks beyond her to the Kava poster – that same fixed stare that Christine interrupted when she saw her in her office alone that day.

Christine swivels her chair and looks upwards. 'It would appear that he can,' she replies. 'Your job is to set social media alight with the truth. I know I can depend on you.'

Another call is coming through as Jessica hurries from the office. This time Christine is able to reassure the marketing executive from a firm that specialises in orthopaedic mattresses that Foundation Stone is the victim of a vicious campaign that is based purely on lies.

She leaves her office and hurries towards Richard. His door is closed, which is unusual. His office is more like an extension of the central hub but, now, he is crouched over his desk, his phone to his ear. 'That was Paul Dorgan.' He replaces the phone carefully back on its cradle. 'He believes Foundation Stone is up for sale.'

'Edward Norris has been in touch.' She sinks into the armchair opposite his desk and presses her fingers to her forehead. 'He's not renewing the Kava contract for the same reason.'

'What the hell is going on?' His shocked expression reflects her own. 'Where is this coming from?'

Another call is put through to him from reception before she can reply.

'I can certainly deny that ludicrous rumour.' Anger sharpens Richard's voice when he responds to the caller. 'We've no intention of selling Foundation Stone. Make sure that that's the only headline you use on your news report, or you'll hear from our solicitor.' He slams down the receiver. 'That was the business journalist from T3X,' he tells her. 'We need to issue a statement before this rumour gains any further traction.'

He knows, as she does, the destructive nature of such gossip. Already, hawk-eyed competitors will be moving into position, preparing to poach their hard-won accounts.

'I'll contact our clients and assure them that everything is normal with the agency and that—' Christine breaks off as Richard's phone rings again. She returns to her own office to field more calls from clients demanding information.

As the day progresses, her rebuttals begin to merge into one long, blurry excuse that sounds less and less convincing. Explaining is losing. She can hear it in her voice, the heartiness of denial. *This is a bush fire,* she thinks, as she checks social media again. The match was lit overnight on Twitter but it is not only tweets that are spreading the lie. As she scrolls through various social media networking sites, she can see that the discussion on the fate of Foundation Stone has spread into an out-of-control inferno.

'Richard has written this statement.' Jessica returns to

Christine's office with her laptop and clicks into a file. 'It'll be read out on the evening business news.'

Strongly worded, the statement is a confident repudiation of the rumour and an avowal of continued support to Foundation Stone's valued clients. Christine hopes it isn't spelling out their death knell.

After Jessica leaves, she brings up Foundation Stone's financial details on her computer. There it is, their future outlined on a spread sheet: current revenue, projected revenue, outstanding accounts, forecasts. She has always been on top of the financial budget, each campaign fully costed, yet all it takes are a few cancelled contracts and a rumour mill to endanger the agency.

Despite Richard's statement, the rumours continue throughout the following days. Foundation Stone has a controversial reputation. Richard calls it 'edgy' and it's true that some of their most successful advertising campaigns have received negative publicity. None of their advertisements have ever been withdrawn or breached the advertising standards yet, now, they are being scrutinised, criticised and the facts distorted on social media. The twisted rhetoric that is being spewed out on various threads could be dismissed at any other time as nonsensical, but it is feeding a frenzy that they have no way of controlling.

Some of the posts are vicious and personal, and are aimed at Richard. He dismisses this hate mail as 'undiluted madness', but Christine can see how shaken he is by these missives and the unrelenting barrage of bad publicity. Her efforts to go through their financial situation with him adds to his distress and she is forced to keep this vital information to herself.

'Do you mind going home by yourself?' He looks crushed and exhausted by the end of the fourth day. 'I'm going straight to the nursing home. I've had a call from Gwen. Dad's had another fall—'

'Oh, my God. Is it a bad one?'

'I gather it's not too serious. But, under the circumstances, that's all I needed to hear.'

'I'll go with you.'

'Better not. It'll make him more confused than usual and you don't need to tire yourself out any further.'

'If you're sure...?' She tries not to sound relieved. Seeing her father-in-law so diminished is more than she can handle today.

'We'll talk when I come home. I promise to go through the figures with you then.'

The sea comes into view as the train pulls into Glencone station. She walks along the coast road to try and clear her head. After calling into the supermarket, she pushes open the gate to Redstone and enters the house.

She had never been conscious of Redstone's spaciousness until Tom moved into the nursing home. Without him and his numerous friends who used to call, it seems like a shell. She removes a lasagne from the fridge and turns on the oven. Dinner is ready and an open bottle of red wine is breathing on the table when Richard rings to say he has been delayed. He won't be home until after ten.

'How is Tom?' she asks.

'He's badly bruised but, thankfully, no bones are broken. He was sleeping when I left him.'

'Where are you going now?'

'To meet Jessica. She's with a reporter friend who's promised to run a piece about us in tomorrow's edition of *Capital Eye*. I'll be home as soon as I can.'

He has gone before she can ask questions. She switches on the outdoor lights and takes her meal out to the conservatory where she can see the garden at the rear of the house. The garden looks dismal and bare right now but soon it will leaf and bloom. It was made for children, long and meandering, with plenty of space to run around, and a warren of hidey-holes in the bushes. Tom took care of it until his disease made that impossible. Since then, Richard has hired a maintenance crew to look after it.

Living here would be different if she wanted a family, but she has never felt comfortable in Glencone, either in her previous apartment or in this old house with its store of memories. High Spires was perfect. She loves the city with its constant motion and noise, unlike Redstone where the sea, viewed from the front windows, is a constant reminder of the unrelenting pull of tides.

Christine pours out a second glass of wine and sips it slowly. Still no sign of Richard. It is almost midnight when she hears his key in the door.

'Your dinner needs four minutes in the microwave.' She lifts her empty wine glass from the coffee table. 'You'd better open another bottle. This one grew tired waiting for you.'

He takes the wine bottle from her and studies the label. 'I was saving this one for a special occasion.' A few drops of wine spill onto her empty plate when he turns the bottle upside down. She thinks of blood spilling and shudders. The heating has gone off, as have the outdoor lights, and the glass surrounds of the conservatory can no longer keep the wintry night at bay.

'Is our current situation not special enough for you?' She sounds calm, which surprises her, but he knows her too well to be fooled by her over-bright smile. 'I'm sorry I'm so late. Jessica rang just as I was leaving the nursing home. She'd arranged to meet her friend, Shay McCabe, in The Bailey. I couldn't turn down the opportunity to tell our side of the story.'

'The Bailey?' She sits upright in the armchair. 'You drove back into the city, from the nursing home, to see her?'

'That was where she'd arranged to link up with Shay McCabe.'

The name is familiar to Christine, as is the tabloid, *Capital*

Eye. Shay McCabe is its crime reporter and has nothing to do with business features. She pauses to steady her thoughts before asking: 'How did the interview go?'

'He was delayed on his shift. Some technical issue with copy. He kept ringing to apologise and promising to be with us as soon as it was sorted. Bottom line, if you'll excuse the pun...' – seeing her expression, he shrugs – 'is that he never made it. But Jessica has given him enough information to run the piece in tomorrow's edition. And that's not all. She's spoken to her father—'

'Last time I checked, Jessica was a copywriter. Since when did she become our knight in shining armour?' Her voice has sharpened and Richard, responding to her accusatory tone, frowns.

'There's no need for sarcasm.'

'I'm simply stating a fact. You've been drinking with an employee—'

'One drink of sparkling water, that's all I had.' He protests too vehemently. 'Jessica had a beer. Do you want to hear me out, or go on a rant? I'm trying to have a serious conversation with you.'

'That's what I've been waiting to do with you for the last four days,' she replies.

'I said I'm *sorry*. But this is important. Did you know that her father owns the Rosswall Heights hotel?'

'I thought he worked in finance?' Despite her annoyance, she is curious.

'He does. The hotel is actually where he lives and is only one of his many business interests. He's the chief executive of SFDN Enterprises. Jessica kept that information to herself until tonight. But I suspect from what she *didn't* say that they've had their differences. She's anxious to establish her career on her own merits but, in this instance, she's willing to accept his help.' Richard roots in the pocket of his jacket and hands her a business card. Embossed with gold lettering on a black background, the card gives only the briefest details of its purpose: *Samuel Newman*

Financier.

SFDN Enterprises and Financial Services

There is a phone number in smaller print along the bottom.

'How does he plan to do that?'

'Jessica believes he'll give us the Rosswall Heights account.'

'Just like that?' Christine tosses the card on the coffee table.

'He'd like to meet us.'

'Us?'

'You and me. Who knows where this could lead?'

He wants her to share his enthusiasm but she is sullen and flushed, argumentative for reasons she is unable to understand. 'Why should a complete stranger want to save our agency?'

'His daughter works for us.'

'That's not a good enough reason. He's a money lender—'

'He's a financier.'

'Is there as distinction?'

'You'll feel differently in the morning. When you're sober.' His excitement has died away and he is fighting to keep his anger under control, as is she. The tight knot of fury she feels puzzles her. Jessica has offered him... them... a ray of hope. Why does that fact fill her with foreboding? Is she capable of rational thought with a bottle of wine churning uneasily in her stomach? She seldom drinks wine and, then, only sparingly. After his phone call, she had been aware of a slight prickling in her chest. Now, it is intensifying. She needs to go to bed before this discussion erupts into a full-scale argument. Her legs weaken when she stands.

'Hold my arm.' Richard moves to take her elbow.

She regains her balance and manages to walk steadily from the room without his help. Her skin feels electrified. Over the years, she had learned techniques to withstand the feeling but tonight it has the upper hand. She shivers, a walking-over-her-grave shudder that comes from nowhere, as mindless fears threaten to overcome her.

Richard is already up and dressed when she awakens in the morning. 'I thought it best to let you sleep as long as possible,' he says. 'You were hammered last night. Take the later train.'

She reaches for the glass of water he has left on the bedside table, along with a packet of Alka-Seltzer tablets. Squeezing her eyes closed then opening them again, she sighs and asks, 'Was I awful?'

'I've known you to be in a better mood.' He smiles across at her. 'I'm sorry for upsetting you. It was the last thing I intended to do. This mess we're in...' – he pauses and leans towards the mirror to comb his hair – 'we've no idea how it's going to end so we need to grab any help that comes our way with both hands.'

'I agree.'

'Then talk to Jessica. She'll fill you in on exactly what her father intends to do.'

Before he leaves, he opens the bedroom window. 'Smells like a winery in here,' he says, although he is kind enough not to add that she is the source.

Even the fizz of the two Alka-Seltzer tablets he provided hurts her head as Christine tentatively eases from the bed, stumbles to the bathroom and turns on the shower.

Soon after arriving at work, Jessica knocks quietly on Christine's office door and enters. 'I hope I didn't upset you by discussing Foundation Stone with Shay McCabe,' she says. 'I wouldn't have done so if the information about the agency hadn't been made public.'

It is impossible to read her expression. Is she apprehensive, apologetic or smugly aware that she has managed to get under Christine's skin?

'I understand,' Christine replies. 'Richard has explained.'

'Shay ran the piece this morning. Unfortunately, it's just a sidebar but it's in the business section and it will be read by those who count. Did Richard tell you about my father's offer to help—?'

'We do not need *help*, Jessica.' She is still hungover and wretched with it. 'Foundation Stone is not a charity case. If your father wishes to advertise with us, we will, in return, deliver a highly professional advertising campaign.'

'I know that.' Jessica steps back, as if Christine's curtness has a physical force. Her eyelashes flutter but otherwise her expression is impassive. 'He's anxious to meet you and Richard as soon as possible. But he can be difficult. I want you both to be prepared. He drives a hard bargain.'

'I'll keep that in mind when we meet him. Thank you, Jessica.'

After she leaves, Christine opens the window. The air is fresh and bracing but the noise of the city smacks against her head. The phone rings. Noel Armstrong, a freelance cameraman, who works for them regularly, demands to be paid immediately. His anxiety echoes other freelancers who have been in touch about fees owed to them for commissions they have undertaken.

By the end of the day, an appointment has been made to meet Samuel Newman for a meal at his penthouse at Rosswall Heights on the following Tuesday.

FOUR

Entering the foyer of Rosswall Heights, Christine feels as if she has stepped into a jungle. Hanging plants cascade from the walls and enormous ceramic containers are filled with birds of paradise flowers, yuccas, ferns and stately palms. Vines twine gracefully across the high-arched ceiling, and cages filled with birds are suspended in mid-air. At first, she believes the brightly feathered occupants are real but when the silence remains unbroken, she realises that they are exquisite fakes. So, too, are the plants with their perfect gloss and dappled shades of green and orange. This jungle should be teeming with oxygen and energy; instead, it has a lifeless sheen that disturbs her.

Samuel Newman, who has been waiting in the foyer to greet them, says, 'You must think this is strange.' He spreads his hands to encompass the plants and cages.

'Working in the advertising industry, I've yet to define the meaning of strange,' Christine replies. 'This is quite a remarkable display.'

'You like it?'

'It's beautiful.' She is not lying. It is a beautiful space. When the background strains of an operatic overture suddenly fills the foyer, it seems as if the birds have finally found a voice.

A handshake is all Christine needs to realise she is in the presence of a strong personality. It isn't just his handshake and his penetrating stare, nor his height – he must be at least four inches taller than Richard's six feet – but something more indefinable. Perhaps it is his confident stride as he leads them through the aviary towards the elevators or his assured expression that tells her he has the power to make or to break Foundation Stone. She can see that his daughter has inherited his taut jawline and chin.

Information on him has proved hard to find. She searched the internet and was surprised by the size of SFDN Enterprises. The companies within the group include a chain of small convenience stores situated along the coastline, two more hotels, a sleek fishing trawler, numerous warehouses and a craft courtyard, all of them supported by SFDN Financial Services. She had no problem finding information on the directors, but Samuel Newman is an invisible figurehead, reclusive and careful of his privacy. She was unable to find any photographs of him online; nor, as far as she can discover, is he involved at any level on social media.

The music dies away when they enter an elevator at the end of the foyer. It glides smoothly upwards, the glass walls offering views of a tree-lined avenue and a wooded walkway. When it reaches the top floor, they step out onto a wide, carpeted concourse. Unlike the foyer, all is silent here. Automatic doors open when they approach the entrance to his penthouse. They follow him into a living room filled with solid, ornate furniture. Imitation Baroque, not antique, Christine thinks, but it is hard to tell the difference. Evening light fills wide picture windows, and double doors lead out onto a spacious balcony with a distant view of the Dublin mountains.

Samuel gestures towards two sofas positioned opposite each

other and a cocktail table in the centre. Pre-dinner drinks are served by staff who glide silently in and out of the room. He seems determined to put them at their ease. The conversation is relaxed, with no hard questions about facts and figures and the disastrous days they have endured. They talk about politics and music, the state of the film industry. He is an effortless conversationalist.

Christine wonders if he has a tick list of subjects to discuss with them before getting down to the real purpose of their visit. She is unable to place his accent. Definitely not Irish, nor English – more neutral, as if his voice has been modulated into an Anglo-Irish drawl that is posh enough to impress but not to intimidate.

Jessica has told him about Tom's deteriorating health and Richard, who is usually reluctant to speak to anyone but Christine about his father's condition, admits to the guilt he feels over no longer being able to care for him.

When their meal is ready, they move to a more secluded area where the table is set for three. Staff silently appear at the appropriate moments to serve each course and remove the dishes as soon as they finish eating. She catches her reflection in a wall mirror that also reflects the chandelier above her. The lighting enhances her features, adds sheen to the fall of her black hair. Her eyes are animated, their brown enhanced by the silk of her burgundy-red dress. She appears relaxed, as does Richard. No outward signs that they are fighting for the survival of their company.

'I hope the Dover sole is to your satisfaction?' Samuel asks, when the main course is served.

'It's delicious, thank you.' The accompanying sauce is subtle yet distinct, the tang of lime and a rich creamy flavour overlaid with dill and shallots. Christine suddenly holds her breath as her stomach heaves. Bile rises in her mouth. For an instant it seems as if the room sways before settling sluggishly back into focus. What is the matter with her? She lowers her hands to her lap. *Clench, unclench, count to ten.* This night must go without a hitch.

The reason for their visit is not mentioned until they finish eating and snifters of cognac have been served.

'Jessica has been very happy at Foundation Stone,' Samuel says. 'I want to thank you both for making her part of your team. She's enthusiastic but inexperienced. She dropped out of college and took time to find her feet, so to speak. She's now decided that she wants a future with your agency.'

'It's the right decision for her,' says Richard. Christine detects his excitement, the buzz he acquires when he is on the verge of signing a new contract. 'Her social media skills are excellent, particularly when it comes to digital marketing. Apart from that, she's good with words and can come up the right ones, the ones with impact, just like that.' He clicks his fingers. The snap sounds loudly in the silence that follows his comments.

Once again, Christine glances towards the mirror. Her reflection gazes serenely back at her. She hopes she imagined a slight unctuousness in Richard's tone. Her hand is shaking when she lifts the brandy glass. She quickly puts it down again. But Samuel has noticed. His keen glance won't be fooled by outward appearances. Something is wrong. She has no idea what it is. All she has to guide her is a growing uneasiness.

'Jessica brought me up to date on your current difficulties.' He holds the snifter to his nose and breathes in the brandy aroma. 'A most unfortunate experience. I believe your agency was deliberately targeted. Sabotage is always difficult to prove and without such proof, how do you find a path back to credibility?'

'Our credibility is sound.' Richard speaks firmly. 'So, too, is our reputation.'

'How many clients have you lost already?' Samuel asks.

'How many will you lose before this second week is over?' His silver hair, still plentiful, has been cut close to his scalp and spikes aggressively above his broad forehead.

'I can assure you—' Richard begins, before he is brusquely interrupted.

'Whoever is responsible for spreading those rumours is waiting to pick over the bones of your agency.' Samuel's accent sounds more clipped and authoritative. 'I don't like vultures, which was why I've decided to help you.'

'Jessica told us you're interested in advertising—'

'Advertising is not something I discussed with Jessica.' He waves his hand to silence Richard. 'Unfortunately for you, an advertising campaign will not be enough to stop Foundation Stone haemorrhaging bad publicity.'

'What exactly are you saying?' Christine asks.

The mood in the dining room has changed from relaxed to tense in a matter of seconds. She can see the physical as well as the mental effort it takes for Richard to respond to the sudden shift in their conversation.

'You know the true worth of Foundation Stone?' Samuel smiles across the table at her and inclines his head. 'How damaging has last week been for you?'

'Our figures are stable,' she replies. 'It's impossible to put a value on our reputation, and that's how we'll survive this attack.'

'Attack is an appropriate word,' he says. 'The advertising industry is a battlefield and when you're bloodied, it's wise to withdraw and consider your options.'

'I was under the impression we were invited here to discuss an advertising campaign, not to analyse tactical manoeuvres.' She is amazed at how calm she sounds. 'I can assure you that our agency will have no difficulties fending off a rear-guard attack – or a frontal assault, if necessary.'

'If you say so, Christine.' Adding to her annoyance, he returns his attention to Richard. 'Jessica is my only child. One day, she will take over my business interests. As of now, she's inexperienced and misguided. Rebellious, even – always had been, since her teens. But with your guidance she can learn how to run a company. I'm prepared to make an offer to buy Foundation Stone for a price we'll all agree is fair. You can both remain as Jessica's mentors. Your salaries will be negotiated and appropriate to your status. She will learn the financial responsibilities of running a company from you, Christine, while you, Richard, will continue to develop her creative skills.'

Darkness has fallen and the blue-grey shadows on the Dublin mountains have blended into the night. Christine is enclosed in a glass bubble that has suspended her high above the world of ordinary things. The fear welling inside her is not normal. She has learned to cope, even to ignore that harrying panic but she is unable to control the dread that grips her now. She is already shaking her head when she glances across at Richard. Why is he still seated when he should be on his feet and walking away from this outrageous offer?

'*Richard.*' Her voice snaps him to attention.

He shakes his head and clears his throat. 'This is not the conversation we expected to have with you when we came here this evening,' he says. 'Jessica led me to believe—'

'What I'm offering you is far more valuable than a one-off advertising campaign to please my daughter. As of now, I've no intention of changing my advertising team. Let me be blunt. I want to buy Foundation Stone for Jessica but if you're unwilling to sell to me, there are other agencies who will only be too eager to accept my offer.'

Christine attempts to speak but the pressure of Richard's hand on hers warns her to remain silent. Perspiration slicks under her arms; she feels it slide down her spine as Samuel Newman calmly, coldly, observes her. She has become an insubstantial shadow, a study in terror as she rises to her feet. 'Excuse me.' She strides quickly from the room and to the elevator. It opens and carries her back down to that avenue of green, lifeless plants. Somehow, they now possess a force that threatens to strangle her in a tangled contortion of vines. The birds of paradise flowers are waiting to stab her with their beautiful, vicious stamens. Above her, the birds in gilded cages are throbbing out a melody that is sweet and terrifying. Their song fades and she is drowning in a rushing space that has no shape, no dimensions, is depthless.

The floor rises to meet her when she pitches forward. It is only when she is able to hide in the descending darkness that the terror drains away and she is safe at last.

FIVE

The sun dazzles her. If she stares at it for too long, it will blind her. Her hand feels heavy when she raises it to touch her face. Her skin is hard, inflexible. A banshee begins to keen. She is waiting to claim Christine's soul... sole... she is choking, gagging, as she claws at her face and discovers that she is wearing a mask. When it is pulled aside, arms turn her sideways so that she can expel the vile contents of her stomach. Gushing... gushing... then breathing again when the mask is replaced. Oxygen. She draws in deep, grateful draughts of air. Reality dawns. A light is shining above her and the banshee wail becomes a siren that waves traffic to one side for an ambulance to pass.

'Richard...' Her voice is barely audible. 'What happened?' The pressure on her arm tightens as a blood pressure monitor takes a reading.

'You collapsed. I thought...' He strokes the hair back from her forehead. 'You gave us quite a scare.'

'Us.'

'We were with Samuel.'

'Samuel?'

'Don't you remember where we were?'

'At the wedding?' Her voice sounds disconnected, distant. She can tell from his expression that he is troubled by her reply.

'She's still in shock.' A woman in a high-vis jacket leans over her and checks the reading on the blood pressure monitor. She jabs Christine's ear with a thermometer and nods, satisfied. 'Do you know where you are, Christine?' Her smile makes Christine want to cry. The urge is a swell, swift as a wave sighting land, and Richard gathers her tears in his hands.

'It wasn't a wedding,' he says.

She knows that. Amy's wedding was the last one she attended and that was five years ago.

The paramedic with the kind smile is beside her again. 'I'm Sarah,' she says, and checks a reading on a machine beside Christine.

She is hooked to a heart monitor, tubes extending from her chest. How can the machine register her heartbeat without it exploding?

'I fainted... oh, my God.'

'Don't worry,' Sarah says. 'Your heart rate has stabilised but you're going to have a bruised face for a week or two.'

A chandelier reflecting in a mirror, picture windows, shadowed mountains, silent, static birds in a dead jungle. She grips Richard's sleeve. 'We can't let him do it... Promise me...'

'Shush... shush. Everything is going to be all right.' He dabs her face with tissues until she stops crying.

At the hospital she is whisked into the emergency ward and Sarah is on her way again. A night knight in a high-vis jacket. Christine is in new hands now. More tests, questions, waiting, endless waiting in a cubicle when she should be at Redstone with Richard, going through their accounts and coming up with a foolproof plan to save Foundation Stone from the clutches of Jessica Newman and her grasping father.

She wants to say all this to Richard but it is impossible to have a private conversation in this frantic, crowded space.

. . .

The sun is rising when Christine is finally discharged. *Stress* – she has been given this information by a considerate doctor who has worked through the night but still finds time to talk to her about meditation, yoga and mindfulness. A panic attack can strike without warning, she says. But there are advance signs, subtle yet helpful if one is aware of them.

Can sabotage cause one? Christine wants to ask. Can piracy and coups be responsible? It all sounds too complicated to query. She is so overwhelmed with tiredness that Richard has to help her into the taxi outside the hospital.

'I have to go the office.' He is apologetic when they reach Redstone.

'I'm going with you.' They have clients to meet today, and courtesy calls to marketing executives or phone conversations to reassure their clients that Foundation Stone is as solid as its name implies.

'You're not going anywhere today except to bed,' he replies. 'I've rung Stella. She's driving over here right now to look after you.'

'That's ridiculous, Richard. I don't need my mother to look after me. You heard the doctor. It's just stress. I can handle that.'

'I beg to differ. You looked lifeless on that floor. Even when you became conscious again, it was impossible to make out what you were saying.'

'That's because I didn't know I was in an ambulance.'

'Before the ambulance came, I mean. You kept talking about feeding apples to a horse. What was all that about?'

'I just remember waking up in the ambulance.' So, not everything about last night is clear in her mind. 'Mum's probably too busy to come over here.'

'Too late,' he says. 'She's already on her way.'

As if on cue, her mother phones to announce that she has

crossed the East Link bridge and will be with Christine in a half an hour. Which activities did she give up this morning to nurse her stressed-out daughter? Bridge, golf, a trek through the Dublin mountains, a jog along Sandymount Strand? Her mother's activities are numerous, her energy boundless. Christine feels the last of her own energy seeping from her as Richard supports her up the stairs. He is right. She is in no fit state to fight the battle that lies ahead. She must recover and grow strong again. She drinks the tea he brings her, eats toast – the elixir of the sick – and lies back against the pillows.

The stale smell of brandy and wine have been washed from him when he emerges from the shower. He dons a crisp white shirt and navy suit. No casual attire today, just armour. He brushes his wet hair and dries it until it falls around his head like a sleek, black helmet. Do battle, she tells him, when he leans forward to kiss her goodbye.

'I will,' he promises. 'You're not to worry about anything. I'll phone as soon as I reach the office.'

'Do you think Jessica will turn up for work?'

'I've no idea.'

'We need to fire her, Richard. She's dangerous. I believe she deliberately—'

A prolonged ring on the doorbell interrupts her. Stella has arrived and Richard blows a kiss before hurrying from the bedroom to let her in. She bounds up the stairs. This is the word that always comes to mind when Christine sees her mother in action – boundless energy, generosity and advice, which she immediately begins to dispense as she shrugs out of her coat. She echoes the words of the doctor with the sleep-shadowed eyes.

'Do you remember Jasper?' Christine asks, when her mother finally slows down.

'Jasper?' Stella looks confused for an instant.

'The horse—'

'Oh, *Jasper*. I do, of course.'

'Did he ever bite me?'

'Not that I can remember.' Her mother kicks off her boots, plumps Richard's pillow against the headboard and sits down on his side of the bed. 'He was a harmless old nag. What makes you ask?'

'Richard says I was talking about him when I recovered consciousness. I was obviously raving. Why would I want to talk about Jasper... or apples?'

'You loved everything about Sheerwater and that included Jasper.'

She used to feed apples to the old horse when he poked his head over the fence surrounding the chalet that her parents rented for a fortnight every July. Their annual family holiday in Tipperary: two exhilarating weeks spent outdoors, no matter what the weather was like. Climbing the mountain, trekking through the forests, picnicking at Rowan Falls and watching her younger sister and brother swimming in the lake. She never joined them, even though her parents insisted that she used to run without hesitation into its chilly waters when she was younger. They had bought Sheerwater when the house was put on the market some years ago, and now spend most of their summer and autumn weekends there.

'I can't believe you didn't come down this year, even for a few days' break.' Stella chastises her mildly.

'I've been so busy—'

'And look where that's got you! Your poor face. Does it hurt?'

Christine gingerly touches her cheek and winces. 'Just a little.'

'Working a seven-day week is a one-way ticket to stress. I've been worried about you for some time now.'

'Stop exaggerating. I don't believe it was stress. I had a reaction to the food I ate last night. You know how much I hate fish.'

'Why did you order it, then?'

'I didn't. We weren't given a choice.'

'Surely there was a menu at the restaurant?'

'The owner invited us to his home at Rosswall Heights. It was a business meal. I didn't like to make a fuss.'

'That didn't exactly go to plan, then, did it?' Stella smiles to take the sting from her comment.

Last night is like a nightmare that lingers long into the aftermath. Christine can't get Samuel's offer out of her mind but she doesn't want to give it voice, not yet. Unspoken, it has no substance.

'What's it like, Rosswall Heights?' Stella asks.

'I was only in the penthouse suite.'

'A penthouse? That's posh.'

'It certainly is. What am I keeping you from this morning?'

'Nothing important.' Her mother brushes Christine's question aside. 'Richard said he was convinced you were having a heart attack. That's not food poisoning or whatever you want to call it. You need to take better care of yourself, my darling.' She tucks the duvet around Christine's shoulders. 'Try and sleep for a while. I'll go downstairs and see to the ironing. After lunch, we'll go for a walk along the coast. Get some colour back into your face.' She strokes Christine's undamaged cheek and smiles. 'You need to stop worrying. Everything will work out, you'll see.'

Her mother gives depth to triteness, but Christine loves her too much to argue.

Downstairs, Stella has switched on the radio. Faint strains of music float upwards as Christine rages into the pillow. Samuel Newman's gaze had been powered with knowledge when he made his offer. He knows their financial situation down to the last cent. Has Jessica been downloading financial files from Christine's computer? The files on their clients? Their upcoming campaigns? That day when Christine came back from lunch and found Jessica in her office, was that what she had been doing? The more Christine thinks about it, the more feasible it seems.

Gradually, the music from downstairs becomes fainter. Four hours have passed when she awakens. Stella enters with a tray. Christine almost expects to find jelly and ice cream on it, and a bottle of Seven-Up, but she is an adult now and her mother has made a chunky vegetable soup which she serves with her homemade brown bread. She returns Christine's phone, which she had slyly taken from the bedside table while she was sleeping. Richard has rung twice.

'All's well,' he says when she phones him back. He sounds too assured to be convincing. 'Stop fretting. Everything is under control here.'

'Did Jessica turn up?'

'She did—'

'Have you fired her?'

'Hold on, Christine. We'll talk about that when I come home.'

'Richard, I want her out by this evening. I believe she and her father deliberately spread those rumours to destroy our company—'

'That's not true.' Richard cuts across her. 'They'd nothing to do with it. I've found out that Andrea Bryth is behind it. She gave a quote to some blogger on social media and that's how the whole rumour machine started.'

Andrea has been running The Bryth Agency for twenty-five years. She knows the industry's strengths and weaknesses, the petty rivalries and cut-throat mentality. She gave Richard his start in advertising, mentored him, promoted him, and was furious when he left her agency and took his clients with him. She warned him at the time that there would be consequences, yet Christine is still shocked by Richard's disclosure.

He ends their conversation. He has calls to make, clients to meet – all sound excuses to avoid discussing Jessica Newman.

After Christine has eaten and showered, and is about to switch on her laptop, Stella returns to the bedroom in full mother-control mode. 'None of that nonsense,' she says. 'We're going for that walk along the coast.' Her voice brooks no argument.

Sighing, Christine changes into a pair of jogging bottoms and a hoodie, and roots out her walking boots from the back of the wardrobe.

The wind is harsh as they walk along Seaward Road. The sea slants towards shore, white horses leaping. The spume settles like chilled fingers on her face when they descend the steps onto the hard-packed sand. She recoils then moves on, her reaction so ingrained that she barely notices it. Today, however, her body is on high alert, an antenna probing the way ahead. The feeling that her skin has thinned, been deprived of a layer, the epidermis, perhaps, refuses to go away.

Stella says goodbye shortly after they return to Redstone, anxious to cross the city before the evening traffic begins to build. Tonight, she is hosting her book club and needs to shop for wine. These friends are from her teens and they have never lost touch with each other. Christine's friends have scattered, while some like her sister, Bernice, and brother, Killian, live abroad. Others have small children who steal their time. She can't imagine any of them having the staying power of Stella's friends. The rough edges of their friendships have been buffed smooth by experiences, and they expect nothing from each other except to drink wine and enjoy themselves when they are together.

'Promise me you'll slow down, Christine,' Stella pleads before she drives off. 'You suffered a full-blown panic attack last night. Don't ignore the warning signs.'

It is useless trying to convince her that stress is manageable or that she doesn't work too hard. Stella knows that her daughter is career-driven and as anxious as Richard to grow Foundation Stone into a major name in the advertising business. Samuel Newman and his daughter will not snatch their future from them.

Alone at last, Christine makes coffee and carries the mug into the living room. She opens her laptop. '*The advertising industry is a battlefield and when you're bloodied, it's wise to withdraw and consider your options.*' Samuel Newman' s words pound against her forehead. She had replied tartly enough but he had known she was lying.

She prints out everything Richard needs to know about their finances. No more ostrich tactics on his part. They can survive this onslaught if they pull together, but Jessica must be fired before they do anything else. Her dismissal will send a clear signal to her father that they are standing strong on their own battlefield.

Richard rings to say he's calling into the nursing home on his way home to see Tom. She should expect him around eight. 'Don't attempt to cook,' he says. 'I'll pick up some Thai in the village.'

It has just turned seven when headlights flare across the driveway. Richard can't have stayed long with his father. Jessica has been on her mind so much that she is convinced the younger woman is an illusion when she steps from her car, zaps it locked and walks towards the house. She usually cycles to work but, tonight, she is driving a BMW coupé.

Christine waits until she rings a second time before opening the front door.

'I had to come and see you.' Jessica rushes the words towards her. 'I heard about last night. It sounds horrendous. How are you?'

'I'm fine, thank you.'

'This has been a dreadful misunderstanding. Can I come

in? Just for a few minutes, please?' Her hair has been cut into a layered style that looks chic enough to have cost her a fortune, as does her black, biker-style leather jacket with its buttery sheen. The desire to slam the door on her pleading expression is obvious enough for Jessica to take a step backwards.

'I'd no idea when I spoke to my father that he had any interest in making an offer for Foundation Stone,' she says. 'If I'd known what was on his mind, I'd never have spoken to him about our difficulties.'

'There's nothing *our* about this situation, nor are there any difficulties that Richard and I can't handle.' Christine leaves the door open and walks back down the hall without waiting to see if Jessica follows.

'I'm aware of that, Christine. I'm *so* angry with him.' She enters the living room and sits down when Christine gestures towards an armchair. 'Since my teens I've been battling against him, but he continues to interfere in my life.'

'Funny you should say that. He made a reference to a battlefield, which is obviously how he does business.' Christine crosses her arms and remains standing. 'I find it impossible to believe you'd no prior knowledge of his offer.'

'I *didn't*.' Jessica faces the accusation head-on. 'You have to believe me.'

'Then why would he make it?'

'It's his way of drawing me into SFDN.'

'What has that to do with us?'

'He knows how much I enjoy working with you and Richard. That's why he wants to includes Foundation Stone in his business portfolio.'

That was more or less what he had said last night: Foundation Stone would be the honeypot, the sweetener, that would shape his daughter into his own image.

'I'm an only child,' Jessica continues. 'My mother died

when I was a baby so he's poured all his love into me. That carries its own burden.'

'I'm sorry about your mother, Jessica. She was young...' Her own mother would be rushing around her kitchen in preparation for the arrival of her friends. All those years of nurturing, the tinderbox of adolescence, the challenges, arguments, make-ups, tears, laughter... she had always been able to take Stella's endless flow of love for granted.

'I don't miss what I've never known.' Jessica shrugs. 'I had a wonderful surrogate mother until I was ten. She gave me enough mothering to compensate for her loss.'

'And afterwards?'

'Just me and my father. I'm a huge disappointment to him. He wanted me to attend a private business university in New York and come back home as a fully formed business executive, ready to sit at his right hand. When that didn't work, he sent me to Trinity Business School, where I dropped out after six months. Since then, I've paved my own way but I was never really satisfied anywhere until I joined Foundation Stone.' She tilts her head, a winsome, appeasing gesture that does nothing to soften Christine's resolve. 'I don't want anything to change. I'm going to demand that he withdraw his offer and keep the promise he made to advertise with you.'

'What's so special about us? With your father's contacts, you could work anywhere.'

'I want to be in control of my own future. Is that so difficult to understand?'

Her bottom lip quivers. Christine is afraid she will start crying. What will she do if she has to hold her, comfort her?

'Did you see the cages?' Jessica asks.

'Impossible to miss them.'

'He collects them. Orders them from antique shops all over the world. The birds, too. All fake, like the plants. He's created a jungle and imposed his own order on it. If he had his way, I'd be caged, also.'

Is this a tactical manoeuvre? A frontal assault on Christine's sympathies? Indecision is tearing her in two. A bird in a gilded cage. Alice, her maternal grandmother, used to sing that song at parties. Christine remembers her voice, sweetly high and wavery with age. '*She was only a bird in a gilded cage. A beautiful sight to see. You may think she is happy and free from care. She's not, though she seems to be.*'

Jessica had escaped his cage but had she escaped him? She hadn't bought that BMW coupé on a copywriter's wage. Nor her luxurious apartment on Grand Canal Dock. Had she ever had to struggle for anything in her life?

Lorraine from graphics occasionally stays overnight in Jessica's apartment. On her first visit, she took photographs of the rooms and showed them to Christine. The curtains in the bedroom are made from the sheerest voile and trail the floor. The mulberry-coloured headboard on Jessica's king-sized bed is mirror-framed and spans almost the entire back wall, while a pink chandelier hangs from the ceiling. The interior has the self-conscious glamour of Rosswall Heights, that same over-attention to ornamental details.

Christine wants to ask if Jessica invaded her office. She can't stop thinking in combative terms. Did she infiltrate the accounts, spy on their clients, sabotage their operations? Looking into her guileless eyes, it is hard to believe she could be so devious. The suspicions Christine feels are based purely on instinct. Usually, she trusts her instincts when there is some rationale to balance them, but she is working purely on emotion here. An emotion she can't articulate. Does she pity her? Despise her? Fear her? Christine dismisses each one and is left with the same unanswered question.

What is it about Jessica that bothers her so much?

'Do I still have a job, Christine?' Entreatingly, she holds out her hands, palms up.

'Yes, you do. Sort this misunderstanding out with your father and make sure he understands that our agency is not for sale.'

'Thank you.' Jessica stands and walks towards a cluster of small paintings grouped together to the side of the mantlepiece. Richard's mother was an artist. She was attracted to water, particularly rivers, where she captured their moods, the reflections of light on stillness, the ominous currents and babbling brooks.

'They're beautiful.' Jessica moves closer to read the signature on the bottom of them. 'Nell Stone,' she says. 'Wasn't she Richard's mother?'

'Yes, she was.'

'How sad to think she died before her final exhibition opened.'

Have she and Richard reached the stage of exchanging family histories? From Jessica's pensive expression as she continues to study the paintings, it would appear so.

'I'll see you in work tomorrow.' Christine's tone is spiky enough to snap Jessica's attention back to her.

The rear lights on the BMW coupé disappear. Christine stands for a moment longer in the darkness. The night is cold, a bitter wind sweeping in from the sea. She hugs her chest as she stands there, still shaky from the vibrations of last night. Every detail seems imprinted on her mind: the opulent luxury of Samuel Newman's penthouse, and the weirdly perfect jungle that seemed to claw at her as she ran towards the exit.

She slams the door with such force that the stained-glass panel vibrates. For a horrified instant, she thinks it will crack.

She opens a bottle of pinot. Nothing special about this label. Richard bought six in Tesco's when they were on special offer. She stands before one of Nell's paintings. Her mother-in-law preferred to paint rivers when they were restless and storm-ridden, but this one is sun-drenched, sparkly. Christine has never asked to have them removed from the walls or felt she had the right to encroach on the dead woman's legacy, but these paintings disturb her in a way she can't articulate. How can she admit to Richard that they repel her? That when she looks at them, she thinks only of what is lying beneath the sheen of the river: the unseen currents and rip tides, the slithery underwater stalks and nibbling fish.

SIX

On the night Richard won the Elora Award, Andrea Bryth's voice cracked with resentment when she congratulated him and Christine. Now, when she puts in a bid to buy Foundation Stone, she sounds clear and triumphant. Her offer is risible, easily dismissed. Two more bids are made and receive the same response. Christine thinks of barracudas, their vicious teeth sinking ever deeper into their dwindling reputation. She is convinced Samuel Newman is behind the destructive campaign. She reads Jessica's responses on social media, her efforts to stem the flood of vitriol from the online community. Is he ruining Foundation Stone at his daughter's behest or is she an unwilling pawn, as helpless as they are against his determination to buy the agency?

She has her computer checked by a computer technician to see if financial files were downloaded. Unable to find any proof of tampering does nothing to alleviate her suspicions.

'This would never have happened if we hadn't hired Jessica,' she says to Richard one evening, when they return to Redstone after visiting Tom. 'We'd never have heard of SFDN and her crazy father would have no interest in us.'

'Are we back to having this conversation again?' Richard crosses his arms and sighs resignedly as he pulls out a chair from the kitchen table.

'It's true.'

'Whatever Samuel Newman is, he's certainly not crazy. He started off with nothing and built his business up from scratch.'

'You seem to know a lot about him.' The daffodils on the table are wilting. She carries the vase to the sink and draws back from the rancid smell when she empties out the water.

'I've done my research—'

'Well, you must be looking in a different direction to me.' Her interruption is brusque and she is taken aback by her anger, the suddenness with which it sweeps through her. 'It's impossible to find out anything about him, unless you're having cosy, confidential chats with his daughter.' She opens the back door and flings the flowers into the bin. She stands outside for a moment and breathes deeply before returning to the house.

She removes two glasses from the kitchen cabinet and opens a bottle of wine. 'I'm convinced she downloaded financial information from my computer and passed it on to him.'

'You've proof of this?' He shakes his head before she can pour a glass for him.

'I don't need proof. I just *know*.' She notices his eyes narrowing when she fills her glass to the brim.

'That's not true. Everything was working fine until Andrea Bryth spoke to that blogger—'

'How can you believe such a ridiculous story? Andrea is a professional. Every word she utters is fact-checked for accuracy.'

'She wasn't fact-checking anything when she told me she'd make me pay for setting up in competition against her.'

His annoyance has risen to match her own. She forces herself to slow down, knowing how much he hates being interrupted when he is speaking.

'That was ten years ago, Richard. Why would she wait until now to damage us?'

His shoulders lift defensively before he speaks again. 'So, what are you basing your suspicions about Jessica on?'

'Instinct.' How ridiculous that sounds. She is an accountant who deals in facts. Two and two makes four. Figures add up and if they don't, there has to be a reason for the miscalculation. That night in the Bailey... the thought of them together in the bar, heads bent close... is her anxiety worse since then? Her hand is unsteady as she lifts the glass.

'Instinct will get you far in a court of law,' Richard laughs derisively.

'You don't believe me?'

'Not when your instinct is based on jealousy.'

'Jealousy? Are you suggesting I'm jealous of Jessica?'

He hesitates, as if searching for an apt reply. 'You've no reason to be... but it's obvious from the way you stare at her.'

'Stare at her? How do I do that?'

'Resentfully.'

'That's not true. If you'd said "suspiciously" you'd be closer to the mark. In fact, you'd be absolutely correct...' Her voice falters. Richard has accused her of drinking too much. It makes her nasty, he said. *Nasty*... that has a sting to it. If Jessica was nasty, she would still look beautiful. Not so with Christine, who feels her expression tighten as the words she wants to hold back trip from her tongue.

'What about you?' She wants to pound him with her suspicions but as soon as she utters them, they sound churlish, fanciful. 'You can't keep your eyes off her.'

'Don't be absurd. She's an employee, nothing else.'

'She's an employee who holds our future in her devious little hands. You know that as well as I do. She's going to take over Foundation Stone and there's nothing we can do about it.'

'We don't even know if her father is still interested.' He

leans his elbows on the table and sinks his face into his hands. He knows, as she does, that Samuel Newman's offer is the only one worth considering.

'He will be.' Christine is as certain of this as she is about Jessica's role in the obliteration of their company. Is she also responsible for the tension in their marriage? The two seem frighteningly intertwined.

As if suspecting her thoughts, Richard apologises and silences her with kisses. She gasps when he lifts her onto the counter and slides up her skirt. They are adept and agile, used to the contours of each other's bodies. Now that Tom has left, they have the house to themselves but this is the first time they have made love in the kitchen.

No need to muffle the sounds of pleasure when they come together, as they always do.

She uncurls her legs from around his waist and slides to the floor. He holds her for an instant longer before releasing her. Short, sharp satisfaction – that's the way it is with them nowadays.

To give Samuel Newman his due, he doesn't play games and reduce his offer when they agree to sell. The deal is quickly concluded. Their world comes crashing down. Crashing suggests a hullabaloo, thunder and clamour, but the sale of Foundation Stone is a quiet business, carried out in the muted offices of SFDN; the pen they use does not even scratch the surface of the contract as they sign their names to it.

They should open champagne but this is not a celebration. It is submission. Christine believes that a bottle of vodka is a more appropriate response. Later, when she is unable to stand, Richard carries her up the stairs to bed.

SEVEN

Foundation Stone closes down for a week to enable what Jessica calls 'the transition'. The name will remain. Despite the battering of bad publicity it received, the brand survives, thanks to a streamlined publicity campaign. Richard retains his office and title as chief executive director. Christine is still the financial director but her name plate is on the door of a spare room that had always been used for storing files and dumping obsolete equipment. Now, cleared out and ready to be occupied, it is a charmless space with no natural light. If she is to move forward, she hopes the walls are strong enough to contain her fury.

Jessica has taken over Christine's spacious office, and it is obvious from the beginning that she has no interest in learning how to balance the books. When Christine tries to explain that it can sometimes be necessary to curb the exuberance of the creative team, Jessica's unwavering stare becomes a mirror that forces her to see herself as someone intent on corralling Richard's imagination with grubby financial restrictions.

Her second panic attack is less dramatic than the first one and occurs a month after the takeover. She hears voices from the main hub and recognises Samuel Newman's accent. He greets Christine when he enters her office, after first knocking politely on the door. He looks even more dominant in this closeted space, his dark, cashmere overcoat adding to his bulkiness. His silver hair is sleeker, the aggressive spikes combed into submission. They exchange a few remarks, nothing alarming or noteworthy. He asks how the mentoring of his daughter is progressing. Christine could have told him that Jessica has no intention of recognising the synergy between finance and design. She could admit that she feels as obsolete as the equipment that once occupied her new office – but her heartbeat is quickening. The floor has suddenly swayed in that remembered oscillation. She clutches the arms of her chair and lowers herself into it. Somehow, she manages a few words that seem to satisfy him. It is only when she hears the door closing behind him that she finally slumps. Deep breathing, Rescue Remedy drops on her tongue, her head between her knees until the dizziness passes.

Her blouse clings damply to her back but no one witnesses her distress as she makes her way to the bathroom. The make-up she used that morning is a mask that hides her ashen complexion. She adds another layer of foundation and blusher, works on her eyes. Nothing can hide the fear she sees there. Confusion, also, and shock that she is once again losing control.

Christine has only been in Amy's house twice since her friend's marriage. The first time was a housewarming party. Everything glistened with newness and Amy, delightedly pregnant, had no idea that the next time Christine visited, little hands would have decorated the dove-grey walls with crayons, and mashed food between the maple floorboards.

This time, the carnage is more evident but Amy seems immune to the damage. She straps Daniel into his high chair and makes coffee. Stretching upwards, she removes a biscuit tin from the top shelf. Joanna, her eldest, and Leo, a year younger, know the sounds of their house only too well. They rush from an adjoining room where a television is audible and Amy sends them on their way again with a biscuit in each hand.

'Anything for peace,' she says, as if she thinks Christine is going to condemn her indulgence. Christine, who has absolutely no idea about the dos and don'ts of parenting, agrees that peace is a dividend that can't be underestimated.

'So, tell me about New Girl.' Amy carries the coffee to the breakfast bar. 'And why you're so unhappy with this new deal. From the way you've explained it, you're still doing what you enjoy yet the buck no longer stops at your desk. After what the agency has been through, I thought you'd be happy with the new arrangement.'

'But *why* did we have to sell?' Christine asks. 'That's the question I want answered. Everything was running smoothly until we employed Jessica.'

'Hardly smoothly. You used to complain about Richard's extravagance—'

'That's normal. Creatives think big. We balanced each other out.'

'Does he feel the same way about the sale?'

'He's working from a bigger budget so it's not surprising that he's adjusted. And Jessica is only interested in design. She wants nothing to do with the financial side of the company.'

'Isn't that better than having her on your back all the time?'

'It's not just that. Richard and I used to meet our clients together. I always sat in on brain-storming sessions and storyboard presentations. Not any longer. And you should see where I work now – it used to be our *dump*. Jessica is deliberately undermining me.' Christine stops herself. She will start whining if she doesn't watch out, and Amy will look as exasperated as

Richard does when she complains again about their changed circumstances.

'What about the perks?' says Amy. 'You're driving a Porsche.' Her lips quiver in a mock-whistle. 'This is the first time I've seen you driving a half-way decent car.'

'The car was part of an agreement we negotiated *under* duress.'

'Some deal. What's Richard driving?'

'A BMW.'

'Which model?' Amy used to work with a car dealership and had plans to set up her own company until she met Jerome and decided motherhood was more enticing.

'What does it matter? Jessica and her father set out to destroy our company—'

'You've proof of that?'

'I don't need proof!'

'If you're going to make those accusations, I'd suggest you do.' Is there a hint of impatience in Amy's voice? 'You told me that a number of people also offered to buy Foundation Stone. Could one of them be responsible?'

Christine thinks about Andrea Bryth and how she threatened to take Richard to court to prevent him bringing his clients with him when he left The Bryth Agency. Could she have been hiding in the long grass for all these years? Impossible to imagine. Christine shakes her head.

'I'm convinced Samuel Newman was responsible,' she says. 'He wore us down first before hitting us with his offer. Just thinking about his tactics makes me *sick*.'

'Have you suffered any further panic attacks?' Amy sounds concerned. Maybe her impatience was imagined.

'Nothing serious.'

'What does "nothing serious" mean? Tell me what's wrong, Christine.'

She has vowed not to tell anyone about the latest episode. It is enough that she recovered without making a scene. Amy waits. They have spent their lives sharing secrets.

She hears Christine out then eases Daniel from his high chair, onto her lap. 'Have you any idea what's triggering these attacks?'

'It's more than panic, Amy. It's fear. But I've no idea why I'm afraid. The worst has happened. We're financially secure and still working, yet I can't shake off this dread. The more I try to manage it, the more acute it becomes. It's obviously connected to Jessica. But it's ridiculous to think she can do this to me.'

She wants to lean into her friend and tell her the truth. But that truth is based only on suspicions and misgivings. She has no proof that Jessica is out to destroy her marriage with Richard, just as stealthily as she destroyed the agency. Neither by word nor glance has Jessica displayed any feeling towards him that could be defined as anything other than respect. *Respect*. How sedate that sounds. How appropriate. He is still the team leader and Jessica seems content to hone her skills on his experience. The advertising campaign for Rosswall Heights will cover print, television, radio and digital. The filming and photography are underway. Christine had been excluded from the planning stages of the campaign, nor was she invited to attend the meetings to discuss promotional strategies with Rosswall Height's marketing management. Samuel Newman is anxious that his daughter's first major advertising campaign will be successful, and no expense has been spared to make it so.

'Would you consider seeing someone about this fear?' Amy asks.

'A psychiatrist?'

'No, that's too extreme. A counsellor, maybe.'

'And say what? I need substance, not perceptions.'

'Maybe your fear is too repressed to understand, and you need someone experienced to help you release it.'

Christine laughs at her friend's response. This is typical of Amy, who believes that the unconscious is a cauldron of childhood fears and unresolved teenage angst.

'I'm too ordinary for repressed memories. I've had a happy childhood and reasonably uneventful teens, apart from some field drinking—'

'Don't remind me.' Amy shudders with mock horror. 'I often think about the night the police chased us over the railway tracks. I dread to think what Joanna will get up to when she's fourteen. That's how parents are punished, you know – they're haunted by abiding memories of their own reckless behaviour.'

'It was good fun, though.' Christine remembers the blissful, hazy space she occupied during those sessions in Fogarty's field. The dancing and singing, the fires blazing. The moon so impassive and distant until it began to fall.

'Yeah, well, apart from the time you were carted off to hospital in a coma.' Amy picks up on her thoughts. 'You drank harder than any of us.'

'It cured me. I was a pillar of temperance from then on.'

That night in the field with Amy, Rob, Dave and Jenny, all of them too terrified to flee after Rob, the only one who possessed a mobile phone, called an ambulance. Stella claimed it was Christine's 'baptism by fire' and her worries that her daughter would drink herself into oblivion again were laid to rest.

Now, though, she drinks alone and with the same recklessness. A morning will come when she can no longer hide the signs. Jessica will then be able to apply the clause in their contract stating that she or Richard can be dismissed if they fail to live up to their stipulated responsibilities.

Maybe Amy is right. She needs someone objective to sort out her head and explain the reasons for this illogical dread.

'Let me check around,' Amy says. 'One of my friends is a

counsellor but she only deals with adolescents. However, she might be able to recommend someone.'

Before she leaves, Christine goes into the living room to say goodbye to Joanna and Leo. Their gaze is fixed on the television screen where a pig with a posh English accent is jumping into puddles. They tear themselves away from her antics and allow Christine to kiss the top of their heads. She wanted to buy sweets for them but was afraid Amy would object. Should she slip money into their hands? She loved getting money from relatives when she was young but she must have been older then – five or six, probably. Better leave it. The land where they exist bewilders her, and besides, they have returned their attention to the pig.

Amy phones a few days later. The friend she contacted has suggested that Christine try hypnotherapy. The term resonates with suspicion. She imagines piercing eyes staring at her and a mesmeric voice ordering her to do whatever he or she commands.

'It's nothing like that,' Amy assures her. 'It's meant to be really good for treating anxiety. Her name is Elaine. I'll text you her phone number. She comes highly recommended. What have you got to lose?'

What indeed? Talking to Amy has helped, yet when she returns home from the agency, she pours a drink and then another. Richard is working late. He acts as though he is still the owner of Foundation Stone and Jessica allows him that leeway. Accounts that they believed were lost have been reopened and new ones established. They have survived the storm and Christine, it appears, is the only one who feels shipwrecked.

This metaphor invades her dream that night. It never varies, this nightmare that comes to her regularly and fills her with horror. She used to hide under the bed and cry out for her parents when she was small but she learned to control her reactions, to understand that it was only a dream and she had the power to awaken from it. But not on this occasion. When she opens her eyes, her mouth is so dry she is hardly able to swallow. This increases the feeling that she is still drowning and it is only when she stumbles from the bedroom to the bathroom that the suffocating sensation passes. Her body is taut with shock as she sits on the edge of the bath and sips a glass of water. That sensation of falling downward towards a depthless river bed is always the same? 'Depthless' is an impossibility, yet that is what she believes as the water closes over her head. All she ever remembers is the struggle, the churning ripples, her silent screams. On this occasion, the nightmare seemed even more charged, as if another shadow had been added to the layers of terror. It is still dark outside and she is afraid to fall asleep again in case the nightmare returns. She slides her arms around Richard, snuggles against the slope of his spine, the angle of his knees. He sleeps on, unaware of her dread. Gradually the warmth of his body and the rhythm of his breathing lulls her back to sleep.

Weeks slip by. Occasionally she notices Elaine Stephenson's number, and plans to ring her as soon as she has time to think straight. Is she making excuses, or is she genuinely too busy to venture into the deeper reaches of her subconscious? She is drinking too much. What was once a social habit has now acquired a new impetus. The relief of unwinding in the evening, pulling the cork on a bottle of wine or pouring a shot of vodka, ice clinking, breathing in the tang of a freshly cut wedge of lemon.

One afternoon, she enters the office she used to occupy and is shocked by the changes. The walls have been repainted, a thick carpet has replaced the wooden floorboards and the furniture has a brash newness that adds to Christine's feeling of alienation. The posters that used to hang on the walls have been replaced with images from the new campaigns. The only poster that remains in place from the old regime is Kava, still hanging boldly behind Jessica's desk.

Christine should have obeyed her own unwritten rule and knocked first. That would have allowed her to continue being duped for a while longer but, now, she can no longer pretend that her suspicions are only in her head. Jessica is sitting at her desk and Richard, stooping behind her, is staring over her shoulder at her computer screen. Their closeness is all Christine sees. His mouth so close to the back of Jessica's neck that he could kiss its smooth length without moving his head. He stands back when he sees Christine and folds his arms, his eyes still on the screen.

'We're having problems with Krisgloss,' he says. 'We underestimated the costs of filming on that lake in Connemara—'

'That was exactly what I told you at the time.' How is it possible to sound so brisk when all she wants to do is scream at them? *What is going on here...? Tell me... no, don't... don't...*

'No need to worry.' Jessica seems unperturbed by the interruption, but Christine is no longer fooled by her guileless expression. 'We've figured it out.'

Krisgloss is a new account. The glassware brand, which is exported globally, is introducing a more modern collection and Foundation Stone has been commissioned to design the advertising campaign.

When it was being envisaged, Christine had argued that expenses needed to be curtailed if they were to work to the fee agreed with the company. Jessica had brushed her advice aside, determined to make an impression on their new client. Christine had waited for Richard to support her. He had always respected her opinion but, on that occasion, the lure of an uncontrolled budget had kept him silent.

Now they have run into difficulties and have spent hours trying to sort out the problem – without consulting her. Would she have even known what was going on if she had not decided to speak to Jessica about another irregularity in the accounts?

'I need to be involved on any discussion on Krisgloss,' she says. 'Show me exactly where the problems have arisen.'

'It's okay, Christine, we have it under control.' Jessica leans her elbows on the desk and sinks her chin into her cupped hands. Why does she keep using the first person plural when referring to Richard? *We... we... we.* 'Obviously, if we've any serious issues we'll contact you immediately,' she continues. 'We're tight on time today so do you mind if we postpone whatever it is you want to discuss until tomorrow?'

Surely Richard must be aware that this is a put-down. Why is he not conscious of her anger? They have been attuned to each other's emotions for eleven years but his eyes are back on the computer, his forehead clenched in concentration when Christine leaves them.

Back in her own office, hemmed in by walls and anxiety, she rings Elaine Stephenson.

EIGHT

Elaine Stephenson's house is terraced and red-brick. From the outside it appears small and poky, an impression quickly dispelled when Christine passes through the narrow doorway into a light-filled, spacious reception area. Health magazines have been laid out on a low table, alongside a water dispenser. Here, as in Samuel Newman's hotel, there is an abundance of plants but these ones release oxygen, and she breathes in deeply as she sits down and waits to be called into the hypnotherapist's consulting room.

Elaine's youthful voice on the phone belied her age. She is probably in her early sixties, slim and slightly built, with a mane of white hair knotted in a single plait. Her handshake is firm, a warm clasp that acts as a conduit, touching nerves and relaxing them. Christine has forgotten how to relax: somehow, it seems important to hold on to her constant, jagged uncertainty. It keeps her alert, sensitive to vibrations that Richard insists are all in her head. But just because he believes that to be the case doesn't make it so. And by the same token, nor does the fact that she is convinced he is falling in love with Jessica turn that belief into a fact.

She exhales slowly as she follows Elaine into a room, where certificates of courses done and awards achieved are displayed on cream-coloured walls. Will she blurt out these feelings as Elaine works her magic charms on her? Will she end up as a blubbering mess by the end of the session?

The hypnotherapist's voice is quiet and reassuring as she explains the process. First, there will be questions to answer, along with information and consent forms to complete. She needs to understand what made Christine decide to seek her help. The questions are not intrusive. Elaine will quietly tick boxes as she builds up a picture that could be at variance with Christine's own image of herself. That is a challenge worth undertaking if it helps her to understand what has brought her here.

Initially, it is easy to address the questions. Christine doesn't take drugs or prescription medication. No one in her family has experienced mental health problems. She doesn't have issues around food but she hesitates, uncertain how to reply, when Elaine asks if she drinks alcohol. This is not a simple yes or no answer. She was always a moderate drinker, apart from the field parties, and that was all part of the teenage experience. More recently, well, yes, Christine stumbles over an excuse then discards it. Yes, she admits. She has been drinking a lot recently.

'How often?' Elaine asks, in her quiet way.

'Every night,' Christine replies, and is shocked to hear herself admitting this out loud.

Has she had blackouts? Elaine's tone is non-judgemental, reassuring.

Could her collapse in that dead aviary be classified as a blackout? No, that was not induced by alcohol, but she cannot say the same about the night Richard carried her up the stairs to bed. Or the night he let her sleep on the sofa and went to work the following morning without waking her. These are incidents she remembers vaguely and now, recalling them, she can no longer pretend they are not linked to a larger picture.

Elaine, guessing, perhaps, that Christine is becoming increasingly nervous, passes on to other less contentious questions relating to her childhood. This is a short-lived respite and soon she is enquiring about work and personal relationships. The questions seem disparate, separate skeins that form the thread which will guide them through this session. Christine is shocked by how many boxes she ticks: lack of concentration, anxiety, panic attacks, anger, irritation. She waits for a question about suspicion but it is not listed.

'Kitten claws tearing at my chest,' she says when Elaine asks her to describe her anxiety. 'Is that a stupid thing to say?'

'It's an excellent metaphor,' Elaine replies. 'How long have you been conscious of this reaction?'

'I don't know...' She hesitates. 'A long time, I guess. When I was a child, I believed it was the way everyone felt.'

'What age would you have been when you first became aware of these kitten claws?'

'Hard to tell,' Christine admits. 'My friends thought I was weird anytime I tried to describe the feeling. After a while I realised it was better to remain silent and accept the anxiety when it came. It was a part of me that would go away again when it was ready.'

It is easy to talk to Elaine and she is calm by the time the hypnotherapist asks her to close her eyes. Elaine has explained that she will guide her into a state where she will feel relaxed and safe.

'Are you comfortable?' she asks. She knows about Christine's fear of losing control but assures her that there is no danger that that will happen. 'In many ways, hypnotherapy may appear similar to sleep from the outside, but you'll be fully aware of what's going on around you.' She makes it sound uncomplicated yet Christine cannot believe that this is possible.

She nods. Already, her mind is drifting. 'Drifting' is a new experience. Usually, her thoughts run on a collision course with spin-off cul-de-sacs in between. Elaine doesn't sound surprised or anything, really. She is used to secrets being shared in this space. Toxins released and absorbed by the leafy, hardy plants. Christine thinks of Samuel Newman' s mock jungle with its suspended cages and sightless birds, but it is his daughter's beautiful face that swims before her eyes. She wants Jessica to move aside but she remains a persistent presence. Which is just what she has been doing since she entered Foundation Stone to be interviewed and turned her smile on Christine.

The scream that rises from her is primal yet it would barely pass for sound. She knows this because she is awake, aware, and what she hears is a child's whimper, muffled, gasping. But, then, how can she be awake when she is living her nightmare? There it is, in all its suffocating intensity, the water closing over her head and the bottomless depths below her.

The hypnotherapist speaks again. Christine has no idea what Elaine has said but it takes her back to the awareness that the chair where she is sitting has firm, secure arms. Essential oils are burning, the scent subtle and non-invasive. She is safe and still in control. There is no ambulance with a banshee siren, no concerned paramedics or frantic Richard.

'I thought I was drowning,' she tells Elaine. 'It's a recurring nightmare, like a... haunting.'

'A haunting?'

'I've never thought of it like that before,' Christine admits. 'A haunting suggests a ghostly alliance with my unconscious mind. This... this...' – she stumbles towards an appropriate description – '*presence* never leaves me alone. It doesn't matter how infrequently it occurs, I know the nightmare will return and it will be exactly the same.'

'Have you experienced it more often recently?'

'I'm not sure. I'm aware that sometimes I awaken with no memory of dreaming yet I know I've had it.'

'How can you tell?'

'That sensation I described, that scrabbling at my chest, it's more acute.'

'Take in a deep breath and as you exhale, follow this sensation all the way back in time to when you experienced it first. Nod your head when you're there.'

There is silence in the room, and then Christine nods.

'How old are you, Christine?'

'Five. Maybe it began after I fell into a river.'

'As you think of this time and you see the river, maybe you can hear the water and feel the air on your skin.' She pauses and waits until Christine nods again. 'Maybe you can recall some of the scents from nature you inhaled at the time, and if you do so, is this scrabbling a new feeling or is it familiar?'

'I'm not sure.'

'So, allow your mind to drift back to an earlier point in time when you experienced this sensation of scrabbling at your chest and nod your head for me when you are there.'

Christine waits an instant before replying. 'No. I've no memory of experiencing either the sensation or the nightmare when I was younger.' She speaks with certainty. 'I was in England at my aunt's wedding when I was five and that's when the accident happened. I was pulled out of the river immediately and was never in any danger.'

The memory of Sharon and Patrick's wedding shimmers when it comes to her. Elaine encourages her to hold on to the images. She is scattering rose petals over the long aisle leading to the altar where Patrick is waiting to marry Sharon. The petals smell like apples, ripe and juicy, her favourite fruit. She dips her hand into her basket and scatters... scatters... The organ is booming out *The Bridal Chorus* and everyone is smiling at Christine as she makes a carpet of love for Sharon to walk over.

It takes so long for the priest to marry them. Sharon and Patrick have to say so many words before they can kiss and everyone can cheer because they are now husband and wife. Patrick winks at her over Sharon's shoulder and the cameras flash and flash again.

But that was before the river. Such a thing to happen. Could the nightmare have originated after the river incident? It was an insignificant slip and a splash of water that ruined her flower-girl dress.

'I'm here with you, Christine. You are free to come back to the safety of this room whenever you decide to do so.' Elaine sounds so reassuring that Christine is able to watch the petals turn from antique gold to crimson. They fall like drops of blood from her hands but the time frame has changed. Instead of the cameras flashing, she is staring into a mirror where the glossy image of a chandelier is reflecting back at her. She recognises the penthouse at Rosswall Heights, the ornate furnishings and elaborate lighting. Before she can grasp what exactly is happening, the chandelier fades and Jessica's face is visible in the mirror. She should not be so beautiful. Her features are too defined, that determined chin and the strong jawline should detract from her beauty instead of enhancing it. A shadow moves over her features, as if she has been superimposed by another presence that is too dense to penetrate.

Why is Jessica doing this to her? She is in a safe place yet the terror that sweeps over her is as uncontrollable as it was that night she collapsed among the lifeless, rubbery plants.

'What's happening now, Christine?' Elaine's voice floats towards her but she is unable to answer. 'Focus on your breathing, Christine. That's good. You're doing great. As you listen to my voice come back into the room now. Eyes open. Look at me, Christine, you are safe in this room with me right now.' The assured voice of the hypnotherapist eases her away from the images that have so disturbed her; Christine holds on to its strength and uses it as a rope to guide her to safety.

'Welcome back,' Elaine says. The session draws to an end with some exercises to elicit a calm and positive state in Christine. Elaine hands her a glass of water and allows her time to adjust back to everyday reality.

The street is quiet when Christine steps outside. She finds a nearby café and sits at a window bench with coffee and a pastry. Elaine's house is visible from her vantage point. How does the roof remain in place? Should it not lift off from the sheer force of energy that is released within those walls? She has been emptied out but, already, the questions come to her on a swell, a torrent that had no source until this afternoon. Is she any wiser than she was before she stepped into those uncharted waters? Probably not, but, somewhere, that shadow is waiting to be illuminated. Jessica Newman, for reasons Christine is still unable to fathom, is a trigger that has unleased something savage and unfinished within her.

NINE

The mood in the agency is jubilant. The Krisgloss management and marketing teams have approved the entire presentation. Jessica stands by the window in the main hub, her face in profile, and opens a bottle of champagne. She usually wears her hair loose but, today, she has tied it in a top knot. Her profile is chiselled, her features more defined.

Once again, Christine is gripped by the certainty that she, herself, is going to crash downwards, and there is nothing to stop her fall. She breathes deeply and holds herself together as glasses are raised in a toast to Jessica and Richard.

He is working late when she leaves the office. It is easier than going home and coming back again into the city to meet his friend, he says. Jamie Coogan is a woodcarver who lives in isolation in Connemara and only comes to Dublin occasionally. Christine has never met him. Nor can she remember Richard ever talking much about him but Jamie, this friend from primary school, is meeting him for a meal tonight.

When Richard is not home by eleven o'clock, she opens a bottle of wine. The glass overflows and spills over the edge of the breakfast bar. Is he lying to her about Jamie and, instead, celebrating the Krisgloss account with Jessica? She empties the wine into the sink and watches it glug sluggishly across the white ceramic surface. Red, deep burgundy, red as roses, red as blood spilling.

She drives back into the city and parks outside Jessica's apartment. This quarter by the docks is popular with young people, especially on a Friday night. Most of the residents will be drinking in nearby bars, dining in restaurants. Lights reflect on the Liffey – green, purple, a glittering gold wavering on the water. How many hearts will be broken tonight? How many betrayals carried out? How many lies leaked into the quivering, stolen hours? Apart from a few illuminated windows, the apartment block on Grand Canal Dock is in darkness. Jessica's car with its low-slung elegance is easy to recognise. Which window belongs to her? Is Richard up there with her, or have they gone elsewhere?

She has no idea how long she sits in that darkened space waiting... for what? Jessica is a disease that is destroying her. Alcohol is only a sidebar, a refuge from this persistent need to rent something aside. A veil that camouflages... what?

Her phone rings.

'Where are you?' Richard sounds anxious. 'Jamie came back to the house to meet you. He had a gift and wanted to give it to you personally. But he's gone now.'

Her anger sags like a deflated balloon. She scrambles for an excuse that will sound reasonable and discards each one. Nothing makes sense any more. 'I'm outside Jessica's apartment,' she says.

She hears his intake of breath then the slow exhale. 'How long have you been there?'

'Too long.'

'Have you been drinking?'

'No.'

'Don't lie, Christine. I saw the empty wine bottle. I'm coming to collect you.'

'I'm sober, Richard.' She turns on the ignition. 'I'm leaving now. We'll talk when I get home.'

The rosewood bowl on the kitchen table gleams and the grain swirls in its own distinct pattern. She will fill it with fruit and think of Jamie Coogan every time she lays eyes on it. That's how it is with gifts. Richard gave her the gift of love – and tonight he listens without interrupting her when she tells him why she waited outside Jessica's apartment. Making such a confession is difficult. No matter how she tries to explain the complexity of her feelings for Jessica – fear, suspicion, resentment – they all merge and sink into the sludge of jealousy. She is younger, more beautiful. Is that what it comes down to in the end? A pathetic meanness of spirit? Surely there is more to it than that?

Richard walks to the kitchen window and stares out at the night. His back is straight, his shoulders squared. 'I've never stopped loving you,' he says. 'And I never will.' His voice shakes. Is he crying? Yes, his eyes are brimming with tears when he turns around. He takes her hand.

'*How many ways can you tell someone how much you love them?*' He whispers it into her ear, the hollow of her neck, the swell of her breasts. In bed, together again, they make love slowly. No rush, they have all night to pleasure each other.

TEN

There is a rhythm to her sessions with Elaine. Christine knows what to expect and is no longer surprised by the emotions each one arouses. Elaine hadn't been surprised when she heard about Christine's near-drowning experience. With her assistance, Christine is beginning to understand why she is haunted by those tumultuous moments when she must have struggled for breath. Traces of this trauma response are still with her. She will need gentle support to discharge them at a pace that is right for her.

She is also beginning to explore the possible origins of her nightmare. The wedding is an understandable connection. But why does she keep focusing on Jessica? Even in a trance, her mind runs in only one direction. Sometimes, Christine sees her standing on the riverbank: Jessica stares into the rapid flow, her gaze unfathomable; or she remains hidden behind a screen of leaves. Even when Christine cannot see her, she is conscious that Jessica is nearby.

During this evening's session, she recalls suffering a similar panic attack to the one she experienced at Rosswall Heights. It occurred when her family was staying with Sharon and Patrick in Dorset. Christine had been an only child at their wedding, but Bernice and Killian had been born since then and Sharon had also given birth to twins. The two families took a day trip to Rillingham-on-the Weir and had lunch in the restaurant at Rillingham Castle, where Sharon and Patrick's wedding reception had been held. Halfway through their meal, Christine had begun to shake and had difficulty breathing. Stella had called an ambulance, convinced her daughter was suffering an asthmatic attack.

An 'onslaught of panic' had been the medical diagnosis. It sounded strange and scary, something that would happen to nervous old women, and Christine, rejecting it with the arrogance of a fifteen-year-old, had been convinced she had suffered an allergic reaction to something she had eaten at the hotel.

When this memory returns, she can recall the sensation she experienced. The struggle to catch her breath, the descending blackness and the muffled roar of the river as it pulled her under. Just before it happens, she sees Jessica. This time she is clearly visible, an inscrutable figure on the riverbank, watching.

'Christine, attend to your breathing.' Elaine's calm voice reaches her. Her ability to recognise when Christine is distressed is a constant reassurance. 'You can come back at any time to this room, where you are safe.'

Christine opens her eyes and allows herself to hear the normal street sounds that filter into the room. She accepts a glass of water from Elaine and tries to articulate her fears. 'I associate Jessica with danger,' she says slowly. 'Subconsciously, I've known that from the first time I met her. That's why I'm so anxious in her company. These panic attacks only began when she came to work for us.'

'Yes, she came to work for you. And *now* you're working for her.' Elaine's quiet emphasis begs a response.

'That irony has not escaped me.' Christine speaks more abruptly than she intends.

'If Jessica were to represent something for you, what would that be?' The hypnotherapist is unperturbed by her tone.

'Call it psychic awareness or just plain intuition... but it's an urge to protect what is mine.'

'And what is it that is yours and needs to be protected?'

My marriage is under threat. Christine wants to shout out this truth. Symbolically, she has figured it out but she is incapable of dealing with the consequences of making such an admission. A short reprieve, that was all she enjoyed with Richard before she was once again watching him with Jessica, noting their darting sidewards glances, their laughter, which always sounds if they have just shared an intimate secret. Suspicion, those spores of jealousy... she can't remember when they attached themselves to her, nor does she know how to prise them loose.Does she regret meeting Elaine? These sessions have forced her to confront reality and she cannot blame Elaine for pulling the wool from her eyes. She wrenched it aside herself, her gaze shaper and more aware than it was when she first walked through the door of this small house. Her anxiety, too, is sharper at times. Any hope that it will abate has gone.

The following Saturday, Christine drives to Sandymount to visit her mother. Jack, her father, is storing his golf clubs in the boot of his car when she arrives. He opens his arms and gives her his usual bear hug. He has grown a beard since he retired, a short, boxed style that feels ticklish against her cheek.

'When are you and Richard coming to Sunday lunch?' he asks. 'It's ages since you've been here.'

'Soon,' she says. 'I promise... *promise*. Work has been so hectic—'

'I don't want to hear the usual excuses.' Jack releases her from his embrace and wags a finger at her. 'Work is secondary to family and you need to slow down. How is Richard?'

'Busy as ever. He's visiting Tom. Otherwise, he'd be here with me.'

As an excuse it can't be faulted but it is only half the truth. Richard is working this morning. Right at this moment, he and Jessica are solving another unexpected 'glitch' on the Krisgloss account. Glitches, tweaks, strategic updates, copy, templates and targets, Christine is familiar with the jargon that dominates her husband's life and keeps him late at the agency on too many evenings. This is the first time he has had to work at the weekend. The seriousness of this latest 'glitch' could not be underestimated, he'd insisted, his forehead creased with anxiety as he explained in detail to Christine what had gone wrong with the art work. He would visit his father as soon as the problem was sorted... or so he told her before absent-mindedly kissing her forehead and hurrying off.

'How is Tom?' Jack asks. 'I thought he looked well the last time I visited him. He talked a lot about his childhood.'

'That's where he spends most of his time now,' she says. 'He had a happy childhood so it's not a bad place to be, I guess.'

Jack nods sympathetically and slams the boot closed. 'I'll call in to see him soon. Give Richard my best. We'll be spending time in Sheerwater now that the weather has improved. Don't let another summer pass without you and Richard coming down for a weekend. In the meantime, fix a date with Stella for Sunday lunch. It's tough with Killian and Bernice living abroad, especially when we have to depend on Skype to keep in touch with our grandchildren.'

She knows he does not mean to make her feel guilty yet that last comment is a reproof, however unintentionally it was delivered. She waves him off then turns to greet Stella, who has opened the front door.

The weather for April is mild and Stella has set the table on the patio in the garden. She serves salad with a smoked salmon quiche and baked potatoes.

'Did you ever worry about Dad's fidelity?' Christine blurts out the question with a suddenness that takes both of them by surprise.

'Why do you ask?' Her mother's gaze is speculative.

'You'll be forty years married soon. It's a long time to remain in love.'

'Love can't be measured by time,' Stella replies. 'It's also mercurial. Just when you think you have it figured out it changes again and, if you're lucky, you manage to hold on to its new shape.'

'You still haven't answered my question? Did you or he ever... *stray*?'

'I'm not sure that's a question a daughter should be asking her mother.' Stella cuts into the quiche and Christine is unable to tell if her mother is amused or uncomfortable by the directness of her question. The garden has come to life, the clematis climbing over the back wall, tulips and narcissuses nodding gently along the borders, and the cherry blossom is already drifting like pale-pink snow to the lawn. Her mother takes care of the planting and her father builds the structures like the patio, pergola and garden furniture that make it such an attractive space to relax. A perfect partnership, like her and Richard. She checks her watch. He should be with Tom now. She will not phone him. Trust... without it their marriage is a shell.

'A simple yes or no will suffice,' she says.

'I've been tempted a few times.' Stella laughs, self-consciously. 'I suspect Jack, too, has had his moments. But, no, we've remained constant.'

Constant sounds cosy but boring yet there is nothing dull about their marriage. Christine has seen them spark with anger and radiate with passion. Their obvious affection for each other embarrassed her when she was a child, yet she never wanted them to change or to be less demonstrative.

'Is everything okay with you and Richard?' Stella asks. This is a tentative question and Christine shrugs as if it is of no consequence.

'Apart from the fact that we don't have a business anymore and I've to report to a woman ten years younger than me, everything's hunky-dory.'

'That's not what I'm asking, Christine. If you need to talk to me, I'm ready to listen.' She knows when Christine is lying, always has. She will be wise and cautious in what she has to say but Christine, by acknowledging her fears, will have breathed new life into them.

'I do need to talk to you but not about Richard.'

'Oh?'

'Why was I beside that river on the day of Sharon's wedding? Did it run through the grounds of the hotel?'

This sudden change of conversation causes Stella to sit back with a gasp. 'Good heavens, that's a blast from the past,' she says. 'I took my eye off you for a moment and you wandered off.'

'A moment?'

'It took time before I realised you were missing,' Stella admits. 'We searched the hotel first before we realised you must have wandered further afield. Why do you ask?'

'I'm curious. I don't remember falling into the river, yet when I have that nightmare—'

'Is it still the same one?'

'It never changes but I can't remember the actual incident. How did it happen?'

'You'd been rescued when we found you.'

'Rescued?'

'It was a fast-flowing river. We almost lost you.'

So, that much is true. A memory has been resurrected but it seems dreamlike rather than an organic remembering. 'How was I rescued?'

'A boy saw you and pulled you out. As soon as we realised

you were missing, we'd organised a search party. He heard our voices and called out to us.'

'Was I able to tell you what happened?'

'You weren't able to tell us anything. Later, after you'd been checked by the doctor, you talked about breaking the roses in the hotel garden. I think Uncle Ned frightened you and you ran off. He was always cantankerous and had no patience with children. Yet he was the first to organise the search. I was convinced I'd find you in the hotel and so much time was wasted before we checked beyond the grounds.'

'You've never told me this before.'

'I often wondered if we should. But you had such happy memories of the wedding. It seemed a shame to dwell on what happened to you afterwards. Why the sudden interest now?'

'I'm seeing a hypnotherapist about my anxiety.'

Her mother looks at her. 'You were five years old when you fell into the river, Christine. I find it strange that your anxiety could be related to that incident...'

'Why should that be so strange?'

'Well...' Stella hesitates. 'Don't you think you should be focusing on the present?'

'Why should I do that if my problem belongs to the past?'

'But does it really belong there, Christine?' Stella clears her throat. 'You're obviously still deeply affected by the buyout. Maybe it's time you considered a change of direction. If you were to start a family—'

'You promised we'd never have this conversation again.' Christine stares at a seagull on the garden wall. Its menacing eyes dart towards the remains of the quiche on the table but it remains stationary.

'I worry that in time you'll come to regret your decision—'

'I *won't*.'

'You sound so certain!' Stella shakes her head. 'Why? It's not as if you had a difficult childhood.'

'Why does there have to be a dysfunctional reason for my decision? A happy childhood doesn't automatically translate into a maternal instinct. You've always known I don't want children.'

'It's the *why* that I've never understood. You like children. Your nieces and nephews adore you—'

'As I adore them. But I'm perfectly happy with the life I've chosen. So is Richard.'

The seagull, sensing its opportunity, swoops to the table and snatches a crust of the quiche. A sliver of lemon falls on the table as the bird takes off. The shock of its lunge is distracting enough to break the tension that has arisen between them.

'Anyway, it's not as if you're deprived of grandchildren.' Christine smiles at her mother. 'Look at you – off to Paris on Monday to see Bernice. What trips has she lined up for you and Dad this time?'

'We've done the tourist trail,' says Stella. 'Our only interest now is spending time with our grandchildren. If only they were nearer to us.' She looks wistful for an instant then stands to clear the table as the seagull returns and brings their conversation to a natural end.

As she carries plates to the kitchen, Christine's anxiety resurfaces. Why did Stella have to bring up the subject of children again? In Paris she will play with her grandchildren and discuss with Bernice why, in the great arena of propagation and nurturing, her eldest child did not inherit the parenting gene. Will Christine's ears burn? Will she even notice?

They part with a hug, neither one admitting that they are handling an unfinished conversation.

Christine's sense of detachment from Foundation Stone grows stronger, even as she is drawn into the wider web that is SFDN. Jessica is expected to deliver a financial report at the board of directors' meeting every month. This should be Christine's responsibility, but Samuel Newman still insists that his daughter familiarise herself with all the financial aspects of the agency. More profit, less outgoings, that is what Alan Martin, the financial controller of SFDN, has decreed. Unlike Samuel, whose presence dominates the boardroom, Alan Martin is colourless. That is the only description that comes to mind each time Christine sees him. His skin is pallid and unlined. She can never imagine him squinting into the sun or allowing the wind to toss the sparse strands of his sleek, blond hair. When he stares at her, his grey gaze is chilling yet he is always quietly spoken, even when he is making decisions to close down companies that are not performing to his exacting standards. Only his mouth, as thin and taut as a wire, indicates the ruthlessness that lies behind his washed-out countenance.

At these monthly meetings, Jessica expects Christine to be a reassuring presence by her elbow as she presents the advertising budgets Christine has compiled for her. Once they return to Foundation Stone, Jessica discards her as casually as a well-worn coat and disappears into Richard's office, where the door is now more often closed than open.

At this session with Elaine, Christine is anxious to focus on the aftermath of the wedding, a desire that is mixed with anxiety and an edginess that Elaine immediately recognises. She is soothed by Elaine's quiet voice as she prepares her to encounter moments from her past, or, maybe, from her imagination.

'Imagine you're sitting comfortably on your sofa, Christine. You're holding the remote control in your hand and you're about to play a home movie from the time when you were a little girl. Now, begin to rewind the footage at just the right speed to where you can vaguely recognise the scene playing in reverse in front of your eyes. You're still unable to pick out the details but keep rewinding until you feel you get to something of interest where you'd like to pause and take a look at what's happening.' When Christine signals that she has paused the video, Elaine invites her to play it in her imagination from that point. She reminds Christine that at any time she is in control and can choose to press fast forward, pause or stop.

Rillingham Castle sits on a height. Christine can make out the turrets and a drawbridge, a moat that looks real enough to be authentic – but there is something too perfect about this configuration.

'What can you see?' Elaine asks.

'Castle Rillingham.'

'Are there any people?'

'Yes. Lots of grown-ups.

'Are you inside or outside?'

'Outside.'

'Is it day or night?'

'Daytime.'

'Are you alone or with someone else?'

'I'm squashed between the grown-ups.'

'What age are you, Christine?'

'I'm five years old.' She answers with certainty.

How small she looks, how vulnerable yet winsome in her purple, flouncy dress and sparkly shoes. It feels safe to sit back and allow the screen to flicker with wraiths that come alive and blaze with colour. Her dress is crushed against the people crowding around her. Leftover petals spill from her basket. She poses between Sharon and Patrick for the photographer and even has a photograph taken on his shoulders. She drinks fresh orange juice but there are no sweets or Rice Krispie buns. Her mother says there'll be real food soon but when is soon? This wedding day feels like the elastic in her flower headband and it just keeps getting longer and longer.

'Just be patient, sweetie,' says her mother when Christine tells her she's hungry. Her father asks the waiter for crisps but the castle hasn't got any, just squiggly things on biscuits that smell horribly. Sharon swishes her dress and kicks up her leg for the photographer.

Christine pulls the head from a blousy red rose and rips the petals from its centre.

'Leave those roses alone, young madam.' Uncle Ned shouts at her. His glasses are perched on the end of his nose and his forehead is shiny from the sun.

She runs away from him and stops when she reaches a wall with a stile built into it. Once she is over it, she runs through a meadow of long grass that swishes against her dress. She can no longer hear voices; only birds, and a rustling sound when the wind shakes the buttercups. She slides through the bars of a gate on the far side of the meadow and laughs out loud when a black horse gallops into view. If only she had an apple. Every summer when she goes on holiday to Sheerwater, Jasper comes to the wall of the chalet and pokes his head over the gate so that she can feed him.

She sees trees beyond the horse field. She is sure the ground there will be covered with fallen apples. She climbs over another gate but the trees are so close together that they hide the sun. Sometimes it peeks down again and speckles the path, but there are no apples, no matter how much she searches.

'What's happening now, Christine?' Elaine's voice is calm and reassuring.

'I'm lost.'

'Is it daytime or night?'

'It's still daytime. I'm at my aunt's wedding but I wandered away.'

She can no longer see the castle, just branches with fluttery leaves, and it doesn't matter which way she turns. Everywhere looks the same. Her hair is loose from the flower hairband and hangs over her cheeks. The curls that Mandy, the hairstylist, made that morning are gone, and her sparkly shoes hurt. She has a blister on one heel but the ground is sore under her feet when she takes them off. Her mother will be so angry when she sees the state of Christine's socks so it's better to suffer the pain of her shoes.

When she cries out, Elaine reminds her of her safe place and to go there in her mind. She thinks of Sheerwater but there is no sign of Jasper anywhere. This adds to her agitation and Elaine gently reminds her that she is safe, snuggled up on a sofa with a rug around her, secure. Unlike the bedraggled, bewildered child she remembers. Her breathing becomes steady and deeper as the session continues. She hears a voice. It is deep and similar to how her father sounds when he's cross. He must be angry at Christine for taking him away from his sister's wedding. She puts her shoes on again and runs down a hollow filled with broken branches. The voice is nearer now and comes from behind more trees. She hunkers behind the tree trunks and peers beyond them to where the ground is flat and stony.

Christine wants to cry out loud because the man who turns towards her is not her father. He is wearing a ponytail but, as yet, she is unable to see his face. He fades into a blur that assumes a new shape and she is staring at Jessica's slender form.

'*Jessica*.' She breathes her name as the picture fades. She is staring at a blank screen that gives a little swish as if her imagination is drawing curtains over what she is no longer able to watch. The trembling starts in her fingers then travels from her arms down through her body.

Jessica, her nemesis. She can no longer ignore the symbolism. Fear has muted her for too long. Once admitted, she'll no longer have the comfort of denial, but the caution she has maintained for so long has deserted her.

. . .

Christine always switches off her phone when she is with Elaine and Richard has been trying to contact her. He is working late. Another problem with Krisgloss.

It is almost midnight when she hears his key in the door. The problem has been solved. He is exhausted yet hyper, adrenaline flowing. Jessica worked late with him.

'Are you having an affair with her?' Christine's steely voice has only the slightest hint of a slur.

He denies it, not once but three times, his impatience growing as she continues to question him.

'Is this what our marriage has been reduced to?' he shouts. 'Suspicion and jealousy? You've no reason to doubt my love for you yet you seem hell-bent on destroying it.' He is rigid with self-righteous anger yet there is something guarded in his denials.

'Don't twist this back on me, Richard.' When she lifts the vodka bottle, her hand shakes. Can a palsy develop from repressed emotions? Far better to have it out in the open. 'I don't make this accusation easily. It's destroying me.'

'No, Christine, it's destroying *us*. Where are you going with this ridiculous obsession about Jessica? She's done everything possible to help us adjust to the buy-out and the terms we agreed with Samuel. Excellent terms, as you know. It's not how we imagined the future but the agency is now in a stronger position than it was when we owned it. Those new accounts – do you honestly believe they'd have come our way if it wasn't for Samuel's contacts?'

The name slides so easily from him. He makes Samuel Newman sound like his best mate. What have new contracts got to do with her question?

She asks it again, slowly this time. Are-you-having-an-affair-with-Jessica-Newman?

How grubby and pathetic it sounds.

He slams his fists on the table, all restraint gone. 'No, I'm *not,*' he shouts. 'No! No! No!'

She perceives a wildness in him, his cheeks flooded with colour, his eyes hungry for Jessica. This is all she sees as he turns from her and storms from the living room. She hears him on the stairs, his furious tread as he crosses the bedroom floor. A few minutes later, he enters the room where her father-in-law used to sleep. He will sleep alone tonight but he needn't have bothered changing bedrooms. She is too drunk and distraught to climb the stairs. She watches television with the sound down. Facial language is her only guide, all those twitches and blinks, raised eyebrows, lowered foreheads, narrowed vision, disdainful nostrils.

Who needs words to establish the truth? As for her heart, increasingly, Christine feels as if the fragile membrane surrounding it is being ripped apart. The kitten claws are never easy, never at rest.

ELEVEN

Richard shakes her awake. The phone call from the nursing home comes in the small hours of the morning. Tom has suffered a stroke and Gwen is waiting at the nursing home for an ambulance to arrive. Christine pulls herself upright on the sofa and tries to comprehend what he is telling her. Last night's argument is not forgotten but is insignificant compared to the news they have just received.

Dawn smudges the horizon as Richard drives towards Beaumont hospital. No traffic, as yet, and the street lamps give off a comforting glow. Gwen meets them in Accident and Emergency. One look at the nurse's expression is all they need to know they have arrived too late. Tom, that lovely, brave man, was pronounced dead when the ambulance reached the hospital.

Richard weeps as he clasps his father's still-warm hands. She wants to hold her husband close but the smell of vodka has created a fetid barrier between them. Self-hatred is a dangerous indulgence. It excuses so much yet Christine is overcome by it as she whispers farewell to Tom. She can't think beyond him right now yet the scene from last night pushes forward as she hurries to the hospital bathroom to wash her face. Haggard, that's how she looks – pale, drawn and blotchy, with bloodshot eyes. She is a stranger, even to herself.

'My card's marked,' Tom told her the last time they were together. His eyes were clear, his words lucid. 'I don't want this to be my final parking space.' He had gestured towards the room filled with family photographs and his favourite albums. 'Take me home when I die and throw a hell of a party for the gang. Tears are strictly forbidden. Remember that.'

When they return to Redstone, Richard phones Jessica and explains that they will not be at work today. Christine doesn't want to listen to a one-sided conversation yet she is straining to hear... what? A cadence that suggests there are secret messages hidden within the professional tone he uses? Suspicion will drive her mad. She must shake it aside and help him prepare the house for Tom's homecoming. He will be laid out in the morning room where he used to play poker with his friends. A view of the sea is visible from the window and that was where he liked to relax in the evenings.

Tom's friends arrive two evenings later to celebrate his life. At first, they are sombre as they stand around his coffin, but the mood soon changes and laughter rings out once the reminiscing begins. Neighbours also call to pay their respects and are followed by the staff from Foundation Stone.

'I'm sorry for your troubles, Christine.' Jessica shakes her hand and sounds just as formal when she offers her condolences to Richard.

Christine is amazed that she can say something so inane yet sound as if she means it. What does Jessica know of her troubles? The longing for a drink overwhelms her but she whispered an oath into Tom's ear when they were in the hospital mortuary and she is not going to break it. She thanks Jessica for coming and moves away with a polite excuse to speak to the new arrivals.

She is experienced at working a room, networking and bringing like-minded people together. But the crowd is varied here and are grouped together by familiarity and shared memories. As the numbers grow, they spill into the larger living room where refreshments and drinks have been laid out on the low sideboard. Laughter and nostalgia, abundant merriment and good cheer – this was the kind of send-off Tom wanted.

She hadn't noticed Samuel Newman arriving. Richard must have let him in. He seems to stand apart from everyone or, maybe, that's just how Christine sees him. Tall and erect, his face in profile and a glass of whiskey in one hand, he surveys the people surrounding him but makes no effort to interact with them. He turns around, and suddenly his jawline is blurring, his features melding, as if his face has turned to wax.

A scream lodges in Christine's throat. It will choke her but so be it: she cannot make another scene... but as she reaches blindly for something to support her, a platter overbalances when she touches the edge of the sideboard, sending cocktail sausages, sandwiches and wraps to the floor. And she falls with them, her legs collapsing with such suddenness that she is unable to save herself.

Samuel comes to her assistance immediately. She sees his concern, his fear that she will pass out again.

'Thank you,' she says, as he lifts her and holds her steady for an instant. 'I'm so clumsy.'

'Not clumsy,' he says. 'Just distressed. It's a sad time.' The sounds of laughter from Tom's friends suggest otherwise and he quirks an eyebrow, as if sharing the irony with her. His cologne, a musky fragrance, reminds her of spices. It must be expensive, he would never wear anything else, yet it smells cheap, repellent.

'You were kind to come.' She struggles to keep her tone neutral.

'Not at all. I was anxious to pay my respects.'

Jessica and Richard move forward and begin to clear up the food. They work in unison, not speaking, their hands touching, then separating. He believes Christine has been drinking. His nostrils flare, as if searching for telltale traces. To admit that she has had nothing to drink suggests she is denying a habit.

She manages to walk steadily from the living room. Once outside, she hurries up the stairs to the bedroom. She collapses on the bed and instinctively curls her body into a foetal position.

Stella taps on the door and enters. Her parents had arrived early for Tom's wake with a platter of food, and wine. 'I've been looking all over for you.' Stella sits on the edge of the bed and takes Christine's hand. 'We're just about to leave. Is everything okay?'

Her glance is too keen to be ignored. 'I wasn't feeling well. I just needed some time alone. I'll go down now.'

'This anxiety, is it bothering you still?'

'I'm managing it. Losing Tom... it's difficult.'

'I can imagine. Dear Tom. He was a lovely man.'

'What was the boy's name?'

'What boy?' Stella is startled by the question.

'The boy who pulled me from the river.'

'Oh... where on earth is this coming from?'

'Did you ever find out who he was?'

'He ran off as soon as we arrived. Your father chased after him. He wanted to reward him but couldn't catch up with him. The boy was scared.'

'Of what?'

'Uncle Ned kept asking him what he was doing by the river. Maybe he was afraid we'd accuse him of having something to do with your accident. Anyway, he took off and we never had a chance to thank him properly.' Stella pauses and brushes some hair from her daughter's face. 'Why all this interest? It was such a long time ago.

'So, you don't know his name.'

'He'd an Irish name, I think. It sounded like Brian O'Neill but when I asked the hotel receptionist if she had ever heard of him, she wasn't able to help me. Honestly, Christine, I'm worried about you. You're not yourself—'

'Who am I, then? Have you a name for this individual?' Her tone is so snappish that Stella hesitates before replying, as uncomfortable as Christine is with the direction their conversation has taken.

'You know what I mean. These panic attacks...' She waves her hand in apology. 'I'm not supposed to know it happened again but Richard was so worried he rang me. He said you'd been drinking and suffered a blackout—'

'How dare he tell such a lie.' Fury scorches her cheeks.

'Why would your husband, the man you claim to love, lie about something so serious?'

'Maybe it's his way of easing his conscience.'

'Oh, Christine! What do you mean?'

Stella's distress presses against her. She has said too much. Far too much. She imagines the cogs spinning in her mother's mind, the worries she will take home with her.

'We're going through a difficult patch but it's nothing we can't sort out.' She sounds convincing, which surprises her. People are beginning to leave. Does she want Jessica standing in her place at the front door and bidding them goodbye? She hugs Stella and checks her face in the mirror, runs her hands over her hair. Appearances are everything.

Downstairs again, she shakes hands, exchanges hugs, thanks people for attending Tom's wake. The noise abates. Samuel has left but Jessica is still there. She stacks the dishwasher while Richard collects the leftover plates and glasses. The synchronicity between them sickens her. She tells herself that Rory and Lorraine have also stayed behind to help with the clean-up but that fact does nothing to ease her mind.

She enters the morning room. Tom is alone now, rigid and still, his features frozen in an unfamiliar mask of sternness. One of Nell's paintings hangs on the wall behind his coffin: curlicues of froth riding high on the fast-flowing Corrib, a lone kayaker battling the currents.

The staff pile into Jessica's car. She beeps the horn as she drives off. The agency will remain shut tomorrow as a mark of respect for Richard's father. Such a gesture is unnecessary.

Richard frowns and steps back from Christine when she makes this comment.

The kitten claws respond... *scratch... scratch...*

TWELVE

Elaine has closed out the evening. The domed shade of a tiffany lamp casts a glow downwards over her hands as they rest on her lap. This time, the scenes come quickly, more clearly. At one point Christine is speaking so fast that Elaine asks her to slow down. Then, the memories are arrested, poised in that instant as she struggles to breathe, exhaling out and in, out and in.

A meadow of long grass and buttercups. The shell-like ruins of a castle rising in the distance. She remembers the exhilaration she felt as she ran towards the horse and how that excitement changed into fear as she ventured deeper into the forest. She sees herself hunkered on the ground, sheltered by broad tree trunks, the river far below her.

This time, Jessica does not appear. Somehow, this agitates Christine even more. She hears the voices again and moves closer. The tall man standing in the clearing is not her father. All she can see is the side of his face and his long, brown ponytail.

Christine moans softly. 'I can't... Elaine... I don't want to be here. I can't... can't...'

Elaine's voice carries authority and reassurance as she

guides Christine back to the safety of this welcoming room. She waits to see if Christine wishes to discuss what she experienced some moments before. Christine shakes her head, the terror the man evoked in her too raw to share, to even begin to comprehend. Perhaps, when she comes again, it will be possible to go back to that shaded forest and penetrate those shadows.

Christine's hands remain steady on the steering wheel as she drives through the quiet streets. Where was Jessica when she was in a trance? Why was she unable to find her? Has she finally moved aside and revealed the real danger? But how can that be defined? Is she allowing herself to be overwhelmed by imaginary fears? This is a possibility she must accept.

Richard has cooked their evening meal. The kitchen is redolent with spices when she opens the door. He has removed a dish from the oven and is carrying it to the table when he notices her. 'What's wrong?' He lowers the dish to a heat plate and crosses the floor to her. 'Has something happened? Did you—'

'I'm fine.' She allows him to hold her for an instant but she is too troubled to relax against him. 'I've just had a very disturbing experience but I'm okay... really, I am.' She slumps down on the nearest chair and grips the arms.

'Where did it happen?' he asks.

'What do you mean?'

'The panic attack—'

'I didn't have an attack. I was with Elaine.'

'Oh, the hypnotherapist?'

'Yes, what's wrong with that?'

'Nothing at all. It's just that you're always on edge when you return from one of those sessions.'

'That's not true, Richard. She's helping me to work through something traumatic that happened to me when I was a child.'

'The river incident?'

'Yes...' She hesitates, uncertain whether or not she should continue. What is real? What is fantasy? How can she possibly trust the scenes she conjures up? Are they genuine recollections or merely images and metaphors offered up by her unconscious mind?

'Tonight, I think I had a breakthrough. I feel as though I've been building towards this discovery for weeks but Jessica kept blocking it—'

'What the *fuck*...? What has Jessica got to do with any of this?' His startled reaction snaps her to attention.

'Nothing,' she says. 'I just meant that she symbolised danger or a threat. Something that I couldn't comprehend, but it frightened me when I was in hypnosis—'

'Funny the way all our conversations come back to Jessica.' He rolls his eyes upwards in exasperation, exhales loudly. 'I don't think this hypnosis is helping you at all. You've lost focus ever since you started going to that woman. You should see someone professional—'

'Elaine is professional—'

'You know what I mean. Someone who can control your anxiety with something more suitable than putting you into a trance where your imagination goes into overdrive.'

'I haven't even told you what I experienced this evening, yet you've made up your mind not to believe me?'

He studies her for an instant before he speaks. 'I think you're overwhelmed by all that's happened to us since the takeover. I've been just as preoccupied and, somehow, we've lost our way in the struggle to adjust. We need each other more than ever. I want you to stop seeing Elaine. Let's do counselling together. We need to plan a new future and this could be our first step.'

He is still talking as he walks towards the hob where rice is simmering and ready to be sieved. Confiding in him was a mistake. Nothing will be solved by blasting him with her anger. Perhaps he is right about her imagination. But she cannot be guided by his scepticism. This is her journey and she will travel it alone.

The chicken curry he made for their evening meal is hot enough to bring tears to her eyes. She has no appetite but forces herself to eat a little. Their silence is laden and when they do speak, it is small talk that is safe enough not to shatter the brittle peace they are working so hard to maintain.

Until now, he was always invisible yet his presence ran like a shudder through her nightmares. This time Christine sees him clearly. Aware that she is dreaming and her terror belongs only to the dream, she forces herself awake. She sits up, her back rigid against the headboard. The rhythm of memory – it thuds like a drum, like a yanked heartbeat.

The sun highlights the dark strands of his hair as he turns his startled gaze on her. He stands above a youth, a boy still in his mid-teens, wearing denim jeans and a hoodie, the hood pulled back to reveal his bowed head. The tall man has a stick in his hand. Black and stubby, how can it be a stick? But that is what Christine wants it to be. The youth is kneeling, his hands joined, as if he is praying. The stick makes a *click-click* sound and the youth falls forward. Blood is coming from his head. It runs over the ground. She has never seen so much red in all her life. She is shadowed by trees. The branches hang heavy with leaves. She must run away from the man with the stick. The ground is covered with twigs. She breaks one with her knees and the crack it makes is so much louder than the *click-click* she heard.

When the man turns around, she sees that he is not holding a stick. She has seen guns on telly when her parents watch films about robbers and that is what he has in his hand. He runs towards her. His eyes open wide and his eyebrows rise up high when he looks at her flower-girl dress and sees how it's all covered in mud.

No time to hide before he catches her and hurls her up under his arm. His face has pimples and there's stubble on his chin. His hand smells of smoke when he covers her mouth.

He curses as he runs past the youth on the ground, runs far away from the blood that flows into the undergrowth. He is running down a steep embankment, pushing his way through branches that drag at her flower-girl dress and she can hear another sound above his curses. It is the river hissing like it wants to bash the rocks out of the way. She wants other people to see what he is doing to her but there is no one else around. The bridge above the river is broken in the middle and the bushes growing along the riverbank are high enough to hide them from view. When he puts her down on the side of the bridge nearest to them, he twists the gun in his other hand then swings his arm towards her. The butt of the gun strikes her forehead. Stars appear and spin before her eyes, then disappear into darkness.

It is cold, as cold as it always is in Sheerwater when she runs into the lake. She usually screams until she gets down. Daddy stays beside her to make sure she doesn't go out of her depth and Mammy waits on the shore with a big towel to wrap around her when she comes out. The river is different. She has no time to scream before the water goes over her head. When she come up again, she sees him standing there watching her. Then he's gone and the gurgling noises fill her ears. Her shoes come off and her beautiful, purple dress rises about her head. Everything is black now and the water whirls her away, tosses her like a leaf, and the loud gurgles grow softer... softer... like they're turning into music, but even that fades away and all she feels is pain.

Someone is hitting her. She feels the thump on her chest and stomach. She is going to be sick. She wants her mother to bring the sick bowl but it is not her voice that tells her to open her eyes. The sick is rising from her stomach and comes out in a great big whoosh. Her eyelashes feel stuck together but she knows she must do what the voice tells her. She forces her eyelids apart but it is hard to see. The sun is white. She will go blind if she stares for too long at it. Then, it is blocked by the person who is hitting her. At first, she thinks it is the man with the gun but he has no stubble on his chin. Nor does he have a gun, just two hands that keep pressing her chest. She wants to touch him to check if he is real but he shoves her on her side so that she can throw up properly. He tells her that she fell into the river and banged her head on the rocks. He lies down beside her and she is able to see him properly. He is soaking wet like her and there is water dripping from his hair. She is lucky she didn't drown, he says. Walking too close to the riverbank is dangerous.

She hears her name being shouted over and over again. The boy stands and cups his hands to his mouth.

'Over here,' he shouts. 'She's over here.'

Her mother hugs her so tight it hurts. Daddy carries her back to the castle and up to the bedroom with the big four poster bed and her own little bed alongside it. The doctor comes and bandages her forehead. He gives her an injection and tells her that she has the cleanest lungs in Dorset. She keeps falling asleep but it is okay because she is safe in Mammy's arms.

'Where did you go?' Daddy asks when she awakens again. '*Tell us* – what happened to you?'

Christine shakes her head. All she can remember are the roses. All those roses with their big, droopy heads and the red petals scattering like drops of blood spilling to the ground.

Richard is still sleeping when she runs to the bathroom to be violently sick. That is where he finds her an hour later. He helps her back to bed.

'I should have died,' she whispers. There is no comfort in denying it. The cut-glass severity of the gunman's profile; his harsh, startled gaze when he turned towards her; his body tensing as he decided what must be done. He is her nightmare made real. She remembers the helter-skelter run down the slope to the riverbank and the stars that spun when he smashed the gun against her forehead. She touches the spot. It is still there. A crescent mark, slightly ridged, barely noticeable. She questioned it once. Stella said it happened when she fell from a swing, that Christine was a clumsy child. It was always easier to believe that lie.

She was unconscious when she was thrown into the river. *Thrown.* The word makes her gasp. Thrown like a twig on the fast-flowing currents. The cold water brought her back to consciousness and an unknown boy dragged her from her grave and gave her back her life.

'I witnessed a murder.' Even as she whispers this truth to Richard, she realises how incredible it sounds.

'Go on.' He sits down beside her on the bed.

'I watched a man being shot in his head—'

'You *what?*'

'I know it sounds crazy... but that's how I ended up in the river. The gunman tried to drown me. How could I have forgotten something so terrible?'

'Christine... Christine, are you listening to yourself?' Richard grips her arms and hugs her close to him. His embrace is hard, unyielding. 'You're describing something that could have come straight out of a gangster film.'

'Let me go...let me *go*.' She frees herself and pulls her hair back from her forehead. 'Look at this scar. That's where he struck me with his gun. He knocked me unconscious, then threw me into the river.'

He angles the bedside lamp towards her face and examines the mark. 'You told me you fell from a swing.' His expression is concerned yet he is unable to disguise his scepticism. She sees it in his eyes but it disappears so quickly it is possible to believe she was mistaken.

'That's what I always believed,' she replies. 'But I was wrong.'

'Are you really giving credence to this... this...' He shakes his head as he searches for the appropriate word and fails to find one. 'Come on, Christine... *please*.'

'You think I imagined it?'

'I think it's part of the anxiety you've been experiencing for months. Along with the stress of losing the agency. That's had such an impact on both of us.'

How can she expect him to accept a truth that she has kept under control for... how long...? Thirty years since she witnessed an execution. Now that the truth is finally uncaged and clawing her, all she wants to do is obliterate it.

Once the tears start, she is unable to stop. His arms are around her again and it is easy to listen to his rational explanations. Her parents were, and still are, hooked on crime dramas: *Miami Vice*, *Columbo*, *Cagney & Lacey*, *Charlie's Angels*, *Hill Street Blues* – they were part of Christine's childhood. Even though she wasn't allowed to watch them until she was older, she would have caught glimpses of high-speed chases and shootings during her early years. Such images must have been fixed in her mind when she was a lost and frightened five-year-old, who accidently strayed from a wedding party and slipped into a river.

She presses her face against his shoulder. What he says makes perfect sense. She wills her body to relax, to let go. Her mouth to open to his kisses. They are kisses of comfort, not passion, kisses that are meaningless... because she knows the memory of what she encountered on that day of happiness and horror is now complete.

The only person who can understand her turmoil is Elaine.

. . .

The following day when Elaine, recognising her distress, agrees to see her, she makes her way to that safe space where demons were kept at a safe distance until Christine was strong enough to face them.

This time, she does not need to be in hypnosis. She drinks camomile tea and remains cocooned in the rug that Elaine had wrapped around her shoulders. She describes, without embellishments, what she saw. A man with a gun, his jaw clenched, his blue gaze, unwavering. A youth in a hoodie kneeling. And a boy who rescued her.

When Elaine, speaking as a friend now, suggests that she might consider seeing a psychologist who specialises in post-traumatic stress disorder, and recommends a name, Christine shakes her head. Later, she will be ready to confront the moment when a stranger turned to face her and decided to take her life but, for now, her only desire is to find Brian O'Neill. She sees his face clearly, his skin pearled from the river as he banged life back into her.

THIRTEEN

None of the profiles on Facebook fit the Brian O'Neill she seeks. It is the same with LinkedIn and the other social media sites she tries. She narrows her search to Rillingham-on-the-Weir and discovers *The Weir View*. For sixty years this weekly broadsheet has been the voice and eyes of the small Dorset town and its hinterland. She contacts the editor and claims to be a writer doing research on the ancient castle that still stands on the grounds of the hotel where Sharon and Patrick were married. Keith Jackson is affable and obliging. She has permission to check the archive, which has been digitised and can be accessed online with a password.

As she checks through three decades of local history, she searches for only one name but draws a blank each time. Many men called Brian have made the pages of *The Weir View* over the years and a sizable number of O'Neills also feature. She reads the death notice of a Brian O'Neill and is relieved to discover that he was a man in his late eighties. His large family whose names had been added to the death notice don't contain a single Brian. Finally, just as she is about to give up, a headline catches her attention: *No More Sleepless Nights for Ryan Niels*.

The feature, written five years previously, is about a software designer, a Rillingham-on-the-Weir local, who invented an app to help people suffering from insomnia.

She remembers Stella's uncertainty over his name. Could Brian O'Neill be Ryan Niels? She imagines a frightened, drenched boy muttering his name when her father asked him for it. This has to be more than a coincidence. She continues reading. The idea for his invention was drawn from Ryan Niels's own experiences of sleeplessness and night terrors.

She locates another article, written two years later, that reported on the successful sale of his app to a company specialising in medical equipment. The thin-faced boy with streeling hair and droplets of river water trickling from his eyelashes has nothing in common with the assertive-looking businessman in the photograph, yet it is worth a try.

Once again, she contacts the editor of *The Weir View* and asks if he can give her any information on Ryan Niels.

'I thought your interest was in the castle.' Keith is politely curious as to why her queries about castle ruins has shifted to an interest in a local businessman.

'I think I might know him,' Christine explains. 'We met when I visited Rillingham as a child.'

'Unfortunately, under data protection regulations, I can't give out that kind of information,' he says.

'I understand. But if you do know how to contact him, could you ask if I can email him? I want to talk to him about a wedding that took place thirty years ago at the Castle Rillingham hotel.'

A week later, Keith contacts her with Ryan Niels's email address.

Christine thinks hard before sending off her own email:

Dear Mr Niels,

Thank you for passing on your email address. I'm not sure if you're the person I need to contact but if you remember saving a young girl from drowning, then I'd love to meet you. I was that child but this memory has only recently returned to me. I'm anxious to thank you in person, if that is possible.

In gratitude,

Christine Lewis

Ryan Niels replies three days later.

Dear Ms Lewis

Thank you for your email. I remember that afternoon. I'm glad I was there when you needed my help. However, I must decline your invitation. I'm dealing with a grave family situation right now and will not be able to meet you. Also, that day is embedded in my memory for other reasons so I'd rather not add to what has always been a distressing period in my life.

I wish you continued good health.

Ryan Niels

She replies to him the following evening.

Dear Mr Niels,

Forgive me for contacting you again. Now that I'm aware you are dealing with a family situation, I apologise for bothering you at such a difficult time. Nor do I want to add to your distressing memories, yet I feel that meeting you is the right thing to do.

My own memories are very confused and I've been attending a hypnotherapist to try to make sense of them. She has helped me to recall my near-drowning but other memories have also surfaced while I've been in hypnosis. I've no idea if they are true or false. Perhaps, by sharing our experiences, we can help each other to make sense of that day. I accept that this may not be possible and if you would rather that I didn't contact you again, I will respect your decision.

Every best wish,

Christine

A week passes before he responds.

Dear Christine,

Your last email intrigued me. If you're still interested in meeting, would you care to arrange a suitable date?

Regards,

Ryan

She responds immediately.

Dear Ryan,

I'm hoping to take some time off work and will be in touch with you regarding dates. If you're free, I'd like to invite you to lunch at Castle Rillingham Hotel where my aunt's wedding took place. I'm really looking forward to meeting you.

Sincerely,

Christine

Richard's expression hardens when he discovers she has been corresponding with Ryan Niels. 'Why didn't you tell me you were trying to make contact with him?' he asks.

'You'd have discouraged me from doing so.'

'With good reason. Honestly, Christine, what are you hoping to find out?'

'If it was an accident—'

'Obviously it was an accident! You can't possibly give credence to something you imagined in that state of hypnosis. Hypnotists can make people believe anything—'

'Elaine is a hypnotherapist and I trust her implicitly.' She answers him defiantly. Lately, all she seems to do is defend herself against his cynicism.

'More than you trust my opinion, it seems.' He grimaces and opens the patio door. The evening is balmy and the south-facing garden is filled with sunshine, despite the lateness of the evening. She follows him outside and sits down with him on a garden bench.

'Let's not have another argument.' She reaches for his hand and squeezes it. 'I need to do this, Richard.'

'When are you meeting him?'

'On the twenty-third. I'll stay overnight in the hotel and fly back the next day.'

'What about the Krisgloss reception? Don't tell me you've forgotten about it?'

'When is that?'

'The twenty-fourth.'

'I thought it was the following week.' She is afraid to admit that the launch of the new advertising campaign had gone cleanly from her mind.

'No, it's that evening, which you'd have realised if you weren't so preoccupied with your own internal drama.' He pushes her hand away, his annoyance obvious.

'Why are you constantly undermining my experience—' she begins.

'Undermining your *experience*.' His interruption is as brusque as his comment. He stands and stares angrily down at her. 'Have you listened to yourself lately? Do you honestly expect me to take you seriously when you talk about gunmen running loose—'

'One gunman who tried to kill me.'

'Give me a break, Christine. I'm not denying that *almost* drowning was traumatising for you. I can understand why you blocked it out. But this insistence that there was more to it than what actually happened... well... I honestly can't buy it. You were a highly impressionable five-year-old and you must have been terrified. I'm not surprised you've dramatised it – not deliberately...' – he holds up his hand to silence her protest – 'but what I suspect has happened is that any imagined fears you had when you were a child have attached themselves to your accident and confused you.'

A sticky-back weed, is that what he believes her memory to be? One with hairy stems that cleave to her imagination and concocts a childish fantasy?

'It can happen easily.' Richard's confident tone is grating enough to bring her to her feet. They are facing each other but she feels as if the space between them is widening with every word he utters.

'I crashed my bike into a wall and broke my two front teeth when I was seven,' he continues. 'Afterwards, I insisted that the brakes had failed and the steering was at fault. Anything rather than admit it was my own stupidity that caused the accident. I fell from a shed roof a year later and ended up in hospital with concussion and a broken collar bone. Later, I was convinced someone had pushed me, which would have been difficult as there was no one else on the roof but me...'

'Have you finished?' she asks when he pauses.

'I'm trying to make you understand—'

'You're trying to patronise me. How dare you preach at me when you know *absolutely* nothing about what I'm going through.'

'I've tried to understand. But the Krisgloss reception is important to me... to us.'

'To us? Are you serious? *Us* hasn't existed since Jessica Newman destroyed our agency.'

'Don't blame her for what's happening here.'

'And what exactly is happening, Richard?' Why is she asking him something that could demand a painful answer? He looks away, as though he too wants to avoid confronting her question.

'Cancel this trip,' he says. 'It's the least you can do considering you undermined me throughout the entire Krisgloss project.'

'How exactly did I do that?'

'By constantly cross-examining my decisions. You tried to reduce my creative concept to a penny-pinching shadow of what I wanted to achieve.'

'Lucky for you that you'd Jessica on-side to undermine *my* decisions, wasn't it?'

'At least she appreciates my commitment to our clients—'

'*Our* clients—? Are you forgetting that you're one of her father's minions? You serve at his daughter's pleasure. How far are you prepared to serve, that's what I'd like to know.' Christine stops, shocked at where this bile and resentment is leading them.

He leaves her alone in the garden and returns to the house. She hears the front door open and the slam of it closing behind him.

The summer solstice is almost upon them. On such occasions, Amy used to dance at dawn on the hill of Tara. Now she feeds Daniel in the first light and communicates with her angel. Christine resists the urge to ring her friend. What can Amy say that will make a difference? Richard is right. What she has recalled is shocking and preposterous. Amy's reaction, if it is similar to his disbelief, is more than Christine can handle.

Walking on the beach always calms him down and when he returns, his apology is terse but genuine. She responds in kind – a truce of sorts. How long will it last? She used to be familiar with the lines and angles of his face, his expressive mouth, the warmth of his gaze. Now, she could be staring at a stranger. Does he feel the same way about her? Strangers who know each other intimately, is that what they have become?

She promises to be back on time to attend the launch of the campaign at the Krisgloss showrooms. Will she be any wiser then as to the state of her mind? Will she know if she has built a fantasy around a traumatising accident or if she witnessed a shocking murder? And if the latter is true... how is she supposed to cope with that knowledge?

FOURTEEN

Castle Rillingham, a cumbersome replica of the medieval castle that once straddled the countryside, looks exactly the same as Christine remembers. She is early for her lunch appointment, and there is time to catch her breath and compose herself with a walk around the grounds.

The rose garden looks so small compared to the enormous space she remembers. The path running along the centre leads to the wall where the stile used to be. A gate, high and spiked, has replaced it. Perhaps her near-drowning was the reason for this precaution. No child would be able to climb over those spikes or squeeze through the bars.

The meadow beyond the gate sways with cornflowers, dog daisies, columbine, cow parsley and harebell. A bee haven, according to Suzie, the hotel receptionist. The owner has an interest in rewilding some of his land.

She recognises Ryan Niels from his newspaper photograph as soon as he enters the restaurant. He, too, seems acutely aware of her presence and comes directly to her table.

'Hello, Christine,' he says.

She stands, breathless at the sight of him. His hands

pumped water from her lungs. His lips breathed life back into her. No wonder the feeling of familiarity when they shake hands is strong enough to weaken her. This time, if she collapses, it will not be from anxiety or terror, but from the untangling of an unknown fear that she can finally understand.

She tries to focus on the lunch menu. The elaborate descriptions of crab pancakes, shiitake tart and cured foie gras are meaningless. In the end, she shakes her head. 'Whatever you're having is fine by me,' she says.

'I was about to suggest the same to you.'

There is a wariness in his gaze that suggests he is equally anxious about the conversation that is to come. They order fish, chips and mushy peas. It is uncomplicated and is served with two beers. Gradually, as they relax with each other, she learns that his father is dead and his mother, who is in ill health, is the grave situation he mentioned in his email. Apart from his face, which is long and accentuated by a pointed chin, his body is compact and sturdy. He has a rugged, outdoor appearance, which is strange for someone who is invested in technology. He lived for years in Australia and the United States, and returned to Rillingham when he inherited a small farm from his uncle. The time he spends out of doors is mapped on his wind-tanned skin and the deeply etched lines around his eyes.

He has moved from the farmhouse back into his childhood home to look after his mother. He is her only child, and will remain with her until she dies. He blinks, as if this reality must be pushed aside.

Christine remembers the vividness of his eyes as he lay beside her on the riverbank. How the water ran like tears down his cheeks. Today they are clear and blue, a man's eyes observing her as he waits for their small talk to end and the reason for this meeting to be made clear to him.

'I remember thinking that staring into the sun would make me go blind.' The words come from her before they are even considered. 'I almost died from drowning yet that was the first thought that came to my mind. My aunt, Sharon, was so happy that the sun was shining for her wedding. She called it a "special delivery". Only for you, I'd never have seen it shine again.'

'Why weren't you at the wedding instead of wandering along the riverbank?' he asks. 'It was quite a distance from the hotel.'

'I was the only child there and I was bored. I remember climbing over a stile and running through a meadow towards trees. After that, I didn't know where I was.'

'That would have been easy to do. The stile's been replaced by a gate. You have to ask for a key to gain entry onto the land now. Safety precautions to do with the old ruins.' He takes a sip of his beer. 'You wrote in your email that you've only recently recalled what happened to you.'

'I did so in hypnotherapy.'

His expression is non-judgemental as she describes her sessions with Elaine. He shakes his head when she asks if she is boring him. A near-drowning and a rescue, that is factual information. To talk about the shooting is too sensational and must wait until later.

'Are you able to remember the spot where you rescued me?' she asks, when their plates have been cleared from their table.

He shakes his head. 'I've only the vaguest recollections of where I was. It's a long riverbank, very wending, and I was quite distressed. Like you, I shouldn't have been there. My parents always worried about the currents along that stretch of water and the river was dangerously high that day. The bank has changed a lot since then. It's more... how shall I put it... more gentrified.'

'I'd like to retrace my steps along it but I understand that you're busy—'

'I'm not busy.' He quickly interrupts her. 'I've no problem

going there with you. You said in your email that there is something else you remembered.'

'There is something...' She hesitates then shakes her head. 'I'd like to find the spot where you rescued me before I say anything else about that day.' She attracts the waiter's attention for the bill and Ryan shrugs good-naturedly when she insists on paying for their meal.

The receptionist hands over the key to the gate, which opens easily. Away from the sheltered walls of the hotel, Christine is drawn to the left-hand path which is visible between banks of wild flowers. The crumbling remains of the original castle, fenced from the public for safety reasons, rises shell-like to their right. No sign of a black horse anywhere. The faint murmur of the river draws her downwards. The sensation that she is being pulled there by an invisible force is impossible to ignore and Ryan quickens his stride to keep up with her.

'Steps leading down to the riverbank were installed about twenty years ago,' he says when the river comes into view. 'It's no longer such a headlong dash down the embankment.'

Instantly, she relives the hurtling rush of the gunman's body as he plunged downwards from the clearing in the forest.

They reach the steps, wide stone slabs that curve down from the high ground to a river path lined with benches, litter bins and dog excrement receptacles. She understands what he means by gentrified. This is so removed from her recollections of clutching branches and tangled undergrowth.

'As far as I can remember, you would have fallen into the water at a spot further on.' Ryan gestures to the right but his voice is subdued. His expression has changed, as if he, like her, is responding to the rushing charge of the river.

'I've taken up too much of your time already.' She walks towards a bench and sits down. 'Elaine has helped me to recall so much about that afternoon but she did warn me that not everything in hypnotherapy should be accepted as factual. Sometimes, it's possible to have a false memory. I remembered something about that day when I was in a trance. I know it's too outlandish to be true, yet it's been planted in my head and I can't let it go.'

'What is it?' he asks when she hesitates. 'I'm interested.'

'I don't believe I slipped into the river by accident.'

The mood between them changes. His intake of breath is audible as he sits down beside her.

'Then how did it happen?'

'I have this memory of a man with a gun... you'll probably think I'm crazy...'

She is conscious that his body has tautened. He must be aware that she is finally coming to the point of their meeting.

'He hit my head with the butt of a gun and flung me into the water.'

On the opposite bank, people are walking dogs along the river path. A group of youths come into view, hoodies and padded anoraks, walking close together. They could be Boy Scouts out of uniform, or runners for a drug ring. How is one supposed to see under the façade of appearances?

'I know it sounds fantastical—'

'A gun.' He turns his head away from her and stares at the racing water. 'He hit you with a gun?'

'Yes.' She swallows, a dryness gathering in her throat. 'When I saw him first, I thought he had a stick in his hand. Now, I know it was a gun and he was pointing it at someone... someone young. He looked like a teenager but I couldn't see his face.'

The sound Ryan makes sounds too strangled to be human – it is more like that of an animal numbed by the snap of a snare. His body is hunched and his hands shake as he rubs his knees in an unconscious reflex action. What she has told him is no longer a false memory but something feral and brutal that has finally found a home. He repeats that primal sound but, hearing himself, he forms a fist and bangs it against his mouth.

'What were you doing on the riverbank that day?' she asks when his breathing has steadied and his hands lie still on his lap.

'I was searching for my brother.' He speaks with an infinite sadness.

In their earlier conversation he mentioned he was an only child. Was that what he actually said, or did she misinterpret his words?

'Did you ever find him?' She knows the answer to her question even as she asks it.

'Paul was never found.'

They sit silently together for an instant. Each of them must gather breath if they are to continue this conversation. A red kite flies into view, the scythe-like curve of its wings visible for an instant before it disappears into the trees.

'Tell me everything you saw while you were in that trance,' he says.

The memory is no longer shadowed, and nor does Jessica's image intrude as Christine brings her mind back to that afternoon. The bluebells are nodding lazily, drowsy from the sun, and birds drift languidly above her. A youth is on his knees weeping. The man standing above him, tall and rangy, is dressed in black; an executioner with a will of iron. No second thoughts or second guessing. He has a silencer fixed on his gun because the sound it makes is muffled, unlike the crack of the broken twig under her knees. She is as light as a feather in his arms and cast into the river just as easily.

Christine grips the edge of the bench for support and Ryan, realising she is in danger of falling forward, holds her against him. She can smell grief on him. It reminds her of mulching leaves or cut grass – sweet-scented yet blooming with mould. Her imagination, she guesses, but she is accustomed to that scent and finds it comforting. He begins to speak about his brother, aged seventeen. A teenager lured at his school gates by free handouts of pills. A fun habit that quickly grew into an addiction to heroin and an ever-increasing debt. Ryan speaks calmly about the money that was stolen from his parents, the wrecking tantrums when it was not forthcoming. He saw his father being beaten up by Paul because he refused to feed his son's habit. He heard his mother crying in the small hours.

His parents threw their son out in the end. Tough love, Dorothy, his mother said. It is the only way. That was after Paul had found the money that Ryan had been saving for a mountain bike by working on his uncle's farm. He had kept his wages in a post office savings account but Paul forged his brother's signature then emptied the account. Ryan still remembers the insults he shouted at him. How he wished his brother was dead. *Dead! Dead! Dead!*

Paul phoned him from a public phone box one morning and begged him to steal money from the uncle who employed Ryan on his farm.

Panic-stricken and crying, Paul insisted that his life was in danger from the Earls. Ryan believed him. He had heard stories about Reggie Earls and his gang. Paul was now in debt to one of the drug dealers and the Earls had a merciless reputation when money was owed to them.

Stealing from his uncle had been easy. The farmer kept a sum of money for emergencies wrapped in layers of cling film and stuffed inside a rusted biscuit tin. Afraid to ignore his brother's pleas, Ryan turned up at the squat that Paul had moved into after his parents had ordered him from their home. The damp, grotty room with its syringes and atmosphere of endless waiting to score, was empty. Those who lived in adjoining rooms shrugged and claimed he had moved on. A young girl with a stick-like figure said he was probably in Rillingham Forest where drugs were often sold.

The forest was dense and criss-crossed with narrow trails. Paul could have been anywhere. Ryan searched for two hours and when he finally emerged from the forest it was late in the afternoon. He descended the embankment that led down to the river where his attention was distracted by what he thought was an otter, its slick head rising above the water as it was swept downriver on the currents. It was only when Christine's purple dress with its flouncy petticoats ballooned on the surface and snagged on the overhanging roots of a tree that he realised a child was drowning.

He remembers an elderly man accusing him of pushing Christine into the river. This frightened him so much that he ran away after muttering his name to her father. Too wet and bedraggled to catch a bus, he trudged home, the money he had stolen still in his pocket. The cling film had protected it and, unbeknownst to his uncle, Ryan returned it to the biscuit tin some weeks later when he believed there was no longer any chance of finding his brother.

Paul's body was never found in a ditch or on wasteland, nor in the dark shadows of a faceless industrial estate. His disappearance gave his parents some hope: in their good moments they could always believe that he had escaped the clutch of the drug dealer and was hiding somewhere, anywhere. It didn't matter how far he had fled as long as he was safe. In their hearts they knew he was dead but such hopes kept them upright throughout those early years. Eventually, even that slender belief became a too-thin comfort. All they wanted was a body they could mourn and bury. The last words his father spoke before he died was to plead with Ryan to keep on searching for his brother.

'Bring me to that place.' Ryan stands and holds out a hand to raise her to her feet.

They walk silently along the riverbank until she stops beneath a tree. The trunk slopes over the water, the angle so precarious that it looks in danger of toppling. She was caught beneath the branches when he rescued her. The roots were exposed, a tangle of fat-bellied snakes, bulging and interwoven, and they are still there, still holding that slanted tree in its grip. She remembers the fluttering leaves, a canopy seen through drenched eyelashes when she opened her eyes but before then – was there really a bridge, split in the middle? It sounds farcical yet Ryan nods as soon as she describes it.

'Newbridge, that's what it was called when it was restored,' he says. 'It's further up the river but, back then, that area was dangerous and out-of-bounds.'

The bridge is a magnificent arch above the river and busy with pedestrians. She stands beside it and looks upwards towards the forest where the trees form a dark silhouette against the blue sky. She is moving with more confidence as they climb the embankment where more steps have also been installed.

They remain silent as they enter the forest. As yet, she is unable to grasp the consequences of what she has revealed. It is impossible to pinpoint the site. The bluebells have withered and the trees that shimmered in the luminous green of late spring have turned a deeper hue. She looks down into a hollow and thinks she has found the spot. A few minutes later she comes to another clearing and hesitates. Her only certainty is that she witnessed a murder. Not a disappearance – that is how Paul Niels has been categorised. Thirty years of wondering. What does that do to a person's psyche? His father died without answers, and it seems likely that his mother will do the same... unless...

The poppies are in bloom. Swathes of red poppies, nodding drowsily in the afternoon's heat. She shudders and grips Ryan's hand. A look exchanged is all that's needed for the information to pass between them. Ryan falls to his knees, his head bowed.

Is he is praying to his brother or cursing his unknown killer? Where did he bring the body afterwards? Paul would have been found eventually if he had been left in the clearing.

Ryan must be asking himself the same question as he gathers poppies in his fist and crushes their redness against his skin. They are crying together. She has shed so many tears lately – tears of regret as her marriage to Richard began to fall apart, and maudlin tears soaked with alcohol. These tears are different. They run from a clear spring; from a truth no longer hindered by amnesia.

She offers her hand and helps him to stand. His skin is hot and clammy.

'Thank you for breaking that terrible silence,' he says.

This time, she is the one who supports him as they walk away from this wildly beautiful place of death.

They return to the hotel bar. Christine orders a brandy for him and drinks a glass of water.

'What will you do with the information I've given you?' she asks. The enormity of the task facing him is only beginning to dawn on her. 'Will you go to the police? Do you want me to make a statement?'

'They won't believe you.' He states this emphatically. 'A remembered memory after all these years is not something they'll take seriously.'

'It should go on the record, even if they disregard it.'

He remains thoughtful for a moment. 'I gathered information on a drug gang who were active in the area at that time. Most of them ended up in jail, some disappeared and many of them have died. I know you didn't get a clear glimpse of the man who killed Paul but the photographs might trigger something in your memory. The file is back at the farm if you'd like to look through it. That way, we'd have something more concrete to bring to the police. I've a friend in the drugs squad. I could contact him and see if he can arrange an interview.'

His phone rings. From the one-sided conversation, Christine understands that the call is from his mother's carer. Dorothy is distressed and asking for him.

'I'm afraid I have to go.' He sounds worried. 'Megan says my mother is anxious and won't settle until she sees me. She seems genuinely upset, which is unlike her. We'll have to forget about the reports—'

'I'm not flying home until tomorrow afternoon. Maybe there'll be time to look at them before I catch my flight.'

'Are you sure?'

'Yes, Ryan. I am. I'd like to help in any way I can.'

'I'll pick you up in the morning then.' They stand awkwardly together, unsure how to end their extraordinary encounter. He leans forward as if to kiss her cheek then shakes her hand instead.

Christine rings Richard as soon as she reaches her room. He sounds harried when he answers. A last-minute Krisgloss hitch has arisen and he is desperately trying to sort it out before tomorrow's launch.

'I've just left Ryan Niels,' she says as soon as he pauses. 'It's been an extraordinary afternoon.'

'How many gunmen did you see?' His short burst of laughter is followed by an apologetic pause. 'I'm sorry, Christine. I'm having a bad day. How did the meeting go?'

'Forget it.'

'No, tell me. I was only joking.'

'And I'm laughing so hysterically I'm unable to finish this conversation.' She cuts the call before he can reply, and switches off her phone.

FIFTEEN

In the morning, she is waiting on the steps of the hotel with her overnight bag when Ryan arrives. She enquires about his mother as she straps herself into the passenger seat.

'Mum knew I was up to something.' He hoists her overnight bag into the back of the jeep. 'That was why she was so upset yesterday. She's always had an uncanny knack of zoning in on any developments to do with Paul. She's a witch, that way. Super-sensitive. In the end, I told her about our meeting. I was worried about doing so but it was the right decision. We spent the night talking about Paul. It was good for her. Cathartic. She was sleeping soundly when I left. Megan will stay with her until I return.'

It doesn't take long to reach the countryside. Thyme is growing in a nearby field. Christine opens the window and breathes in the spicy fragrance. Ryan turns in through an open gateway and drives along an avenue of poplars towards a farmhouse. The roof is thatched and the walls ivy-covered. Beyond the farmyard, the fields have been converted into allotments. Garden huts have been painted in different shades and a large, hand-built pizza oven looks as if it is used regularly. Gardeners, at work on their allotments, stop to wave and shout greetings to Ryan.

Once inside the kitchen, he puts on the kettle then reaches up to the highest shelf on the dresser to remove a stiff blue folder. Inside, translucent plastic files are clipped together, each one containing newspaper reports or handwritten sheets of foolscap. The reports date back over thirty years, the paper yellowed with time.

Local Businessman Arrested in Drug Raid

Cocaine Worth £6m Found in Fertiliser Bags

Rillingham 5 Arrested for Alleged Importation of Drugs

Notorious Rillingham 5 Boss Faces Murder Charge

As Ryan makes tea, Christine turns the pages and begins to read. Even a village as picturesque as Rillingham-on-the-Weir was not immune to having its heart torn out by an influx of drugs in the eighties and nineties. Ryan has charted the rise and fall of a gang called the Earls. Led by Reggie Earls, the gang was sub-divided into six units, each once controlled by a deputy, appointed by Reggie. The dealers, nicknamed 'The Rillingham 5' by the media, gazed sullenly from the front and inside pages. Four men and a woman, who had struck at the heart of the community by flooding the town and the surrounding areas with cannabis, cocaine, ecstasy and heroin.

'If justice had been properly served, they would have been known as the Rillingham Six,' says Ryan. 'They were betrayed by one of their own. Thanks to this informer, and the information he supplied, the police were able to catch those at the top of the drugs chain instead of just the usual small-time operators. But it meant that one of their main operators went into a witness protection programme and disappeared.'

Notorious Gang Leader Vows Death on 'Rat'.

This last headline, in various forms, screamed from the tabloids when Reggie Earls was accused of murder and sentenced to life imprisonment. The other four received lengthy prison sentences for being accessories to a murder. Or murders, claims Ryan. He brings the teapot to the table and pulls his chair closer to hers.

'It was years after Paul's disappearance before the police finally broke up the gang.'

Christine can see the impact opening this folder has had on him. How often has he studied it over the years as he tried to piece together the last hours of his brother's life?

None of the men photographed look familiar to Christine. But how can she tell for definite, when all she has are fragmented images of a figure, his features blackened against the sun until he turned his eyes on her? And terror had blinded her to his face as he ran with her towards the river.

'The informant was never named,' he says. 'He gave evidence behind a screen and was whisked away at the end of the trial to go into a witness protection programme.'

The prosecution, in an effort to achieve a life sentence, had focused on only one murder. Protesters had gathered outside the court. Their sons and daughters had also suffered over the years and some had died at the hands of the gangs. Other sons disappeared without trace. Ryan points at one couple among the protestors: William and Dorothy Niels. His mother was a heavily built woman whose mouth was stretched as she shouted furiously at a police van that was being driven through the crowd.

The Rillingham 5 were dead, according to reports published years later. Two were killed in prison, another two moved to Spain and lasted a year before they were shot. Reggie Earls was released early on a legal technicality and died from drowning off the Irish coast shortly afterwards.

Ryan's phone rings. He excuses himself after a quick glance at the screen and leaves the room.

'That was my friend from the drug squad,' he says when he returns. 'He warned me last night that I shouldn't expect a quick answer and he was right. His request has to go through a process that will take time. He's not hopeful of a positive outcome.' Ryan doesn't sound surprised or even angry.

'But he hasn't said *no*?'

'Not yet. Paul's disappearance is history. It's going to take something substantial to instigate a cold case investigation. Craig's a good copper. If there's anyone who can push against regulations, it's him.'

'It would help if I could recognise anyone from the photos in the newspaper reports. I've had no luck so far.' She points at another headline. *Rillingham Woman Dies after Hit-and-Run.* The victim was young, early twenties, she guesses. Although her photograph is slightly blurred, it is obvious that she was in the prime of her life when she was struck down. 'Why is she in the folder?' Christine asks. 'Had she anything to do with the gang?'

'Grace Cooper.' Ryan takes the clipping from her and studies it. 'No, she wasn't a gang member. Unfortunately for her, she fell in love with the wrong guy and paid the price.'

'The "snitch"?'

'Yes. The Earls vowed to take him down but he was protected twenty-four seven by the police. Grace was the one who paid the ultimate price. The driver got away with it. There was a lot of suspicion at the time but nothing could be proved.' Ryan unfolds the page from *The Weir View* and spreads it over the table. 'All five were on remand in jail awaiting trial but it would have been easy enough to organise something like that from inside... though Bessie Cooper, Grace's mother, has a different view of what happened to her daughter. She thinks the boyfriend was responsible for Grace's death. She hated him from the beginning, so it's hardly an objective opinion.'

'That's horrendous.' Christine can't take her eyes off the black and white photograph. An arm was draped around Grace's shoulder but the rest of the body of the person beside her had been cropped. Was that the 'snitch' boyfriend? she wonders. 'Are there photographs of her boyfriend on file?' she asks.

'No. He was held under maximum security before and during the trial. The media was prevented from using his photograph or his name, but everyone in Rillingham knew he was Mr Allsorts or, to give him his correct name, Dougie Barnes? He earned the nickname because of the assortment of drugs he could supply. The police had to keep him safe until he gave evidence against the gang. After the trial he disappeared and that's the last anyone heard of him.'

'What about his family? Did the gang go after them, also?'

'His mother was dead from a drug overdose and he never knew his father. If they were responsible for Grace's death, it was the only way they could get to him. She'd just given birth to a baby a few months previously.'

'A baby... oh, my God! What happened to her child?' So much violence is contained within this folder.

'She disappeared after Grace died.' Ryan, sensing her distress, reaches across and opens a window. Once again, the aroma of thyme is wafted on the breeze. A ginger cat leaps onto the outside ledge and stares unblinkingly at Christine.

'She was rumoured to have been taken by her father but, as he was in witness protection, we don't know if that's true.' Ryan gathers up the newspaper clippings and returns them to the folder.

'I'm sorry I couldn't identify any of them. The sun was in my eyes—'

'You've no need to apologise, Christine. What you've done...' He closes the folder. 'Just knowing, that's enough.'

'I didn't see any mention of Paul among those newspaper clippings.'

'He was never even listed as a missing person. It was simply assumed that he'd run away.'

'I'm sorry I wasn't able to come forward earlier... before your father died.'

'You're here now and that's what counts.' He glances at his watch. 'We'd better move. You don't want to miss the bus to the airport.'

The cat darts into the jeep as soon as Ryan opens the door and sits majestically on the passenger seat.

'Shoo. Out you get, Hennessy. Not today.' The cat mews in protest but does as Ryan orders.

'Hennessy?' Christine asks, as they drive off.

'Named after my favourite brandy. Imagine my consternation when Hennessy gave birth to five kittens. I'm a townie by birth so I guess my ignorance was excusable at the time.'

She laughs at his rueful expression. 'Are you still a townie?'

'I'm somewhere in between.'

'A man of the soil and a designer of apps. That's quite a mix.'

'Mixed up is the right word.' He glances across at her. 'What about you?'

I'm so mixed up, I'm not sure I know who I am anymore. That is what she wants to say but it is too late to trade their life stories. All she knows about him is that he has a dead brother and a mother who is fading fast. Has he a wife, children? She saw no signs of a family in his farmhouse, no toys cluttering the floor, no feminine touches to soften the lines of his practical kitchen.

The bus is ready to leave. Ryan parks at the entrance to the terminus and removes her overnight bag. She is stepping down from the jeep when his phone rings.

'It's Mum,' he says. 'Excuse me for a moment.'

'No, that's not going to happen,' she hears him say. 'Out of the question. She has a flight to catch.'

Although it is impossible to make out what is being said at the other end of the call, it is clear that Dorothy Niels is anxious to meet her.

'Maybe I could see her the next time I come over,' Christine says, when he ends the call. 'Hopefully, the police will want to talk to me.'

He nods, noncommittally, too polite to tell her that his mother will not be alive by then to hear the details of her eldest son's final moments.

How many gunmen did you see? Richard's mocking tone and his conviction that she is deluded still stings. It is one of those remarks she will find impossible to forget, and helps bring her to a swift decision.

'I'm in no hurry to return home,' she says. 'I'd like to meet Dorothy today.'

'Your flight—'

'Can be cancelled and rearranged for tomorrow.'

'No, no, I can't let you do that.'

'Then let me do it for Dorothy.'

Dorothy Niels draws Christine into her small house. She is frail yet stalwart. Arthritis has stooped her once tall frame and the weight she has lost to cancer is apparent in her bony face. After what she has been through, cancer is a burden she is able to carry.

She makes tea and empties a packet of Hobnobs onto a side plate. Christine eats one to please her and sips a cup of scalding tea.

'Paul was such a good boy,' she says, as she rummages in a sideboard for a photographic album. 'Never in trouble in school. His teachers expected great things from him and then it all went wrong.'

'Mum, there's no need—' Ryan attempts to take the album from her but she swipes him aside with the back of her hand.

'Just a few photos,' she says. 'I'm sure Christine would like to see what Paul looked like.'

She turns pages that chart his growth from babyhood to his teens. Christine sees his innocence bloom then harden into defiance. Dorothy lays her hand on the last photographs and says, 'He was gone his own way by then. My poor, lost boy.'

She asks for a description of the man who killed her son. Christine can only describe this faceless killer in broad strokes: long, brown hair tied in a ponytail, his taut jawline, his face turned from her as he fired a gun into a young man's head. How can she describe such an aching scene to this elderly woman? She recalls his blue, startled gaze and slack mouth when the snap of dead wood spun him around. Strong arms – that, also, is unforgettable, as is his forward dash towards the river.

'Would you like to visit Paul's grave?' Dorothy accepts that the memory of that instant is too traumatic to be retold.

'His grave?' Christine is startled by her question and Ryan, sitting opposite her, is embarrassed as he takes the album from her. 'Christine's had a difficult time—'

'I needed a place to mourn him after William died.' Dorothy ignores her son's protests. 'I decided that Paul should have his name on the same headstone as his father. It was acceptance of a kind, I suppose. Without William to keep it alive, hope was no longer possible.'

'I'd like to see his grave.' She catches Ryan's eye and nods reassuringly. If her journey here was difficult, it can't even begin to compare to the emotional roller-coaster he has been on since they walked by the river.

Ryan helps his mother to her feet and holds out her coat.

. . .

The graveyard gate is unlocked and it seems as if the peaceful hush of the afternoon has been waiting for them to arrive. Sounds are distant, muted, and the only birdsong is the low, sweet call of doves. There's a dovecote nearby, Dorothy says.

The older tombstones give way to modern ones that stand erect and carry images of beloved family members. They slow their footsteps to accommodate Dorothy, who walks with two sticks. She stabs them fiercely into the ground, her body rigid with determination. Christine is amazed, yet again, that she and her son are willing to trust the memory of a petrified five-year-old. She hadn't expected Dorothy to give her the same open-minded acceptance as her son has done. Perhaps, they seek certainty and closure will follow. But how can they move on until there is a body they can mourn?

The photograph Dorothy used for the headstone is that of a younger Paul in his mid-teens. Nothing brash or streetwise about him then. Christine holds her sticks and Ryan supports her as she pulls a cloth from her pocket and rubs the images of her son and husband. The resemblance between Ryan and his father – the same oval-shaped face and alert gaze – is strong. William's eyes were grey and Ryan's are a darkish blue, so it's not their colour that creates this resemblance but, rather, an awareness that the answer they seek lies somewhere beyond their vision.

Christine gives herself a mental shake. She must stop projecting. What does she know about the inner turmoil of this family?

Ryan must have picked up on her uneasiness, as he takes his mother's sticks from Christine and steadies Dorothy when they begin their slow walk from the graveyard.

Jessica, never far from her thoughts, suddenly seems to emerge from the depths of a black, marble headstone. Christine stops so suddenly that Dorothy staggers before she is steadied by her son. On closer inspection, Christine discovers that the similarity is less apparent. The shock of recognition has to do with the earlier photograph she saw of Grace Cooper. The newspaper image was grainy but the vibrancy of this oval-shaped photograph suggests it could have been taken yesterday, instead of twenty-five years ago. Christine forces away the impression of Jessica – that's the way it is these days: She sees her everywhere. A toss of russet hair, a frown, a laugh, a gesture. Even walking behind someone, she glimpses her in the assured stride of a stranger.

Ryan drops Christine off at the hotel, where she has booked a room for another night. Dorothy, in the passenger seat, murmurs a sleepy goodbye as he steps down from the jeep and walks Christine to the entrance.

'I hope Dorothy...' Christine searches for the appropriate words as they prepare to part. 'I hope her passing is easy.'

He should wince at such a cliché but, instead, he takes her hand in both of his. 'You've made it possible for her to leave me.' He states this simply. 'People always say that death brings peace, but peace in life is more important. You've answered the question that has tormented her for so long.'

'Will you let me know when she dies?'

'I will.' This time he kisses her cheek then stands back and releases her hand.

Castle Rillingham, despite its comforts, is an uneasy cradle, especially during the small hours. Sounds from that long-ago afternoon fill her ears. The swish of grass, rustling leaves, the crack of dead wood, the thud of a bullet muffled in its velocity – all seemed dream-like until she came here. She hears Paul Niels's terrified pleas, his cries for his mother. His voice is a false echo. What she witnessed was remote and wordless yet, now that he has a face, a history, she's unable to stop conjuring his dying words, their unbearable eloquence.

She opens the mini bar and stares at the neatly ranked miniature bottles. If she opens one it will undoubtably lead to another.

Richard is furious with her. He refused to listen to her excuses. This time he was the one who hung up. She settles on a super-sized bar of chocolate and carries it to the window. Pulling back the heavy curtains, she fills the room with moonlight and gorges on sugar. Bloated and sated, she crumples the wrapper in her fist. The lights lining the avenue to the hotel are switched off. What acts of brutality are being carried out in hidden places, she wonders. And when such acts are done, will the perpetrators ever be able to make peace with themselves?

PART 2

SIXTEEN
JESSICA
LONG ACRE PRISON

Fifteen Months Later

The birds are singing when Jessica awakens in the mornings. She hears the robin first. Shrill as an alarm clock, it is soon joined by a whistling thrush and the song of a lone blackbird. Then the overture begins in earnest and continues until the world is up and about its business. Since arriving in the prison, she has learned to value little things. Crumbs of comfort have become her staple diet. Small mercies are a bonus. So, she considers herself lucky to have a cell close to the perimeter of Long Acre where she has a chance to enjoy those snatched songs that will soon be lost in the chorus of dissent when the prison awakens.

She usually rises around five thirty or thereabouts. It takes an instant before reality kicks in. In that brief, half-dreaming lull, she imagines opening the curtains in her apartment, running a shower, choosing what she will wear for the day, something understated yet chic, and that's when the memory of Christine bears down on her. The lurch that follows shudders her back to the reality of four tiled walls and a light that never goes out.

Maria Divine, her cell mate, is still sleeping. Undisturbed by the birds, she is snoring heavily and will carry on until it is officially time for breakfast. They sleep separated by the width of a small communal table. Each has a locker with two shelves on the other side of their beds. The toilet is discreetly hidden behind a steel panel and allows a modicum of dignity. Boundaries don't exist here. Privacy is a more precious commodity than phones or drugs, yet is harder to source. Jessica finds it amazing how they have adapted to their lack of privacy; but when the aberrant is normalised, everything is possible.

Yesterday, she had an appointment with a prison psychologist. Eoin Cronin is a quiet man, weary of ticking bureaucratic boxes, and always hoping he will see a face before him that is not instantly recognisable – reoffending is a problem Long Acre has never managed to solve. He believes Jessica doesn't mix enough with the prison community and is becoming insular. He is wrong to see that as a problem. Insularity was a given on Cullain and, as Jessica believes her early years to have been the most formative, she has never shrugged off her island mentality. She has promised to attend his twice-weekly group therapy sessions and Eoin seemed relieved that he could tick another box.

He believes that the therapy group will help her to stay sane. Can it be that easy? Her sanity is a fragile thing. It balances on the point of a knife, a tippy-toed ballerina, unsure of its footing yet knowing that to fall will be the end of everything. Eoin has not said so in as many words, yet he expects her to be cooperative in the circle of nine that he has formed. Does that mean sharing? Weeping? Howling? Confiding her innermost thoughts and feelings? Recalling her life story?

How should she begin such a story when there is no point of entry? She lived on an island but was not born there. Whenever she asked her father for details about her birthplace he simply said, 'Across the water.'

What kind of answer was that? The ocean between Cullain and the mainland is vast and restless. She had to assume she didn't float to the island in a reed basket but, as she was only six months old, could such an assumption be made? Even when she was older and answers were forthcoming, the information always felt mercurial, insubstantial. She had a different name then, and a different identity; one that separates her from the person she is today. She has no guarantee that the memory of Rachel Cox is capable of joining the two halves of her childhood. Does she have the courage to wade through the lies and deceptions, the betrayals and presumptions, until she scratches the surface of the truth? Such a lot of scratching to do until she can figure out what led her to that momentous deed.

A split decision and it was done. A life taken.

Murderess... the word gathers momentum each time Jessica repeats it. She should be used to the sound by now, the harsh sibilance at its tail giving it impetus, like the hiss from a pantomime villain or the too-late warning from a snake before it releases its venom.

Murderess... *sss... sss...*

SEVENTEEN
RACHEL

On Cullain, she was usually awakened by budgies. They sang in cages in the little parlour but the walls of the cottage, though sturdy, were always damp and the birds died easily, despite her father's best efforts. For their brief lives they were called Figaro, Isolde, Aida, Giovanni, Carmen and other names from his favourite operas. At night, she heard his stereo playing, the voices of sopranos, altos, baritones and basses competing against the wind bellowing in from the ocean. Sometimes, she had difficulty distinguishing between the sounds.

Whenever he went to the mainland, Margaret played Joni Mitchell, a choke in her voice when Joni sang 'Morning Morgantown'. Rachel was able to sleep beside her then. She would curl into the swirl of her soft warmness and listen to Margaret's stories about prehistoric giants who once hurled the rocks of Cullain at their enemies on the mainland, or the hags who wove their island magic within the cavernous caves.

When the sun flashed between the rocks it was easy to see giants marching between the granite pillars. Shadows playing hide-and-seek on mica, she understood the tricks of sunlight on rock yet she was convinced she could hear them marching across Devil's Reach. In the wind's rage, she heard the hags cackling from deep inside the caves that burrowed beneath that overhanging headland.

The boat that carried her father home always came at night. Margaret claimed he ran a fish processing plant somewhere on that vast and distant mainland that Rachel could never see, no matter how hard she strained her eyes. The following morning, she would awaken in her own bed with only the fuzziest memory of being carried back there by him. A gift, wrapped in glitter paper, would have been left on her pillow: sometimes dolls, skinny yet busty, and with flowing blonde hair; or My Little Pony figurines with their startling manes and soulful eyes.

He disapproved of Margaret's imagination, especially when Rachel awakened from nightmares and ran to their bedroom to be comforted. He insisted they were safe on Breaker's Sound. No giants or hags would dare come near their cottage. The sounds she heard in her dreams, the roars and screams and the dulled, muffled thuds, were just echoes of the wind chasing the waves to shore. On those nights, if she cried out in her sleep, Margaret would reach for her hand and squeeze it. She knew the shape of the calluses on Margaret's palms, the knobbles on her knuckles, and the life lines she would read to her when she was in the mood.

Margaret's life story changed many times. Sometimes, she claimed to have been an orphan reared by nuns, or a wild child who ran away from cruel parents when she was thirteen. Her most outrageous claim was that she was the only daughter of trapeze artists who abandoned her when they discovered she was afraid of heights.

Knowing Margaret's fear of heights, Rachel had no trouble believing this story. On the cliff top overlooking the ocean, she would sway and hold her hands to her eyes as Rachel clambered over the serried rocks surrounding Breaker's Sound, confident that to keep her safe, Margaret would overcome her terror and come after her. She was a puzzle Rachel eventually stopped trying to solve. It was easier to just love her and be folded in her strong, plump arms when the shadows surrounding them became too dark to penetrate.

Margaret drove her to and from school. Breaker's Sound was far from the town where most of the islanders lived. Rachel was unable to invite friends to sleep over, nor did she visit their houses after school. She didn't understand loneliness and when it touched her, she didn't have the vocabulary to articulate it. They never had visitors, apart from the men who came occasionally by boat to meet her father. He liked his own company and never mixed with the islanders or the tourists, who arrived by ferry every summer. He also ignored the 'blow-ins' – the painters, musicians, writers and photographers who came and went, attracted to the island by its remoteness and towering granite formations. Rachel was familiar with the sight of them moving across the windswept terrain, or standing star-struck on Devil's Reach as the sun sank into the ocean. But they always departed for the mainland when the winter gales keened too loudly for them.

The last budgie her father brought home was Figaro. Cheerful and melodic, he was a flutter of blue feathers and a white, cheeky face. Sturdy, also, Figaro seemed capable of surviving the harsh winters and did so for two years. His presence cheered her father, who trained him to walk over his shoulders and perch on top of his head. This amused him so much that he would laugh out loud, an unfamiliar sound and one that filled her with lightness when she heard it. He was happy then, and it meant that, for a brief while, he had forgotten to be sad about her mother's death. He only ever referred to her as 'Alyson'.

Margaret claimed he carried her ghost on his shoulder. It was easier to fight a live rival, she would tell Rachel, but impossible to compete with the dead, especially when the ghost was a 'blonde bombshell'.

To think of her mother as a blonde bombshell seemed strange yet she understood why Margaret would describe her as such. In the photograph her father gave her to frame and place on her bedside table, Alyson reminded her of a remote and dazzling film star. Tendrils of silvery, blonde hair fell to her shoulders and her eyes seemed to follow Rachel around the bedroom. Perhaps that was wishful thinking and it was their shade, that luminous spring green, that seemed to reach out from the photo and captivate her.

'You have Alyson's eyes,' Margaret used to say every time she saw the photograph. 'Your mother gave you her greatest gift.'

A gift that was not a doll or a toy pony. Rachel studied her eyes in the mirror and wondered what it would have been like to have a blonde bombshell cooking her meals and washing dishes. Would Alyson have held her close at night in the shivery blackness of the island where sound never settled until the waves carried her father home again? Whenever she pleaded with him to tell her stories about Alyson, he did so with an obvious reluctance, and the catch in his voice made it difficult to continue questioning him.

She was ten years old when he decided to leave Cullain. They would travel light, he told her. That meant without Margaret. Such a thought was inconceivable, yet when Rachel listened to them arguing she knew it was going to happen. Margaret accused him of showing more compassion to Figaro than to her. In bed one night, she heard glass breaking and slaps, but the following morning there were no shards anywhere. Only for the redness on her father's cheek, she could have imagined the smack of skin on skin.

On the night of departure to Rosswall Heights, Figaro was found on his back in his cage, his tiny claws in the air. Margaret was stony-faced when she wrapped his tiny body in newspaper and added him to the debris they were leaving behind.

'*Bitch.*' Her father spoke softly, yet the word had such bite that Margaret's eyelids flickered, as if she must bat away his anger. Would there be more slaps? Rachel buried her face in Margaret's soft stomach. Her father had to prise her loose when it was time to leave.

No looking back, he said. To do so was to emulate Lot's wife and would turn her into a pillar of salt. It wasn't a good joke, not even a remotely funny one, and she did turn back. Margaret was standing in the doorway, the light shining on her wild, dark hair, her cries drowned by the ocean, the sting of salt on her cheeks. One last glance back was all Rachel had before she was bundled onto a boat. Her father held her close as the sea broiled around them. His body was rock hard, strong and determined, when he told her he was going to build an empire. It would take time but when it was ready, she would be its empress.

EIGHTEEN
JESSICA

She was adrift in Rosswall Heights, wandering through spaces that had no boundaries; no pillared rocks to fence her in, no ocean to sing her to sleep at night. The trees on Cullain were scattered and rare, wind-tortured and stubby, but at Rosswall Heights they marched over the grounds of the hotel and oppressed her with their rolling greenness. In school, she kept her head down when the teacher said, 'Are you paying attention or daydreaming again, Jessica Newman?'

Jessica. Her new identity constantly took her by surprise. This name she acquired overnight had the same unfinished veneer as the hotel. The hotel that now belonged to her father had been lying empty for a decade. A grand, half-built scheme that went awry when the money ran out and the property market collapsed. He bought it for a song. What song, Jessica wondered? Certainly not one that Joni would ever sing.

In this new reality they entered, her father answered to the name of Samuel Newman. An appropriate surname, Jessica thought, as he changed gradually from a bearded, solitary island man in thick woollens and baggy jeans into a businessman in suits with button-down shirts and gold cufflinks. His scraggy blond ponytail, usually covered by a cap, was cut so short she could see the outline of his skull and it was hard to believe his manicured nails were once rimmed with diesel oil.

The hotel underwent that same, slow transformation. Margaret used to say he had the fingers of a musician; long and supple fingers that never touched the keys of a piano yet were sunk deep in every pie. As the damp and decaying building was transformed into a glittering, glass palace, Jessica began to understand what Margaret had meant.

Many of the men who had visited them in Cullain arrived at Rosswall Heights to meet with her father in his penthouse office. Some of them held important positions in the companies he acquired. Alan Martin, the financial controller, was a rougher diamond when he used to come to Cullain, but a university degree in business studies had polished him to a colourless sheen. She also recognised Taig O'Meara, who drove them in a van from a deserted Mayo pier to Rosswall Heights. He bullied and bossed a crew of workers into transforming the derelict hotel and, now, as operations manager of SFDN, he was as ruthless as Alan was when it came to him axing a company that failed to perform.

'I'll find you, even if it means searching the globe,' Margaret had whispered when she hugged Jessica for the last time. 'Look out for me wherever you go. Never forget that I'm out there waiting for the chance to hug you again.'

After she moved into Rosswall Heights, Jessica left her mother's photograph in the bottom drawer of her new dressing table. It was enough to know that she once had a mother who was beautiful but destined for an early grave. Instead, she grieved for Margaret, who had been flesh and blood, not a phantom. Jessica kept expecting her to step into view from behind a wall or a tree, to be waiting outside the school gates. The panic she felt on losing her was mixed with terror and grief, emotions too complicated for a child of ten to understand. Whenever she heard Joni singing, it seemed as if her chest was being rent apart and she was haunted by that last glimpse of Margaret standing in the doorway.

Gradually, this image was overlaid by the belief that Margaret had left the island and built a new life for herself in Australia. She had married a sheep farmer who adored her, as did her twins, a boy and girl named Noah and Chloe. It was a perfect happy ending, as fantastical as the stories Margaret used to tell her about rock-slinging giants and spell-binding hags. Who invented this scenario? Did she create it, or did her father give her tidbits to build her own fantasy? It would take many years before Jessica asked herself such questions but, back then, as she made the transition from shy island child to rebellious teenager, this vision of a happy and contented Margaret blurred the edges of Jessica's forced separation from the only mother she had ever known.

Shortly before the opening of Rosswall Heights, her father returned from a trip abroad with a magnificent budgerigar. It perched on a swing and stared out at Jessica from glinting, plum-coloured eyes. Rodrigo would never die, he said. It was easy to see why. Made from Murano glass, the fake bird was housed in an elaborate cage, decorated with wrought-iron flowers, their centres studded with coloured gems. When the refurbishment on Rosswall Heights was complete, Rodrigo was displayed in the foyer and was soon joined by other birds, parrots, cockatoos, parakeets and a brilliantly coloured loriini. Their ornamental cages were suspended from the foyer ceiling and artificial plants in giant containers added to give the impression that visitors had entered an exotic aviary. When he was in the mood, music from her father's favourite operas emanated from the cages and it seemed as if the entire foyer had become an auditorium. He liked the order of his 'jungle,' as he called it.

No dead weeds to pull up, or birds who turned their claws to the light and died.

Sometimes, when they argued, Jessica accused him of wanting her sedated and compliant in one of his cages. One with enough space for her to roam freely until he decided the time was right to lock the cage door.

NINETEEN

She was in her mid-teens when she learned the truth about Alyson's death. A hit-and-run accident. She tried to imagine her mother's beautiful body lying broken and abandoned on a bridge somewhere in London, where, Jessica had eventually discovered, she was born. But she was unable to equate such a piteous image with the vibrant photograph she had hidden away. She took it out and studied the face she had tried to forget. Her mother's gaze held a new intensity, a fearlessness that defied a drug dealer's son to take her life away so carelessly. Yet that was what had happened. The only son of a gangster had knocked her down and left her to die alone.

As soon as her father unearthed that information and reported his discovery to the police, he had become a target for the gang, he told her. They almost ended his life, and hers, when a gunman, riding pillion on a motorbike, fired bullets into the car he was driving. He had just collected Jessica from her crèche and she was strapped into the back of the car when one of the bullets passed through the padded arm of her car seat. Her life was saved by a steel bar that diverted the bullet away from her. Her father was shot in his shoulder and crashed into a wall when he lost control of the wheel. He told her that she had been crying but unhurt when she was cut loose from the wreckage.

Knowing that a second attempt would be made on their lives, he fled with her to the island and only emerged from that secluded outpost when he believed their new identities were strong enough to protect them.

Sometimes, Jessica had flashes of those moments but could never tell if it was her imagination recreating the scene from his recollections or the imprint of a genuine baby memory. What were the odds of memory stretching back that far? Was it the reason for her night terrors? Had her dreams been filled with muffled thuds, the revving of an exhaust, the squeal of tyres, the crush of steel against brick? All Jessica knew for certain was that the attempt on their lives had turned her father into an obsessively suspicious man who believed that even shadows were capable of betrayal.

Occasionally, the mask he wore would slip and she glimpsed his fear behind the all-embracing protection he lavished on her. Falling in love for the first time when she was fifteen pushed it to the surface, but she was too enthralled by Justin Wright to heed the signs. Justin sat beside her in the school canteen. His eyes burned into the back of her neck during Maths and English. They held hands when they walked through Rosswall Park on their way home from school.

'Who is this boy?' her father asked when she returned to the hotel an hour later than her allotted time. 'Tell me his name.'

'Why are you asking me when you know it already?' She was petulant and strident then, aware that he tracked every move she made. What had begun as a flickering defiance was growing into a rebellious flame. She was fed up waiting to be gunned down by an unknown assailant. Boredom had replaced fear. The feeling of being protected from harm was as irritating as a contagious rash. She wanted to make her own friends, not those chosen by her father from the families of his business partners.

'All I care about is your safety,' he said. 'It's vitally important for both our sakes that we don't keep secrets from each other. The Wright family have connections to dangerous people.'

'That's not true,' she protested. 'Justin's family are only distantly related to those criminals. They're fifteenth cousins once removed or something like that and it's not *fair* that I—'

'Listen to me, Jessica.'

The tone he used, forceful yet caring, silenced her. 'You're too young to know what it means to be in love. Your guard is down. You're susceptible to sharing secrets. You want to know everything about the person you love and they want the same from you. It's a natural inclination and you will be unable to resist that kind of pressure. Do you think I wanted to live in Cullain? All those years of waiting until I felt it was safe for us to take a step back into the real world with identities that could keep us safe from harm.'

'All I understand is that you want to keep me in a cage forever!' Defiance was the only way she knew how to respond to him in those days. Later, she learned to hold fire, to pick the battles that were important to her and the arguments that were winnable.

But with Justin it was all heat and passion. The thrill of disobeying her father added an extra frisson to the thrill of lying beneath a canopy of leaves in the park and opening her mouth to Justin's kisses.

He was beaten up when he was walking home alone from the Rosswall Snooker Emporium where he had been playing snooker with his friends. He was taken to hospital with fractures and serious bruising. Local youths were blamed. No one knew for sure who was responsible and there was talk about his distant family connection to a criminal gang. He had told

Jessica it was impossible to disown the connection, even though his mother was a police sergeant and his father ran marathons for charity.

To accuse her father of planning such an attack was ludicrous, yet that possibility haunted Jessica. The next time she saw Justin he was on crutches and in too much pain to care that she was ending her first tentative experience of falling in love.

After Justin, there were others. Eamon Branagh, whose house was spray-painted with the words *A DRUG PUSHER LIVES HERE* when Jessica shared a joint with him at a barbecue held in his parent's back garden when they were away for a weekend. Once again, the school corridors were alive with speculation. Jessica walked close to the wall and kept her head low. She knew by then that the first boy she loved had been brutally beaten up for no other reason than that she was the daughter of Samuel Newman. That was the beginning of revelation and the end of innocence.

A finger in every pie. As SFDN expanded, Jessica was reminded of the many-headed snake, the Hydra – the mythological beast that continued to grow new heads even as other ones were chopped off. Her father sat on top of this pinnacle and seldom strayed from his private, penthouse office, apart from attending a monthly board meeting.

Money made money. Expansion was the way forward; the cut and thrust of business laid down by Alan Martin in jargon that was as dreary as his personality. What was hidden behind this acquisition of wealth? Was it drugs, not fish, that gave her father the capital to fund SFDN? This suspicion, no matter how often Jessica rejected it, kept returning like a worrying scab that needed picking.

His comings and goings on the island had been the same as the other fisherman, yet she had known even then that he was different from those sturdy, ruddy-faced men in waders and woollen caps. On market days, they spread their glistening catches along the harbour on containers of ice, or returned from the mainland hotels with empty boats. She had never seen her father's catch and never questioned why his boat didn't smell as pungently as those that listed by the harbour wall.

Eight years after leaving the island, she was determined to resist his efforts to groom her into his own image. She refused to study in New York and dropped out of a business degree course in Trinity College before completing her first year. During another heated argument about her future, she demanded to know the truth about his activities on Cullain.

Drugs. She battered him with that one word and only fell silent when he eventually admitted that Cullain had, indeed, been a cover for a smuggling operation. But not drugs. He was adamant that they were never part of his cargo. He smuggled merchandise – clothes, handbags, cigarettes, computers and car parts – an assortment of 'grey' cargo that would be taxed and vatted if it came in through official channels.

She chose to believe him even as she struggled against the constraints his history had placed on her. What if an overpriced designer handbag or a jacket that had probably been produced under sweat-shop conditions in some off-shore factory had to compete with the counterfeit imitation brought ashore by her father and his friends? He worked in a shadowy middle-world that made him enough money to wash it clean and establish a new future for them. Yet the past was never far behind them.

Under the pristine white shirts he wore, he carried a scar. She saw it once when he was exercising in the gym that he'd had set up in the penthouse. He was bare-chested as he exercised and unaware that she had entered the gym. His body, slick with sweat, was toned yet not overly muscular, and the scar was an angry red ridge against his pale skin.

She had left the gym before he noticed her. When she saw him again, he was dressed for business and that fleeting glimpse of his scar could have been imagined. A knife, not a bullet, was responsible for that puckered slash of skin but she never questioned him about it, knowing what his reply would be.

'We don't talk about the island, Jessica,' he would have said, his gaze as hard as his words. 'The past can't be undone and dwelling on it turns it into something it never was.'

He could always close down their conversations with a curt command. As if memories could be repressed so easily.

All Jessica had to do was close her eyes and she became Rachel Cox again, a terrified child in a nightdress, all alone at midnight in an empty cottage on the island of Cullain.

The unnerving silence had driven her from her bed and into the room her father shared with Margaret. Their bed was empty, the duvet neat; the pillows still had the smoothness of Margaret's hands when she plumped them in the morning. The fire was out in the kitchen and the clock on the wall showed that it was after midnight. Her father must still be on the mainland, but where was Margaret? Why was the front door unlocked? It was always locked at night, even though the chances of a burglar finding their isolated cottage were remote.

She had searched each room, unable to believe that Margaret would have gone out in the dark. Her father, yes – so much of his work was done under cover of darkness – but Margaret was always a reassuring presence when he was away.

The torch was missing from its usual place above the mantlepiece but she found a second one in a drawer. The beam sliced across the road outside the cottage. It was little more than a lane, filled with pot holes that regularly punctured the wheels of their jeep.

Figures came towards her. She thought of giants, their voices loud and urgent, but that was just wishful thinking: she knew immediately that something terrible had happened.

A figure rushed towards her and grabbed the torch, swung it

away from the hunched figures. *Margaret.* Her grip was tight on Rachel's arm as she yanked her back into the cottage. This was another side to Margaret, one that Rachel had never seen until then; this new Margaret, with her rough, cross voice, had seemed in tune with the terrifying sight of her father being carried into the cottage by two men, their arms acting as a stretcher for his limp body.

'Go to your room and stay there,' Margaret had shouted. The cottage light was merciless on her face. 'Your father had an accident on the fishing trawler and we need to make him well again.'

What happened... why is he bleeding... so white and still... his eyes rolling mad in his head? But these questions were not to be asked; already, Margaret was directing the men into the dining room where they laid him down on the table.

'Are you deaf or what?' Margaret was still shouting at her. 'Didn't I tell you to go to bed? Your father is going to be as right as rain in the morning.'

In bed, she had pulled the duvet to her chin and listened to unfamiliar noises. The voices sounded frightened. She was shocked by the words she heard. Boys used the same language when they fought at the back of the school. It was a shocking sound when Margaret cursed but she spat out the words as easily as the men did, and sent one of them rushing into the night to fetch the doctor.

After Dr Wallace arrived, she crept along the corridor and inched the dining room door open. From that vantage point, all she could see were the soles of her father's boots. He was still stretched on the table and Margaret had been leaning over him. She recognised Dr Wallace from his visit to the school where he talked to the pupils about the importance of clean hands and sneezing into their elbows. Alan Martin was standing too close to him. He was one of her father's friends and he kept on shouting into the doctor's ear about the importance of silence until Margaret ordered him to shut up. She pushed him away from Dr Wallace and things were quieter then.

In the bathroom, a man was washing blood from a knife. He was a stranger to her, unlike Alan Martin, who came regularly to Cullain. She knew the shape of that knife handle.

In the flare of a torch beam, she had seen it sticking out of her father's chest.

'Boo,' the man shouted when he saw her standing in the open doorway. He had bared his teeth in an exaggerated snarl. His laughter followed her all the way back to her bedroom.

Later, after the doctor left, she heard the men talking about earls. Earls were important people. Margaret had told her about the royal family, princes and dukes and earls, and darling Princess Di, who made Margaret cry for three days when she died so young and tragically. What was an earl doing on her father's boat and why was he swimming with the sharks that Rachel sometimes saw in the distance, their sinister fins breaking the waves? They had laughed about it, Alan, and the man who had shouted, whom Alan called 'Hawk'. They clinked their glasses, ignoring Margaret's warning that her father was sedated and needed to rest.

The cottage was spotless in the morning. It would have been easy to believe last night had never happened. In the kitchen, the fire was blazing and the men had disappeared. Her father, pale and motionless, lay on his bed. He reminded her of a statue, so still and rigid, his skin warm when she touched him, his chest rising and falling. She could tell from the slump of Margaret's shoulders that he would be okay. When she asked why his clothes were covered in blood, Margaret shoved them into a bucket and told her she was away with the fairies. It was her favourite expression when Rachel asked questions she wasn't prepared to answer.

'Your father had a serious fall on his boat.' She repeated this so often that Rachel began to wonder if she had imagined the knife. Why would anyone stab her father? When she asked Margaret why they must keep his accident a secret, she said he had broken his fishing quota and should not have taken his trawler out. The police would come from the mainland and ask questions. They must leave the island as soon as he was strong enough to travel. She had no awareness then that he was planning to leave without her.

When he was strong enough to tell her his time on the island was over, Margaret kept talking about the ten years she had shared his bed. Was this to be her reward? She demanded an answer to this question many times. He said he would leave her the cottage and the jeep, and enough money to begin a new life in Australia.

'Thanks for nothing,' she shouted, her voice rough with the unfamiliar sharpness Rachel had heard when she came through the darkness, her clothes stained with his blood.

TWENTY

Her father was right. Dwelling on the past turned it into something it never was. Margaret, content and happy in Australia with her loving husband and twins, would have remained there in Jessica's imagination if she had not met Siobhán Doolin on Grafton Street one Saturday afternoon. If Jessica had seen her first, Siobhán would not have recognised her. Jessica had perfected the ability to blend like a chameleon into her surroundings. Slumped shoulders, her face folded into blankness, eyes down, she went unnoticed in the throng. But Siobhán saw her first and called 'Rachel!' with such certainty that she didn't have the nerve to fob her off with the usual jokes about doppelgängers and how she was always being mistaken for someone else.

Siobhán had been one of the older pupils at the small island school, the daughter of the principal. With an ambition to become a teacher like her mother, she had often helped the younger pupils with their school work, and would have been aware of the isolation that must have clung like a caul to the young Rachel Cox.

'London is my home now,' she said. 'Two children, two

marriages, three homes and one career in teaching. But who's counting?' Siobhán laughed and asked Jessica if she had ever been back to Cullain.

'It's a bit of a stretch from New York so, no, I've never been back,' Jessica replied. 'We moved to the States after we left the island. I've just flown into Dublin for a conference.' She lied with confidence. *Eye to eye when you lie.* This was one of her father's aphorisms, short and pithy.

'Sounds like you lead an exciting life,' said Siobhán. 'New York is a far cry from Cullain, as is London. It took me years to become accustomed to the clamour.'

'Cullain has its own clamour.'

'True enough.' Siobhán nodded. 'The wind and the waves. They're still a soundtrack in my head. How is your father?'

'He died some years ago.'

'I'm *so* sorry to hear that.' Her surprise was evident when she paused. 'Like Margaret, he was too young to die,' she continued. 'You must have got an awful shock when you heard about her death.'

'Death?' Jessica was stunned by the brute force of this information. *Never betray emotion. Opening a chink in your armour exposes your heart to the coup de grâce.* Her father's warning held her upright as she struggled to follow what Siobhán was saying. *Lies, all lies.* Jessica wanted to tell her about the sheep farmer and the twins, about love being precious when it was reciprocated, but she knew with a stinging certainty that what she had just heard was true.

'Good God, Rachel, you're as white as a sheet.' Siobhán's surprise was mixed with apprehension. 'Didn't you know Margaret died? I'm so sorry to spring the news on you so suddenly. It never dawned on me that you weren't aware of what happened.'

'When did she die?'

'About a week or so after you and your dad left.'

'What happened to her?'

'She went into the sea off Devil's Reach. Her body was washed up on the rocks the next day.'

'Devil's Reach?' Jessica's voice shook. 'Margaret hated heights. What was she doing up there?'

Buskers were performing nearby, a man singing sad, rebel songs and, further up the street, a trio of students were playing violins, yet all Jessica could see was the foreboding plateau where the islanders who'd had enough of the mist and the isolation went. She used to climb up there and stand on the edge. Teasing Margaret, forcing her up the lower reaches before skipping downwards and into her arms.

Siobhán was still talking, answering questions Jessica didn't want to ask but must. An inquest had been held. A coroner claimed she took her own life but that was an easy label, Siobhán said. It could just as easily have been an accident.

Jessica could have sought more information but what else was there to know? They said goodbye and lost themselves in the Saturday afternoon crowd.

All those years of missing Margaret, and Jessica hadn't even felt the shiver of her passing.

Her father was working in his home office when she reached Rosswall Heights. His jaw clenched when she mentioned her meeting with Siobhán. It told her all she needed to know. He unlocked a drawer on his desk and removed a buff envelope containing a death certificate and a coroner's report. There it was in blunt, official language. *Suicide.*

'I didn't tell you at the time because you were desperately upset at leaving her.' He tried to console Jessica. 'Then, when you finally settled in Rosswall, I wanted you to move on with your life, not look back—'

'Pillar of salt, was that it?'

He looked puzzled for an instant then nodded. 'I did what I believed was best for you. You had such a tendency to brood on the past—'

'Margaret was like the mother I never had! How *dare* you make that decision for me.'

He stood back and surveyed her. 'I can see how upset you are. That was an unfortunate way to discover the truth.'

'*Unfortunate*? The least I would have expected from you was the truth. But I guess that was a big ask.' Her encounter with Siobhán had ripped a bandage from a wound that had never healed. She felt light-headed, untethered from the belief that Margaret's story had had a happy ending.

He drew back, as if she had smacked his face. 'I thought our fighting days were over, Jessica.'

'Obviously not,' she snapped back. 'Why didn't you take her with us when we left Cullain? She loved you so much. Did she not fit in with your new image? Were her hands too rough from all the scrubbing she had to do in that hovel?'

'*Enough*, Jessica.' His face was flushed, his eyes widening as she snatched the certificate from him and tore it in two. 'Margaret died by her own hand. I didn't walk her up those rocks. Nor did I order her to jump from them. She had her own reasons—'

'What reasons? Unrequited love? Was that it? Or was it because we had to leave Cullain so suddenly? Why was that? Was it connected to that night—'

'Stop it.' He caught her wrist and held it tightly. 'Don't you dare say another word. Someday you'll understand the pressures I was under to keep us alive. Margaret could have endangered our lives. I'd stopped trusting her. She made friends with the women on the island. She drank with them. All that music and dancing loosened her tongue. She brought danger to our doorstep and that was why I had to leave her behind. Since then, I've done everything I can to build a future for both of us.

If we can't trust each other, then the sacrifices I've made to keep us safe are worthless.'

Jessica moved into her apartment shortly afterwards. The vast, glassy hotel with its operatic overtures and flamboyant birds had become too small for both of them.

Strictly speaking, the apartment was never really hers, however: it belonged to SFDN and, as Jessica wasn't allowed to change the décor, she felt as if she had simply moved into an annex off Rosswall Heights. And she was conscious of being watched, of being encaged by love, protection and the tyranny of invisible eyes.

TWENTY-ONE

Unrequited love was for losers, Margaret used to say, the bitterness of her own experience etched on her face. If Jessica had listened to her, would things have turned out differently? Or were the choices she made set on a predestined path that was bound to lead her, sooner or later, into Foundation Stone and face to face with Christine Lewis and Richard Stone?

She was at the cinema with Shay McCabe when she saw the advertisement for Kava perfume. Played out on a giant screen, the shock of recognition tore at her heart. Cullain was laid before her in all its rugged splendour. The soundtrack had captured the orchestral music of wave and wind, and the wild scream of seabirds, a sound that instantly transported her back to her childhood.

She was intrigued enough to find out the name of the advertising agency who had chosen such a remote and unknown location. No surprise to discover it had been made by Foundation Stone. She knew the details of the wife and husband team from reading about them in tittle-tattle *Zing* features and well-researched business ones. They had met by chance on a train and built a hugely successful partnership from that encounter.

Working for *Zing* magazine she was writing about celebrities: short, trite features that she could write easily but with utter detachment. Another dead-end job. She had no problem finding such jobs, and left them just as easily. Her love life followed the same pattern. Shay McCabe lasted longer than the others. Their on/off relationship consisted mainly of drinking binges and bedroom aerobics. Feel the burn... wasn't that what Jane Fonda urged those sinewy eighties women with their leg warmers to do? She and Shay burned each other out so quickly that, when it was over, Jessica found it hard to remember anything that was notable about those wasted months.

She attended the Elora awards with him and watched as Richard held aloft the trophy for the 'Outstanding Advertisement of the Year' Award. Shortly afterwards, when she heard they were advertising for a senior copywriter, she applied for the position.

They were seated together on one side of Christine's wide, impressive desk when they interviewed her. Their arms touched occasionally in a way that seemed too familiar to be noticed yet emphasised their togetherness. Richard was dressed casually in jeans, an open-necked shirt and a pale blue jacket. His full lips had a natural upwards curve, made for smiling, though the strong thrust of his chin suggested a forceful personality behind his easy smile. Christine wore a caramel-coloured trouser suit, no blouse, the jacket showing some cleavage, its starkness lifted by strands of gold knotted into an intricate pattern at her throat.

Jessica understood enough about financial controls to know that Christine was the more powerful one in that partnership, yet her awareness was focused on Richard. It was as if she had suddenly acquired a third eye that followed the fold of his arms as he sat back in his chair and allowed his wife to control the conversation. She asked what Jessica could bring to the agency. Her tone suggested she had heard more than enough from the previous interviewees about commitment, creative energy, loyalty, innovativeness. A challenge or a question lurked behind her cool brown gaze, but he had smiled at Jessica, as if encouraging her not to be unnerved by Christine's brisk questioning or the rise of her elegant eyebrows.

Jessica figured she had failed the interview but he rang her later, his voice startlingly seductive, and welcomed her to Foundation Stone.

TWENTY-TWO

At first, working alongside Richard, she believed it was adrenaline that fuelled those moments with breathlessness. He energised her imagination. She would throw out a suggestion and he would catch it in mid-air, build it into a concept that they could pull apart and put together again. But when, in the middle of a strategy discussion, she found herself wondering what it would be like to kiss his wide, generous mouth, she was shocked into the realisation that she was falling in love with him; headlong love that rang warning bells, yet there it was. It was a meteorite she hadn't been expecting and when it whammed into her, she felt as if the very air they breathed had sweetened.

At night she could let go. Her dreams were fevered, yet when she arrived at the agency, no one would have guessed at the thoughts tumbling through her mind... except, perhaps, Christine. She always appeared to be hovering over them. Even when Jessica was alone in Richard's office, she was still aware of her presence. Watchful, that was how she had seemed then. Her laser stare reminded Jessica of her father. She gave off the same aura, as if she could scan Jessica's thoughts and expose them, belly up.

Her father guessed, of course he did. 'Tell me about your employer,' he said, when they met for lunch one afternoon.

Knowing his ability to read a situation, Jessica was immediately on her guard. 'Which one?' she asked. 'I have two.'

'As your interest has always been in men, most of them unsuitable, I've to assume it's Richard Stone who's captivated you.'

'I'm not captivated—'

'Jessica, *stop*.' He waved the backs of his hands at her, a gesture he used whenever she tried to argue her way out of *his* truth. 'We've never kept secrets from each other and we're not going to start now. Is he married?'

She shrugged. No use pretending. 'Yes. He's married to Christine but she uses her single name. She looks after the financial side of the business.'

'Are they happy?'

'I guess so.'

'Make it your business to know,' he said. 'Your end game must always be crystal clear before you even reach the starting line.'

His homemade aphorisms made her cringe. 'The enemy you allow to survive could be your future assassin,' was his favourite, closely followed by, 'Why settle for nickel when you can have a silver spoon in your mouth?'

Her 'silver spoon' was SFDN Enterprises. How naïve she had been to believe he would give up so easily. He pulled strings with his long fingers and others danced, but she'd had no idea what tune he was playing when he offered to save Foundation Stone from closure.

She had driven directly to see him on the night Richard rang from St Vincent's Hospital to tell her that Christine had collapsed at Rosswall Heights.

'I never offered to advertise with Foundation Stone,' her father said when she demanded to know why he had changed his mind. 'You were so intent on impressing Richard Stone that you only heard what you wanted to hear. I told you I was prepared to help them overcome their current difficulties, and would put a proposition to them when we met.'

'I wasn't trying to impress anyone,' she said. 'I'm part of a team and I was trying to help them to save their agency.'

'You will never be part of a team, Jessica,' he said. 'You are my heir. Everything I've achieved will become yours in time. You constantly under-achieve and talk about being caged when what I'm offering you is the freedom to fly as high as you aspire. Foundation Stone will never move beyond its limitations. This past week has proved how unstable it is. One shake and it falls. I'm giving you an opportunity to explore its full potential. Don't turn it down because of misplaced loyalty. Do you honestly think Christine will tolerate your presence in her company much longer? She observes everything and she believes you are a threat to her marriage.'

It had been there from the beginning. A triangle of confusion, an awareness that their paths were crossing in ways they were unable to fathom or even acknowledge. She would catch Christine staring, a quizzing gaze that was as puzzling as it was discomforting. But her father had a way of knowing things, of recognising a weak link and how it could be further destabilised. The perfect balance of their marriage could be tilted under different circumstances and he would give Jessica the power to do so. She had already seen the tensions in their business partnership: Christine's intractability when it came to finance, her tight-fisted approach constantly at odds with Richard's creative ambitions.

As she drove back to her apartment that night, Jessica knew that her father had orchestrated the misinformation that was strangling the life from Foundation Stone.

When she called into Redstone the following evening, Christine was no longer the poised, intimidating woman that Jessica had come to know. She seemed shrunken, her eyes bloodshot and cloudy, the side of her face badly bruised. Her bottom lip was swollen and split. Richard had said she bit down hard on it when she fell. She wasn't expecting Jessica to visit so she had no opportunity to gloss over her appearance with make-up, as she did in the days that followed.

Initially, she seemed prepared to give Jessica the benefit of the doubt but as the pressure continued to mount on the agency, Christine no longer believed she was an innocent bystander. The agency was hollowed out by then and Christine – so impeccably made-up that it was hard to believe the skin underneath was mottled brown and blue – continued to insist that the day would be saved.

At the signing of the contract, her hand was steady when she wrote her signature. Jessica had never been able to interpret her stare, but what she saw that afternoon was fear. A naked streak of fear that stretched her lips as she glanced at Jessica's father then back at her. Richard had the hangdog look of someone who had been pummelled repeatedly. Had there been arguments between them? Impossible to imagine otherwise.

At Rosswall Heights, her father suggested opening a bottle of champagne to celebrate her entry into SFDN. Jessica wanted to shout, 'You mean my capitulation,' but that would have been hypocritical. He had made her an offer she was unable to resist and, from then on, she knew she would be in thrall to him. She had convinced herself that there wasn't a cage wide enough to contain her, but her wings had not proved strong enough to keep her afloat.

TWENTY-THREE

Christine and Richard had seemed invincible as a couple. When their marriage began to fall apart, the signs were imperceptible to everyone except Jessica. She saw the cracks when they had barely formed. Then, for a short while, it seemed as if these fissures had closed over and they were happy again. They took coffee breaks together, fifteen minutes morning and afternoon, sitting close together on the coffee deck, his finger stroking her cheek or whispering something into her ear in the intimate way of lovers who were still carrying the heat of the morning's sex. But that was just a short respite, like a terminal illness that arrests itself temporarily before entering the final stages. Hypnosis was the problem, and Christine was lost to its suggestive powers.

Working late on the Krisgloss account or grabbing a quick lunch on the coffee deck, Jessica learned to hear what wasn't being said when Richard spoke about Christine. She could tell from his expression, his gestures, a shrug of his shoulders, that he was worried about her. He became increasingly suspicious of the hypnotherapy sessions she was attending. Mostly, they focused on an accident she'd had when she was a child, a near-drowning that she was only beginning to recall. He also admitted that she was drinking heavily as a reaction to the buy-out of the agency. When he apologised for boring Jessica with the details of his troubled marriage, she pounced on the word 'troubled'. It had reverberations, a hint that promised more than he was willing to admit.

They had stayed late at the office to work on the Krisgloss campaign. Jessica had ordered an Indian takeaway which they had eaten at her desk, washing it down with beers sent up from the bar next door. Aware that she was tapping into a reservoir of frustration, she was a sympathetic, listening ear when he spoke about Christine's obsession about this childhood accident. Somehow, it had grown from an accidental slip from a riverbank into a deliberate attempt by a gunman to drown her. She was demanding that Richard believe this outrageous possibility. No wonder he was struggling. When this fixation was combined with her drinking and her suspicions… Richard had stopped at that point, his discomfort obvious.

'Why is she suspicious?' Jessica asked.

'Oh, it's nothing to worry about,' he replied. 'It's just that she's always been so self-assured but now… well, it's hard to know what's going on in her head. I've never given her any reason to…' He hesitated, and she, sensing his embarrassment, knew that she was the cause of Christine's suspicions.

She was aware of his quick-fire glance at her, and the swamping sensation in her stomach deepened.

'Has it to do with the takeover?' she asked. 'I feel responsible—'

'You're not responsible for Christine or what happened to the agency.' He hesitated, then shrugged. 'Christine has her own issues and they have nothing to do with Foundation Stone.'

'Does she worry about us working late?'

'She has no reason to do so. And she knows from experience that sometimes it's necessary. When she went to your apartment…' he stopped, flushed suddenly, and slapped the side of his head. 'Drink talking… forget I ever started this conversation.' He gathered up the empty beer bottles and the food containers. 'I'm going to call a taxi. You should take one too. Cycling around the city at this time of night is risky.'

'Don't worry about me. I'm capable of looking after myself. Just tell me what's going on with Christine. If it concerns me in any way I need to know.'

That was how she discovered that Christine had sat outside her apartment one night. Eyes on her. She had been the object of their dangerous intent – a reality that had framed her childhood. She felt the familiar tingle of fear, the goosebumps rising. How long had his wife stayed in the shadows, suspicious and jealous?

Richard tried to play it down but it was obvious that Christine considered her a threat.

A threat that became a reality on the night of the Krisgloss reception.

Christine chose to stay away and miss an event that meant so much to her husband. Richard's mouth had an unfamiliar hardness when he spoke about her decision to find the location where this childhood near-drowning had occurred. He was vague on details, reluctant to admit Christine had travelled to a dark place in her mind and left him behind.

After the reception ended, the staff from the agency moved on to a bar close to Jessica's apartment. One by one, the others left until only Richard remained with her. When she suggested a nightcap at her apartment, there was a heartbeat pause before he nodded.

The tide was high on the Liffey, the wind soft. He put his arm around her as they crossed the Samuel Beckett bridge. Below them, the river flowed on a quavering stream of light that trapped the tall, glass towers and the laid-back belly of the exhibition centre; an aurora borealis wavering on the dark ripples.

The stars, aligned that night and high above them, glistened with promise.

In the lift, she touched his cheek. The rasp of his dark stubble against her palm, the leaden desire of his breath as he sighed and gripped her wrist. His lips on hers had the aching familiarity of a dream that was about to become real.

She'd had lovers, of course – some clumsy, some who looked upon sex as an acrobatic feat, and others who believed it gave them the right to wake up beside her the following morning. She had climbed heights of pleasure and, sometimes, been left cold, adrift from her body and the one above her.

When Richard came to her bed, it was as wild and electrifying as she had anticipated.

Afterwards, as they lay in each other's arms, she was too sated to notice his guilt, a parasite forcing its way between them. When she raised herself on her elbow to look down at him, she saw his pleasure evaporating. Instead of words of love, of reassurance, all she heard were apologies. He had taken advantage of her. That was exactly what he said.

She felt a cruel pleasure in reminding him that, as she was his employer, the boot, so to speak, was on the other foot. His face froze. Until that moment he had never fully appreciated that their business relationship had fundamentally changed; unlike Christine, who had been aware of her loss of status from the beginning.

He left shortly afterwards and returned to his empty house to await his wife's arrival home.

Christine seemed different when she returned from England, more relaxed than before she left. Her trip had gone well, she said. She never mentioned the real reason why she was there and Richard shrugged when Jessica enquired about the river incident.

'She's sorted it out in her mind,' he said. 'I'd prefer not to discuss it.'

'Is she still stalking me?' The question needed asking and he winced, uncomfortable about the ease with which he had spilled such secrets into her ear. 'I told you it only happened once. I should never have mentioned it.'

'But you did. And I have to protect myself from her.'

'*Protect* yourself?'

'She's unbalanced, Richard. You said so yourself.'

'Don't distort what I told you. She was trying to find answers to something that happened to her a long time ago, which is perfectly understandable.' It was obvious that he regretted turning Jessica into his confidante.

Over the following weeks, he avoided being alone with Jessica. His haunted expression killed the joy she had experienced in his arms. She wanted to hate him. Hate would give her strength. Without it, she was that most pathetic of creatures. A victim of unrequited love. The rage that came over her when she imagined Christine lying next to him at night shocked her. Rage was dangerous, destabilising. Her father had impressed this fact on her from her childhood. Decisions, when made, must come from the cold depths of logic. Action, when taken, must not be endangered by fury's heat. She asked him once if she was the daughter of a robot. He laughed then, something he seldom did, and told her that what defined him from a robot was a heart that burned with protective love for her.

PART 3

TWENTY-FOUR

LONG ACRE PRISON

Despite obvious differences – one of them being an open door – Jessica has discovered that Long Acre has similarities to her life on Cullain and at Rosswall Heights. One was rugged, the other glossy, yet each had a small community at its centre, while a flow of anonymous visitors circled the outer edges. And in here, it's the same. The community of shop-lifters and drug dealers, con artists, corporate fraudsters, hackers, counterfeiters, and one murderess, form a dangerous nucleus; a molten core that only needs a spark to explode.

Listening to the women's stories in the therapy group, Jessica is electrified, terrified, saddened and amazed by the sharing that takes place in the circle of nine. She welcomes the sensations that rip through her. They provide proof that she is still capable of emotion. Despite Eoin Cronin's attempts to stress that she is of no more, or no less, importance than the others in the group he has formed, they don't believe him. Her crime has set her apart, but she will not be unlocked so easily. Her father had cloaked her world in secrets, and Jessica has lived within their shadow all her life. Her shell is rock hard. She allows the women glimpses of her rebellious years but they are not interested in hearing how she dropped out of college. They do not want to know about the dead-end jobs that filled her with inertia or the men she loved briefly but eased from her bed before morning. Maria, her cell mate, egged on by the others, is beginning to demand facts. Eoin's gaze is keen, his antennae on high alert. He knows when Jessica is shamming, when she is removed from what she is saying, free from any emotional reaction her words might arouse... but not this morning.

Never one to miss an opportunity for self-promotion, Shay McCabe has written about their relationship in *Capital Eye*. Who is this woman with her neediness and mood swings, her jealousies and insecurities that he has profiled? Jessica could be reading about a stranger. One she would cross the road to avoid. In Long Acre, introspection is inevitable and she wonders if he has described the unadorned Jessica Newman, stripped of illusions, wiles, charms and deceits. Did he pluck all her feathers until only her bare carcass was exposed? That is what this circle of women would like to find out. They know what she did to Christine and now, in this cloistered community, they want a blow-by-blow account of the night that howled. Does Jessica feel regret, shame, sorrow? Most importantly, they want to know what brought her to that finite moment. So far, no one has had the nerve to put that terrible question to her but one of them will do so, sooner rather than later.

How will she answer them? Is an answer even possible?

A pillar of salt. What good ever came from a backward glance?

TWENTY-FIVE

Has Jessica lost her lustre? Her energy seems low, her attitude indifferent when she gathers the staff for a meeting in the Hub, the nickname for the central office. Halfway through the meeting, she excuses herself and hurries towards the staff bathroom. She is still there when Christine enters ten minutes later. Her cheekbones look even more defined than usual as she brushes them with blusher. She appears to have lost weight but, maybe, she is simply skilled at contouring her face?

'Are you okay?' Christine asks.

'I had a late night,' Jessica admits. 'It's catching up on me.'

'I hope it was a good one.'

'It was unforgettable.' Jessica applies lipstick and uses her fingers to fluff out her hair. 'I want you to look at the Kava account. Can you meet me in my office this afternoon?'

'Of course. Is there a problem?'

She stares through the mirror at Christine, her gaze unfathomable. 'Richard is underestimating the cost of the new campaign.' She puckers her lips, a slight moue of discontent as she runs a finger along the edge of her bottom lip to wipe a lipstick smudge. 'I'd like to check the figures with you before I speak to him about it.'

Her irritation with Richard is a surprise. Is the gloss of his creativity beginning to dull? Christine wonders, as the bathroom door swings closed.

On her arrival home from Rillingham, she had briefly answered his questions about her meeting with Ryan. He seemed satisfied to be told that he was a boy who just happened to be in the right place at the right time. The shooting...? He had quirked his eyebrow and tried not to let his disbelief show. The rawness of her experience was still too real to share and when she attributed it to a false memory, he nodded as if that was the answer he expected.

She has never lied to him in the past, nor kept secrets from him. This awareness adds to her discomfort, especially as the weeks pass and any inclination to tell him fades. She will not allow his sarcasm, or even his clumsy attempts to understand her, discredit the time she spent with Ryan and Dorothy Niels.

She enters the nearest toilet cubicle. The scent of Jessica's perfume is strong in this enclosed space. Suddenly, Christine feels it again: that quavering uncertainty, the belief that the floor is about to fling her off balance. She breathes evenly. She has learned techniques from Elaine and is able to withstand this sudden surge of anxiety.

Christine's meeting to discuss Kava with Jessica is concluded quickly. She can see the problem with the costings and how it can be rectified. Richard's office door is shut – again.

He looks up from his computer when she enters, his gaze loose and unfocused. The edge of the screen is visible and he appears to have been staring at an X-ray.

'Christine, hi. You startled me.' He clicks out of the image and runs his fingers over the keyboard.

'I've just been talking to Jessica about Kava,' she says. 'You're over-reaching again. I thought you two worked well together.'

'Apparently not.'

'Is something wrong?'

'Everything's fine.' He stands too quickly and presses his hands flat on his desk. 'Let's get a takeaway tonight. We'll just chill out and plan a short break. We're both severely in need of one.'

'That sounds like a plan—'

She is interrupted by Lorraine, who calls out to Richard from her desk that she is having trouble with her graphic software.

'I'd better sort this out.' He sighs and shrugs, waits until Christine walks before him from his office.

Later, when she is taking a break at the coffee deck, he enters Jessica's office. She finishes her coffee and waits. Fifteen minutes pass without any sign of him emerging. The uncertainties she tries so hard to control are triggered again? She glances at her phone when it bleeps. An email has arrived. She will check it later on her computer.

She is about to put her phone down when she reads the subject line. *Richard's Future.* The sender is a Mary Murphy. This ubiquitous name is commonplace enough to belong to her wide list of acquaintances yet Christine is unable to bring a single Mary Murphy she knows to mind. She tries to ignore the email as she pours another espresso. The subject line is a taunt that, finally, proves too much to ignore. No message has been written in the body of the email but there is an attachment, which she opens.

The image she sees is just a squiggle. Initially, she can't make it out. Is she looking at a dormouse? Tiny as a comma, it lies on its back in a partially-lit burrow. Her mind has become a shock absorber that withholds from her an instinctive recognition until she is able to breathe again. She has been shown this image often; three times by Amy and Bernice and on another two occasions by her brother, Killian.

She hurries into her office, her fingers fumbling on the keyboard of her computer as she opens her email account. The picture is clearer now. She is seeing it with X-ray precision. She remembers Richard's expression earlier, his slack-jawed shock when he looked up and saw her standing there. And that instant of panic in the toilet cubicle, her antennae primed but without direction as she breathed in the cloying smell of perfume. Had Jessica sprayed it into the air to hide the evidence of morning sickness?

It seems preposterous, yet the attachment that was sent to her is a relentless flash before her eyes.

As the afternoon progresses and the world maintains its normal rotation, it is possible to convince herself that her imagination is in overdrive. She has deleted the email and emptied her trash. What she saw on her computer could have been anything. A quickly drawn sketch for a new advertisement; the crude representation of the ultimate new beginning.

For five days Christine exists on denial. She is as strung out as a voodoo doll with pin pricks, only she is the one inflicting the wounds. She watches them avoiding each other. Jessica snaps at him at a team meeting when they are discussing Kava, and insists that he work within Christine's budget. It is so deliberate yet no one else seems aware of the great pretend.

At night, she drinks to alleviate the pain of knowing, not knowing. By day, she waits. If her suspicions are correct, something has to give. On the sixth morning Jessica rings the agency and tells Jean at reception that she is taking the morning off. A short while later Richard enters Christine's office to announce that he is meeting a client. He speaks too fast, spilling out information she doesn't need to hear about the potential value of this meeting. He expects to be back within two hours. All going well, he should have good news. His smile is strained as he departs. She watches from the window of the main office as he walks down the steps and turns left.

She follows him. He enters a coffee shop with a glass frontage. The aroma of coffee and freshly baked pastries wafts past her but all she can smell is the rank odour of an upturned stone. He is not holding hands with Jessica when they emerge. If the space between them is an indicator of separation, then Christine should have nothing to fear. But she knows better than that. She is behind them all the way. Occasionally, Jessica turns her head to speak to Richard but, mostly, they are silent as they walk through Crown Alley and along the quays, over the Liffey and up O'Connell Street.

They walk by a grey building with Palladian pillars and arched doorways, past black wrought-iron railings and around the corner where an in-patients clinic with a brash modern face and an automatic glass door that swallows them into the interior. She recognises the maternity hospital. Richard was born there and he is back again in the role of a father. What other reason could he have for entering the Rotunda Hospital with Jessica Newman at his side? Christine responds to this reality with a sensation that is akin to relief. A relief that is false and will be short-lived, but she will no longer have to endure those clamorous suspicions, those side-tracks from the truth.

TWENTY-SIX

She waits for them on the opposite side of the road. They are still not holding hands when they emerge, but she can tell there is something different about them. Have they appreciated her agony? Surely it must travel across this busy thoroughfare and smack them to a standstill. Apparently not.

They turn back the way they came. When they stop to wait for the red traffic light, Richard puts his arm out to hold Jessica back as she steps too hastily onto the road. This is a protective gesture, a man guarding his future; in that instant, he must have known he was saying goodbye to his past. He glances back, as if he feels the burn of Christine's eyes on his spine. She ducks quickly behind the burly figure of the man in front of her and when she looks again, they are heading back down O'Connell Street.

What drove them into each other's arms, and deeper still? It is too soon to confront them. She will need courage to listen to their excuses, their lies. They enter the Gresham Hotel. She follows a few minutes later and sees them in The Writers Lounge, sunk deeply into armchairs, a waiter taking an order for refreshments. No champagne. A pregnant woman would not be so irresponsible.

Christine walks on. The pub she enters is empty, apart from a barman and an elderly woman with raspberry-coloured hair and the pitted nose of a habitual alcoholic. She glares at Christine, as if she has disturbed her unbroken routine, then returns her attention to the morning newspaper.

Three hours later, Christine turns her phone back on. Ten missed calls from Richard are listed, three more from Jessica.

'Richard's been trying to contact you for ages.' Jean at the reception desk leans forward to greet her when she returns to Foundation Stone. 'So has Jessica.'

'I'll explain everything shortly.' She swings her tote bag onto the reception desk and removes a bottle of champagne. 'Go to the meeting room and collect enough champagne glasses for everyone,' she says. 'We're going to have a celebration.'

'What's the occasion?' Jean hesitates, uncertain.

'Go... *go*!' Christine slaps the bottle down and the receptionist hurries towards the meeting room to arrange glasses on a silver tray.

Jessica is standing beside the Power Point screen when Christine enters the Hub. Richard stands on one side of her and the others are grouped nearby or relaxed in easy chairs. Every head turns towards Christine when she holds the champagne bottle aloft. She enjoys the moment, the knowledge that she has supreme control over the situation. Richard hurries towards her then draws back slightly, startled, she guesses, by the smell of alcohol on her breath. She envisages it as a vaporous, rainbow-streaked bubble enclosing her and, again, she has the sensation of being lifted high above the world of ordinary things.

'Were you drinking?' he hisses. 'For Christ's sake, Christine, what have you been doing? I've been trying to contact you for hours.'

'I was unavoidably delayed by unanticipated consequences.' She almost sings the words at him. 'Ah, Jean. You've got the glasses. Everyone, please gather around. I've an important announcement to make.' She is skilled at releasing champagne corks with a celebratory pop and does so now. Her voice rises as the champagne fizzes over the neck of the bottle.

'Apologies for not returning your calls.' She addresses Jessica directly. 'As I've explained to Richard, I was unavoidably delayed by unanticipated consequences.' The words no longer sound free and easy. Her tongue is too clogged with grief and the rainbow-hued bubble bursts with an inaudible splatter.

She holds the bottle outwards and the champagne runs like a spill of rain across the surface of the tray. She is reckless with hate and hurt. Is that how murders are committed? A snap decision that allows no room for second thoughts?

The staff, sensing an unfolding drama, have gathered around her. She steadies her hand and pours, waits while each bemused member removes a glass. Richard is unable to hide his nervousness but Jessica looks composed. How does she do it? Where did she get that self-possession; the ability to bear such an earth-shattering secret so blithely on her shoulders?

'Jessica, you're not drinking,' Christine says. 'But that's perfectly understandable under the circumstances.'

Richard grabs her arm but he is unable to silence her. 'Congratulations on your pregnancy.' She holds her glass upwards and takes a sip. 'And a toast to Richard, the proud father.'

Silence makes such a powerful statement. It covers shock, stupefaction, anger, despair, incredulity and general all-round amazement.

Jessica is speaking. Her eyes are cast down, her cheeks glistening with tears. Finally, her mask has cracked, or is that simply another layer to hide the real person? Richard's fingers dig deeper into her arm. His face is ashen, crushed with a dreadful truth. His lips are moving. He is telling her something but it is too late... too late.

Christine ignores the babble of voices and wrenches her arm free. Cheap, that is how she feels. Nothing triumphalist about pulling such a tawdry stunt. Now, all she wants to do is run for cover.

On her journey to Glencone, the taxi driver remains silent. Taciturn or sensitive, it matters not, she is just thankful she doesn't have to waste words. Richard arrives shortly afterwards. He insists on explaining, demands the right to do so. He is not a man who carries condoms in his inside pocket. It was never a requirement until that night when everything changed.

'Once,' he says. 'It was a moment of madness that happened only *once*.'

Is *once* supposed to make a difference? They had been drinking shots. Did he think he was twenty again, carefree and reckless? And now Jessica is pregnant. What are the odds? Christine wonders. Calculated or bad luck? Richard never wanted children. Was that what attracted him to Christine? A woman unconcerned by the expectations of society would make a compliant partner. No agonised arguments about the tick-tock clock and that all-invasive maternal instinct.

Once...once...*once*. He keeps repeating this fact as if it has enough muscle to break Christine's resolve. She doesn't ask where the *once* took place. It is enough to know they made love without a surrounding canvas adding colour and texture.

The breaking up of their dream agency has been silent and resigned; the break-up of their marriage follows the same pattern, but only after they have nothing left to say to each other.

They shout, rant, hurl boulders of accusations. He wants this child that he and Jessica have conceived during those moments of madness at her apartment. That was where her husband slept. It slips out during one of their arguments and now she can image the headboard and the pink glister of the chandelier casting its glow over their naked bodies. On which side of the bed did he lie? Or was he unable to sleep, a brief and tumultuous satisfaction souring into guilt as he dressed quietly and slunk home to await her arrival from Rillingham-on-the-Weir?

She should be writhing on the floor, gripped by another panic attack. Instead, she is cold and rational. Her heartbeat is steady. She has realised a startling fact.

The truth has set her free, but freedom from pain is not part of the deal.

The tide is out, the sand roiled and glistening when she leaves Glencone. Throughout the years she spent in Richard's old house, she has missed their apartment, where life pulsed with energy and had a soundtrack of traffic and clattering footsteps. She is back there now, the city throbbing outside her window, the bells of Christ Church Cathedral within earshot.

TWENTY-SEVEN

This tiny creature, whose cells had been multiplying unbeknownst to her, could only have one father. Jessica was realistic enough not to expect Richard to swing her in the air and cover her face with kisses, but his disbelief, disappointment, shock and yes, ever horror, was worse than she anticipated. He assumed she would have an abortion. He was persuasive; after all, his area of expertise was applying gilt to the hard skin of reality.

She awakened one morning to find blood on the sheets. As she sat in the out-patients clinic waiting for attention, it seemed as if nature had made the decision for her. But a heartbeat told her otherwise, a faint flutter yet steady, and when she emerged with the scan of her baby on her phone, she drove directly to Rosswall Heights.

'How long?' her father asked.

'Eight weeks,' she replied.

'Richard Stone?'

'Yes.'

'Does Christine know?'

'No.'

'Is he going to leave her?'

'No.' The tears she had been holding back flowed. When she showed him the scan of his grandchild, he gathered her into his arms and hugged her with a gentleness she had forgotten he possessed.

He told her not to worry. 'I'll deal with Christine,' he said. 'Leave everything to me.'

A week later when she returned for a check-up scan, Richard came with her. He did so reluctantly, still refusing to accept that one misstep should turn his world upside down.When they emerged from the hospital, the swash-swash rhythm of their baby's heartbeat sounding in their ears, Christine was waiting. Richard, staring straight ahead, didn't see her trampled expression but Jessica saw it and knew there would be consequences. How could it be otherwise?

It didn't take long to find out how Christine would react. She left Redstone and Foundation Stone, and was living at High Spires when she broke into Jessica's apartment.

The childhood fear that unseen eyes were watching Jessica returned when she opened the front door and surveyed the damage. All the rooms had been trashed. Most of the damage was done in her bedroom. The chandelier had been pulled from the ceiling, the glass shattered and scattered, the mirrored headboard, also. The curtains had been dragged to the ground and ripped into shreds, the duvet and pillows slashed. Her clothes had been pulled from the wardrobe and bleach poured over them. The jewellery her father had bought for her over the years was untouched. She knew immediately that this was not a random robbery. She had often left her keys lying around the central office or on the coffee deck. Having a copy of her apartment key made would have been easy to do. Only one person could be responsible for such a frenzied attack. She imagined Christine assaulting her with the same ferocity.

Jessica had taken her agency and her husband. If Christine was considering an eye for an eye, she still had a lot of ground to make up.

Her father came to see the damage. Like Jessica, he was in no doubt as to who was the culprit. She was reluctant to call the gardaí but he insisted it was necessary to involve them. A dour-faced man and a younger, female police officer arrived and asked for evidence to back up their belief that Christine Lewis was responsible. Jessica was able to tell them that she had been stalked on at least two occasions, once outside her apartment, and at the Rotunda Hospital.

The gardaí had just left when Richard entered the apartment. He refused to believe that Christine could have been responsible for the break-in and was furious when he heard that a report had been made to the police.

Since her teens Jessica had been straining against her father's iron control, but that evening, as she stood among the wreckage, she was grateful for his strength, his purposefulness. Was Richard more concerned about protecting his wife's reputation than looking after the woman who was carrying his child? he demanded.

'Ignoring my daughter's needs is no longer an option,' he warned Richard. 'Jessica is now homeless. I expect you to take care of that situation immediately.'

Richard could have argued that Jessica would never be homeless when Rosswall Heights was at her disposal but hearing the flint in her father's voice, that hard lash of anger, and a barely concealed threat, he bowed his head in agreement.

TWENTY-EIGHT

The gardaí who call to interview Christine, are in uniform. They are polite but firm when they ask her to account for her movements on the previous day between 8 a.m. and 5 p.m. A full working day that she would normally have recorded in her desk diary, each hour filled with purpose and decisions. Not so, now. She seldom leaves her apartment. It is easier to drink in private, to order takeaways when she allows herself to feel hungry. Unhealthy living is such a simple move to make. A slippery slope isn't even involved, just a quick tumble over the edge of caring.

Someone has broken into Jessica's apartment and trashed it. They show her photographs taken at the scene.

'Why are you interviewing me about this?' she asks. 'Am I a suspect?'

'We believe you've been following Ms Newman on a regular basis.' The male policeman has introduced himself as Garda Roberts.

'That's untrue—'

'A woman answering your description and driving a

company car leased to SFDN Enterprises was seen outside Ms Newman's apartment on the night of June the fifth. We have CCTV evidence to corroborate this report.'

'Yes, I was there.'

'What was the purpose of your visit?'

'I'd no intention of visiting her. I simply needed to check if my husband was sleeping with her that night.'

'I see.'

'I doubt very much that you do, Garda Roberts.'

'You also followed them to the Rotunda Hospital.'

'Yes, I walked behind them all the way from Temple Bar.'

'With what purpose in mind?'

Christine throws back her head and laughs, hands on her hips, a 'fisherwoman' stance, as her grandmother would have said. 'Surely that must be obvious.'

'Please tell us in your own words.'

'I wanted to see if she was carrying my husband's child.'

The female police officer purses her lips as she takes notes. She is young, probably just out of training college.

'Was that why you attacked Jessica Newman's character in front of her staff?' Garda Roberts asks.

'Attacked? You're wrong. I congratulated her and my husband on her pregnancy. Have you ever had to live with lies, Garda Wilson?' Christine addresses this question to the young woman, who is scribbling in her notebook.

Garda Roberts, being older, remains impassive. 'We ask the questions, Mrs Stone—'

'Ms Lewis, if you don't mind.'

'Ms Lewis, bad blood spills eventually. Please provide us with details of your movements yesterday. Otherwise, you'll have to oblige us by coming to a garda station for questioning.'

She remembers now. She walked through the Phoenix Park in the rain and spoke to an old man with a dog. Later, she phoned her mother and Amy. She has no idea of the conversations she had with them but it should be easy for the gardaí to fix her location. A visit to an off-licence in the afternoon – that should be on the owner's

CCTV. She thinks she called into a supermarket. She rummages in the pocket of the jacket she had been wearing and finds the receipt for Supervalu and the off-licence. What else? A conversation – she spoke to someone in the elevator. Female, late twenties, hair braided, Dublin accent with a soft Nigerian roll to her voice. She should be easy enough to trace, though Christine is unable to remember her name. The day in question becomes a mosaic that is painfully assembled and complete enough to satisfy the police that she was not anywhere near Grand Canal Dock on a frenzy of revenge.

Garda Wilson has put away her notebook and even manages a tentative smile when Garda Roberts is looking the other way.

She phones Richard after they leave. 'Did you tell Jessica that I'd parked outside her apartment on that night you were out with Jamie?'

He hesitates, clears his throat. She hangs up before he can reply. He rings back and insists on meeting her.

'I didn't come here to start another argument,' Richard says, when he enters the apartment. 'And I can't keep on apologising. At this stage, it's a meaningless gesture. I have to come to terms with what's happened and make decisions for the future. Jessica—'

'Ah, yes, Jessica. How is she after the break-in?'

'Still shaken. That's what I want to talk—'

'How could you allow the police to question me?'

'I'd nothing to do with that. Neither had Jessica. I didn't believe you'd be so vindictive as to trash her apartment. But you're a stranger to me when you're drunk... and you've been so angry. That stunt you pulled with the champagne—'

'If anyone is a stranger in this marriage, it's you. Now, get out. This conversation is over.'

'Jessica is moving into Redstone.' He states this bluntly, no emotion. 'She's no longer safe at her apartment.'

'Is she afraid I'll come after her with a machete?'

'Please, Christine, don't make this any harder than it is.' He flinches from her anger. 'Will you come to the house and remove what belongs to you? It's difficult enough as it is.'

He wants to say more but apologies, excuses, explanations... they are water under the bridge now. His discomfort grows.

She laughs out loud when he tells her that Alan Martin is demanding that she return the Porsche. 'In my contract it states that I can keep the car should my employer fail to live up to her obligations to create a harmonious working environment,' she says. '*Her* failure to do so gives me every reason to keep the Porsche.'

'You're twisting words—'

'I'm not giving it back, Richard. Tell Alan Martin he can demand all he likes, but it belongs to me now.'

After Richard leaves, Christine opens a bottle of wine. She is still stretched on the sofa by the following afternoon. From that vantage point she can see two empty wine bottles, a half-full bottle of vodka beside them. She counts three empty pizza cartons, and numerous mugs still filled with coffee. A drink will ease her pain. Her body screams that essential message, yet she continues to lie there. She begins to list the steps she took that brought her to this moment. Every time the scream became unbearable, she counts again; a litany that is both repetitive and soothing.

It is dark outside when she pulls herself upright. She stumbles to the bathroom with the stiffness of an arthritic and stands under a cold shower. Neighbours must be able to hear her gasps and the hysterical sobbing that follows. In that enclosed space, she endures the pressure of water that feels ever colder as her body temperature struggles to adjust. Finally, unable to cope with the icy sensation, she adjusts the temperature control and shampoos her hair. Her fingers dig into her scalp, nails clawing through the sodden strands.

Huddled on the sofa in her dressing gown, she allows herself to understand why the fact that Jessica is moving into Redstone has upset her so much. It is the garden with its abundant shrubs and trees, the maze of leafy trails and igloo-shaped hidey holes. A garden for curious children to explore and build their own fantasy worlds, hidden from the eyes of adults.

Too late... too late... she never wanted children. Never wanted to trace the roots of that decision. Elaine with her finely tuned intuition has helped her to release that information. It was there within her, if she had been willing to embrace it, but she rejected it until now.

Terror. Just one word. The terror of being responsible for the safety of a defenceless child. The fragility of life. The whims of fate. The stumble into the wrong place at the wrong time. So many dangers that she would be unable to avert.

Such fears had buried themselves in her unconsciousness and paralysed her.

A week later, Samuel Newman contacts her by phone. 'We need to have a conversation,' he says. 'Just you and I. It's important that we meet.'

'I disagree.' She has forgotten his accent, that posh blend of vowels and consonants that have nowhere to land. 'We've nothing to say to each other.'

'You're wrong, Christine. I've never believed in sticking my head in the sand. All that does is put grit in your eyes. You and I need to be clear-eyed to discuss what has happened.'

The thought of walking through those lifeless plants and static birds revolts her. She is about to refuse when he suggests they meet in Jury's Inn; it is close to her apartment. He has an offer to make, one that he needs to discuss in person with her.

He is dressed casually in a leather jacket, a black open-neck shirt, jeans and loafers when they meet. He looks younger and more relaxed, yet that does nothing to ease her apprehension.

'How are you?' His handshake is on the verge of becoming painful when he releases his grip and waves her into an armchair opposite him.

'I presume that's a rhetorical question.' She is not in the mood for small talk.

'You're hurting badly,' he says. 'The sin of betrayal is the hardest one of all to forgive.'

'Who said anything about forgiveness?'

'Indeed.' He smiles thinly. She figures he is unfamiliar with the concept of clemency.

'Allow me to congratulate you on your impending grandfatherhood,' she says.

He puckers his forehead then nods. 'I didn't expect to become a grandfather quite so soon.' He raises a finger and a waitress comes immediately to their table to take an order for coffee.

'I'm a protective father,' he says when they are alone again. 'Too protective, Jessica claims. She's pulled against the yoke ever since she was a teenager, and look at her now. Pregnant by a man who doesn't love her. Richard will support their child but he won't commit to her. Not as long as he has any hope of winning you back.'

'I'm not a lottery ticket, so don't refer to me as such.'

'Is he still in contact with you?' His question has the precision of a blade.

'Whether he is or not need not concern you, Mr Newman. Why have you asked to meet me?'

'Samuel, please. Let's keep things civil between us.'

'Please answer my question, Samuel.'

'The reason is obvious. We have a situation that affects us both.'

'Ah, yes. The situation.

'You're a pragmatist... may I call you Christine?'

She nods, anxious for him to get to the point of their meeting.

'I recognised that quality in you as soon as we met,' he says.

'There was nothing pragmatic about collapsing at your penthouse.'

'Whatever those reasons were, they were not personality-driven. I respect you. It was your business acumen that established Foundation Stone's success. Richard received the awards but creatively withers without the financial structures to support it. I want to appeal to that intelligence. You've just admitted that your marriage to him is over. Your heart is breaking right now, but you'll recover. I've experienced much heartache in my life. I never believed it was incurable and neither should you. I came here today to offer you a position with SFDN. We've established a subsidiary financial hub in New York—'

'I'm not interested.'

'Hear me out.' This is a command, not a request. His gaze is laden with intent. The voices surrounding them fade, as does the clink of crockery and glasses. All she can hear is the cascading crash of water. This can't happen to her, not now. He seems unaware that her attention has drifted from him and falls silent as the waitress sets cups on the table, a coffee pot for two.

Christine's forehead is damp. She is unable to decide if the heat is coming from her over-excited imagination or his close proximity.

'We need a chief financial advisor,' he says when the waitress leaves. 'I'm offering you that position. Along with your salary, you'll have a relocation fee and accommodation expenses.'

He bought Foundation Stone for his daughter when she requested it. Now, he intends to buy a father for her baby.

'What a generous offer,' she says. 'I'd no idea it was so rewarding to be *disappeared*.'

'I hope that's not how you see it,' he replies. 'I prefer to call it an amicable agreement. I don't make the offer lightly. It's genuine. I wouldn't consider you for the position if I didn't believe you were capable of handling it.'

'I'm flattered by your belief in me. Thank you but no. I've made my own plans and they don't include a handout from you.'

'Think carefully, Christine.' He pours coffee for himself and waits, the pot tilted, to see if he should fill her cup. She shakes her head and pushes the cup away. 'Richard will love his child, and his love towards Jessica will flow from that abundance.' He adds a sugar lump to his coffee, watches it absorb the amber liquid and dissolve. 'You, on the other hand, will be unable to move on from your fury, jealousy, revenge, or whatever it is that gets you out of bed in the morning. I've seen the toll it takes at first hand and learned from it.'

'The lesson learned being that all your problems can be solved by money.'

'With your background, you should know that to be true.' He makes no effort to stop her when she stands to leave. 'You're angry with me now. But please consider my offer. The challenge it represents. I don't look back, ever. New beginnings are always possible. We just need to recognise them when they present themselves.'

She has to walk only a short distance to her apartment. She glides upwards on the elevator to the third floor. At night, lights glow from windows. Thuds and clangs alert her to the fact that people live above and below her, yet she never sees them.

She doesn't need to go to New York to experience the loneliness of occupied spaces.

TWENTY-NINE

Dorothy Niels dies towards the end of October.

'She spoke about you often and always with gratitude,' Ryan says, when he rings to tell Christine what she had been expecting to hear. 'You helped her to die peacefully. In the end, all she wanted was to be with my father and Paul.'

The catch in his voice causes her own grief to well up again. Her path in life was changed by a chance encounter on a train. Now, she needs to travel in another direction. She has no idea where it will take her. Elaine says the knowledge will come when the time is right. How will Christine know? Is there another internal clock, besides the biological one, that signifies those illuminating moments, booms with recognition when the penny drops?

'I'd like to attend Dorothy's funeral but I don't know...' It seems right to do so, given the circumstances of their brief acquaintance, yet Christine is nervous of intruding on this family ritual.

'No, no, please don't feel under any obligation to do so.' Ryan misunderstands her hesitation. 'I understand it could be difficult to take time off work—'

'That won't be a problem.'

'If you're sure...?'

'Yes, Ryan, I'll be there.'

She stays with her aunt, Sharon, who is discreetly sympathetic about her marriage break-up. No intrusive questions about how it went so wrong, apart from telling her that she is ready to listen if Christine feels like talking.

Dorothy's funeral is well attended. She was a popular woman in her community and also well-known as an activist for Our Lost Sons – the name given to the parents who sought justice for the young men whose murders and disappearances were never resolved.

In his eulogy, Ryan speaks eloquently about his mother's courage, energy and humour. At the graveside, he sprinkles a handful of earth over her coffin. Others follow suit. Christine hangs back, aware that she is a stranger among his close-knit crowd. As they walk from the cemetery, she is once again struck by the number of headstones bearing photographs of young men, who were barely out of boyhood, their hair bleached or in spikes, some with partings down the middle. They are frozen in an era, victims of the Earls, their lives ended before they'd had a chance to live them. Some of the graves are neglected; others appear to receive constant attention.

Once again, she is caught unawares when she passes Grace Cooper's grave. On the last occasion she was there, she was on tenterhooks waiting for something to happen without knowing what shape it would take. Now, Jessica's features no longer overlie this tragic young woman's image.

Grace Cooper had been attractive in a pleasing way but not beautiful: her nose too narrow, her mouth too wide, her chin undefined. Her green eyes were her most striking feature. Christine's palms are suddenly damp, her breath short. She shakes off a sudden trepidation. What has she to fear when she has nothing left that can be taken? She had no idea why she has such an interest in Grace Cooper yet the urge to know more about her is strong. She hangs back from the crowd and removes her phone from her handbag to discreetly photograph the gravestone.

The funeral reception has been organised at Castle Rillingham. The crowd breaks up into small groups and settles around the tables. Ryan has reserved a seat for Christine beside him but is soon waylaid by Dorothy's friends, who wish to express their condolences. A woman on the other side of Christine introduces herself as Cathy. She is curious about Christine's connection to Dorothy or, indeed, to Ryan. Christine distracts her by admiring the brooch on the lapel of the woman's jacket and Cathy is happily distracted into discussing the antique shop where she buys her jewellery. Ryan casts an apologetic glance at Christine then turns his attention back to an elderly man with a high colour and a ferocious moustache. The conversation surrounding Christine has the easy sound of people who are familiar with each other. No one notices her leaving the function room.

Outside, the clouds are an ominous grey but the rain is holding off. The ruins of the castle are visible from the back of the hotel. They stand on a massive rampart that must once have dominated this small town. She walks towards the wall separating the ruins from the public. The gate is unlocked, though there is a trespassing notice beside it. She hesitates before opening the gate. She is alone and unobserved. The path to the castle leads her to fencing at the foot of the rampart. One section of fencing has split and the separation of the two jagged edges forms a narrow entrance. She slips through the gap and climbs towards the ruin.

The walls are still solid, the shape of the castle clearly defined. Inside, there are circular steps and narrow passageways, crumbling arches and slitted openings. Outside, collapsed headstones, worn smooth by centuries, are half-buried under moss and snarls of ivy. Withered leaves and thistles mulch beneath her feet and the deadness of her surroundings sends a chill through her.

She is startled when her name is called and turns, expecting to see Ryan. The man who appears in the arched doorway is a stranger. She remembers seeing him among the mourners, a solidly built man who looked uncomfortable in a suit and tie. Now, wrapped in a padded jacket, he is flushed from the climb up the rampart.

'Apologies, Christine, did I startle you? I'm Craig, Ryan's friend.'

'I was afraid you were from the hotel and about to reprimand me for trespassing,' she says. 'I know the ruins are out of bounds but I was curious about them.'

'It's an understandable curiosity,' he says. 'The castle is a massive piece of Rillingham history. Plans are in progress to make the ruins safe for visitors. Has Ryan mentioned me to you?'

'Yes, he has.' She extends her hand. 'He says you're one of the good guys.'

Craig smiles and shrugs off the compliment. 'I'm sorry I wasn't able to do more to help him when you were here before.'

'I'm sure you did your best.'

'I did what I could. But your account of what you claimed to witness was a strange one to sell to a team of hard-nosed investigators. They had no problem accepting that you went into the river and were rescued by Ryan. However, I could see the whites of their eyes when I mentioned hypnosis and retraced memories.'

'Did the fact that Ryan and Dorothy believed me not make any difference?'

'Unfortunately, no. The general feeling was that they were

desperate for closure and seized on your recollections for that reason.'

'The same thought also entered my mind,' she admits. 'I was amazed by Dorothy's trust.'

'You saw what happened through the eyes of a confused child. Innocence, ignorance and truth combined, that's what Dorothy recognised.'

Christine nods, slowly. 'Once the memory came back to me, every detail was clear, except for his features. That's the infuriating part. I don't know if I wasn't able to see his face or if I'm still blocking the memory.'

Craig sits down on a low wall and folds his arms. 'I was heading the same way as Paul Niels. My name could have been on one of those bullets if I hadn't got lucky and managed to find my way out. Dorothy helped me to do that. That's why I'm anxious to help Ryan. I've always believed there was a cover-up at the time. All the police were concerned about was nailing the Rillingham Five on a murder charge they could prove. The witness who worked with them gave enough evidence to put them away. Job done. The senior officers involved are either retired or dead, and those who've replaced them are unwilling to put in the resources. If you think of anything further, no matter how insignificant, let me know. Sometimes what we believe to be of no importance can be the most vital link in the chain of evidence.'

'I'll remember. Thank you for giving me the benefit of the doubt.'

'Ryan sent me out to look for you so we'd better head back to the wake.' He stands and sucks in his breath. 'If you think the climb up that rampart was hard, wait until you're going down.'

The funeral reception is ending, the last mourners departing when they return to the hotel.

'I'm sorry we had so little time together,' Ryan says.

'Don't apologise. You had to look after everyone. Dorothy was a popular woman.'

He nods. 'It's going to take time to fill the space she's left behind. I intend to carry on her work. I ran away from it all when I was younger. Couldn't hack the grief, the endless waiting for news. But it came with me no matter where I went. It's part of me now, and I've made peace with it.'

'Are you married, Ryan? Children?'

'None of the above.' He smiles, shrugs. 'I almost married once but she ended it before we made it to the altar. She said I carried too much baggage.'

'I never realised I carried baggage until I experienced hypnosis. My husband...' She pauses. Her throat muscles work as she struggles to continue. 'We're no longer together.'

'I'm sorry, Christine. I'd no idea. Has this happened recently?'

'Two months ago.'

'Since you were here then?' Ryan looks shocked at the suddenness of their separation.

'Yes. It was a mutual decision.'

He waits politely to see if she will reveal any further information. She could spill it all out in a confessional rage. Tell him that she chose his mother's need to talk about her dead son above the promise she made to Richard. She shoves the thought aside. Ryan has enough on his mind without feeling he inadvertently played a role in the break-up of her marriage.

'There's someone I'd like you to meet if you have time before you leave,' he says.

'I'm staying overnight with my aunt in Dorchester. The bus isn't due for a few hours so I'm free until then. Who am I meeting?'

'Bessie Cooper. She worked hand in hand with my mother on Our Lost Sons.'

'Is she the woman whose daughter was killed in the hit and run accident?'

'Yes, that's her. She's still recovering from a hip operation, otherwise she would have been at the funeral. When she heard you'd be here, she asked if she could meet you.'

Bessie Cooper lives in a horseshoe-shaped cul-de-sac of bungalows. She moves awkwardly on a Zimmer frame which is difficult to manage in her overcrowded living room.

'Do you have children?' She stands beside Christine as they survey the photographs cluttered on the sideboard; photographs that chart Grace's childhood and brief motherhood. The baby she holds in one photograph is new-born and Grace's face, as she stares down at the swaddled bundle in her arms, is suffused with love.

'No,' Christine replies. 'No children.'

'Then you're spared yourself a lot of heartache.'

'It's a courageous thing to have a child and take on that heartache. I'm not brave enough to do that.'

'My heart broke the day Grace died but I've never for a minute regretted those years I had with her.' The woman fumbles in her cardigan pocket and pulls out a tissue.

Christine picks up a photograph that is almost identical to the one of Grace and her baby. It was taken a generation earlier when Bessie was a new mother. The baby in her arms could be Grace but it is impossible to stamp any definable features on the tiny, scrunched face. But Bessie... Christine is struck by her beauty. The years since then have ravaged her face. Her long, brown hair with its warm tones is now thin and white, her eyes sunken.

Christine replaces the photograph as Ryan returns to the living room with mugs of tea. 'Tell me about Grace.' She takes a mug from the tray and sits down at the table.

'She was my sunshine,' Bessie replies simply. 'What more can I say?'

'What happened to her?'

Bessie pulls open a drawer in a cabinet. The newspaper report she hands Christine is the same one she read in Ryan's folder: *Rillingham Woman Dies after Hit-and-Run.*

Christine sips slowly as she once again reads the details. 'Who was that?' She points at the truncated arm around Grace's shoulder.

'Spawn of the devil,' Bessie says. 'I warned her about him from the very start.' She stares at the newspaper clipping then returns to the open drawer to rummage again. She finds another photograph – the one from the newspaper, but now Christine is seeing it in its entirety, a trinity comprising mother, father and child. Grace's slim frame is encircled by the man's arm. His hand dangles over her shoulder, long fingers, a ring on each one: brash, chunky rings that are aggressive enough to act as knuckle dusters. There is something possessive about the way he embraces Grace. The baby is swaddled in a rug and the young mother's vulnerable expression sends a tremor through Christine.

In the background she can see a tall cabinet with a drop-down shelf stacked with beer bottles. The photograph must have been taken at a party. A birdcage appears to be suspended from the ceiling.

Bessie stands behind her. She leans across Christine's shoulder and spits at the photograph. Her spittle lands on the man's face.

Christine pulls away from her and tries to stand. Her legs give way as she collapses back to the chair. She can't faint here, not in this house, which is redolent with bitterness and sorrow. She tries to steady herself, to think straight as Bessie bursts into a tirade.

'Dougie Barnes... spawn of the devil... spawn of Satan. You

killed her and stole my little granddaughter... my little Lisa... Lisa... Lisa.' Her spittle is a wet stain on his face but it does nothing to diminish his tough, handsome features.

But Christine has moved beyond the old woman's hatred, moved beyond her scattergun words. Her voice is drowned out by the howl of the river, the endless, surging river.

She is being lifted high in his arms... Dougie Barnes... she has a name for him now... light as a feather she is lifted... lifted... his fingers... she remembers them now, sharp and scratching... rings that flash and dazzle... that dig onto her legs as he rushes down the slope towards the riverbank. Light as a feather... spawn of the devil...

Bessie, hearing her cry out, stares open-mouthed at her.

The river grows louder. It batters her ears and drags her down, tumbles her over, whips her along a corridor that froths and bucks and will, eventually, release her.

Christine knows she must hold this last thought in her head, because a journey she believed had come to an end is only just beginning.

It is important to take one step at a time. Her suspicions must not destroy any clarity she has left. The first step is that she has recognised Paul Niels's killer. She is in no doubt about his identity, and convinced, also, that there must have been other victims. His own life must have been threatened when he became a state witness – he would not have done so out of compassion, regret or shame.

These are not emotions she has ever witnessed in Samuel Newman.

Her stomach lurches as she allows herself to breathe his name. This suspicion, for that is all she allows it to be, is based on nothing other than a photograph of a man who bears an uncanny resemblance to him.

She looks at the photograph again, searching for something that will assuage her suspicions. Otherwise, she is facing into a crisis of unimaginable depths.

Grace is still smiling down at her baby, and Dougie, holding her possessively, stares challenging at Christine, daring her to continue this line of thought. Dougie and Grace, their features merging together, and all she can see is Jessica's beautiful face rising from the photograph and forcing a terrible truth upon her.

Keep it simple... keep it simple... This is the one thought she allows herself to heed as she studies the photograph. Bessie, unable any longer to look at the face of Dougie Barnes, takes the tray out to the kitchen. Quickly, before she returns, Christine photographs this sundered family unit. She is aware of Ryan's curiosity as they say goodbye to Bessie.

Twilight has stippled the clouds into streels of orange. They remind her of claws, ripping claws that tear at her chest as she reveals her suspicions to him. He phones Craig, who is waiting for them in his car when they reach the house where Dorothy kept the flame of Our Lost Sons burning.

Once inside, Christine shows them the photograph she took on her phone, enlarges the rings with their menacing glister. For now, that is all the factual evidence she can offer them.

Neither man appears surprised that she has identified Dougie Barnes – Mr Allsorts, a strutting, confident drug dealer and a leading figure in the Earls, until he betrayed them and brought about his own disappearance.

'Can you scan those newspaper clippings you have at the farm and email them to me?' she says to Ryan. 'I'd like to study them again in more detail.'

She understands so much now. Her abiding anxiety around Jessica and the unconscious struggle to familiarise herself with the features of a murderer. The essential profile that filled the eyes of a five-year-old child. The panic attack in his penthouse and the minor ones that followed, all stemming from that same source. How is she to move forward from her conviction that he and Samuel Newman are one and the same? It still defies belief. How could Dougie Barnes, thug, murderer, state witness and father have become the polished businessman she hates? Is this hatred, and the hatred she feels towards his daughter, distorting her reality?

Has she stumbled upon a terrible truth, or is she lost in a tangle of her own imagination; an unstable, embittered, betrayed wife, who is having a nervous breakdown?

THIRTY

Richard glances approvingly around her apartment. Does its pristine appearance and lack of empty wine bottles ease his conscience?

'How is Jessica?' she asks.

'Keeping well, thank you. And you?'

'As you can see, sober and clear-headed. Thank you for coming to see me.'

'I was surprised when you contacted me. Is it about the car? I know that Alan is putting pressure on you—'

'It's nothing to do with the car. I want to talk to you about my trip to Rillingham.'

'Ah, yes. The trip.' He sighs. 'Did either of us guess it would have caused such a seismic change in our lives?' His expression is wary, a frown already gathering as he pulls out a chair, sits down heavily.

'I wasn't being honest with you when I returned from England and told you I'd met the person who rescued me from the river.'

'What did you leave out?'

'That I *did* witness a murder.'

'Christine.' Richard's tone is measured. It is clear that he is anxious to avoid another argument. 'I came here to see if you were okay but I'm not prepared to go through all this with you again.'

'Look at this.' She hands him the newspaper clippings that she has printed out. He rifles through them, glancing at headlines and the dates they were published. His uncertainty grows as the depths of the gang culture that was endemic in Rillingham at the time becomes clear to him.

'Where did you get all this information?' he asks.

'From Ryan Niels. I witnessed his brother being murdered.' She looks into the eyes of the man she has loved since the day they met on a stationary train. She watches how he struggles to comprehend what she is telling him. He is prepared to listen now, and does so until she runs out of words.

He believes her. She can see this conviction in his expression. His eyes reflect the deepening awareness of all they have lost. She hands the photograph, printed and enlarged, to him.

'That's the man who killed Ryan's brother. He was placed on a witness protection programme and never charged with any of his crimes. The police got the results they wanted and his case is closed, as far as they are concerned. Does he remind you of anyone?'

He studies the photograph then hands it back to her. 'No. Why on earth should he?'

'Look at him again. Imagine him as an older man. More polished, sophisticated, his hair a different colour?'

He squints at the image then shakes his head. 'What am I supposed to be looking for?'

'I know you'll think I'm crazy...'

'Go on.'

'He reminds me of Samuel Newman.' Saying his name aloud increases her fear but, also, her uncertainty. It is an outlandish comparison to make, yet she has released his name and, now, must wait for Richard's reaction.

His gaze remains fixed on the photograph, his shoulders bowed, his mouth resolutely closed. The silence stretches. He had always been able to use it effectively when she challenged or questioned him in the past.

How strange that sounds. The Past.

'How very convenient.' He finally speaks. 'A ready-made villain. How much tortured thinking led you to this conclusion?'

'You don't see it? Nothing reminds you of him. *Nothing?*'

She pulls the photograph towards her, stabs her finger into the chin with its slightly extended thrust, the inflexible jawline that could suggest authority or brutality. 'What do we know about his background before he took over Rosswall Heights? There's nothing online about his previous life. I've searched—'

'And found absolutely nothing that links him to this... this *thug*. I accept that you've had a traumatic experience and I deeply regret not believing you when you tried to discuss it with me. But I don't for one minute accept this vindictive accusation you've made.'

'It explains so much—'

'Explains what? Listen to yourself!' Richard's expression is one of total incredulity. 'You use one photograph and some imagined resemblance to make this crazed leap. Hatred and jealousy, that's what it stems from! That you'd expect me to believe one iota of what you've just implied beggars belief. I stood up for you when Jessica's apartment was destroyed. Seems I was wrong. Deal with your past, Christine, but don't dare involve me in this vicious lie.'

She has never seen him so angry, his face engorged and flushed, a vein pulsing at his temple. He presses his hands to his chest, as if protecting his heart against the onslaught of her accusation. Then he is gone, his furious tread fading as the door slams behind him.

THIRTY-ONE

Initially, after Jessica moved into Redstone, Richard slept alone in his father's room. Penitence. He seemed to relish it in those early weeks. Both of them avoided the main bedroom where he and Christine used to sleep. Jessica was willing to use the guest room and give him space. One thing she had learned from her father was that patience brewed its own reward. It would be only a matter of time before Richard accepted the new reality their recklessness had forced upon them.

But Christine was everywhere, or so it seemed to Jessica as she adjusted to living with Richard. She kept coming across books Christine had read, albums and DVDs she had enjoyed, walking shoes she had discarded but never thrown away, accessories and jackets hanging from hooks. These constant reminders of Christine's one-time presence in the old house became unbearable. She discovered Richard one night on his knees before a storage container where she had packed some of Christine's possessions. He had unwound a scarf and was bending his face towards it when she entered the room. Hearing her, he flung the scarf back into the container and pressed the lid down on it. Patience, she realised, was a cold companion when she heard his bedroom door close behind him. And in the dark hours, lying on her own, it was impossible not to imagine what life would be like if Christine was no longer around.

One evening, before they left the agency, he told her he was going to see Christine: she had contacted him to say she had something of importance to discuss with him. He insisted that Jessica take the train home without him. He sounded impatient, weary of having to reassure her that his marriage was over.

By midnight, furious and tormented with images of him and Christine together, she had gone to bed and fallen into a fitful sleep. He returned to Redstone in a rage. Rage was good. It wrenched him from a stupor that made him believe he would awaken some morning to find that time had moved backwards and his life, as it was before Jessica, had been restored.

He entered the spare bedroom where she had been sleeping until his fierce footsteps on the stairs awakened her.

He smelled of brine, his skin cold from the spume of waves. She remembered the same smell on her father when he came home from a trip to the mainland. His skin was tanned then, and roughened by the wind, but Richard was pale, a ghastly shade that frightened her. He told her that, after he left Christine, he had been walking along the seashore for hours. Trying to get his head right, that was how he put it, and when he gathered her into his arms, murmuring her name over and over again, he made love to her with a barely controlled ferociousness. Jessica, too, was driven by that same covetous desire, biting hard into his lips, his neck, her mouth seeking and finding the driving force of this rage, and when he came, the sound he made was anguished, as if pain and pleasure had merged to become one.

He spoke about divorce as they lay together in the aftermath, legs and arms entangled, their bodies still hot and already aching for more. It would take time but he was determined to rid himself of Christine. She sounded unhinged, still caught up in that past trauma from her childhood. When Jessica asked him if he was referring to the drowning, he shrugged, as if it was of no consequences, and said he needed to pee.

Would he come back to her bed or return to his father's room? The door opened and he was beside her again, tender, attentive.

When they made love the following morning, the cool light of day replacing the hotness of the dark hours, she was convinced it would only be a matter of time before Christine's presence was fully eradicated from the old house.

Redstone was an extension of Richard, the home where he was born and where their child would also enter the world. His childhood had been uneventful compared to her own. Jessica was content to listen to his anecdotes about growing up in Glencone but when he asked about her early years, she could feel that familiar fist tensing in her chest.

'A Londoner?' He sounded surprised when she told him she had lived in Barnet until she was ten. 'You don't sound like one.'

'Elocution lessons. My father wanted me to assimilate when we moved to Ireland.'

'What was it like growing up in Barnet?'

'I was ten when I left, so most of my growing up was done here.'

'Was it difficult being without your mother?'

'I had Margaret. She loved me as much as any mother could love a daughter.'

'Where is she now?'

'In Australia. She's the mother of twins. A boy and a girl.' She was sinking deeper in a mire of her own lies. She wanted him to stop asking questions. What did the past matter? It was the future, their future, that counted. She hadn't appreciated how much she needed to skirt around the truth during even the most ordinary conversations. Her sanitised version of life in the Greater London area was so sterile she was amazed he believed anything she told him. Instead of describing adventure playgrounds and cinemas in Barnet, leafy parks and crowded classrooms, she longed to tell him about the island and how the gales used to hurl their music through the cottage windows to soothe her to sleep.

THIRTY-TWO

Hi Christine,

Thanks for your email. It's good to know you are well and staying strong.

There has been some development in the Dougie Barnes case. Craig has finally made contact with one of the detectives who was involved in bringing the Rillingham 5 to justice. Ivor Williams retired years ago and is now in a nursing home. He is suffering with dementia and, though he has periods of lucidness, what he told Craig must come with that caveat.

According to Ivor, Barnes was a police informant even before he turned state witness. If that is true, it explains why no serious investigation ever took place into Paul's case, along with other crimes that were never solved.

Ivor is confused as to where Barnes went after he entered the witness protection programme. I think only a few people would have had access to that information. He mentioned the Scottish Highlands but later he seemed convinced it was somewhere in Glasgow, which suggests that Barnes could have been hidden at an isolated location or in an anonymous, crowded city. Either way, it didn't work out for him. The Earls found him. According to Ivor, he was tortured, then killed and his body dumped into a loch or buried in cement – which makes either location possible.

Needless to say, I'm sickened by the news of his death. Ever since we lost Paul, I've had this burning need to bring my brother's killer to trial. The fact that Barnes received rough justice doesn't bring me any comfort.

Regarding your query about the baby, Craig has been unable to find any evidence that Barnes entered the witness protection programme with the child. The general belief is that she was adopted and moved to London.

So, that's the latest update. Whether we can go any further is debatable. It's been a long and torturous journey to reach this stage but, thanks to you, I can now put a face on the man who killed Paul.

I wish you the best of luck with the choices you have to make, Christine. Do keep in touch. It's always a pleasure to hear from you.

With warm regards,

Ryan

Christine's first thought after reading Ryan's email is to go to the nearest off-licence and buy a bottle of vodka: by the time she finishes drinking it, she might just be able to eradicate all memories of her argument with Richard.

She is ashamed, embarrassed, shocked... and sober. No amount of alcohol will deaden the impact of the accusations she made, the seeds of suspicion she must have planted in his mind.

He has not been in touch with her since he stormed from the apartment. Perhaps he decided to treat her claims with the contempt they deserved and has wiped them from his mind. Is that even possible? She tries to compose an email retracting everything she said about Samuel Newman.

> *Richard, I've been a fool... blinded by grief... by jealousy... by my crazed imagination... by stress... fury... terror... suspicion...*

She deletes repeatedly, unable to read over her contrived, stilted sentences. If she phones Richard, perhaps it might be easier to explain how she came to such a disastrous conclusion. A meeting might be a better option. Would she be able to cope with his scorn, his rejection?

And yet... her fingers lie still on the keyboard as she recalls those irksome flickers of recognition; the memory that is always just beyond her grasp. She checks the photograph that triggered her recognition. By now, she knows every line and angle of Dougie Barnes's face. Ivor Williams is an old man whose hardened memories are being distilled by the onslaught of dementia. She remembers Tom and how he struggled through his confusion to moments of extreme lucidity. Is it possible that Ivor is mistaken in his belief that Dougie Barnes is dead? Her mood fluctuates as the days pass. Finally, unable to put off the moment, she rings Richard.

'What is it this time, Christine?' he demands, before she can speak. 'What new fantasy have you concocted about Jessica?'

'I said nothing about Jessica. It was her father—'

'I'm well aware of our conversation. The claim you made is despicable. Jessica's never set foot in Rillingham. Never. Are you listening, Christine? She's a Londoner by birth, and only came to live in Ireland when she was ten.'

'Listen, Richard, I'm deeply sorry. Those things I said about Samuel Newman... I was wrong.'

'I'm well aware of that.' The flatness in his voice suggests that speaking to her is an ordeal he is forced to endure.

'I'm trying to apologise—'

'Okay. You've apologised. Is that it?'

'What else do you want me to say?'

'That you're seeking professional counselling.'

'I don't need—'

'After the accusation you made, I believe it's essential to help you move on with your life.'

'Move on? How easy you make it sound.'

'It's not easy but it's necessary. You're spending too much time alone and that's not good for your mental state. You need to start working again.'

'I signed a contract not to seek employment in advertising for a year—'

'I can get that changed easily.'

'You're an employee, Richard. You don't have the authority to change anything.'

She ends the call before he can reply. Her embittered words leave a sour taste in her mouth but the conversation is forgotten when another email arrives from Ryan.

Hi Christine,

Your disappointment on hearing that Dougie Barnes is dead is understandable. I'm still trying to come to terms with that information but part of me refuses to accept it. For that reason, I decided to visit Ivor Williams today. He's grown used to Craig's company but he clammed up when he discovered I wasn't a member of the force. He's not that old, mid-seventies, still strong, also quite truculent. He has that restlessness some people develop with dementia and is unable to sit still for any length of time. We must have walked the hospital grounds three times before our visit ended. It turned out to be a useful exercise, mentally as well as physically, because he suddenly began to talk about his youth just as I was leaving.

Turns out he's Irish but came to England when he was a

teenager. He was born on a small island off the coast of Donegal. Apparently, when he was Barnes's handler, he mentioned it to him. Barnes said it sounded like a drug smuggler's paradise. The name of the island is Cullain. It's possible that that was where Barnes was killed. That's if he is *dead. I can't help thinking that I'd feel it in my bones if he'd stopped breathing.*

I'll let you know if I hear anything further.

With warm regards,

Ryan

Christine remembers with clarity the afternoon she returned to her office after lunching with Amy and found Jessica standing before her desk, her eyes fixed on the Kava poster. Her gaze had been unfathomable, yet there had been something heavy in the atmosphere that day, as if Christine's arrival had disturbed her concentration, which seemed fixed on that dramatic coastline.

THIRTY-THREE

The ferry to Cullain is only half full. It is too late in the year for tourists and the passengers are mainly students, who are weekly boarders at the secondary school on the mainland. They are joined by some locals with crates of provisions and bags carrying the names of department stores. Three women artists, with easels, palettes and backpacks, are searching the skyline for a glimpse of the island. The students, returning home for the weekend, are giddy and noisy. They are familiar with the tilt and heave of the ferry, unlike Christine, who stays on deck to combat the nausea brought on by the smell of diesel and the choppy waves.

Cullain remains hidden from view and there is nothing to break the greyness of sea and sky. One of the women leans over the side of the ferry and adjusts her camera. She clicks busily, though what she can be photographing is a mystery to Christine; but, then, she is not an artist, as Richard often reminded her.

The island seems to dance through the haze, an in-and-out manoeuvre that finally shapes itself into the curves she remembers from her previous visit. That was during the summer season, and the weather had been kind to them. Now, the gradients of rock and craggy cliffs are unflinching and stark as they cradle the buffeting waves.

The roads on the island are not built for heavy traffic. Christine and the women artists have left their cars on the Donegal boarding pier; tractors, jeeps and vans are mainly driven by the locals, and a small number of cars are available to rent to tourists. The Cullain Bay is still the only hotel on the island and is now under different ownership.

The receptionist and part-owner, Justina, is a tousled Lithuanian blonde with pale blue eyes and radiant teeth. 'Vilnius,' she says, without being asked. 'My capital city. Big change, eh?' She is obviously used to being questioned as to how she got from there to here, but Christine is too preoccupied to wonder. Since receiving Ryan's email, she has been unable to think of anything else.

Justina hands her a map of Cullain and a key to her room. The window overlooks the harbour. The pier is now deserted and a flotilla of seagulls settles on the backwash of the departing ferry. The WIFI signal is good and she has no difficulty rereading her email from Ryan, though, by now, she could recite its content by heart. After removing an envelope of photographs from her case, she sits on a seat by the window and studies them.

When the directors had arrived for their November monthly meeting at SFDN Financial Services, she had been waiting for them. They drove around the side of the building to the car park and emerged a few minutes later to enter through the automatic doors at the entrance. Hidden from view behind the trees that lined the pavement, Christine had focused her camera and clicked. She used a zoom lens to capture a close-up of Jessica's face. She was followed by her father shortly afterwards. A second man appeared as he was about to enter and stopped to speak to him. His arrival blocked Christine's view but she was able to take a better shot when the men separated. Samuel paused before stepping through the doors and glanced over his shoulder at the man who was still in the background. It would have been impossible to see Christine yet she pressed her back against the knobbly bark of a trunk. Did he suspect he was being watched, or was he simply displaying the intuitive reaction of the hunted? Even after he entered the building, she waited another ten minutes before emerging from her hiding place.

Now, as she studies the photographs, she notices how tense Jessica looked. Unable to stand the sight of her, Christine pushes the photographs back into the envelope and slides the clearest print of Samuel Newman into her handbag.

The dining room, which also serves as a bar, is empty when she enters. Justina, who waits tables as well as the reception desk, shrugs apologetically. 'The island is in hibernation,' she says, in perfect English. 'You must come again when the season opens. Then the bar is leaping... is that how you say it?'

'Jumping, yes. Sounds like fun.'

'Oh, how they sing. All night long these tourists, they sing about love and liberation, and cute little birdies. Are you here to paint, Christine?'

'No. I'm anxious to find out about a man and his daughter who used to live here. I've lost track of them and I'm hoping someone on the island might know where I can contact them.'

'Did they live in the town?'

'Town?'

'Here.' Justina smiles somewhat ruefully. 'This is now my capital city.'

'What brought you here?' Finally, she asks the inevitable question.

'Love, what else?' Justine beams and crosses her arms on her chest. 'My husband, Michael, swept me off my feet and landed me here. We run the hotel together. How long since your friends left Cullain?'

'A long time ago. Sixteen years or more, I reckon. But someone might have a forwarding address for them. Will anyone else be here tonight?'

'Some of the locals, they come later to *ceili*.' She waves her hand towards the bar. 'It's like their nightclub but no disco music. You should talk to Bertie. Big beard. He'll be here with his bodhrán... boom... boom... boom.' She smacks her chest, throws her eyes upwards. 'Poor goat. To lose its skin for such a sound.' She hands the menu to Christine. 'You have two choices this evening and I would recommend the fish. Fresh from the harbour.' She kisses her fingers at her mouth. 'Fish is delish.'

'Thanks, but I'll go for the other option.' Christine's stomach is still unsettled, and the memory of the meal she shared with Samuel Newman adds to its uneasiness.

Michael comes to her table after Christine has finished eating but he, too, has only been living on the island for three years. He agrees with Justina. Bertie with the beard is her best option.

The locals drift in after ten o'clock. The weather has changed and they are wrapped in oilskins. The women artists follow them. They are renting a cottage nearby and are flushed from wine and wind. She knows Bertie immediately. His beard is a fiery red bush, streaked with grey, and a bodhrán rests comfortably against his expansive stomach. An elderly woman produces a set of Uilleann pipes and two fiddlers tune up.

The music takes off and continues until after midnight, when people begin to leave.

'Justina says you want a word.' Bertie is drinking a pint of milk at the bar when Christine sits beside him. The milk has left a rim around his moustache which he wipes away with a hefty fist. 'How can I help?'

Christine has a vague recollection of meeting him on her last visit. He was drinking whiskey then, she remembers, flushed and swaggering at the bar, but still playing with that same discipline when the music began. He, too, must have a story to tell, but his attention is fixed on the photograph of Dougie Barnes that she has placed on the counter.

'Who's this, then?' He pulls a pair of glasses from an inside pocket of his gilet and examines it.

'Do you recognise him? I believe he spent some time living on Cullain.'

'Can't say I remember seeing him. Are you sure it was Cullain he lived on?'

'To the best of my knowledge, yes.'

'What's his name?'

'Dougie Barnes. He's English, probably from Dorset, though I'm not sure about that.'

'We don't have many Brits staying here. Was he an artist? We get a lot of their kind. It's to do with the light, they say. Not that they hang around for long when it dims.'

'No. He doesn't paint. I'm not exactly sure what he was doing on the island, but I suspect it was illegal.'

'Ah...' He draws back slightly. 'Are you a guard?'

'No, I'm not from the police.'

'What's your area of expertise, then?'

'Finance. I used to run an advertising agency with my husband.'

His eyes narrow slightly as he registers the past tense. 'I'm no good with finance. The only notes in my head come from music.'

'Be thankful for the grace notes, Bertie. I heard you playing when I was here before. We were filming an advertisement—'

'Ah, the perfume ad. Very impressive shots of the island.

Brought a lot of tourists our way. Hard to recognise beauty when you're facing it day and night. I took off out of here as soon as I hit my sixteenth birthday. Ended up in the arse end of New Zealand. The only difference was the magnitude. Same fucking rocks everywhere, so I came back to make my living among my own. Now, I run boat tours in the season. Sorry I can't help you, Christine.' He finishes his milk, raps a tattoo on his bodhrán and heads into the night.

Bertie is sitting at the bar the following morning when she comes down for breakfast, another glass of milk at his elbow.

'I've been thinking about the photo,' he says. 'I want to have a proper look at it in the morning light.'

The air is clear outside. A brisk wind scuttles clouds across the bright sky. Bertie sinks his heavy frame onto the window sill and studies the photograph closely before shaking his head. 'I had a notion last night after I got home that it might be Frankie Cox from Breaker's Sound out by the lighthouse. But you said a different name.' He carries his glass of milk to her table and sits beside her. 'What was it again?'

'Dougie or Douglas Barnes.'

'That's a name I'd remember so it's not him. It's just that Frankie had an English accent and, like I said last night, the Brits don't come here much. He kept to himself, did Frankie, and the woman and child. Never mixed, apart from the kid who attended the local school. The woman would come into town to buy groceries and occasionally stop off here for a coffee or something stronger if the mood took her.

I saw him a few times down on the harbour but he mostly kept his boat out at Breaker's.' He taps the knuckle duster-like rings on Dougie's fingers. 'Frankie Cox never wore rings, and that's a fact. My mother, may she rest in peace, was pious enough to frown on what she called "free love". She never missed a trick, that woman, and she'd noticed, first time she set eyes on Frankie and his woman, that neither of them had weddings rings.' He passes the photograph back to Christine. 'Apart from that, Frankie was blond and had them punk spikes.'

She stares at Dougie Barnes's shoulder-length, brown hair and the unruly fringe covering his forehead. Is it possible to imagine him with silver hair that spikes aggressively, despite his best efforts to maintain his smooth façade? Bertie is still talking, a natural chatterbox. She can imagine him regaling tourists as he motors around the island, hoping for a glimpse of whales or dolphins.

'The woman was a quiet sort. Didn't mix that much with the community, but friendly-like with some of the women. Must have been hard for her out there alone on Breaker's Sound. God love her, she ended up on the rocks.'

'What do you mean?'

'She either fell or jumped.'

'Oh, my *God*.'

'It happens, girl. Whether it's by accident or design, no one knows, and it's always kinder to believe a foot slipped. Easy enough thing to do.'

'The poor woman. What a tragedy for her family.'

'He'd gone by then, him and the kid. She'd stayed on after they left. I don't know if she intended meeting up with them again, but she was dead a week later.'

'Is she buried here?'

'She's in the local graveyard. Where else could she go when no one claimed her body? We never knew her surname and it couldn't be Cox because of the rings, or lack of them, as was the case. We just put "Margaret" on the cross and some of the local women always lay a few fresh flowers there. Just to remember her, like.'

He sinks his beard into his chest and studies the glass of milk before sighing and downing the remains in a noisy gulp.

'Would Frankie Cox have looked like a younger version of this man?' Christine shows him the photographs she printed of Samuel Newman walking towards the entrance of SFDN Financial Services. The collar of his heavy overcoat was pulled up around his ears but she had managed to snap him full-faced when he glanced over his shoulder before entering the building.

'He's hardly one and the same dude, is he?' Bertie points to the photograph on the table of Dougie Barnes.

'It's possible that he is. That's what I'm trying to find out.'

'You swear you're not from the guards?'

'Swear to God.' She crosses her chest, brings her finger to her lip. 'I'm currently driving a car that could be classified as stolen, depending on who's making the accusation, of course.'

'That's neat. What kind of car?'

'A Porsche.'

'Wow! You're choosy when you steal. Is it on yonder pier?' He nods a vague salute towards an invisible mainland.

'That's where it is. Actually, it's a company car. We're currently having a disagreement over the rights of possession.'

'Who's winning?'

'They are. It's a weight I don't need to carry. I'll return it when I get back.'

'That's if it's still there. There are a few light-fingered lads on the mainland who've been known to hot rod some of them tourist cars.'

'Really?'

'No need to worry. Mostly, they just bring them on a joyride and do a few fancy wheel spins or doughnuts to impress their peers. The cars are usually back in place before the ferry lands.' He blows out his lips, a splutter of thoughtfulness as he studies the Samuel Newman photographs. 'This dude looks nothing like Frankie Cox but... well... that guy beside him looks familiar. I'm sure I saw him on the harbour a few times when Cox was living here, and even afterwards. Not that much in recent years but there's something about this island that always draws people back.'

Christine studies the man who had stopped to speak to Samuel Newman and been inadvertently photographed. A full, heavy face and a massive chin, eyes sunk behind sagging eyelids. 'Do you know his name?'

'Can't say I ever remember hearing it. The cottage where Cox lived is empty, if you wanted to take a drive out to Breaker's Sound. No one else bothered with it. Too far from the centre of the town. I see it when I take the boat out, just a chimney and part of the roof, so I guess it's still standing.'

'I'm renting a car while I'm here. How would I get there?' She shows him the map of the island and watches as he draws a line from the hotel across to the foremost headland on the island.

Once away from the centre of Cullain, the road narrows and minor roads – little more than trails – lead weblike towards isolated houses, some deserted, others defying the elements with brightly coloured exterior walls. Christine keeps to the main road until she reaches a signpost for Breaker's Sound. Pebbles rattle under the wheels of the car when she turns left. Gusts of sand blow across the windscreen. She slows to a crawl, the car rising and dipping along a wending trail that seems endless. Occasionally, she glimpses the lighthouse or a flash of the sea but they are like illusions, disappearing when she drives around another bend. How was it possible to create a home on this desolate landscape?

She brakes when she notices a jeep. It looks as though it was driven off the road and lies on its side, the frame rusting, the glass shattered, the bonnet pushed upwards. The sight of it adds to her growing anxiety. She climbs downwards from the road, moving cautiously, the thought of a broken ankle too terrifying to contemplate. The registration plates to the front and rear are missing. No sign of them among the broken glass or beneath the flattened wheels.

She drives on until the road twists sharply and there it is. Breaker's Sound roars before her. A drug smuggler's paradise, Dougie Barnes had called it, and he was right.

The jetty jutting into the water is now raddled with neglect, a useless piece of cement clumsily assembled and now breaking apart under the pressure of waves. The cottage was built into the protective shelter of rocks. Like the jeep, its exterior walls and windows have suffered the buffeting elements yet, once she pushes open the door, the interior is surprisingly intact. She attributes this to the sturdy, wooden shutters that remained in place, despite the broken window glass.

She moves from room to room. Two bedrooms, a kitchen, dining room and bathroom; a confined space that someone once managed to turn into a comfortable home. Intruders have been here, youngsters with spray cans of paint and sixpacks. She picks her way between empty cans and bottles. A mattress and two duvets are spread across the floor in front of a fire grate filled with dead ash. The duvets are grubby and dank, and she can make out the prints of My Little Pony figures on a smaller one. The curtains in a bedroom have the same pattern. She finds one of the little toy ponies, stripped of colour and sparkle, under a sagging bed. In the main bedroom, she studies the double bed where Frankie Cox and Margaret must have slept. The wardrobe is open, clothes scattered on the bed and floor. The smell of mould forces her to step back as she looks at a jumble of clothes, tops and jeans, some dresses, jackets, a collection of beanies, two pairs of sturdy walking boots, a frivolous pair of high heels that defy the reality of this woman's living conditions, and underwear – the flimsy and the sensible. No-Name Margaret. Her make-up is still on a dressing table with a cracked mirror. Someone has used the lipstick to scrawl initials inside love hearts and a few expletives across the glass.

Christine continues her search but she is unable to find any evidence that Frankie Cox, if that was his name, ever lived here. Nor would she know of the child's existence, apart from the soft furnishings in her bedroom. Where are the photographs in frames? This woman would have had them sitting pride of place on the shelves. She would have had paintings of the island on the walls – but there is nothing left, apart from a religious picture above the kitchen fireplace.

She finds a birdcage behind an armchair, rusted and severely dented. It is not enough, not nearly enough, to cause her heart to thump violently yet that is what happens as she bends to examine it. She swipes her mobile phone to bring up the picture of Dougie Barnes with his girlfriend and baby, a birdcage suspended behind him. No, she shakes her head. The two cages are different and the jump to make the connection is widening. She continues searching the cottage and is unable to find anything of significance. She photographs each room and takes the toy pony with her when she drives away from this place of arrested time.

THIRTY-FOUR

The Sunday morning ferry has been cancelled. Overnight, a storm blew up and the captain, Aiden, goes into the hotel to inform Christine personally that it will be tomorrow morning before the conditions improve. She finishes breakfast and emerges from the hotel an hour later. The wind instantly catches her off balance. She steadies herself against the low wall of the hotel, knots her flapping scarf inside her coat and pulls her woolly cap down over her forehead. Justina has given her directions to the graveyard and warned her not to risk an umbrella, in case she ends up like Mary Poppins.

The graveyard lies on a sloping embankment overlooking the ocean. No shelter from the wind in this exposed spot, but what a view. Lashing waves and screaming seabirds, the dark clouds laden with menace as they tear across the sky. As she clambers up the steep path to the graveyard entrance, it is easy to believe that the essence of those who lie below the clay has been infused into these majestic elements.

She finds the cross with a single name. The only person there who has no identity. Christine traces her fingers across the carved letters and tries to find a sheltered spot to protect a vase of flowers that has blown over.

Back in the hotel, she discovers that the WIFI system is down. She settles into an armchair in the lounge where books, left by residents, are displayed in a bookcase. She tries various titles but is unable to settle on any of them.

The storm continues throughout the night but the siren-song of the gale has blown itself out by morning time.

Aiden is ready to sail. The students are quieter now, their weekend spent and five days of study ahead of them. The island is soon lost from sight and the journey to the mainland seems shorter than the outward one. Aiden glides the ferry into Balmoylan harbour and shakes her hand as she disembarks.

Christine walks towards the pier where she left the car and quickens her pace when she realises it has been vandalised. The lock is broken, the alarm disabled. Whoever took it on a joyride must have scraped it along a wall. The metal is gouged on one side and the door so dented that Christine is unable to open it.

Aidan, noticing her distress, comes ashore to help her. 'A hard boot up their arses, that's what those feicers need,' he mutters, as he wrenches open the door. She winces at the screech of metal but her main concern is the engine.

The battery is dead, not even capable of a splutter.

'Paddy McGann from Balmoylan Auto Repairs is your man,' says Aiden. 'He's a good friend of mine and will get you sorted out in no time at all.' He has the number on his phone and is soon speaking to Paddy. As he explains the problem, Christine walks around to the other side of the car. Apart from dust and muck, it's intact.

'He's organising a tow,' say Aiden. 'Could take a day or two to sort out. I'm sailing shortly but I'll be doing the afternoon run if you want to come back. Or you can stay here. I can recommend a good hotel—'

'No, thanks.' Christine makes a quick decision. 'I'll take the ferry back later. Justina and Michael have made me very welcome.'

'The pair of them have brightened up the hotel no end since they took it over, right enough,' he says. 'See you later, then.'

Christine is waiting at the harbour when Aidan returns. The engine trouble has been sorted and the damage to the body of the car will be repaired by tomorrow afternoon.

She has refused to report the damage at the local garda station, despite Paddy's entreaties that she do so. These joyriders will continue on their merry way unless action is taken against them, he argues, but she remains adamant. No garda report. Her journey to Cullain must remain a secret. She has not found anything that would link Samuel Newman to the island, yet that lack of evidence has done nothing to alleviate her suspicions.

Justina welcomes her back with open arms. Her effusive greeting is followed by coffee and freshly baked scones, which she serves in the little lounge where a fire burns and copies of yesterday's newspapers are available.

Christine is skimming through *The Sunday Independent* when she is interrupted by a soft, apologetic cough. Looking up, she recognises the woman who was playing the uilleann pipes on the night of the *ceili*.

'I'm sorry, am I disturbing you?' She hovers at the door, then enters when Christine shakes her head.

'I heard about the car,' she says. 'Hooligans. They'll kill themselves on those roads one of these nights and who'll be left to mourn them? Broken-hearted parents, that's who.' She extends her hand. 'I'm Sabina Doolan.'

'I'm Christine–'

'I know who you are. I recognised you the other night. You were here with the film crew when they were making that advertisement.' She has a vigorous handshake. 'I'm a great believer that every cloud has a silver lining. I'm hoping you share that view.'

'It's been difficult to find the silver lately, but I believe that thought has some credence.'

'Well, I hope you'll be my silver lining tonight and talk to my women's group. We meet on a Monday night in the schoolhouse. You passed it on Saturday when you were driving to Breaker's Sound.'

Has she done anything on this island that has not been observed? Christine images a network of intelligence linking every resident, yet she is no nearer to finding any link to Dougie Barnes.

'Thank you for considering me but there's no way I can do that. What could I possible say that would be of interest to your group?'

'You can talk to us about advertising. How you plan a campaign. Make decisions, like deciding to film here. That caused a fair amount of chat at the time, I can tell you.'

'That's not remotely interesting—'

'Why don't you let us be the judge of that?'

'Why not ask the artists?'

'We've done them.' She dismisses the three women with an airy wave. 'They come here every year. You've a gorgeous voice, Christine. It's made for radio, and that's not a word of a lie.' She piles flattery upon flattery until Christine capitulates. Sabina will collect her from the hotel at seven-thirty.

She arrives as planned and bundles Christine into her jeep. The women, who have gathered in the assembly hall of the small, one-storey school, fall silent when Christine enters. She is conscious that the talk she is expected to deliver will sound dry and filled with facts that can be of no possible interest to this cloistered island community. The artists have also arrived, their expressions set with expectation. Before

Christine has time to consider the enormity of this responsibility, she launches into an anecdote about Ellie Stokes and the young model's fear of heights. Little has changed on the island since the team from Foundation Stone filmed here. The stir they caused among the locals – all of them astonished and amused that they would consider Cullain a suitable location for advertising perfume. Christinc describes how she climbed the rocks with Ellie and crouched just out of sight of the cameras, reassuring her until Ellie's professionalism took over and the model looked as though she was wedded to the bleakly beautiful terrain. By the time the filming ended, it was Christine who was petrified and Ellie who coaxed her down.

The audience laugh obligingly and, after that, it is easy. The questions flow naturally and Christine can see their interest grow, especially as the artists begin a discussion about how art and advertising draw from each other in ways that are not always recognised.

Cups of tea and coffee and an array of cakes are produced at the end of the session. Christine has enjoyed herself, as has the audience, who thank her profusely before they leave.

'Definitely, you've a voice made for radio.' Sabina speaks with the smug satisfaction of someone who has discovered a rare nugget among the gold tailings. She opens the exit door for Christine and the wind that rushes along the corridor rattles the framed photographs of past pupils that hang on the walls.

And that's when Christine sees it: the missing link that had seemed out of reach. Jessica is staring out at her from among a group of classmates, her hair braided in two neat plaits, a shy smile for the camera, her shoulders raised slightly, as if she finds it difficult to stand so close to others. No mistaking those eyes, the shimmer of green, cat-like in their intensity; the same brilliant eyes her grandmother Bessie Cooper possessed before tragedy leached the colour from them. The same colour that radiates from an oval photograph on a well-tended grave in Rillingham cemetery.

'Just a moment, Sabina,' she calls after the older woman, who closes the door and starts talking to one of the women artists.

Christine shivers. She has her answer and it terrifies her. Samuel Newman' s suave façade hides a murderous past and she has stumbled directly into its path. His links to the island could easily bring him back. And the second man in the photograph... this heavy-set stranger, who has the ear of Samuel Newman, could easily find out about her visit and pass on the information to him. Bertie said he had been back to Cullain and could return. All her movements since she arrived here have been observed and she has made a further impact on the islanders with the talk she has just delivered. Samuel Newman could only reach one conclusion. To him, she is simply a woman who stood in the way of his daughter's happiness. Someone who was easily deposed and could just as easily be dispatched – as Paul Niels, kneeling and begging for mercy, was.

Sabina is still chatting with the artist when Christine takes out her phone. Checking that she is unobserved, she uses the camera to zoom in on the image of Jessica. She then photographs the school group with the banner about them that states they are fourth class students at Cullain National School.

'Are you okay?' Sabina walks back towards her.

'Just admiring the children. How innocent they look.'

'I was principal here when that was taken.' She peers at the photograph. 'Most of those wee ones have emigrated, same as my own daughter. Hard to keep them here when the mainland beckons. It's the curse of all small-island communities.' She shakes her head and then looks at Christine. 'I heard you were asking about Frankie Cox? That's Rachel, his kid.'

'Where?' Christine feigns innocence.

'That wee one there.' She points at Jessica. 'Shy little thing, quiet as a mouse. How do you know Frankie?'

'I don't. I was mixing him up with someone else.' Now, that her suspicions have been confirmed, she feels trapped and scared, anxious to put as much space as possible between herself and Cullain.

'Just as well he's not the man you're searching for. He was an unfriendly sort when he arrived and stayed so until he left. He chose to live out by Breaker's Sound for whatever reasons brought him to the island. Bit of a wheeler dealer was the general opinion. His partner was a nice woman. Brought up in care, God love her. She was glad to cling on to any bit of affection that came her way. What she saw in Frankie Cox is anyone's guess. She only stayed with him for the child's sake. Looked upon Rachel as her own kin and she was heartsore when Frankie took off.'

'Bertie said she fell from the rocks.'

'Aye, she fell all right.'

'You think it was... deliberate?'

'Not on her part, if that's what you mean. All I know is that she was taking the ferry the following morning and was going to turn hell over until she found Rachel. That was never to be, sadly.' She takes Christine's elbow, nudges her towards the door. 'Come on. You're shivering. Back to the hotel with you. You've earned something stronger than a cup of tea. A drop of brandy is the ideal answer to a night like this one.'

Sabine is right about the brandy. Christine is warmed through with a shot and has no desire to take another one; no desire to drown her thoughts in a frenzy of self-doubt and inexplicable fears. The bogeyman is out of the cupboard now. A man with different faces and identities. Dougie Barnes became Frankie

Cox, who became Samuel Newman, for reasons she is finally beginning to penetrate.

Drugs would have been landed on that old pier at Breaker's Sound then smuggled to the mainland and distributed onwards. SFDN would have been founded on the proceeds. It is too outrageous to consider yet, now that she has framed it, it makes sense. Her definition of outrageous no longer has any meaning. She strayed from a wedding and has ended up here.

Anxious not to leave a trail behind her, she uses cash, removed from an ATM in Balmoylan, to pay Paddy for the repairs to the Porsche and is back in Dublin by the late afternoon. At SFDN Financial Services she hands over the car keys to the receptionist. Outside on the street, the wintery sunshine feels like a splinter on her skin. She rings Richard as soon as she reaches High Spires.

'What's wrong, Christine? You sound upset.' The concern in his voice is like a remembered echo that no longer has any meaning.

'No, I'm fine. I've dropped the car back.'

'Thank goodness. Alan Martin's been wrecking my head about it and I've been—'

'Richard, forget the car. I took your advice and sought professional counselling. I realise I said some ridiculous things to you about Samuel Newman.'

'That conversation is best forgotten.'

'I was in a very dark place at the time. Confused as well as hurt. I'm ashamed to think I made such a preposterous accusation. I hope you didn't discuss it with Jessica?'

'Of course not. How could I even begin such a conversation?'

'Did you mention anything to her about the sessions I had with Elaine? Those memories I told you about? The drowning... and that shooting I saw?'

'No.' He answers too readily. She wants to tear into him,

shake loose what he is hiding. The closeness they once shared, their ability to gauge each other's thoughts and express them simultaneously, when did that begin to change? Jessica... it always comes back to Jessica.

'Are you telling me the truth, Richard? I know how worried you were about my mental state at the time. Her father offered me a position with SFDN in New York. I refused it but it would be hugely embarrassing if he discovered what I'd said about him. Tell me exactly what you told Jessica.'

'Very little,' he admits. 'Just broad strokes about what you were going through. Nothing about Samuel. Are you considering New York?'

'Unlike you, I don't know what I'm going to do.'

'Christine...' He pauses, the silence lengthening until he finally breaks it. 'I feel as though I'm on an express train. I've no idea how I got onto it and even less idea how to get off. It just keeps getting faster and the thing is this...' – he swallows, a gulping, audible sound then clears his throat – 'I suspect that even if I tried to jump, I wouldn't be allowed to do so and that's—'

He stops abruptly when his name is called, the sound faint enough to come from the Hub. She recognises Jessica's voice, the accent that carries the intonations her father acquired. With Jessica it is her natural voice but he must spend his life checking his vowels and consonants, touching his skin to make sure it is still a secure membrane.

'Don't talk to her about me, Richard,' she whispers. 'I can't bear it.'

She sits with the phone in her hand, her eyes fixed on the home screen. An image of the two of them together smiles back at her. She needs to change it. Ridiculous that she hasn't done so already. She searches through her gallery and finds one she took of Bernice and Killian's children when the families were together on holidays two years ago. What a contented aunt she had been, happy to take them shopping, go to the cinema and theatre, loving them yet forgetting them easily when they left. So detached from her real emotions and, now, consumed by them, she wonders if she has the strength to rise.

She has to believe Richard. Broad strokes, he said: crazy wife, drinks too much, sees a hypnotherapist who is filling her head with nonsense about a gunman on the loose and a teenager with a bullet in his head. Her skin begins to crawl as she imagines Jessica, her head tilted in that winsome way, a slant of hair falling across her cheek as Richard unloads his concerns about his wife's mental instability. What did she make of that?

Enough to bring it to her father?

Mud is rippling under her feet, unseen, unfelt. The underworld is a bustling sphere that she and Ryan are only beginning to penetrate. Money makes money, and laundering is needed to wash it clean. Ryan is constantly in touch with her. She has no idea how he is accessing the information he passes on to her, but suspects he is working with Craig and hacking into SFDN's system. They have strayed together into dangerous territory and, perhaps, that is why Christine is unable to shake off the impression that she is being followed.

Walking along the quays, she turns suddenly to check who is behind her and faces an inoffensive woman wheeling a child in a buggy. Passing under the arch of Christ Church Cathedral, she confronts an elderly man, who passes her by, his thoughts on other things.

The elevators in High Spires have broken down. A notice informs residents that a repair crew is on the way. She climbs towards her apartment without seeing anyone until the Nigerian woman comes towards her, on her way down. Aisha is her name, she says, as they pause on the landing to complain about the breakdown. 'Such a strange thing to happen,' she says, as she smiles brightly at Christine, 'the lifts are usually so reliable.' She is a nurse on her way to her shift. A long night lies ahead and she hopes the elevators will be fixed by morning. Footsteps sound behind them.

Christine hurries upwards and slams the front door of her apartment. What is the matter with her? Nothing she has seen or heard points to her being the target of someone's eyes, yet her wariness persists. If she confides in Richard, he will see it as further evidence of her paranoia. Her mother will believe she is suffering a delayed reaction to his betrayal. Even Elaine, with her open-mindedness and understanding, will be hard put to understand this hair-prickling sensation of being observed, especially as Christine will be unable to offer any evidence to support her suspicions.

The bells of Christ Church peal joyously on Christmas Day. Christine spends it alone at High Spires. Her parents are eating turkey under a radiant Australian sky with Killian and his family. Bernice, in Paris, is unable to persuade Christine to join her. So, too, is Amy. It is easier to lie than to keep making excuses and Christine tells them she is spending the holiday on the Costa del Sol. The bells ring again to welcome in the new year.

THIRTY-FIVE

Jessica had sensed her father's anger as soon as he entered her office. Outwardly, he appeared calm as he sat down on an armchair opposite her and stared upwards at the image of the island.

'What have you told Richard about Cullain?' His question was harsh and interrogative. 'Think carefully,' he said. 'It's easy to leak secrets when you're sharing the same pillow. Why else would his wife visit that godforsaken lump of rock?'

Paddy McGann, owner of McGann Auto Repairs, had traced the owner of the Porsche through the registration plate and made contact with him. The Porsche had been vandalised on Balmoylan Pier and Paddy had carried out the repairs. The woman driver had paid cash but he had overcharged her by mistake—something to do with VAT and he wanted to let her know that he intended sending on a rebate. Jessica lost track of the details, all of them irrelevant.

'I've no idea why Christine went to Cullain but I can assure you it had nothing to do with anything I said to Richard.' Facing her father down, she sat a little straighter and hid her astonishment. 'I've never *once* mentioned Cullain to him.'

'How can you be certain? Whether you like it or not, they had a life together before you disrupted it.'

'Are you suggesting *you* had nothing to do with their break-up?'

'Don't change the subject, Jessica. I need to understand why Christine went there.'

'It's not as if she's a stranger to Cullain. It's where the Kava advertisement was filmed.'

Did nostalgia bring her back? No, that was a leap too far. She could think of only one reason why Christine would leave the company car parked on Balmoylan pier, next stop Cullain: she was intent on vengeance.

'You don't believe that and neither do I.' Her father, as always, was reading her thoughts. 'Christine is as dangerous as a wounded animal and she is determined to destroy your relationship with Richard. You've seen what she's capable of doing and now she's investigating your childhood. There's only one way she could have found out about Cullain, and that's through Richard.'

'You're wrong.' Her anger rose to match his own. 'Thanks to you, all I do is lie to him about my childhood in *Barnet*.'

'Why are you talking to him about Barnet?' His stillness, so instant, seemed to suck the air from the room.

Richard's questions about her childhood had become more persistent. Where did she go to school? Was she still in touch with childhood friends? Did her father always work in finance? In hospitality? These questions, scattered as they were throughout their conversations, seemed harmless, and they should have been easy to answer. Instead, Jessica viewed each one with a growing awareness that Richard was venturing further into her past than anyone else had ever done.

'Just the stuff normal people who are in love share about their childhoods,' she replied. 'All I share with him are lies, and that's *your* fault.'

'What is it you want from me, Jessica?'

'A true explanation as to why I can't be honest with him.'

'Our lives have always depended on secrecy,' he said. 'Security before happiness. Even love must come a poor second.'

'And that's exactly where it comes. I lie to Richard because of *your* life choices. You've forced a past on me for your own reasons and I've no option but to live by them.' She was swept by a wave of nausea. Nothing to do with morning sickness. That stage passed months ago and she was now experiencing movements that juddered her stomach. 'It's ironic, actually. I can't talk to him truthfully about my childhood, but all Christine did was overload him with traumas from hers.'

'What exactly was she traumatised about?' He raised an eyebrow, as he always did when he believed she was exaggerating.

'She almost drowned when she was a kid.'

'Almost drowning would certainly qualify as trauma but surely Christine can hardly still be affected by it?'

'She'd forgotten all about it until the memory came back to her during some weird therapy she undertook. It's obvious that she slipped into the water but she built it into a huge drama and claimed she was deliberately pushed.'

'Pushed?' He pulled his chair closer to her desk.

'She was a flower girl at a wedding, for goodness' sake. It's all quite ridiculous but by the time she'd sorted out her head, Richard had had enough. It was her obsession that disrupted their marriage... *not* me.'

'What else did he tell you about this obsession of hers?' Her father glanced towards the door, as if expecting someone to enter, then nodded at Jessica to continue.

'That's all I know. Richard believed those therapy sessions exaggerated what was an accident and Christine imagined the rest.'

'The rest?'

'The shooting. That's what she claimed she saw. As if she could witness something like that and forget about it for over thirty years. I still remember every detail of the night you were—'

'That's *enough*, Jessica.'

The drumming of his fingers on the desk irritated her. She wanted to put her hand over his to still his restlessness. The past was forbidden territory; a mainland, misty and floating on lies she could never penetrate. Playing it so often in her head, denying it repeatedly until it would erupt again. The same demanding questions, the same cloying denials. She didn't want to listen to his explanations about 'grey' markets. His market was as black as midnight. He had built his empire from the proceeds. Dirty money washed clean. Wasn't it ever thus? And Christine, with her thoughts on revenge, her ability to read the bottom line, was preparing to denounce her to Richard.

She thought about her wrecked apartment. The viciousness with which the curtains had been slashed, the dangerous glint of glass shards, the bleach Christine had poured over her clothes. Christine had convinced the police of her innocence but Jessica had not been fooled so easily.

Last week she had returned with Richard to the Rotunda for another scan. His mouth had softened when he stared at the monitor. Their baby was visible and so defined: mouth, ears, nose, unique finger whorls. When they emerged from the hospital, Jessica half-expected to find Christine waiting for them, even though she could not have known about their appointment. Her fear was unfounded yet the feeling of being under observation persisted. Eyes watching... was she ever to be freed from this feeling that an unseen enemy was only a few steps behind her?

'Christine's decision to go to Cullain could be nothing or

everything.' Her father was still talking, concentrating, as always, on the present. 'My duty is to protect you and my grandchild. If she tries in any way to drive you and Richard apart, she'll have to deal with me.'

PART 4

THIRTY-SIX

LONG ACRE PRISON

Soon after she arrived at Long Acre, Jessica was beaten up for trespassing onto the private space of another prisoner. No markings had defined this space and she had yet to learn the unwritten rules of the hierarchy that existed within the prison. Now, she knows how to avoid the invisible boundaries, the unscalable walls, the pitfalls and quicksand. She is a chameleon, turned beige... but the colour beige is not tolerated in the circle of nine.

Today, Maria, her cell mate, finally demands an answer from her: what is it like to break a taboo and play God? Eoin reminds Maria that sharing is a voluntary act but these women with their hard, wounded eyes are tired waiting for her to give them something they can understand. Why did you kill? The question runs like a collective nerve through them and, now that it is out in the open, Jessica can no longer ignore it.

'I did what I believed was necessary to protect my future.' It sounds so banal, so brutal, and when she begins to tell her story, she is reminded of a river riding roughshod over secrets that seldom rise to the surface. The deadly intent with which she pulled the trigger overwhelms her. She wants to atone, but how is that possible when she is unrepentant?

All that talking... exposing her soul... it should allow her to walk with a lighter step, to sleep as deeply as Maria does. But even that sweet relief is denied and she is forced to lie awake and listen to the snores from the other bed.

She turns restlessly and disturbs a photograph that is part of a collage on the wall beside her bed. Soon she will run out of space, but seeing those photographs first thing in the morning and last thing at night keeps her from grating her fingers against the cell door. She picks it up and recognises the scene from the Krisgloss reception. The photograph captures the midnight-blue shimmer of her dress as she steps into the spotlight to make a speech. Richard, familiar with such formal occasions, wears his tuxedo with an easy elegance as he stands beside her. Behind them, the Krisgloss advertisement is being played on a projection screen. His smile hides the anger Christine aroused in him when she rang and told him she was 'unavoidably delayed'. A trite excuse, yet it created the tremor that would detonate the perfect order of her world.

THIRTY-SEVEN

Amy rings and invites Christine to dinner. No arguments. A visit is long overdue and she wants to hear about her friend's life as a singleton.

Her house on Oak Valley reminds Christine of a suburban oasis plonked slap in the middle of a rural landscape. It is also a warren of identical roads. Most houses don't have numbers or, if they do, it is too dark to see them. The car behind Christine appears to be equally confused but the driver passes her when she, having recognised her friend's distinctive red front door, brakes outside the gate.

Amy, Jonathan and the two older children rush out to inspect her new car. She is then escorted into a steamy kitchen where Amy has cooked a beef casserole laced with wine. She calls it 'comfort food', which she ladles onto Christine's plate and orders her to eat every bite. Slimness can easily change from elegance to haggardness when too many meals are missed, she warns Christine. This must be the tone of voice she uses on her children when they play with their vegetables.

Apart from a mild reprimand, Amy is willing to forgive Christine for neglecting her. It would be easy to bitch about

Jessica, to fulminate over Richard, but what will that achieve? She can describe the ache that loneliness hollows out of her but Amy will simply tell her to hit the singles bars or go online.

Amy asks her when she is going to resume her career and talks longingly about crowded commuter trains, the office gossip pool and the upward climb towards the glass ceiling. 'Don't get me wrong,' she says. 'Parenting is an amazing experience and I love my kids to bits. But it comes with a health warning and a notice to fasten your seatbelt before take-off.'

It is easy to steer the conversation towards the children and, then, to look back, as they always do, to their own childhoods and the friends with whom they have lost touch.

'We must do this again soon.' Amy sees her to the front door. 'Promise you won't leave it so long the next time.'

'I promise.' Christine hugs her friend and drives from Oak Valley with Amy's instructions directing her onto Kindling Road.

This is where the houses end abruptly and give way to green fields on either side. According to Amy, the land is due for further housing development. Hedgerows, overshadowed by bare trees, line the road and only an occasional street lamp pools the darkness.

She drives cautiously. Some development work has already begun and the surface of the road has been damaged by heavy machinery. When the headlights illuminate the figure of a woman standing on the edge of the road, she slows even further. The woman raises a hand as if signalling for a lift but collapses to her knees in the same instant. As she falls forward in front of the car, her long blonde hair streels behind her in an almost coquettish swirl.

Her fall is so sudden, so shocking, that Christine believes she is hallucinating. But this is not a mirage and the screech of tyres as she stamps on the brake is real enough to horrify her. So close... so close... her head slumps and her hands, clenched on the steering wheel, shake as she tries to release her grip. Her breath escapes, a wheeze of relief. Her life would have been destroyed if she had struck this unconscious figure. To have blood on her hands, the thought is unbearable.

The lower part of the woman's body remains on the pavement but her torso is angled on the road, the unruly mane of hair covering her face. She is motionless as Christine bends over her. She is wearing skinny jeans and a padded black anorak. The ridged patterns on the soles of her upturned ankle boots are visible. Tough boots that are caked with mud. Boots that a man would wear. Before Christine can register this fact, the figure stirs and springs upwards. The face is bony and angular, youthful, too. She sees his features clearly in the headlights, his expression frozen with determination. How could she ever, even for an instant, have mistaken that fallen body for anyone other than a man with criminal intent on his mind? The gun he holds, a short, stubby weapon, is pointed directly at her waist. His other hand is gloved.

'Get into the car and drive,' he says.

Too stupefied to move, she continues to stare at him. He walks swiftly behind her and grabs her arm with his free hand. The gun is pressed against the nape of her neck and her arm twisted upwards in a sudden jerk. Keeping her in this grip, he pushes her towards her car.

The engine stalls when she tries to start it. She only purchased the car a few days previously and is still becoming accustomed to it. It cuts again on her second attempt. Her foot is too heavy on the accelerator and his commands, interspersed with expletives, add to her confusion.

Carjacking – she has heard about it, of course, but not on a deserted road where there is more danger of crashing into a stray deer or running over a fox. Finally, she manages to accelerate. She drives slowly, cautiously. She could have killed him if she has been driving faster but, now, it looks as though he could kill her. The gun is pressed against her side. At his command, she indicates left when she reaches a T-junction. They are not going towards Dublin, then. She glances across at him. Mid-twenties, but he could be younger. His eyes have the flintiness of hard experiences, yet his mouth is soft, almost pouty, incongruous in a face that is scarred and whittled down to the pale stretch of skin over bone.

'I could have run over you,' she says.

'No fuckin' danger of that,' he replies. 'I gauged it well.'

'Lots of practice, then.'

He laughs. 'Practice makes perfect.'

She has read enough about stolen cars to know the drill. He could have left her on the roadside and driven off by himself. Why has he not done so? For some reason, he wants her behind the wheel. She is useful to him as long as she keeps her foot on the accelerator. After that, what? Thinking forward is bad. The present is all that matters for now.

She isn't frightened. Disbelieving, yes, and shocked. Has the fear that consumed her when she believed she would drive over him depleted her store of terror? Or is she still numbed from the suddenness of his actions?

The road widens. She passes another turn-off sign for the motorway but he advises her to ignore it. They are heading west by the back roads. No chance of being caught on a speed camera or photographed at a toll booth.

He leans forward and switches on the radio. His hair brushes her arm, that deceptive, blond shade that forced her to a standstill. Rap music fills the car. The words thud against her head. She is unable to make out the lyrics but they seem appropriate for the occasion. He rasps his hand across his chin. Dark stubble, two days' growth, she reckons. He is naturally dark-haired, the regrowth stark against the bleached strands. Dougie Barnes flashes into her mind. His hair would have looked the same, if he had allowed his roots to show. But that would not have happened. Becoming Frankie Cox had been a seamless transition and later, switching identities again, he would have paid the same precise attention to detail.

Now, the fear comes, consuming her with its lateness. This is a carjacking. She must concentrate on this fact. An opportunistic incident that could have happened to anyone unfortunate enough to be on Kindling Road at that time. She is not an intended target. Her feverish thoughts swing from one grotesque possibility to another. Robbery, rape, murder? Each one is entirely feasible. Even as she contemplates them, she continues driving robotically past scattered houses where lights glimmer like embers in the darkness. Samuel Newman has nothing to do with her abduction. As long as she believes this, there is hope that she can survive.

Her jumbled thoughts begin to clear. She, too, is in control of a weapon. One that could wipe them both out. She presses harder on the accelerator. His gasp as she turns a corner at high speed sends a rush of adrenaline through her.

'Take it easy,' he yells, as she swerves wildly over the central white line.

'Or what?' she shouts back.

'Or I'll put a bullet through your fuckin' head.'

'You think I care?' She steals a sideways glance at him. His cheekbones are quite pronounced. All the best heroes have them but they look dangerous on a villain: sharp, like blades.

'If you don't, you should.'

'Try it, then. See where that gets you.' She drives faster. 'You deliberately targeted my car. Why?'

Could there be a connection between the car that stayed behind her when she was searching for Amy's house? And that feeling of being followed in the city? Is this the final play?

'Slow down... slow *down*.' His mouth, the disturbing pout even more pronounced, reveals a vulnerability that is at variance with his hardened features.

'Who organised this?' she shouts.

'Stop fuckin' asking questions and keep your eyes on the road.'

'If I'm going to be killed, I've the right to know who's responsible.' Trees, black and skeletal, hurtle towards her as the road rises and falls.

'Your *right*?' He lifts the gun and jabs it against her cheek. 'What the fuck is that supposed to mean?'

Her kidnapper is sweating. She can smell his fear, a whiffy pungency that catches in her nostrils. The car swerves, just a slight twitch, but she is going too fast and it will take only one mistake to spin it out of control. She could end up paralysed, or in a vegetative state and dependent on a life support machine. She wants a clean, swift ending. The man beside her is capable to administering such a fate when they reach their destination, but she will have a fighting chance of survival. She must slow down.

For the time being, as long as she is at the wheel, he is unable to harm her.

'Where are we going?' she asks.

'You'll find out when we get there.' His tone is final, no use questioning him any further.

She is driving fast but safely, and the pressure of the gun's nozzle against her head eases when he moves it back down to her waist.

The siren comes from behind them. She has slowed the car but she is still driving above the speed limit. Blue lights whirl in the rearview mirror.

'Fuck... you *stupid* bitch.' The gun remains in position but the bulkiness of his anorak hides it from view. 'This is all *your* fault so you'd better sort it out fast,' he says, when she brakes. 'One wrong word out of your mouth and I'll shoot you first, then the fuckin' cops.'

The squad car passes her by then stops a short distance

ahead. She pulls in behind it and turns off the engine. A female officer walks back towards Christine and shines a torch at the front window, checking the tax and insurance discs. All in order. She nods down at Christine, who has lowered the window.

'Are you aware of the speed limit on this road?' she asks.

'Sixty kilometres,' Christine replies.

It will only take a fraction of a second for him to remove the gun from under his anorak and fire. The prod of the nozzle against her ribs reinforces this threat.

'Then why were you driving at eighty kilometres an hour?' The garda speaks in a brusque tone of authority.

'I'm sorry, Guard. I wasn't aware that I was doing so.'

'How is that possible, especially along this stretch?' She gestures towards the side of the road where a white cross is visible in the headlights. 'Do you want one of those erected as a memorial to your recklessness?'

'No, of course not. I'm—'

'Your lack of awareness suggests to me that you weren't paying attention to one of the most basic rules of the road. Can I see your driver's licence, please?'

She examines the licence and hands it back to Christine. 'Have you been drinking?'

'No.' Will the liberal use of wine in Amy's casserole register if she has to take a breathalyser test?

'Where are you coming from?'

'My brother and I were visiting a friend in Kildare. I'm driving him to his home in Portlaoise and staying there overnight.'

'Then drive within the speed limit,' she advises Christine. 'You've just gained three penalty points and you'll be receiving a fine in the post. I'd advise you to pay it on time.'

Christine turns on the engine and steers carefully past the squad car. A second officer is visible in the passenger seat. What would have happened if she had blurted out the truth. Would her kidnapper have carried out his threat and, if so, how many bodies would he have left in his wake? He slumps, just a slight rounding of his shoulders, but she is attuned to his every movement as the squad car disappears from sight.

He leans forward, his attention on the road rather than on her. When he orders her to turn into a gap that becomes visible between the hedgerows, she knows he has reached a decision. A sob rises up inside her. It will stop her breath if she doesn't control it. Her heart races with hard, painful thuds.

The lane she enters is barely wide enough for the car to pass through it. Branches whip against the sides as the wheels judder over the uneven surface.

'Stop the car,' he says, after she has travelled a short distance.

When she does so, he again raises the gun to her cheek and traces it along her jawline. Will he deliver the bullet through her head? Swift, merciful? Will he burn her car or leave her body in the boot? Will she ever be found? It won't matter if she is dead. But what if she isn't? She has no way of knowing what this armed stranger is capable of doing.

Fear sweeps in waves over her yet she feels remote from it, as if it has become someone else's burden to carry.

He shoves the gun inside his anorak and opens the passenger door. 'Consider this your lucky night, bitch,' he says. 'But your luck will change if you attempt to report this to the fuckin' cops. Don't think I'm kidding. I'll be at your back but you won't know I'm there until it's too late. That's all you need to remember.' He steps into the night and is immediately swamped in darkness.

The minutes pass. Christine waits for him to return. Waits for a bullet to shatter the windscreen. Waits for the gun to fire if she steps from the car or turns on the engine. Her heartbeat slows down, as does her breathing. The silence – waiting, expectant – hurts her ears. She reaches towards the ignition and starts the car. She drives forward, headlights blazing as she searches for a space to turn. Is this how a fox feels in the seconds before the hounds arrive? The relief of escape tempered with the knowledge that the enemy is still within the distance of scent?

The lane eventually opens out into a yard, a long-deserted, overgrown space fronting the ruins of a two-storey farmhouse. She turns the car cautiously and heads back up the lane, still unable to believe she is free. Her mind is beginning to clear. He is a professional – someone who recognises the moment when the risk of discovery outweighs the planned objective. The garda with the officious voice has saved Christine's life. She has a record of where Christine was at a precise time. Until that moment, when she was pulled over, everything her captor did was out of sight but his clean trail was muddied by Christine's speeding.

She can report him. Allow the police to search her car for fingerprints. They will find nothing. The gloves he wore fitted him like a second skin. Her description of him will be equally useless. He has faded into the night and when he emerges into daylight, he will have a new persona. His mentor will have trained him well.

THIRTY-EIGHT

The last of Christine's possessions were packed in storage containers, the lids securely fastened. If only she could be contained so easily. When Richard discovered that Jessica intended contacting a courier service to deliver them to High Spires, he insisted that he should be the one to bring them to her. He rang Christine to arrange a date and left a message on her answering machine. She responded with a text that stated she would be in England for a few days and would contact him on her return.

Once again, she was chasing ghosts from her childhood. And that meant her apartment was empty. Jessica found a key to High Spires in a drawer in Tom's cluttered bureau. When Richard was lunching with a client, she entered his office and flicked through the pages of his notebook until she found the code to enter the apartment complex.

The following evening, she told him she was working late. When everyone had left the agency, she took a taxi to High Spires.

The front door to the apartment unlocked easily yet Jessica hesitated before stepping over the threshold, fearful suddenly of being overwhelmed by images of the lives Christine and Richard had once created there.

The furnishings were simple, the colours cool and easy on the eye. The sofa in the living room had a soft curvature to its line and the armchairs were mismatched yet harmonised perfectly. Jessica had no idea what she had expected to find as she prowled through the rooms. She searched for evidence of Richard's visits to the apartment and found none. The only photographs on display were of children, probably Christine's nieces and nephews, and family groups but, even there, he was nowhere to be seen.

The restful atmosphere of the living room was missing from the kitchen. Signs of busyness were evident: an ironing board still in an upright position, the unplugged iron on the stand. She removed the lid from a saucepan on the hob and stood back when the smell of decaying food reached her. It was difficult to tell what lay beneath the layer of grey film – probably a pasta sauce of some kind. She pulled down the door of the dishwasher and saw unwashed dishes. This seemed out of order in comparison to the rest of the apartment, but she soon forgot this anomaly when she entered the main bedroom.

Christine must have wept a storm of tears on that bed and spliced the air with hatred. Such hatred, all of it directed at Jessica. When she opened the wardrobe door, she recognised some of the outfits Christine used to wear to work. The urge to pull them from the hangers and replicate the damage Christine had inflicted on her clothes disappeared as fast as it came. She was after information, not revenge.

She noticed a Jiffy envelope on the upper shelf of the wardrobe. Pulling it out, she dislodged a small item beside it. It fell to the floor, bounced once and came to rest at her feet. She picked up a My Little Pony toy, tatty and worn, the colours on its mane barely discernible. She knew immediately where Christine had found it. Unearthing the past in an effort to destroy her, Jessica could no longer have any doubts about Christine's reason for visiting Cullain. She left the toy on the bed before turning her attention to the envelope.

She pulled out a folder filled with photocopies of newspapers clippings. She spread them across the bed and studied the headlines. They referred to a drug gang and the imprisonment of its ring leaders at the end of a trial. The Rillingham 5. The newspapers had been published decades previously, but they might as well have been published yesterday. The same sordid, merciless struggle for control, the same wasted lives and wanton killings.

She almost missed the photograph. It fluttered to the bed when she held the envelope upside down. Christine's neat handwriting on the back of the photograph was easy to recognise. Jessica stared at the names. *Dougie Barnes=Frankie Cox=Samuel Newman with Grace Cooper and daughter Lisa Cooper=Rachel Cox=Jessica Newman.*

Suddenly, her palms were slick with perspiration. It gathered on the nape of her neck and beaded her forehead. It seemed as if the room was filled with shadows, yet light was streaming through the window. Was it the obscuring of her reality that created this illusion and blinded her to the images on the photograph until she was ready to look at them?

Ready was the wrong word. *Forced* would be more accurate.

She turned the photograph over and allowed the darkness to lift. A father, mother and child, three distinct images that, together, united the whole. Why had Christine affixed her father's name, and Jessica's, to this family grouping? She must have discovered that their real name was Cox when she was on Cullain, but who was Dougie Barnes? Kneeling at the edge of the bed, Jessica scrabbled through the clippings for a mention of a name that had been unknown to her until that moment.

She read through each news report carefully, searching line

by line for some reference to him but he was not mentioned anywhere. Dougie Barnes... Dougie Barnes... was he the 'rat' whom Reggie Earls had been determined to execute? The 'witness' who collaborated with the police and betrayed his own? Why had Christine linked him to her father?

Unable to find an answer, she stared at an image of a headstone until her eyes stung. A young mother with only one identity. Her story was stark, final. She read the newspaper report on her death and studied the head and shoulders shot, the same one that had been used for her grave. She had been cleaved from the side of Dougie Barnes and it was impossible to tell that a baby had once rested in her arms.

A hit-and-run.

The term resonated with a terrible awareness.

She searched the young woman's face for a sign that would release her from an appalling suspicion. She longed to tear the photograph in two. And tear it again until it was reduced to tatters that she could scatter to the wind. But such a gesture would do nothing to dispel those faces, those names with their equalising symbols attached to them. And if she did reduce that image to shreds, where would they fall? What new picture would they form?

That was how her history seemed in those moments: a snapshot that was in danger of being ripped apart and reassembled.

Outwardly, there was no resemblance between Dougie Barnes and her father. Her earlier childhood memories were of him standing on the rocks and looking out to the ocean, his hair shining gold in the sun. She remembered his thinness, the outline of his ribs, his face hollowed; how could he be compared to this fleshy, brown-haired man with his ostentatious rings and de rigueur gold chains? And yet... and yet... each time she examined the photograph, Jessica saw something she recognised. A direct stare into the camera, a determined mouth and, compellingly, that birdcage hanging in the background.

She lifted out another photograph. The boy in a grunge T-shirt and denim jacket was young. Mid-teens or slightly older, she guessed. His hair straggled over his forehead and shaded his eyes. He looked disgruntled, a sullen boy waiting to become a man, one foot pressed against a wall covered with graffiti, his hands deep in the pockets of his jeans. The photograph had a dated look. She reckoned it was taken sometime in the late eighties or early nineties. Christine's handwriting was recognisable on the back of it. *Paul Niels, a month before he was killed by Dougie Barnes.*

Her baby kicked, hard and forceful kicks against her ribs, yet Jessica found it impossible to distinguish between her furious heartbeat and those tiny, ramming heels. She had invaded Christine's space but Christine had plundered hers.

In the photographs spread before her, she saw herself posing shyly amongst the island schoolchildren. She recognised Sabina Doolin and Aiden's ageless face, burned raw from the salt and wind. Bertie still played his bodhrán in the hotel bar, but the woman with the shaggy blonde hair was a stranger to Jessica.

Christine had gone to the small cove at Breaker's Sound where Jessica's father and his accomplices – Jessica refused to call them his friends – used to gather. She gasped when she saw the cottage. How small and desolate it looked yet it had once been the centre of her world.

Christine had photographed her outside SFDN Financial Services when she was heading into a board meeting. In another photograph, her father was standing with a second man, their heads bent towards each other, as if what they had to say must not be overheard. Jessica recognised Hawk Davitt immediately. He was heavier than she remembered but with the same flabby, undefined features that had frightened her so much on the night he arrived in Cullain. She remembered his bared teeth, his manic laughter as he washed the blood from the knife that should have killed her father.

Christine's apartment had grown warmer. She must have the central heating on a timer. The heat was clammy, cloying. Jessica needed air or she would collapse. The noise of the city rushed up to greet her when she opened a window and breathed in great gulps of air. She found Christine's laptop open on a small table in the living room. The battery had died and the screen was dark. She found the charger but the nauseating overload of information made it impossible to remain any longer in the apartment.

She took the laptop, the blue folder and the toy from her childhood with her and left High Spires. No one had seen her enter or leave the apartment. Let Christine wonder and worry when she returned to High Spires. Jessica wanted her to be afraid. To understand what it was like to believe that footsteps followed soundlessly behind her.

Richard had gone to the gym when she reached Redstone. She searched for a loose floorboard. The house was old and had many planks of wood that creaked and bent underfoot. She chose the spare bedroom where she had slept until she moved into the newly decorated main bedroom with Richard.

That night she dreamt about Margaret. She was standing with her back to the cottage. Jessica's joy at finding her was boundless but when she called Margaret's name, the face that turned around belonged to Grace Cooper. Jessica awoke, haunted by a name that was unfamiliar yet had a resonance that shook her to her core. What was Christine planning to do with information that, somehow, connected Jessica to this woman? How would she live with the consequences if Christine dismantled her history?

. . .

Richard was surprised when she informed him at breakfast that she was flying to London to meet a potential client. He demanded details, annoyed that she would make a decision without consulting him.

'It's too early to discuss details at this stage.' Jessica could feel a shift in the balance between them, a change in the dynamic of authority. 'This is my project. I'm going to handle it my way.'

THIRTY-NINE

Darkness falls early and the crisp morning sunshine is sharp enough to dazzle her. The view from the front window of Sheerwater overlooks the field where Jasper once grazed. Christine thinks she sees him lumbering through the high grass and thistles but the play of light is deceptive at this time of year, and terror has dazed her perception. She is safe here for the time being. The trail leading to her parents' holiday home is gated and she has added a padlock for extra security. Her car is out of sight behind one of the outhouses and, in the evenings, she pulls the curtains closed. Not that anyone can see the windows. Sheerwater is surrounded by trees and invisible from the main road.

When her parents bought the Alpine-style chalet, they gave Christine, Bernice and Killian keys to the front door, along with an invitation to use the holiday home whenever they wished. The irony is that her siblings, who live abroad, have spent more time holidaying there than Christine. Always so busy, so focused; travelling abroad with Richard to ski or sunbathe, which he preferred to the leafy solitude of Sheerwater with its glassy lake and forest trails.

The lake is sheeted in a thin layer of ice when she walks along the shore each morning. In the afternoon, she treks through the forest, which is still hooded in winter. It seems as if nature has stopped breathing; yet her own breath is a vaporous sign that she has escaped from the clutches of Samuel Newman once again.

At night she sleeps with a cricket bat beside her. A feeble weapon against a gun, but it is all she has for protection. She never returned to High Spires. His face is before her, behind her; wherever she looks, she imagines his presence. She jumps at sudden sounds: the clatter of an overbalancing cup on the draining board, a dog barking, the wind against the window, the swish of bare branches when she is walking through the forest. He would have been waiting when she returned to High Spires, ready to carry out the contract he had undertaken or, if not him, someone else equally indifferent to her existence.

Going to the police is not an option. He made that perfectly clear. After he released her – how confident he must be that she is within his grasp when he decides the time is right – she had driven for an hour. Eating up the miles, she braced herself for a bullet every time a car passed her out. She booked into a hotel for the night and, the following morning, bought essential clothes and groceries at a local shopping centre. She purchased a laptop and two new phones.

Before destroying her old phone, she notified her mother that she would be spending some time in England. Richard had left a message on her answering machine. He had boxed the possessions she had left behind in Redstone and wanted to drop them over to High Spires. They needed to talk.

She texted him the same information she had sent to Stella, then destroyed her phone. It seemed symbolic, sacrificing all her contact details. They had seemed as essential to her as a limb but were suddenly irrelevant. Survival must do that, she thought, as she stamped the phone underfoot and disposed of the shattered pieces in a ditch.

Since her arrival in Sheerwater, the only person who knows her whereabouts is Ryan. Her supplies are running low but will last another few days before she has to think about shopping. Her hair is red and spiked, and her face seems thinner, bonier. No time for regrets when her thick mane of black hair ended up on the floor and was then burned in the Aga. Catching herself unawares in the mirror, she is still startled by her appearance.

For days she lives like an animal who has found a safe burrow and is afraid to peer beyond the perimeter. Somehow, Samuel Newman has made the connection between her and the river. The information would have come from Jessica, who heard it from Richard. No other explanation is possible. She imagines the conversations they must have had when her marriage was floundering. He would have described her paranoia, histrionics, obsession, her fascination with Elaine, the hypnotherapy sessions, and, in doing so, created a Chinese whisper that finally reached the ears of Jessica's father.

Now, Christine is focused on only one thing. Alan Martin has established a virtual paper trail that is as complex as a spider's web. Each skein is independent of the next, yet they lead to a central hub that is SFDN Financial Services. Ryan continues to gain access to the group's financial system, and Christine works tirelessly on her new laptop to penetrate the sophisticated network of accounts. The pieces are not yet in place but, in time, they will be and then the entire edifice upon which Samuel Newman has built his wealth will collapse. Caught up in this adrenaline-pumping undertaking, she is able to believe that he is within their sights – yet she also knows that what they are doing could suddenly implode and expose them.

One false move, that is all it would take.

FORTY

Rillingham-on-the-Weir was exactly as Jessica had imagined: cobbled streets filled with galleries and restaurants, brash modern shops rubbing shoulders with the distinctive windows and decorative wooden beams of old Tudor buildings. Impossible to believe evil had ever rippled its serene surface.

She stood on the bridge where Grace Cooper had died and looked down at the weir that gave the town its name, and wondered what secrets lay under the surface of the rushing water. Unable to hold off the reason for her visit any longer, she hailed a taxi to take her to Rillingham cemetery.

She walked among the old tombstones with their faded, moss-shrouded faces. Impossible not to feel the peace that lay over these slanted slabs of memory. The modern section of the cemetery had yet to mellow with the passage of time and she paused, stricken by the sight of a recently dug grave with a blue teddy bear on top, a helium balloon attached to its arm.

She continued walking until she recognised the black headstone in the photograph.

In memory of our beloved daughter
Grace Cooper
1972–1992
You will always remain in our hearts

How could the young woman in the oval frame possibly be the 'Alyson' of Jessica's imagination? The blonde bombshell that Margaret had envied and admired? Grace Cooper was pretty in an unaffecting way. Women would have liked her, trusted her, but they would not have envied her or seen her as threatening, a predator in their path.

'Are you okay, dear?' An elderly man was arranging flowers in a vase at the grave beside her. He stood up and brushed earth from the knees of his trousers. 'Pardon me for intruding but you seem upset.'

'I'm fine, thank you. It's just... she was so young when she died.' She touched the oval-shaped image.

'She was indeed. Far too young but that's life. My wife passed last year. She'd lived her full three score and ten, with a few more years added on. Not my son, though. Nineteen, that's all he was when he left us.'

'I'm sorry to hear that.' Her hand was still resting on the image of Grace Cooper. 'Did you know Grace?'

'I knew her from the time she was a baby. A sad business. Her mother never recovered from the loss of her only child. She'll be here tomorrow afternoon and she'll be chatting away to Grace, as she always does. Are you sure you're all right, dear?' He glanced at her stomach then stared down at the grave he had been tending. 'You never expect to bury your child. I hope yours has a long and happy life.' He touched the peak of his cap to her and walked away.

. . .

The following afternoon she once again entered the cemetery. An hour passed before a woman on a walking frame appeared. A gardening bag hung from the handle of the frame and gardening tools clanged as she pushed it over the uneven ground. She was coming directly towards Grace Cooper's grave and Jessica, turning quickly, walked in the opposite direction. On the parallel aisle, she watched the woman stop and sit on the seat of her walking frame. Her voice, faint yet distinct, reached Jessica.

'I'm good to go for a while longer, pet. That's what Dr Klein says. The operation made all the difference. I bet you're laughing your head off at the idea of me using this bone shaker. Who'd have believed it but, then, who can believe anything...?' Suddenly aware of Jessica's presence, the woman looked over towards her. 'What's troubling you, miss? Are you looking for a grave?'

'No, thank you. I'm okay.'

The woman removed carnations from her bag and stabbed them into a vase. She was bone thin yet there was strength in her arms. The grave was well tended and only a few weeds needed to be removed. She took out a trowel from the bag but almost overbalanced as she attempted to kneel.

'Let me help you.' Jessica crossed between the graves.

'I'm used to managing on my own, thank you very much.' She stuck out her bottom lip as she concentrated on bending down but the effort caused her to breathe heavily. This time, when Jessica came to her assistance, she allowed her to pull up the weeds and dispose of them in a nearby bin.

'She was so very young.' Jessica bent down until she was level with the woman. 'Is she your daughter?'

'The good die young,' the woman replied. 'Isn't that what they say? Did you ever hear such bullshit in your life?'

'It is bullshit, I agree with you there.'

'Look around you. We call this the nursery. Hardly any of

them saw their twenty-first birthdays. No keys to the door for them. Keys to the gates of hell, more likely. Those poor lost sons.'

The headstones bore photographs of young men who were barely out of boyhood, all of them frozen in an era that had blighted their youth.

'What happened to them?' The question had to be asked.

'Drugs. They paid the price for their foolishness. I can tell you're not a local lass.' Her sideways glance at Jessica suggested she was only just acknowledging her presence. 'What did you say your name is?'

'I didn't. It's Jessica.'

'Ah, that's a sweet name. I'm Beatrice. Everyone calls me Bessie.'

'Do you want to talk to me about Grace? How did she die?'

'They all said it was an accident. A hit-and-run. If it was, I could have accepted it. Grieved, yes, and been heartsore to my own grave, but not the way she went.'

'What do you think happened to her?'

'I believe she was silenced, like those lads in their graves. She wasn't compliant, you see. Always headstrong, was Gracie. The boyfriend, now he was a bad one. Spawn of the devil.' She stood and pushed the walking frame forward with such force that it hit the marble edge of a grave. Before Jessica could catch her, she had fallen on her hands and knees. Her thin frame shuddered as she was helped her to her feet. Her hands were grazed but thick woollen trousers had protected her knees.

'You're a good lass,' Bessie said, as Jessica brushed clay from her coat.

'Do you live far from here?'

'Just a short trot.'

'I'll walk with you.'

'That's kind of you. I'd like the company if you've time to

spare.' Her eyes settled on Jessica's stomach. 'When's the big day? If you don't mind me asking.'

'I've another two months to go.'

'Boy or girl, do you know?'

'We decided not to ask.'

'I agree. Too much information can be a burden.' She made no further comment as Jessica accompanied her from the graveyard.

'Do you want to come in for a cuppa?' she asked, when they reached a small cul-de-sac.

Standing on Devil's Reach, Jessica used to slide one foot forward until only her heel was touching the edge of the plateau. Her stomach would lurch from the thrill of knowing how close she was to plunging downwards into the flailing ocean. In that quiet cul-de-sac, she experienced the same sensation.

'I have to go... my bus... it'll be here soon.' Stammering apologies, she was aware that her baby was rolling over; frightened, perhaps, by the thud of Jessica's heart, and the dread that heaved through her at the thought of the information this pent-up, grieving woman could reveal.

When Jessica arrived home on Saturday morning, she was greeted by the sight of a note from Richard on the kitchen table.

No word yet from Christine. I know you're anxious to remove those storage containers. I'm leaving them in her apartment. Hope your trip was successful. Will hear all when I return.

FORTY-ONE

Two hours passed, then three, and still Richard had not returned. What was keeping him? Had Christine lured him back? Was a reconciliation taking place? Were they in bed together? Sheets in tangles, bodies arched or sunk in pleasure? Jessica's rage passed and was replaced by anxiety. Christine would not bring him to her bed. She would not be waylaid so easily from the path of revenge. She would tell him about Cullain and expose the lies that Jessica had heaped upon him.

His phone went to voicemail each time she rang it. She tried Christine's phone. An automated voice announced that the number was no longer in service. When he still had not returned by seven o'clock, her anger was a keg, primed and ready to explode. Unable to wait any longer, Jessica decided to drive to High Spires.

The wind was blowing hard when she reached the city. Traffic streamed along the quays and the tucked-in, wintery glow of pubs and restaurants lit the darkness. She found a parking space and walked towards the apartment.

Two squad cars were parked outside the complex. No mistaking their hi-vis colours and the word GARDA printed on the sides of each car. All her anger, her fantasies and suspicions were replaced by dread. Her legs weakened and she was forced to stop and lean against a wall.

A woman muffled in a scarf, a hat pulled low over her forehead, stopped beside her. 'Are you okay, lady?' Her dark brown eyes swept over Jessica's stomach and widened with concern. 'You should not be out on such a night.'

'What's happened?' Jessica could barely speak above a whisper.

'There was a shooting, earlier,' the woman replied. 'My friend texted me about it as I came off duty. I live at High Spires. I'm hoping I'll be able to get into my apartment.'

'That's where I'm going, too.' Jessica realised the woman was in scrubs, the bottoms visible under her parka jacket. 'My partner was visiting someone earlier. I haven't heard from him...' She paused, tried to force saliva into her mouth. 'He's been gone too long and he's not answering my calls.'

'Then you must speak to the gardaí.' Her voice was rich and deep with understanding as she helped Jessica to take a tentative step, then another.

They were close to the entrance to the complex when two police officers emerged through the arched gates that fronted the parking bay.

'Officer, my name in Aisha Bello,' the woman said. 'I live at High Spires. This lady is worried about her partner. He was here earlier today but he's not answering his phone.'

'What's your partner's name?' One of the officers addressed Jessica directly. Even as she spoke Richard's name aloud, she was convinced she was over-reacting; yet she was watching the garda's response, his darting glance at his companion, the urgent way he brought his walkie talkie to his mouth. Images of her trashed apartment, the glinting shards of pink glass, the slashed curtains reduced to ribbons with a knife that had cut cleanly through the heavy fabric tortured her.

If Christine could wield a knife with such malice, what could she do with a gun?

'Who was he visiting?' the garda asked her.

'Christine Lewis.'

'Come with us, please.'

Jessica walked between them into the foyer of Block 6. The light was too bright for her eyes. She cried out and held her hands over them as she was led to a chair. Aisha sat beside her, her arm around Jessica's shoulders, her accent textured with a splash of Dublinese as she told her that everything would be grand... *grand.*

She knew Christine, not well, Aisha admitted, just enough to say hello to her when they passed each other in the corridor. Aisha hadn't seen her for a few days but that was not unusual. There was probably a perfectly innocent reason why Richard had been delayed. Her voice flowed over Jessica as they waited for the senior officer to arrive.

'How long have you to go?' she asked, as Jessica was forced forward when her back was engulfed by a cramp.

'About two months.'

'Then you must take better care of yourself. You are Christine's friend, yes?'

'We worked together. She is far from being my friend.'

A female officer stepped from the lift and came towards them. 'Ms Newman, I'm Detective Sergeant Mulhall. Can you come with me, please?'

'Where am I going? All I want to know is the identity of the person who's been shot. Is it Richard? Tell me... tell me!'

'Please, Jessica, we need to talk privately.' She nodded towards Aisha, who squeezed Jessica's shoulder reassuringly.

They entered an office where a bank of cameras revealed various locations within the High Spires complex. Jessica could see the parking bay. Why were the cars cordoned off? The figures moving in and out of view, some in uniform, others in forensic suits, answered her question.

She must have screamed then. How else could she have reacted? Screamed until she was voiceless, but Jessica had no memory of doing so. The senior officer repeated what she had been saying. Richard was discovered shortly after he was shot. But for the timely intervention of the security manager, who was monitoring the cameras on the parking bay and managed to stem the bleeding while they waited for the ambulance, Richard would be dead.

He had never reached the apartment. The shooter had fired at him as soon as he stepped from his car. High Spires was now a crime scene and all residents would be questioned by the gardaí.

They were wasting their time. Jessica knew who was responsible. Intuition would never pass for evidence, but she was able to give Detective Sergeant Mulhall the information she needed about Richard's history with Christine.

Her father came as soon as she phoned him. Her bulwark. Jessica longed to sink into his arms. His expression reminded her of the night they left Cullain: that same rigid inflexibility, his face stripped of vitality, honed down to its harsh essence. He held out his arms to her and swept her into a fierce embrace. It was the first time she had ever seen tears on his cheeks.

Finally, the questioning ended and he ordered a taxi to take them to the hospital where Richard was undergoing surgery.

Christine's mother was already in the family room with her husband when they arrived: Stella Lewis was listed as the second emergency contact person on Richard's medical file. She had been phoned by a member of the hospital staff when Christine was unreachable. Jessica remembered meeting her at Tom's wake. The friendliness Stella had shown that afternoon had turned into an icy politeness as she relayed the necessary information on Richard's condition. In the absence of his *wife* – her lips clenched on the word – it was Stella's responsibility to consult with his medical team. Richard was in theatre. He had taken a bullet in his chest and, though it came close to penetrating his heart, he was expected to survive.

'Where is Christine?' Jessica asked. 'Why isn't she here?'

'I'm not prepared to discuss my daughter with you.' Unable to control her agitation, Stella paced up and down the family room.

Where was their murderous daughter hiding? Jessica pressed her hands to her stomach, conscious that her coat was stretched tightly, and that Stella's gaze had flickered towards the telltale bump. She would not show weakness in front of this stiff-mouthed couple, who believed they had more authority than Jessica to speak with Richard's medical team.

'You may not wish to discuss your daughter with us but her whereabouts may be relevant to the police.' Her father's bluntness added to the tension in the room.

'What exactly are you implying?' Jack Lewis was on his feet instantly.

'Are you aware that Christine had already been questioned by the police for stalking Jessica and destroying her apartment?'

'Christine had no difficulty clearing her name on those trumped-up charges.' Jack Lewis was flushed and angry when Stella intervened and ordered the two men to sit down.

A doctor arrived in the same instant with an update on Richard's condition. He was out of theatre and in the intensive care unit. The next twenty-four hours would be critical.

Detective Mulhall and another officer arrived at the hospital. As Christine's parents were taken to another room to be interviewed, it was clear to Jessica that the investigation was heading in only one direction.

FORTY-TWO

In the evening she reads from the books Stella has bought over the years. Occasionally, when she feels the need to connect with the outside world, she watches the evening news. And that is how, on the fifth day since she reached Sheerwater, Christine discovers that her husband had been shot the previous day.

The details unfold across the television screen like a slowly moving nightmare. A crime correspondent is standing outside High Spires. Christine barely has time to recognise the building before she is staring at Richard's face. Her handsome husband, his vibrant smile, white teeth against his snow-tanned face. She took that photograph two years previously when they were on a skiing holiday in Italy.

She recognises the crime correspondent. He has the impassive face of someone who is no longer shocked by the reports he delivers daily. For years she has watched him relating other people's tragedies and, now, she is at the centre of his report.

The news rolls on. Figures move in and out of her line of vision. Wars are raging elsewhere. Bodies are loaded into ambulances, buildings collapse, people riot. When she finally moves, her body is rigid. If she bends, will she snap? *Dead wood break-*

ing. She imagines Richard driving into one of the two parking bays that were assigned to their apartment. She had intended cancelling one of them when she moved back to High Spires but had not got around to doing so. Tall and slim, like her, he would have been indistinguishable in the gloom when he stepped from his car – the security manager had mentioned the lack of lighting in the news report.

She is under no illusions. The gunman would have been determined not to fail the second time. Richard's shooting was a case of mistaken identity, yet she is in the crosshairs of the police investigation. They want to dismiss her from their line of enquiry. How benign that sounds. How deceptive. Richard was dropping off personal possessions at the apartment. What does that mean? Vaguely, she remembers a message he left on her answering machine. Something to do with storage containers. Had she replied? Yes, she remembers responding with a text, but has no idea what she wrote.

She must ring the hospital, find out how he is. They will only give that information to his next of kin. If she comes forward, can the garda protect her if her abductor decides on a third attempt to kill her?

She and Stella are listed as Richard's contacts in case of a medical emergency. Unable to trace Christine, someone from the hospital must have been in touch with Stella already. The police, also – they would have questioned her about her daughter's whereabouts. Christine must ring her immediately.

But as soon as this thought forms, it is overshadowed by suspicion. Could Stella's phone be bugged, not by the police but by Samuel Newman's associates? She must take this risk and find out how Richard is.

She stands beside the lake and rings Stella's number. 'It's me,' she says when her mother – sounding cautious, as she always does when an unfamiliar number shows up on her screen – answers.

'My God, Christine, where are you?' Stella gasps, and cries out to her husband to come to the phone. 'We've been out of our minds with worry. Are you aware of what's happened to—?'

'I know about Richard. I've just heard it on the news.'

'Just heard... my *God*, Christine! How can that be? He was shot yesterday. We'd no idea where you were. The police have interviewed us. The questions they asked... we don't know what to tell them—'

'You can't think I'd anything to do with Richard's shooting?'

'It's not what I think that matters. You need to talk to them. Clear your name and stop those terrible rumours online.' Stella is on the verge of tears. 'Where are you? We'll pick you up and go with you to the garda station. Jack has been talking to a solicitor—'

'Mum, I can't stay on the phone. I'm okay. That's all you need to know. I love Richard and I would *never* harm him. Tell me exactly – how is he?'

'He's seriously injured but his medical team believe he'll pull through. That woman...' Stella hesitates, her voice hardening when she continues. 'She's there with her father all the time. Oh, Christine... I'm so confused. Please tell me – what's going on?'

'Someone is trying to frame me for reasons I can't explain. I have to stay out of sight until I believe it's safe to talk to the police.'

'Safe? Are you in danger? Where *are* you?'

'I'm with Jasper.'

'*Jasper?*'

'You remember my friend from way back when I was a child? I'm staying at his place.'

'I remember Jasper.' Stella still sounds distressed yet an awareness of what Christine means is evident when she adds, 'I'm glad you're safe with him. Your father wants to talk to you.'

'No, Mum. No more talking.' Jack's questions will be rapid-fire and cover the same ground as Stella has done. Her mother is still protesting when Christine ends the call. Her burner phone is a firefly flash in the darkness as she hurtles it towards the lake. Only the faintest of ripples disturb the water as it sinks from sight.

By the following morning, the story has changed. She listens in disbelief to the radio.

'Gardaí have arrested a suspect in connection to the High Spires shooting incident that left advertising executive, Richard Stone, fighting for his life. The suspect, as yet unnamed, but known to the gardaí, is helping them with their enquiries.

'An urgent garda appeal has gone out for information on Christine Lewis's whereabouts. New evidence has come to light regarding her movements after she left Amy Watson's house on the night of the twenty-fourth of January. She was apprehended by a garda petrol car and pulled over for breaking the speed limit and driving in a dangerous manner.

'The garda press office has refused to confirm if the passenger in the car with her is the suspect currently in garda custody. She introduced him as her brother to the garda who questioned her and stated that she was driving to his home in Portlaoise where she intended spending the night. Gardaí have since confirmed that her only brother is living with his wife and family in Sydney, Australia.'

Christine is unable to listen any further. Huddled in an armchair, her arms around her knees, the silky filaments of Samuel Newman's web clings to her as she listens for sirens, the screech of tyres, the authoritative barks of command.

Ryan comes when she contacts him. He catches the first flight available and arrives at Sheerwater under cover of darkness.

She opens the front door when she hears his car. The sky is clear, the moon full and blue-veined with mystery. Tomorrow morning, there will be frost on the ground.

He brings supplies – bags of groceries that he unpacks and insists on cooking for her. She eats when he orders her to do so, swallowing obediently until her taste buds kick in and she realises she is ravenous.

Later, unable any longer to bear the loneliness, he provides her with warmth when she comes to his bedroom in the small hours. They hold each other, not as lovers, just co-conspirators, knowing there is no room in their relationship for anything else. His arm is around her still when she awakens, his eyes closed, his breathing deep with sleep.

The longing to sink into the newness of his body surprises her.

She has cooked breakfast when he comes into the kitchen, freshly showered, his hair glistening as it was on that fateful day when he pulled her from the river.

FORTY-THREE

Shay McCabe was in touch constantly with the latest information on the police investigation. They used each other, no pretences between them. Give and take. Jessica gave him angles to use for his news reports: her wrecked apartment; the stalking incident; Christine's fury when she discovered her husband was in love with another woman. In return, he gave her the name of the suspect who was in garda custody. His name was Billy Macken and he had made a statement claiming he had been contracted by Christine to kill her husband.

When Richard was stable enough to be taken off the ventilator and moved from intensive care, Jessica was waiting in a private ward for him. Her face was the first one he saw when he opened his eyes. He was confused, high on morphine and antibiotics when he called her 'Christine'. Her name slipped from his lips and hung there until it dropped into the space between them. His eyes were cloudy, the sclera yellow and veined. That was the moment she felt as if she had become an actor in a drama that was scripted by a stranger.

On the third day after his operation, he was interviewed by

the police. While the interview was taking place, Jessica waited in the hospital café. She ordered a sandwich with a cup of herbal tea. Camomile. It promised calmness but did nothing to soothe her. She bit into the sandwich. The cheese tasted like rubber, a lump in her mouth that she eventually forced down.

'You're upset.' A man sitting at the next table leaned towards her. 'Can I help you?' When he handed a paper serviette to her, Jessica realised that her face was wet with tears.

'Hospitals do that to us,' he said. 'They unhinge our reality. Can I get you another tea? That sandwich looks inedible. Would you like a pastry or something lighter?'

'No, thank you. I'm fine.' She was embarrassed at being so exposed, conscious of her streaming eyes, the angry blotches on her face.

'If you don't mind me saying so, you're far from fine, Jessica.'

She sat up straighter, surprised that he knew her name.

'I've heard what happened to your partner,' he said. 'Secrets don't last long in this cocooned environment, especially when there are uniformed police outside his ward. I hope you don't think I'm intruding...' He hesitated, as if he was waiting for her permission to continue.

'No, I don't think that,' she replied. 'I appreciate your concern.'

'I've some understanding of what you're going through,' he said. 'The wait for news can become unendurable. How is Richard doing?'

Thinking about his murderous wife, Jessica wanted to shout. *Whispering her name when he awakens and wishing she was by his side*. She dried her eyes and told this stranger that Richard was still seriously ill but strong enough to be interviewed by the police.

'If he's able to cope with an interview of that kind, it has to be a positive sign.' He held out his hand. 'I'm Brian.' His grip was firm and oddly comforting. 'Let me repeat my offer. Can I order something for you? I haven't eaten since early this morning, so I'm going to check what's available.'

'I'd like another camomile tea,' she said. 'Though I'm not sure it does what it says on the tin.'

His smile was sympathetic as he rose and walked towards to counter. Early to mid-forties, Jessica guessed. A solidly built man with an outdoors complexion, his skin tanned by wind, not sun, his hands roughened yet his nails were trimmed and well maintained. He was dressed in jeans, a navy crew-neck jumper, and a leather jacket. His clothes looked comfortable and well worn, like his black walking boots. He had left his overnight case propped against his table.

'What part of England are you from?' she asked, when he returned and sat down opposite her.

'The West Country.' He shrugged out of his jacket and hung it from the back of the chair. 'I'm here to see a friend who's ill.'

'I'm sorry to hear that. I hope it's nothing too serious?'

'I wish the same for your partner. He's fortunate that he was found so quickly. You must be relieved that the person who's responsible is in police custody.' He had obviously decided that the café food was not to his liking and had ordered only a coffee.

'The main person who's responsible is still at large.'

'Christine Lewis, do you mean?'

'Yes.'

'Have the police any further leads on her whereabouts?'

'I believe they do. It's only a matter of time before she's arrested. When that happens, I hope they throw away the key.'

He drew back, as if he could feel the power of her venom then nodded, understandingly. 'Vengeance is a heavy burden to carry,' he said. 'You need strong shoulders for the task.'

'Is that what you've discovered?'

'It's what's brought me this far,' he admitted. 'But it's been one hell of a ride.'

Jessica waited for him to continue, convinced she was going to hear his life story. It happened every time she entered the hospital café and someone with a need to offload their personal tragedies sat down beside her. He was right about hospitals unhinging people from reality. Ships passing in the night but, as always, she had no intention of sharing.

Once given away, your information will be bent into a boomerang that will take out your face on its return. She may have been sick of her father's sayings, but she was never able to ignore his advice.

The man sitting opposite her asked if she could recommend a hotel he could book for a couple of nights. Whether he would stay any longer depended on his friend's progress.

'My father owns a hotel,' she said. 'It's in Rosswall, which is only a short distance from the city.'

'It sounds perfect,' he said. He looked expectantly at her. 'What's the name of his hotel?'

'Rosswall Heights. If you're interested, I'll call reception and see if there's an available room.'

'Thank you. That sounds ideal. O'Neill is my surname.'

She booked him into the hotel for two nights and told the receptionist to keep another potential reservation available in case Brian O'Neill decided to stay longer.

Her father entered the café just as she ended the call. She raised her arm to attract his attention and Brian, glancing back, half-stood, as if aware that their time was over. He reached for the handle of his case but it fell over, the long handle catching the edge of the table and overbalancing his coffee cup. Dregs of coffee splashed over his boots as the cup shattered on the floor. A woman immediately came from behind the counter and hurried across to them with a roll of kitchen paper, along with a mop. He apologised as he straightened his case and bent over to help her clear up the broken pieces. Flushed with embarrassment, he seemed unaware of her father's presence until the clearing up was done.

'That was clumsy of me.' He shrugged. 'Difficult days always lead to bad coordination.'

Her father barely acknowledged Brian's presence when Jessica introduced them. She sensed his tension – it was becoming more apparent of late – and Brian, also, seemed affected by it. He nodded goodbye and left immediately.

'Are the police still with Richard?' Jessica asked.

'No. He terminated the interview—'

'Terminated? What do you mean?'

'He stopped answering their questions.'

'I knew it was too soon for him to be interviewed,' she said. 'He's still heavily sedated?'

'The police are taking that into consideration but he won't budge from his belief that his shooting was a case of mistaken identity. He refuses to believe Christine had anything to do with it.'

'But they have evidence. A confession—' She needed to make Richard understand what had been done to him.

'Richard refutes it. He's not prepared to make a statement.'

'I have to talk to him. The morphine he's taking has confused him. He's no idea what he's saying.'

'Not now,' he advised. 'A physiotherapist is working on him. His lungs are giving him trouble. She should be finished shortly.'

She had to pee, the pressure constantly building on her bladder. Her body seemed alien, a force with its own demanding momentum. She could never imagine it belonging wholly to her again.

. . .

Jessica's father was finishing a phone call when she returned from the bathroom.

'Don't look so worried, Jessica.' He seemed more relaxed. 'The evidence the police have compiled against Christine is irrefutable. She'll be behind bars before long.'

'How can you be so certain?'

'I have my sources,' he replied. Of course he did. His long fingers, everywhere. 'Christine is staying with a friend, an ex-boyfriend, apparently. His name is Jasper. The police don't have a surname as yet but it's only a matter of time before they identify him. Talk to Richard. He probably knows who this Jasper character is. This nightmare will soon come to an end and be forgotten.'

The physiotherapist had finished working with Richard when they entered the ward. Some colour had returned to his face, just enough to remove that death-mask pallor Jessica had found so frightening. His eyes were more alert when he looked at her but his attention soon shifted to her father. The wheeze in his breathing was loud enough to alarm her. An IV drip was attached to one hand and a catheter tube was visible at the side of the bed. They could have explained his discomfort at being so exposed yet she saw his fear when her father moved closer to the bed. His skin felt dank and cold when she squeezed his hand.

'I want to be left alone with Richard,' she said.

Her father seemed about to protest but one look at her expression warned him she was serious.

'I'll be waiting outside for you,' he said, before turning to Richard. 'I'm sorry you've had such a stressful interview. But, as we discussed earlier, it's not only your safety that's at stake; it's also my daughter and your child that you have to consider.'

'He believes Christine did this to me.' Richard's distress was palpable when they were alone, his voice barely audible.

'It's what everyone believes.' Jessica held a glass of water to his chapped lips.

'What about you?' he asked.

'We nearly lost you, Richard.' She brought his hand to her stomach and saw his eyelids flutter when their baby kicked. 'Christine has to be brought to justice.'

'Christine would never hurt me. *Never...*'

'Yes, Richard, you're right. She hired someone else to do it.'

'That's nonsense... I'd be dead if I'd been the target.' His eyelids fluttered as he forced himself to concentrate. He was unable to stay awake for long and could fall asleep in the middle of a sentence.

'What stopped him putting a bullet in my head?' he asked. 'I saw his feet. He knew I was alive. There was no one else in the car park yet he just walked away. Christine was the target, not me. I can't understand why she's being framed for a crime she didn't commit.'

'Why doesn't she come forward if she's innocent?' His refusal to accept the truth was unbearable. 'You must have heard the latest news reports. A police officer saw her with the man she contracted to kill you. His name is Billy Macken.'

'What if she's dead?' The jerk of his hand almost dislodged the IV drip. 'What if this gunman went after her and... and... did what he'd been paid to do?'

'She's *not* dead. She's living with an ex-boyfriend.'

She leaned over him until their mouths were almost touching. 'Listen to me, Richard. You almost died on me. Our baby could have been born without a father. Christine has to be stopped. The police expect to arrest her as soon as they locate her ex-boyfriend? His name is Jasper. Do you know where he lives?'

Now that he knew Christine was alive, his face had slackened and he appeared calmer. 'Jasper... Jasper...' He was drifting from her, his breath warm on her face when he repeated the name again.

'Where is he, Richard? You have to tell me where we can find him.'

'Long dead... poor old Jasper... she used to feed him apples...' His breathing deepened as his eyes closed, and his words, slurring and indistinct, slipped away from him.

The IV tube clicked as it dripped into the intravenous line and the heart monitor bleeped so fiercely that Jessica ran into the corridor to call for a nurse. When Richard's vital signs were checked and found to be stable, Rosita, the senior nurse, ordered her to leave the ward. Richard needed to rest and Jessica was too tense and exhausted to be of any use to him. She sternly reminded Jessica that her first consideration had to be her baby's welfare.

Her bedroom at Rosswall Heights was still caught in the fug of teenage years. Posters of singers whose songs had seen her through her teens were still on the walls: Rihanna, Beyoncé, P!nk. They had cast off their surnames, but Christine had loaded Jessica with three. She wanted to return to Redstone and pull up that floorboard, pour boiling water over Christine's laptop, set a match to those clippings and watch the evidence she had compiled go up in smoke.

The memory seemed to come from nowhere. A sudden lurch of knowledge that told her exactly where Christine was hiding. When she had met Stella Lewis at Tom's funeral, she had mentioned a holiday chalet and expressed her disappointment that Christine had no interest in using it. She had talked about long ago holidays when her children used to feed a horse with apples and carrots. 'Poor old Jasper,' that was the exact phrase Stella has used.

Sheerwater, she had called the chalet.

Her father's reaction when she rang him was difficult to gauge. He agreed it was a possibility. He would take it from there and pass the information to the police. They had planned to eat together in the hotel restaurant, but he asked if Jessica would mind dining alone.

She was relieved not to have to make conversation with him. Sooner or later, she would have to confront him with the contents of the folder. How could she even begin that conversation? Their relationship had been built around information he had kept from her. Now, it was the other way around – and Jessica had no idea how to adapt to their changing roles.

The restaurant was busy, mainly filled with accountants who had been attending a conference at the hotel. Brian O'Neill, the only diner eating alone, rose to his feet when he saw her.

'I hope everything in the hotel is to your satisfaction,' she said.

'I'm very satisfied.' He looked more relaxed than earlier, his dark stubble shaved and a white, open-neck shirt emphasising his tan. His jeans and jumper had been replaced by casual trousers and a dark blue linen jacket worn over a T-shirt. 'Give my compliments to your father. He runs an excellent establishment. Are you dining with him?'

'No. He was called away on business.'

'Why don't you join me?'

'I'm not very good company at the moment.'

'Let me be the judge of that.' He pulled out the chair for her and waited until she had lowered herself awkwardly into it before sitting down again. Sheila, the restaurant manager, came immediately to the table to greet Jessica and explain the menu dishes.

Brian O'Neill was easy company. He worked in IT and had lived most of his life abroad. Did he have children? A wife? She suspected not. His interest in the woman who was ill suggested more than friendliness, but he didn't mention her during the meal. His accent had a familiar rhythm that tugged at her memory: dropped h's and swollen vowels – sounds her father lost when they moved to Rosswall Heights. Hearing pronunciations she had forgotten, she realised how much her father's diction had changed since then. Dougie Barnes came to mind. An ugly eruption, like a boil about to burst.

'Where exactly in the West Country are you from?' she asked.

'Dorset,' he replied.

'Are you familiar with Rillingham-on-the Weir?'

His attention was distracted by the accountants who had grown more raucous as their meal progressed. For an instant Jessica thought he was going to ask them to quieten down, but Sheila was heading purposefully towards their table.

'It's a small town, very picturesque,' he said, when the noise level dropped.

'Why are you asking?'

'I'm certain Christine Lewis has some connection to it.'

'In what respect?'

'It's not important. She'll be arrested soon and I can get on with living my life.'

'Arrested?'

'Thankfully, yes. The police have new information. It's just a matter of time before they move in on her.'

His attention was focused on his plate yet he made no attempt to eat. 'You sound very certain,' he said. 'I stopped trusting in the ability of the police a long time ago. Perhaps it's different over here.'

'There are cock-ups here too, but not this time.'

'How so?'

'It's something Richard said when I spoke to him earlier. I've figured out where she is.' Her stomach curdled with loathing towards the woman who had tried to destroy her future.

'Are you okay, Jessica?' His face was taut with concern as he stared at her. 'Delayed shock can hit suddenly. You won't feel safe until this woman is apprehended. Where do you believe she's hiding?'

'Tipperary. A place called Sheerwater.' The words slipped out so quickly she hardly realised she had spoken aloud.

'And you've passed that information on to the police?'

'My father has done so.'

The accountants were kicking off again. Egged on by his friends, one of them began to sing. His deep baritone voice rang through the restaurant and Sheila, squaring her shoulders, headed towards their table again.

In the hush that followed, Jessica realised that she was talking to a stranger about matters that were of no concern to him. Her back arched when she stood and Brian immediately moved to assist her.

'I really do need to lie down,' she said and he nodded, the indentation between his eyebrows deepening.

He walked with her to the exit. Once outside the restaurant, she turned towards the private lift leading to her father's penthouse. Brian went outside. He said he would be unable to sleep unless he took a walk around the grounds. Two men in overalls and peaked caps were working on the aviary. They had removed some of the containers and was arranging new ones with different plants. The green vibrancy of the ferns and umbrella tree plants were so life-like that Jessica had to touch them to believe they were artificial.

'They're amazing,' she said. 'Where did these ones come from?'

One of the men ignored her, the other shrugged and muttered something in a language she didn't recognise. Jessica left him to his work and walked through the aviary her father had created. The dead-eyed birds watched her go, their iridescent feathers unruffled, their throats frozen on a note they would never sing.

She looked back once. Snow was falling, and Brian O'Neill was standing outside the glass doors, his phone to his ear.

FORTY-FOUR

They came quietly. No sirens or flashing lights. Christine is unaware of their arrival until she hears the knock on the door, a loud rat-a-tat repeated twice. A glance out of the window reveals a squad car parked at the front of the chalet. When she checks the back window, she discovers a second squad car at the rear. She scribbles a brief note to Ryan and leaves it on the table. *Squad car has arrived.* It started to snow earlier, swirling in from the north in a blizzard that wraps itself around her when she opens the door.

Two policemen in uniform stand before her. One is young and stern-faced, the other middle-aged and paunchy. He tilts his head quizzingly when he sees her, sizing up her short, red hair, which is a disguise that will only fool those who are not intent on finding her.

'Christine Stone, I'm Sergeant Meehan and this is Garda Slaney,' he says. 'Come with us, please.' His broad face has spread into his substantial double chin but his height adds to his authority.

'Are you arresting me?' There is something nerve-prickingly recognisable about him, yet she is too frightened to pin it down.

'We're asking you to accompany us to the garda station for questioning in relation to the attempted murder of Richard Stone,' he replies.

'Can I see the warrant for my arrest?'

The younger policeman moves towards her but stops when the detective sergeant lays a hand on his arm. 'We don't need a warrant, Mrs Stone—'

'My name is Lewis. *Ms* Lewis.' She is annoying the younger man, who stares at her with barely controlled impatience.

'Under these circumstances, we don't need a warrant, Ms Lewis,' the older man says. 'We simply ask you to be cooperative so that we don't have to handcuff you. But if you insist on doing things the hard way, that will be our only recourse. You've successfully evaded capture but now it's time you answered some questions.'

'I need my coat—' She is reaching towards the coat rack when Garda Slaney shoves the door open and pins her arms to her side.

'No, you don't. Not where you're going.' Her wrists are cuffed before she has time to resist and she is led outside.

'Are you taking me to Nenagh garda station?' She has to shout above the wind that gusts against her as she is shoved towards the squad car.

'Yeah... yeah...' The younger garda has taken control. He leans around her and opens the back door. Snow covers the car's roof and has already obliterated the windscreen. This is an unexpected blizzard. He presses his hand down on her head as he herds her into the back seat. *Like all the best cop dramas*, she thinks, struck by the theatricality of his gesture. He fixes the seat belt around her before sitting into the driver seat. Why didn't they use her correct surname? It should have been written on their documentation. The door slams, a clunk sound telling her it has locked automatically. And it comes to her then, the older garda's familiar appearance, but it is too late to do anything except cower in the back seat and remember.

On the morning she photographed Samuel Newman when he arrived for a board meeting, he had been approached by this man. His bulky frame had prevented her from taking the photograph she needed but when he moved to one side, she had photographed them both. He wasn't wearing a garda uniform then. Maybe he was off duty, a corrupt cop talking tactics or passing on information. In her bones she knows otherwise, though everything about the two men looks authentic. Anyone seeing them will simply assume that the law is going about its duty – not that anyone is abroad on this stormy night.

The car that was waiting at the rear of the chalet comes around the side of the building and heads before them through the front gate. Almost immediately, it is lost from sight. The younger man turns his car around and follows.

Snow has piled up on the inner road, smothering the hedgerows and embankments. He mutters expletives in his punchy Dublin accent when the car skids. He shouts at the older man, whom he calls Hawk, to keep his opinions to himself when he is advised to stop pressing so hard on the brake. Of the two men, the younger one is the more merciless, she thinks. Too young to understand the torment of a conscience and, more than likely, he won't live long enough to endure one. He has the same jittery personality as the blond-haired man who fell into her path and would have killed her only for the intervention of the police.

Richard is alive because he failed to carry out his contract for the second time. These two men won't fail.

The driver slows at the T-junction. A right turn means that they are heading towards Nenagh; left will bring them to the mountain. Slievenamon. It sounds as beautiful as its English translation. *Mountain of the women* seems like a hideously appropriate place to dispose of her body on this wild night.

Until the moment he turns left, she has clung to a faint hope that they are genuine members of the garda force, that she only imagined Hawk's resemblance to the man she photographed, that the coke-fuelled energy of the younger man is purely youthful ambition. Such an illusion is no longer possible. Her skin tingles from the knowledge that a journey to the mountain means only one thing. Her stomach, responding, cramps in fear. She hiked through the mountain when she was a child. She knows its beauty and its dangers – so easy to hide a body in the gullies and undergrowth. She tastes blood when she bites down on her bottom lip.

The driver swerves again and, as she is thrust forward, Christine feels the nudge of her phone against her thigh.

'You're not going the right way to Nenagh,' she shouts. 'Where are you taking me?'

'You'll find out soon enough,' the driver shouts back. 'Now shut up and enjoy the scenery.'

No sooner have the wipers cleared the windscreen than it is covered again. The road is a blank white canvas. It is impossible to see any traffic markings and the cats' eyes are buried beneath the snowfall.

'You're not from the police.' She is still shouting. Her voice is her only weapon. 'Did Samuel Newman order you to kidnap me?'

Hawk turns around. The peak of his cap is low over his eyes. In the gloom of the car his features appear to have melded into his fleshy face. 'Be quiet, or I'll be forced to do something I may regret later,' he warns her.

Her phone rings. Only one person knows her number. She moans inwardly as the ring tone reaches the men in front. The wheels churn but the tyres hold the road and the driver manages to bring the car to a stop.

The heat of Hawk's anger – she feels it burning her face, but that impression is dispelled when he opens the passenger door and steps outside. In the dazzle of headlights, the snow dances to the choreography of the wind and the blast of cold air chills her to the bone.

He yanks at the back door, throwing himself into the car with such force that their foreheads collide. She is slammed back against the seat, dazed and disoriented as he scrabbles at her jumper, then her jeans. He feels the phone immediately and pulls it from her pocket. He stares at the lit screen and presses his index finger on the off command. 'We'll check the caller ID later,' he says, before he powers off her phone.

Back in the passenger seat, he flings the phone into the compartment between the two front seats and grunts at the driver to restart the car. Snowflakes melt on the shoulders of his uniform and the wipers are working at full speed to keep the windscreen clear. They don't speak to each other. Both are focused on what has to come. She begins to pray, as Paul must have done before Dougie Barnes pulled the trigger. She is not religious, not in the sense that she believes there is a divine deity with compassionate eyes and bleeding palms watching over her, yet she conjures him up as she used to do when she was a child, convinced that she had been singled out for his attention.

What is Ryan thinking right now? Will he believe the storm has cut her signal? He rang her earlier in the evening to reassure her that Richard had been moved from intensive care into a private ward. He had spoken to Jessica and had faced Samuel Newman. A man much changed by circumstances and time, yet Ryan still recognised him. His eyes, he said: watchful, calculating, merciless. Impossible to hide behind the mirror of the soul.

Tears run unrestrained down her cheeks and drip onto her chest. The handcuffs chaff against her wrists and the strain in her arms is painful.

'Take it easy,' Hawk warns the driver as the car skids to the centre of the road.

'Just shut the fuck up and let me concentrate,' the younger

man snaps back. He sounds nervous, out of his element on this desolate country road.

She lifts her legs and kicks at the back of his seat.

'Stop that,' he yells.

She does it again, this time gaining so much traction that the seat rocks slightly. She screams at the same time. It comes from deep within her gut, a wall of sound that rushes into the space behind him. When he increases his speed, it seems as if the noise she is making has acted like an accelerant.

Hawk pulls open the glove compartment and reaches inside. 'Stop the car and let me silence this bitch once and for all!' The gun he holds is barely visible in the car's murkiness but there is no mistaking his intention when he raises his arm and points it at her.

She kicks again, the drumming of her heels drowned out by her screams. The driver feels the thuds on his back as he attempts to slow down.

'Shut your mouth and put your feet up on the seat or I'll blow your fucking head off right now!' Hawk roars.

He keeps the gun trained on her as she lifts her left leg, then her right, and plants her feet on the seat. She is scrunched in this disjointed position when the car veers to the far side of the road then skids back again. The driver pulls hard on the steering wheel. A curved steel barrier comes into view. It serves as a safety guard against the steep drop below. They have reached Rowan Falls, which sits at the bottom of a slope and is a popular picnic area. The barrier is visible in the headlights for an instant before the side of the car catches it.

The sound of steel grating against steel silences her as the car is buffeted against it.

The curved rail comes to an end with such abruptness that there is no time to react before the car leaves the road and plunges downwards towards Rowan Falls. Branches lash against the doors before a rock, protruding like a bulbous nose from the descending embankment, catches against the chassis and topples the car over. Christine is hanging upside down for an instant, her body held tightly in place by the seat belt. It feels like an eternity but is only a few hurtling seconds before the car rights itself and slams against the wide girth of a tree trunk. The last sounds she hears before she loses consciousness is the crack of glass shattering and the crunch of steel that had nowhere to go but inwards. Her body is jerked violently, her knees rising to slam against her forehead. She is going to die and all she feels is disbelief. No past life flashing, no divine rapture or beckoning white light. Just disbelief that her life can be ended so randomly, so carelessly.

FORTY-FIVE

When she opens her eyes, she emerges from one darkness into another. She believes death is an abyss, a black nothingness. But, if there is any truth to the steadfast belief in optimism, it can also be a journey towards a higher awareness. This one is filled with pain and when she moans – a thick, groggy sound – she is able to deduce that she is alive. She is living, breathing, and the wind sweeping through the broken windscreen, the snow riding on its breath, is unendurable enough to be real.

The men in front are silent. She waits for them to make a sound. The airbags should have protected them but all she can hear is the ragged wheeze of her own breath. Unable to use her cuffed arms as leverage, she wriggles her body in a desperate effort to free herself from the seat belt. She manages to partially lie down along the back seat. Every time she moves, pain shoots through her chest. *Cracked ribs*, she thinks, and grits her teeth even harder as she continues to squirm against her constraints. She manages to free her upper body and digs deeply into her pain to allow her that extra manoeuvrability to release her legs. At any second, she expects Hawk or the driver to turn on her. When she has freed herself from the safety belt, she sits up straight and wriggles along the seat. The angle of the car has only slightly dislodged the passenger seat and there is a narrow space there for her to lower her legs. She slides forward, bending her head against the slant of the roof, then stretches even further until her face touches Hawk's back. His jacket is covered in snow. She feels the curve of his shoulder and the ice-cold stump of his neck. His hat is still on his head. Stooped in that same space, she carefully raises her head to feel the ceiling. Every movement she would have done effortlessly before is a torturous procedure as she painfully contorts her body. She remembers noticing an overhead light that might still be working if the electrics have not been destroyed. She locates it and pushes against it gingerly, ribs shrieking, in the hope that such pressure will activate it. After a few failed attempts, the light comes on.

The scene that meets her eyes is too grotesque to grasp in its entirety. She must view it in fragments. First, the young man slumped so rigidly over the steering wheel, his hands clasped clawlike around it. The window on his side is shattered and, for some reason, his airbag didn't inflate. A shard of windscreen glass is buried in his neck. All Christine needs is a quick glance to realise that he has bled to death.

Hawk's head is sunk into the airbag that has now deflated. He is also unmoving. She discovers the reason when she sees that the window on his side has been shattered by the edge of a boulder. His body must have taken the brunt of the blow. Unlike his companion, he is still breathing.

She needs her phone. In the plunge down the slope, it fell from the compartment where Hawk had left it. She uses her feet to try to locate it and finally feels it under Hawk's seat. She traps it under her shoe and drags it forward. Somehow, she must find a way to use it or she will die in this blizzard.

Slipping off her trainers, and then her socks, she is able to grasp the phone between her feet. She manages to lift her legs upwards and drop it on the seat beside her.

She must not think about the men in front. The younger man can no longer harm her but the older one is stirring, groaning as he lifts his head, only to let it fall again against the deflated airbag. On her knees now, she uses her chin to steady her phone, which lodges in the gap between the seat and the backrest. She presses her teeth to the power button. The screen lights up. Facial recognition is all she needs to activate it but will it bypass the damage to her face? Her eyelids have swollen, and it is difficult to move her jaw.

Her luck holds, and she is able to draw enough breath to speak to the first responder.

Hawk is upright now, his shoulders hunched bull-like as he moves his head from side to side. She has to get out of the car. Did he re-lock the door after he took her phone from her? She checks the window frame and weeps with relief when she sees that the locking mechanism has not engaged. Lying flat along the seat, she hooks her foot under the handle. He groans loudly as he bends forward. His hat falls off and she is able to see the blood in his hair and on his neck, blood spilling down the side of his hi-vis jacket. His gun lies against the leg of his dead companion.

Hawk is reaching for it when she manoeuvres the handle and the door partially opens. She bangs it with both feet and wriggles frantically along the seat until she is able to fall to the ground. Her phone has disappeared in the scramble to escape and she has no idea if it is still in the car or lost in the snow. Darkness is a shield, but it is also a trap – one that skids her to the ground when she tries to run in her bare feet.Hawk fires the gun, his heavy body silhouetted against the interior car light. Another failed attempt on her life will be intolerable to his boss.

She stumbles on, sinking deeper into the drifts. The gun goes off again. He is firing wildly into the night but there is no reason why a bullet won't bring her down. Random happenings and chaos, that is how the world spins.

When lights appear on the horizon, she is convinced they are part of the white world where she will be buried. Even the sirens belong to the wind that is whirling shapes towards her, and luminous colours, horrifyingly familiar, surround her. Gardaí, she realises, dazzling in their hi-vis jackets.

More shots are fired. She has no idea who is firing them. Her legs sink her into the snow as a floodlight illuminates the sky. She watches snowflakes falling. Millions and zillions, each one uniquely sculpted, each one drifting with her into infinity.

She wants to think about Richard but it is Ryan's tough, rugged features that emerge from the luminous night. Will he ever know what happened to her? Even when voices call out to her, she is unable to do anything except lie where she fallen and hope that her words reach them.

'My name is Christine Lewis. I'm ready to answer any questions you need to ask me.'

FORTY-SIX

Snowstorm Shootout with Gardaí
By Shay McCabe

Two men are dead and a woman has been arrested following a car crash that occurred last night on a deadly road bend in Tipperary. Gardaí were called to the scene when they received an emergency call from the distraught woman, who had been injured in the crash. The names of the deceased men will not be released until family members have been notified and their bodies formally identified.

The name of the injured woman has also not been released. She was suffering from shock, cracked ribs, severe bruising and hypothermia when found by gardaí after she made the distress call. She was brought directly to Nenagh General Hospital.

The garda press office is unable to confirm that the dead men were disguised as garda officers and driving a fake squad car when the accident occurred. Nor can they confirm that their identities are already known to the gardaí or that the female passenger was in handcuffs...

Unable to continue reading the online morning report from *Capital Eye,* Jessica closed her laptop and wrapped her arms around her stomach. She did not need to ring Shay to find out the identity of the unnamed woman. Nonetheless, that was what she did.

Information, a priceless currency.

'I thought I might hear from you,' he said. 'How are you, Jessica?'

'I've just finished reading your report,' she replied. 'Is Christine Lewis the injured woman?'

'I can't divulge that information. My source—'

'Just tell me, how seriously injured is she?'

'She'll live.'

'How did she end up in the company of criminals when the police were tipped off about her whereabouts?'

'The police didn't receive a tip-off.' He sounded confident, well-armed with knowledge. 'The first they knew about her whereabouts was when she called them for help.'

'That's not true. The police were told—'

'No, they were *not*. I know that for a fact. What I don't understand is how she managed to contact them when she was in handcuffs. She's lucky to be alive. Hawk Davitt was notorious—'

'Hawk?'

He paused, then spoke more slowly. 'I shouldn't be talking to you about this. My source—'

'Did you just call him Hawk?' Her breath whistled through her teeth.

'It's a nickname, short for "Tomahawk". He was originally a money lender. A hatchet was his weapon of choice when collecting debts.'

'I see.' That, of course, was a lie, but she was incapable of questioning him any further.

. . .

The snow was banked heavily on either side of the gritted road when Jessica drove to the hospital. Richard was propped up against pillows, and copies of the morning newspapers were spread across his bed. The senior nurse had spoken to Jessica on the corridor. His blood pressure and temperature had reached dangerously high levels after reading the reports on the shootings. He had refused to relinquish the newspapers and had spent the last hour searching online for the latest updates.

'Jasper.' His gaze, direct and accusatory, was aimed at Jessica. 'The fact that I'm pumped up with morphine could have something to do with the fact that I couldn't figure it out for myself.' His hand shook as he tapped the print copy of *Capital Eye*. 'But you put two and two together and this is the result.'

'What are you talking about?' Jessica shrugged out of her coat and sat on the edge of the bed.

'Are you going to lie to me again?'

'I've never lied to you.' She lifted the copy of *Capital Eye* and studied the photograph of the damaged car. It must have been taken in the haze of first light. The gaudy yellow and blue paintwork reminded her of an obscenely twisted dragonfly that had collapsed into a wonderland of snow. 'What has any of this got to do with me?' she demanded. 'You don't even know that that woman is Christine.'

'Stella phoned me. Who did you tell?'

'Tell *what*?'

'Where Christine was hiding.'

'How could I have known where she was hiding?'

'Because *I* told you.'

'Richard... what are you talking—?'

'I distinctly remember telling you about Jasper before you left.'

'You were out of it, Richard. *Hardly* conscious. The morphine—'

'Don't lie to me, Jessica. Did you pass that information on to your father?' His curt interruption tautened his face with pain or, perhaps, it was hatred that stretched his mouth into a grimness that was unbearable to see.

'Those men who were with Christine last night were criminals. Why would my father have anything to do with them?'

'That's what I need to know.'

'What you need to know is that Christine hangs out with dangerous people. One of them is currently in police custody and has made a statement that he was hired by her to kill you.'

'Christine was dragged from the chalet by murderers. But for that crash, her body would be hidden somewhere on the mountain and probably never found. Those men were professionals. They hadn't reckoned on the snow storm. That's the only reason she's alive.'

'Neither my father, nor I, had anything to do with what happened to her.' She sounded convincing, forceful, her voice an inflexible shield against his suspicions. 'I've never lied to you, Richard, and I'm not going to start now. I spoke to Rosita on the way in. She said your temperature was through the roof this morning. You need to calm down and start making sense. My father is a hard-nosed businessman but if that was a crime, then most of the corporate world would end up inside. I can't understand why you've linked him to Christine's accident and are blaming me—'

He leaned forward in the bed and grasped both her elbows. 'Swear to me that you didn't tell your father where Christine was hiding.'

'I swear it.' She spoke with conviction and held his gaze until her eyes began to sting from the effort of lying to him.

'Or that he had anything to do with tracking her down?' he demanded.

'I swear to you that my father had nothing to do with it.' Her mind was clear, a canvas wiped clean of all illusions. 'If you don't believe me, I'm walking out of here and you'll never hear from me, or your child, again. *Ever*. Do you understand what I'm telling you?'

Richard was silent as he studied her face. She knew he was searching for the crack: a faltering tear; a skidding, sideways glance; a revealing tic. He lay back against the pillows and reached for her hand. The lies she had told him lay like lead on her tongue. Strong shoulders were needed to carry secrets. Hers would never sag.

Jessica waited for her father to return to Rosswall Heights that night. He was not a noisy person – staying below the radar required stealth – but her ears had been attuned to his comings and goings from a very young age.

Unable to sleep, she rang the hospital. Richard was 'comfortable' according to the night nurse. No mean achievement, considering that a bullet missed a major artery by a millimetre, she said. Jessica didn't want to think about what could have happened if that millimetre had not saved his life. To live without him would be intolerable. Love was a consuming force that made one strong or enfeebled those who were afraid of its control. It had made her weak until she had decided to take action. Her father had proved that his reality was what he decided to make it. She, too, must have the strength to bring Richard with her into the new reality she intended to create for them.

She awoke at three in the morning and thought she heard her father moving around his office. It was next door to her bedroom and out of bounds to everyone, even her. She used to be familiar with the sounds from there: a phone ringing, the slam of a drawer, the clack of a keyboard. These sounds she heard were more muted, soft enough to be imagined or caused by the whisper of ghosts seeking revenge.

One night, when she was in her mid-teens, she had opened the door without warning and found herself facing a gun. He had calmed her down and explained the importance of always being ready to defend her from those who pursued them.

This time, before entering it, she called his name. The silence that followed waited to be broken by a sigh or a muffled cough. Her own breath was suspended as she switched on the light, expecting to find him sitting in the darkness counting his sins. What else could he do in the dragging small hours?

And it was exactly as she imagined when she saw him slumped across his desk, his head cradled in his arms.

'Where were you all day?' she asked.

'Business meetings.' He blinked, his stare unfocused as he stood up and faced her.

'Exactly what does that mean?'

'It's nothing that should concern you.'

'Everything you do concerns me,' she said. 'You never contacted the police about Christine. I told you where I believed she was hiding but you didn't pass the information on to them.'

'Don't lecture me, Jessica.' He raised a hand, palm out, warding her off. 'I did report your suspicions and I've since been informed by the police as to why she was abducted. It's a drug-related feud. Christine has discovered that when you sup with the devil you need a very long spoon.'

He always lied so smoothly, honey on his tongue, but this time he lacked conviction.

'How long should that spoon be?' Jessica asked. 'And who decides on the devil's identity?'

'What exactly is that supposed to mean?'

'I don't need to explain myself but I'll do so in case you're under any illusions that I'm still a child. You never contacted the police, so don't insult me by pretending otherwise.'

'I'm not pretending anything. What's the matter with you?'

'Richard accused me of informing you about Christine's whereabouts and bringing those thugs to her hiding place. He was right, of course. I've denied it. Utterly. If you ever tell him otherwise, I'll have no hesitation in going to the police and exposing the truth about you.'

'And what exactly is that truth, Jessica?'

She held his gaze, though she wanted to gouge out her eyes rather than look at him. His mask was torn off and all she could see was the brash, cruel face of Dougie Barnes.

'Listen carefully, because we're only going to have this conversation once,' she said. 'I know that Hawk Davitt was behind Christine's abduction and that you were in contact with him. In return for my silence, I want Richard to have full control of Foundation Stone. Also, I want nothing further to do with you or SFDN. Is that clear enough for you to understand, or would you like me to elaborate further?'

'This is madness personified,' he said. 'I refuse to continue this conversation. You need help—'

'I'm sane enough to know that my entire life has been based on a lie.'

'You don't know what you're talking about, Jessica. All I've ever done is keep you safe when others would have harmed you.' His excuses rang with the same familiar refrain but, underneath, she could hear his desperation. Unable to listen, she walked towards the door. 'I'm returning to Redstone tomorrow,' she said. 'Don't try to follow me or make contact with me or Richard, except to sign the papers for the transfer of the agency to him. That's all I have to say to you. Goodbye.'

It was easy in the end to leave him. If a cord snapped between them, it made no sound.

. . .

The sun continued to shine above a hazed world of whiteness. A snow plough had cleared the hotel driveway and the soft mounds on either side of the road shimmered in the wintery glare. The flittering clawed feet of birds had patterned a black filagree across the courtyard. She thought of Christine stumbling through the drifts, her hands cuffed behind her back, nothing to stop her fall, nothing to penetrate the darkness into which she had fled.

FORTY-SEVEN

Christine is allowed one phone call from the hospital, where she is under police surveillance. Ryan answers immediately. She hears his relief, a sob of gratitude that he turns into a cough. He agrees to contact her parents and ask them to organise a solicitor for her. She wonders if her mother will recognise his name. Will she associate Ryan Niels with the frightened youth she mistakenly remembered as Brian O'Neill?

Briefly, he fills her in on what happened after he tried to contact her. He had panicked when she didn't answer his call and had emailed a warning, hoping she would see it on her laptop. When he was still unable to reach her, he drove to Sheerwater, a two-hour journey that became increasingly treacherous as the snowfall increased. He had passed the scene of the accident. Squad cars were parked at the side of the road and below, on Rowan Falls, floodlights flared as figures moved through the snow. The dents and scrapes on the steel barrier, and the ragged gap in the hedgerow, showed where the accident had occurred.

He continued driving to Sheerwater where he found an open front door. Snow was heaped in the hallway and he found a note on the table that simply read, *Squad car has arrived.* Knowing that the police would not leave the door open, and seeing her coat on the clothes peg, he knew immediately that she had been abducted.

The first reports of the accident had gone online. Two men dead, one female survivor, critical but stable. He had taken her laptop with him before he left, knowing that its contents would add further to her problems, and returned to Rosswall Heights.

She is unable to find words to describe her ordeal. Only clichés come to mind. *I thought it was all over... death was staring me in the face... I'd lost all hope* – how inane such phrases sound. He, too, seems incapable of expressing his relief. 'I was frantic wondering if you were safe...' He stops, as if aware that his feelings are insignificant compared to her experience. 'If anything had happened to you...' he falters again and his voice shakes when he says: 'I don't know what I would have done.'

Two days after her ordeal, Christine is deemed well enough to be discharged. Once again, she is in handcuffs. The police officer glances sympathetically at her wrists. Bandaged to protect the cuts and grazes left by the original handcuffs, they look as though she had made an attempt on her life.

She is brought to Dublin for questioning. The journey from Tipperary is a silent one and the noise of a busy city centre garda station hits her between her eyes when she is escorted into the building.

Her solicitor, Anna Leeson, a specialist in criminal law, is waiting. Before they enter the interview room, she asks Christine to begin at the beginning. That soon proves problematic. The tentacles of Christine's story go back too far and she is flailing as soon as she tries to explain about a lost memory, a wedding and all that has stemmed from it.

'Keep your answers simple and specific,' Anna advises her.

'The evidence they have on you is circumstantial. You were never charged with breaking and entering Jessica Newman's apartment. You were never charged with stalking when you parked outside her apartment. As regards the carjacking, it is your word against a criminal who has been jailed on two occasions for grievous bodily harm. He abducted you. You were afraid to inform the garda who stopped you because he had a gun and threatened to shoot her. You were in hiding from him at Sheerwater. Those are the facts. Stick to your story and don't deviate from it, no matter what possibilities they throw at you. That's all they are – possibilities to frame their own narrative. If you are uncertain in any way about your answer, simply say "No comment."'

Anna is a big woman, as solid as she is tall, and has an expression that suggests she would be equally at home on a war front. Christine wants to lean into her and sob but Anna's arms are made for flinging grenades, not for comfort, and, so, she squares her shoulders as they walk towards the interview room.

The detective who interviews her is a fast speaker, his voice lilting up at the end of each sentence, which makes it sound like he's asking a question even when he's not. She is told that the man who abducted her on Kindling Road is called Billy Macken. *Billy is a child's name*, Christine thinks. *Innocent sounding, almost playful.* She stares at his photograph and nods in recognition, even though it is an old image and his skull has the beginnings of black stubble. His sharp cheekbones and too-wise, hooded eyes are instantly recognisable.

The questions come hard and fast. How would Billy Macken have known she would be driving along Kindling Road at that precise moment? Why would he fall in front of her car and kidnap her with the intention of shooting her? Why would he release her? Why, despite being freed, would she go into hiding? Was he a gun for hire, as he insists? Was there an ongoing gangland feud between him and the dead men that resulted in Christine being taken hostage as an act of revenge? The suggestion should be nonsensical enough to make her laugh out loud but, like Alice in Wonderland, she has strayed down a rabbit hole where anything is possible. She feels the heat of Samuel Newman's breath on her neck.

Anna is a quiet guide beside her. The assertion that Christine is involved at any level in a gang feud is quickly dismissed. Her interrogator picks at the lobe of his ear, which is flaking. He seems unaware that dead skin is falling to his desk. It is a wide, strong table, made to withstand lies, grief, guilt, exhaustion.

Hawk's real name is Wayne Davitt, but the young driver had not lived long enough to earn the honour of a nickname. He was known simply as Joel. Hearing his name, Christine bursts into tears. He is dead because of her. She forced him off the road and, in doing so, saved herself. Should that absolve her from blame? Too soon to know and Anna's tone sharpens, a warning to Christine that she is endangering her situation by such an emotional reaction. She passes a box of tissues to Christine and demands time for her client to recover her composure.

The door of the interview room opens. A uniformed woman enters and speaks quietly to the detective, who rises and leaves the room with her. The remaining officer checks his watch. Four hours have passed and Christine is entitled to a break.

'Something has happened.' Anna can feel it in the air, an instinctive awareness that is based on experience. Christine drinks tea and tries to eat the sandwich she is offered. She doesn't share Anna's belief – Billy Macken has been forced to hand himself into the gardaí for only one reason: failure to carry out orders. And he will bring Christine down with him.

But when the detective returns to the interview room, it is Anna's instinct that proves to be correct. Christine is free to leave. The gardaí will be in touch with her again but, for now, she can walk unescorted from the station.

FORTY-EIGHT

When she first suspected she was being followed, Christine found such a possibility unbelievable. Now, every sound carries a warning, every shadow is a potential assassin. She has to become invisible again, but where to go? Her parents cannot be endangered, nor can she risk seeking help from Amy. She could go to Bernice or Killian. They could help her to begin a new existence far from here. Even as the thought registers, she pushes it aside. It cannot possibly be a coincidence that Samuel Newman came back into her life so many years later. She has come to believe it is something deeper, more profound. She cannot run. He must be brought down before he attempts to vanish her again.

Anna explains the reason for her release but she still can't believe it is that simple. Craig is responsible. Kind, solid, plodding Craig, who analysed all the data she and Ryan have been able to compile on SFDN and fed it into his own investigation. He contacted the gardaí in Dublin to pass on the information he had collated; information that mirrors a similar investigation into money laundering that is underway with their own investigative team. This is the first time the name SFDN has been brought to their attention.

Under pressure, Billy Macken has admitted to the carjacking and to falsifying a statement claiming that Christine was involved in the High Spires shooting. He was a lone wolf. No one believes him, Anna says, but he refuses to divulge names. He would prefer to face prison rather than a cold grave.

Ryan parks his car on the far side of the Liffey and they walk across the bridge towards High Spires, passing under the ancient arch of Christ Church Cathedral and turning right. Is the parking bay where Richard was attacked still cordoned off? Christine will never use it again; nor will she be able to live at her apartment. She keys in the entrance code and has just stepped inside the foyer when Aisha appears. She is wearing her scrubs and must be on her way to work. Her smooth forehead puckers when she sees Christine. She pauses, as if struggling to remember a name, but there is no recognition in her expression as she buttons her coat and steps outside into the icy wind.

The sense of invasion is strong when Christine opens the door to her apartment. The police must have fine-combed every room in their search for evidence. The books in the bookcase lie at an angle, the cushions are scattered, and drawers are only partially closed. She recoils from the stench that reaches her when she takes the lid off a saucepan. *They could have thrown out the rotting food*, she thinks, as she wraps the Bolognese sauce in a resealable bag to dump in the bin outside.

Ryan stands ill-at-ease in the middle of the kitchen. Like her, he must feel the negative energy the police left in their wake. Her laptop is missing. She remembers where she left it before she headed to Amy's house. The police would have taken it with them. Now that she is no longer a suspect, does she have the right to claim its return?

In her bedroom, she flings clothes into a case: casual sweaters and jeans, trainers. No suits and crisp blouses; high heels also belong to her old life. She reaches for the folder of information on Dougie Barnes and touches empty space. The My Little Pony figurine is also missing. Why did the gardaí take a folder of newspaper clippings, and what have they made of the contents?

She rings the garda station and asks to speak to the detective who interviewed her. He is off duty and the officer who speaks to her insists that he is the only person who can answer her questions. Her message will be passed on to him.

At the hospital, Christine has fifteen minutes to see Richard and convince him of her innocence. Her heart pulls her towards him; her head warns her to stay away.

In the end, it is easy to do. She waits until the text comes from Ryan: the coast is clear. Fifteen minutes is the length of time Jessica stays away from the ward. A pot of camomile tea and a sandwich, often left uneaten, that is the pattern she follows.

Richard is sitting on a chair beside the bed when Christine enters the private room. His eyes widen. He sees beyond her stark, red hair and the glasses that are dramatic enough for people not to look beyond the multi-coloured frames.

'Christine.' He breathes her name on an exhalation and tries to stand. 'Thank God you're safe.' Pain stretches his face as he grabs the side of the bed to prevent himself from falling.

She moves to help him but he has collapsed back into the chair. 'I can't stay long.' She is trembling, on the verge of tears. 'But I had to see you again. I'd never harm you—'

'Stop...' He leans towards her. 'I never for a moment believed you had anything to do with the shooting. But what the fuck is going on? Tell me what happened to you.'

'It's Samuel... you must know that by now. I've information on him and he wants me silenced. It's as simple yet as unbelievable as that.' She stops, braces herself against his disbelief, his denial, but sees only a grim acceptance. Like her, he has faced death and is only alive because of circumstances beyond their control. She tells him about the carjacking and what followed. Time is short. She glances at her watch and hopes that Ryan can hold Jessica in the café for a few moments longer.

'Does Jessica know what her father does?' she asks.

'I've no idea what she believes.' Two spots of colour darken his cheeks, yet he is sickly pale, diminished by weight loss and dread. 'What I do know is that she's deliberately lied to me about her past. I can't break through the façade she's created and yet I have the feelings she's constantly struggling to escape from it.'

'Do you love her?'

'I love you—'

'That's not the question I asked you.'

He hesitates, then sighs. 'I could grow to love her. It's what she wants more than anything. But how could we possibly build a future with her father shadowing everything we do?'

'Take her away. Go somewhere that's as far away as possible from here and start a new life together.'

'I want my life with you back again.' His cry is plaintive, a useless call that reaches beyond the small ward to encompass everything they once had and have now lost.

A text comes through from Ryan. Jessica is on her way back to the ward.

'I have to go,' Christine says. 'Find somewhere safe. It's your only chance to have a future together without being contaminated by Samuel Newman's evil.' Evil has a melodramatic ring to it, yet it is the only description she can apply to him.

'What about you?' He holds her hand, reluctant to let her go.

'I'm also leaving.'

'Where are you going?' His grip hurts her hand but he won't let go. 'I can't accept this... I *won't*.'

She pulls free from him and hurries from the room. She is halfway down the corridor when she recognises him. Sleek, silver hair, a dark overcoat flapping open. He is speaking into his phone and she has time to open the door nearest to her.

'Can I help you?' A woman looks up from behind a computer screen and frowns. 'Are you lost?'

'I'm looking for the X-ray department,' Christine says.

She is barely listening as the woman gives her directions. The office door has a window. She waits for him to pass and clear the way for her escape.

'Would it be possible to have a glass of water?' she asks.

'Not here, I'm afraid,' the woman replies. 'You'll have to use the café.'

'Where exactly is the café?'

'It's on the ground floor.' The woman rests her hands on the keyboard and waits impatiently for Christine to leave. 'You must have passed it on your way in here.'

'I don't remember. I've had such an upsetting day. My husband... he's been ill...' She falters when she sees his shape through the glass. A sideways glance, that's all she needs to recognise a profile she had locked away in the deep recesses of her mind.

The woman has risen and entered a room beyond her office. She returns with a glass of water and passes it to Christine. Does exposure to death lessen rather than increase fear? Christine wonders. She sips the water slowly, killing time before it kills her. Does it harden resolve and strengthen the spine?

Samuel Newman has passed by and she is able to release a long, slow breath.

'Thank you.' She hands the empty glass back to the administrator and opens the door. The corridor is empty. She hurries towards the elevator which has just arrived. Jessica is among those who emerge. Christine veers away from the group waiting to enter and pushes open the door leading to the stairs.

She leaves through an emergency exit some distance from the main hospital concourse. She rings Ryan, who arrives after a few minutes. He slides his arm around her and she buries her face in his shoulder to avoid being spotted by the security cameras as they hurry towards the car park.

Once away from the hospital, the air seems lighter, breathable again.

Ryan has booked them into a small hotel on the north side of the city where they stay overnight. She is safe behind a locked door, but the hairs on the back of her neck warn her that there is no time for complacency. Ryan adds the contents of a USB key to the laptop he removed from Sheerwater. When that is combined with the research Christine has done on the group's finances, a picture emerges that astonishes them with its breadth and audacity.

SFDN Financial Services is a thinly disguised money lender with investments in the property, hospitality and retail markets. The reach of the group is far-flung, and it is near impossible to penetrate the financial network Alan Martin has established.

'He's a financial genius.' Dispassionately, Christine can admire his ability to funnel money through intricate channels that remain within the law, yet she knows he runs a money-laundering operation and that every company within the group is linked in some way to that overall digital network. The craft courtyard puzzles her until she spots the link eventually: a pottery that specialises in large, ceramic planters and, next door to it, a workshop where fake plants made from organic materials are produced. She has seen pictures of the other hotels owned by SFDF Enterprises where such planters are also on display in the foyers. Slowly, her thoughts are coming together. Could these hotels, acclaimed for their hospitality, be centres for the distribution of drugs?

'You could be onto something there.' Ryan nods when she mentions this possibility. 'On the night you were taken...' He pauses and exhales slowly. 'I remember that a van was parked at the side of the hotel. I thought it must have something to do with the aviary because it was decorated with a bird of paradise plant. I was so intent on contacting you that I hardly paid any attention to what was going on. A side door into the hotel was open. I assumed it was a trade entrance. And I overheard some workmen speaking to each other in a foreign language.'

'We have to go there,' she says.

'Where?'

'To Rosswall Heights.' Her heart is racing, adrenaline flowing through her. Fight or flight, which is it to be? She thinks about Billy Macken and the gun he held on her. The journey through the snow when she believed she would die on the slopes of a mountain. Have these experiences made her immune to fear? The risk of what she is about to do seems nullified by such terrifying events.

'The only time I was in his hotel, I collapsed because I was afraid of him,' she says. 'I didn't understand what was happening to me but I've come a long way since then. I have a hunch about that place. I suspect it's more than a hunch but I need to see what is going on there. I intend to destroy him utterly. It's either that or I spend the rest of my life hiding from him.'

'We'll be taking a huge risk.'

'You don't have to come—'

He presses his index finger to her lips to silence her. 'You can't believe I'd let you go there alone.' He is grim and quietly determined. 'I'm with you every step of the way.'

FORTY-NINE

The porter who welcomes Ryan back to Rosswall Heights hotel refers to him as 'Mr O'Neill'. His manner is professional yet warm when he smiles at Christine. She remembers him rushing towards her in the seconds before she collapsed in the aviary but the porter, who has introduced himself as Danny, shows no sign of recognition as she forces herself to smile back at him.

When they reach their room, Ryan produces a blueprint of Rosswall Heights that he has managed to download. They study it together before returning to the foyer. The sun is shining, a wintery glare that will be short-lived, Danny says, when they tell him they would like to walk through the grounds. He apologises for the weather, as if he is personally responsible, and hands them a leaflet marking the walks. Snowdrop Trail or Heather Vale are apparently worth a visit.

Once outside, they turn towards the side of the hotel and stop beside the exterior wall where the van had been parked. Unlike the rest of the hotel with its smooth surfaces and expanses of glass, old bricks belonging to the original building were preserved and used to build this wall. Evergreen creeper spurts from the crevices and cascades so profusely that only an occasional glimpse of the brickwork is visible. It would be easy to miss the outline of a door within this abundance of green, but slight signs are visible. Withered and broken stems prove that the door was recently opened.

They move on without speaking towards Snowdrop Trail. Above them, the glass walls of the penthouse glint aggressively. The feeling that they are under observation is impossible to ignore yet they know from information Ryan has hacked, that Samuel Newman is attending a meeting of directors at SFDN Financial Services.

Danny is on the phone when they return to the hotel. Lilian, on the reception desk, is busy registering guests. Christine sits on the edge of a cube-shaped planter. The wide-spanning leaves of an umbrella tree filter light onto her fingers as she dips them into the sandy soil and touches the hard surface underneath the thin layer. Does Jessica know what lies behind the old bricks that her father preserved? Is she aware that there is a door that when opened gives access to a basement used for storage? Studying the blueprint of the hotel, it is possible to see where the aviary is positioned above the basement. She suspects there is a trapdoor that allows direct access to the planters with removable bases that arrive empty and leave with their precious commodity packed tightly inside. Like everything about SFDN, the regular delivery of new fake foliage in large planters is a slick and highly professional operation.

All around her the splendid ferns and rubber trees disguise their roots in the white loam. And birds with jewelled eyes watch everything, but see nothing.

FIFTY

Alone in Redstone, Jessica prised up the floorboard and removed Christine's laptop. While she waited for it to boot up, she examined the contents of the blue folder once again.

The first time she read the newspaper clippings Christine had compiled she had been too shocked to check the notebook tucked into the back flap of the folder. Removing it, she flicked through the pages. They mainly contained short reminders written in Christine's handwriting.

Must check The Weir View *archive again.*
Must email Ryan about Rillingham 5 court case.
Is Ivor Williams's memory of Dougie Barnes to be trusted?
Need to ask Craig about Ivor's reference to Cullain.
A relief to talk to Ryan tonight. He always makes me see things in perspective.

What perspective? Jessica wondered. Who was this Ryan whose name appeared so often in her notes?

Need to dig deeper into Sabina Doolin's suspicions about Margaret's death. Did she commit suicide or was she murdered?

Jessica snapped the notebook closed. What gave Sabina or Christine the right to question Margaret's death? Anguish welled inside her as she examined a photograph of Margaret's headstone. Shocked by its bleakness, she thought back to her encounter with Siobhán on Grafton Street, and tried to remember exactly what she had said. Suicide or an accident? Siobhán had not suggested anything other than those two tragic options.

Christine had dared to suggest a third element and sow doubts where none were needed.

She reads another note.

First meeting with Ryan Niels. Will the certainty of Paul's death lessen his grief? It can be a comfort but also a compulsion to find closure through revenge. Was I wrong to seek him out and let loose the dogs of war... Get a grip, Christine... no need for dramatics... focus... focus...!!!!

Was she drunk when she scribbled those words? That thought barely registered before Jessica saw the photograph underneath the note.

It had been taken on a riverbank. Whorls of froth raced along the surface of a river. She could tell by its speed that it was deep and dangerous. A tree leaned over the water at an angle that seemed impossible to maintain yet bulging roots held it steady. She was reminded of a Nell Stone painting, the violence of the water barely contained. In contrast, the man standing beside the tree seemed relaxed, his hands in his pockets, a half-smile on his face as he tilted his head towards the photographer.

She was staring at the face of Brian O'Neill.

The resemblance was unmistakable. Yesterday, she had ordered her usual pot of camomile tea when he entered the café and sat down beside her.

'I understand how angry you must feel,' he said, when she told him that Christine had been released from custody. 'When you know someone is guilty of a crime but they remain unpunished, it eats into your soul. Richard must be devastated that she would want him dead.'

'He doesn't...' Jessica had stopped, unable to admit that Richard was still in denial.

'He doesn't believe she's responsible?' This was a flat statement from him and she had nodded, still shocked that Christine's police interrogation should have ended so abruptly.

'I can't understand it. The gunman she ordered to shoot Richard is still under arrest—'

'Have you ever considered the possibility that she could be innocent?' His sharp interruption had taken her by surprise.

'Why should I consider that, when all the evidence points the other way?'

'You have no doubts?' he asked.

'None whatsoever.'

There had been something edgy and off-kilter about him, his expression harsher, judgemental. She had left him abruptly. At the exit she had looked back but he was already texting on his phone. She had gone to the ladies before returning to the ward. Queuing for a cubical, she had felt faint and the women before her, seeing her distress, had ushered her to the front of the queue. A short while later, stepping from the elevator on the third floor, she thought she saw Christine among the cluster of visitors waiting to enter it. Not that the red-haired woman with the zany glasses, who turned away from the crowd and headed for the stairs, bore any resemblance to her, apart from an arrogantly tilted chin and the self-assured stride of someone who knew exactly where she was going. But the sight of her was enough to panic Jessica. She was almost running by the time she reached Richard's room. Her father had been and gone. A flying visit. The papers for ownership of the agency lay on the bedside locker.

She had expected gratitude from Richard but, instead, she got tears. He was finally allowing himself to let go, all his pent-up shock released in explosive sobs.

He had no interest in reforming Foundation Stone. The agency would be sold and they would go abroad. Far, far away, he said. Their baby must grow up in a different environment, where there were no unanswered questions or unexplored lies.

The photograph she was holding shook in her hand. Brian O'Neill... Ryan Niels... the similarity of their names was obvious, as was the realisation that they were one and the same person. What was his connection to Christine? Could he be one of the Rillingham 5? According to the newspaper reports, all five were dead. She searched for Ryan's name in the clippings and finally found it. A fluff piece about a local boy made good with an app that he sold on for a large amount of money.

Why had he stalked her, deceived her, lied to her about a sick friend who didn't exist? He must have known she would suggest her father's hotel to him and then, later, in the restaurant, how skilfully he had coaxed the information from her about Christine's whereabouts. He couldn't have warned Christine on time. When he was standing outside the hotel, his phone pressed to his ear, Christine must already have been a prisoner in a fake squad car.

The laptop had enough charge to function. As soon as she entered 'Ryan Niels' into the search bar of Christine's email account, his emails came up immediately. One email after another, each one laying bare the many faces Dougie Barnes had possessed: drug dealer, executioner, witness for the state, businessman, father... and soon-to-be grandfather.

They exploded any belief Jessica had left in the history her father had created for her. Shrapnel everywhere. Which piece to pick up first? Which piece to ignore?

Outside in the garden, Christmas lights were still slung around the trees, lanterns hung from branches. She had been too distraught to contact the maintenance crew to remove them. Her first Christmas in Redstone, she had tried so hard to make it perfect. But Richard's face had been shadowed by memories of the other Christmases he and Christine had shared there with Tom.

Jessica had imagined the Christmas to come. Their baby would be old enough to experience the magic she and Richard would create between them. But this... she bent to pick up the notebook, that had fallen to the floor, and read it again before shoving it back into the folder. Bile rose in her throat. Why couldn't Christine have left well alone? Why the need to unveil a childhood trauma and force it into the light?

A river flowing all the way from there to here had finally reached its destination.

FIFTY-ONE

Jessica had known Danny Pearson all her life. Like Alan Martin, he had lost his rough edges but, whereas Alan had acquired a pallid self-importance, Danny, always a talker, had developed an affable and obliging personality that made the guests at Rosswall Heights believe that their care was his only priority. Earlier, when she rang to check that her father was home, Danny said he had returned late from a meeting in a bad mood and had chided her for upsetting him.

'You're the only one I know who can ruffle his feathers,' he'd said when she asked why he thought she was responsible for his moodiness.

The porter was alone in the foyer when she arrived and the hotel was hushed in the breathing space between midnight and the early hours.

'I don't think it's a good idea for you to be running around this time of night with the condition you're in, Missy.' He laid the book he had been reading on the desk and eyed her knowingly. 'Go on up now and take the weight off your feet. Be nice to your da. Family is everything. I see your friend is back with us again.'

'My *friend*?'

'Yeah... what's his name? I saw you dining with him a few nights back.'

'Brian O'Neill?'

'That's him, right enough.'

Jessica leaned on the desk and dislodged the book Danny had been reading. It hit her ankle as if fell to the floor but she was hardly aware of the impact.

'When did he arrive?' she asked.

'Signed in this afternoon. He'd company with him this time. Nice woman, friendly-like.'

'Really. I wonder if I know her. Is she tall with long black hair?'

'No, not this lass. A redhead, punkish. Hair much too short for my liking.'

'Can I check the register?'

One glance at Jessica's expression was enough for Danny to scroll down the screen until he came to Brian O'Neill. The woman's name was Caroline Harte.

'I'll play the CCTV footage,' he said. Guests never looked beyond his welcoming smile. Had they done so, they would have noticed that his gaze was sharp enough to cut through any façade.

Short hair and zany glasses may have been an adequate disguise at the hospital but, looking at the recorded images, Jessica had no difficulty recognising Christine as she glanced upwards towards the camera then away again.

She and Ryan Niels were sharing Room 206.

The penthouse was silent and empty. As she expected, a line of light was visible under the door to her father's office. She knocked and called out his name.

He was standing behind his desk when she entered. Had

she ever known his true skin? she wondered. He seemed shrunken, a shake in his hands when he pressed them to the desk to steady himself.

'Why have you come back?' he asked. 'If it's to fight with me, then please wait until morning. I'm tired and in no mood for another confrontation. The papers are with Richard. Not that he showed much gratitude...'

Her expression caused him to falter with an unfamiliar nervousness.

'I'm not here about Richard,' she said.

'Then why—?'

'I want to know if any of it was true.'

'What exactly are you asking me, Jessica?'

'My mother... the hit-and-run... did it really happen the way you've always told me?' The question was finally out there, in all its ugliness. 'Or was that another lie?'

'Why are you calling me a liar?' He drew back, as if she had smacked his face. But his hurt was manufactured. She could see him constructing it around himself, creating a shield that would bounce her questions back at her, as he had always done in the past.

'I'm asking you to explain the mystery of my childhood. Did Alyson ever exist, or was that some cheap, celebrity photograph you gave me to pine over?'

'Sit down, Jessica.' He waved her towards a chair. 'Take a long, deep breath before we continue this conversation.'

'My breathing is fine.' She remained standing. 'I want you to admit that Alyson never existed anywhere but inside your head.'

'How can you doubt her existence?'

'Tell me her real name.'

'Alyson—'

'*Stop* lying to me.' She knew what needed to be said but once the words were spoken aloud... what then? So many lies to confront. 'I'm aware that she existed and that she's dead. But her name was not Alyson. It was Grace Cooper.'

'Where did you get that information?' He poured a drink from the water cooler and took a long draught. His Adam's apple bobbed convulsively when he swallowed. 'Answer me, Jessica! What have you been doing?'

'I got the information from a source who told me who you really are.'

'Who am I, Jessica?' His question was a challenge she could no longer ignore.

'Dougie Barnes.' She tasted his name on her tongue then let it go. She ached for him to be puzzled by its sound but he was unable to control the flinch of recognition.

'Oh, my dear child... why are you doing this to yourself?' She heard the crunch of plastic splintering when he crushed the empty water container in his hand.

'I want to understand why we had to live on Cullain.' Her legs could no longer support her. She reached behind her towards a chair and sank clumsily into it. Her blood pressure must be sky high. At her last consultation her obstetrician had told her she needed to keep it under control. Plenty of rest and relaxation was the key to a healthy pregnancy. She needed to remain calm but the wildness in her could no longer be contained. She took the blue folder from her bag and pushed it across the desk towards him. 'Read it.'

At first, she thought he would ignore her request. He splayed his hands and laid them across the cover but he was unable to control the tremor in his fingers. Aware that she had noticed, he opened the folder. 'Where did you get this?' he asked, when he had skimmed through a few newspaper reports.

'I took it from Christine's apartment.'

'What do you mean?'

'Her apartment was empty. She was hiding from you in her parents' chalet.'

'She was never hiding from me. How often—'

'*Stop* it.' She spoke quietly, afraid that if she screamed at him, the sound would be unstoppable. She flicked through the clippings until she found one about a protest organised by parents whose sons had disappeared and thrust it towards him. 'This is about you. Don't deny it. I can't listen to your lies any longer. If we are to have a future, then you must come clean and tell me about the past. How am I supposed to reach you if I don't know who you are... who I am?'

'Jessica, my love, we should not be having this conversation. What I did in the past has no relevance today.'

'It's catching up with you now. All the personas you acquired will not be able to hide you any longer.' She tapped a finger against the newspaper clipping. 'Read it and tell me if it's about you. For once, be truthful to me.'

'This has nothing to do with me,' he said, after giving it a quick glance. He crumpled it in his fist and flung it back on the desk. 'Take his filth out of my sight. I don't know what's happening to you—'

'I'm trying to save your life.' Jessica removed the photograph that had been taken by the river. 'Do you recognise this man?'

He studied it closely then nodded. 'You introduced him to me at the hospital.'

'Can you remember his name?'

He shook his head and shrugged. 'For God's sake, Jessica, I don't understand where this conversation is going—'

'His name is Ryan Niels. His brother was called Paul. He's been carrying a grudge against you for a long time. An eye for an eye, that's the only justice that'll satisfy him. He knows everything about you, thanks to Christine. She witnessed you killing his brother.'

'Stop it this instant!' She watched him recoil, as if she had released lethal fumes into the room. 'Have you any idea what you're implying—'

'I'm trying to make you face reality. I've read her emails. They intend hacking into your software system and exposing your entire operation.'

'Ah...' His breath rushed from him on a harsh exhalation. Lines on his face that had scarcely marked his age suddenly seemed ingrained and stark, his cheeks blotched red. She had struck a chord with this statement: maybe the hacking had already been done, or the warning signs were becoming visible.

She watched his struggle. His instinct to deny so entrenched. Her life had been dominated by those lies until she discovered he was the pursuer, not the pursued.

'It was one of the last of the Rillingham Five who came after you that night on Cullain, wasn't it?' she said. 'He left a knife in your chest, but you left him swimming with the sharks.'

He half-stood then slowly lowered himself back to his chair. 'The truth is a strange animal, and not always recognisable to those who find it.' He pointed to the folder. 'Thank you for bringing this to me. What you have there is only a small part of my past. I lied to protect you but that time has passed. I underestimated your ability to cope with a harsh reality. I can see that now. Tomorrow is a new day. I promise I'll tell you everything then.'

'You've protected me in ways I've never appreciated until now,' she said. 'That time when my apartment was wrecked, I know you organised it. And the scan – you sent that to Christine. Foundation Stone... that, too. You never allowed me to want for anything. What are you going to do with the information I've shown you?'

'I'll contact Alan and let him know about the hack—'

'With *Christine*, I mean?'

'She can't prove anything—'

'Then why did you try to have her killed?'

'I *never*—'

'No... *don't* lie to me anymore,' she said. 'I can't bear it. This has to be a new start for both of us. She was five years of age when you tried to drown her. I know about Billy Macken and Hawk. They failed you. But *she* won't fail. She won't rest until you're behind bars.'

He closed the folder and shoved it into a drawer in his desk. 'Go back to Redstone, Jessica. This conversation never happened. Do you understand me? It *must* be forgotten.'

'Selective amnesia. Is that how you live with yourself?'

'It's how I survive.'

'I saw her at the hospital. I'm convinced she went there to poison Richard's mind against you. That's why he's no longer interested in the agency. He's made me promise to run away with him and never see you again. You're my father... my family...' The sob that broke in her throat felt like a ligature.

He came towards her, his arms outstretched. When she walked into them, he held her with a fierceness that snatched her breath away.

'I'm going with you to their room.' Her baby's heels beat out a rhythm that demanded a future unclouded by fear and deception.

'Jessica...'

'I'm ready,' she said, when they drew apart. 'Isn't this what you've always wanted from me? To be at the heart of your operation?'

'*Not* like this. I created an environment where you could be free—'

'I'm free to do as I choose. Either we end this together, or I do as Richard demands and never see you again.'

When he bowed his head in agreement, the shift that took place between them felt physical, an almost sickening lurch forward into a shared future. He walked to the safe at the back of his office and removed a gun. His hands no longer shook when he attached a silencer to the nozzle.

'What number is their room?' he asked.

'206.'

He handed her the master key card that would allow them admittance to all the rooms in his hotel. The corridor was empty when they emerged from the lift. When had he last pulled the trigger on a gun? Many years, Jessica suspected. Long fingers, clean hands, but this time it was up close and personal.

Their room was dark. He turned the dimmer knob and a faint glow gave enough light to see their faces on the pillows. The glasses Christine had worn earlier were on the bedside table. Ryan lay beside her but apart, a distance between them. She knew immediately that they were not lovers. No heat of passion had tumbled them onto the bed. They were merely resting before they began again to target her father, and destroy her in the maul.

FIFTY-TWO

Christine is running along the top of a cliff. Sheer and white, it braves the sea, but the grass snags her feet, slowing her down. She does not know who is chasing her, only that she must stay ahead, even if that means jumping across the cleft that opens in front of her. The gap is wide, the drop bottomless. She has no option but to jump. She springs forward and flies through space, one leg spread to reach the other side. She is almost there when the chill of steel touches her forehead.

She awakens on the struggle between dreamtime and reality. Her pursuer is no longer an invisible threat. The gun he holds is steady and is pressed against her left temple. If her dream had lasted, she would have fallen into the cleft. A leap into the unknown is always a risk and, now, seeing his face looking down at her, the thin, pitiless slice of his mouth, she feels, again, the terror of the five-year-old child who struggled so hard to escape from him.

Then, as now, that has proven to be impossible.

'Stay quiet.' He presses a finger to his lips but Ryan stirs and stretches his arm across the space between them. He awakens in the same instant, his body vibrating with shock as he tries to pull himself upright. 'Make one move and I'll shoot her,' Samuel Newman warns him.

'He means it.' Jessica moves into view. She is wearing wide-legged trousers and a black stretch top that emphasises her stomach. She seems composed as she picks up the pair of glasses on the bedside table and stares through the lenses at Christine. 'A good disguise,' she says. 'But coming here was a mistake. I wish you hadn't done so.'

Earlier, Christine had talked to Ryan about a future. It had no shape and was shaded by uncertainty, yet it seemed possible to think ahead. Another mistake. An underestimation of the forces ranged against them. They will pay the price for being reckless. She must find her voice and beg for her life. But remembering Paul, the pleas and cries he must have offered up, she knows the uselessness of words.

'Let her go,' Ryan speaks directly to him. 'This is between us. She has nothing to do with it.'

'On the contrary, Christine Lewis is the axis of everything,' Samuel Newman replies. 'The past is another land. We never trespass there. It's unfortunate that both of you ignored that fact. What were you hoping to achieve?'

'Justice for my brother.'

'Ah, justice.' His tone is conversational. 'I'm familiar with the concept but, as the law is an ass, I never found a use for it. Your brother was a junkie. He would have wiped out his family in exchange for his next hit. And for his wasted existence, you thought you could bring me down?'

'I saw you kill him.' Christine will have her say even if these are the last words she speaks. 'He was crying for his mother when you put a bullet through his head.'

'Listen to me,' says Ryan. 'For your own sake, *listen*. Killing us is not going to make your problems go away. Tomorrow morning your IT data is primed to flood into police stations here and abroad. I can stop it happening. Let Christine go and I'll decrypt—'

'She's not going anywhere.' His finger is tense on the trigger. Christine senses the pull of flesh against steel. 'But you'll decrypt my system or end up with your brains on the floor.'

Ryan moves slowly, aware that any sudden movement will further endanger her. What does it matter? Soon she will be dead. It will be instant and he, also, will be dispatched with the same efficiency once he has ended his usefulness.

'Give the gun to me.' Jessica's smile is thin and merciless.

'Stay out of this.' Her father moves protectively in front of her. How did she persuade him to allow her to be his witness?

'Total commitment,' says Jessica. 'I have to finish this. Otherwise, Richard and I can never have a future.'

'No—'

'Give the gun to me.' She repeats the command. Like her father, she has become the executioner. Death can only be cheated so many times before luck runs out. She holds out her hand to him. 'I need to be the one to pull the trigger.'

FIFTY-THREE

Christine's eyes reminded her of amber, dangerous secrets caught in their dark depths. Her eyelashes fluttered but she refused to lower them when Samuel Newman handed the gun to Jessica.

Her anger had left her. In its place was acceptance. She had heard that people who were determined to end their lives gained peace of mind once the decision was made. Was that same calmness possible when a decision was made to take a life?

Such strength, such conviction as she pulled the trigger. One bullet to the head. She had to do it swiftly or she would falter; do it so fast that her father would not feel pain, shock, surprise, disappointment or betrayal.

She loved him. She hated him. The weight of her feelings held no imbalance and, in the end, she had no choice but to bring his story to an end.

He died instantly yet he seemed to take an eternity to fall. Christine's head was thrust deep into the pillow, her eyes finally squeezed closed. Ryan was frozen, his body half in and out of bed. They seemed suspended in the horror of that single, muffled sound.

Jessica dropped the gun. It hit the floor at the same instant as her father collapsed. She sank to her knees and tried to gather him into her arms. His body was soft and warm but heavy, so heavy. All she could do was cradle his head. His expression was blank, his face stripped of emotion. The wound was small, neat, almost, but there was blood, slick and flowing over her hands, drowning her in grief, tossing her on a current she would never be able to escape.

I need to be the one to pull the trigger. Her last words to him. Had he known what she intended to do when he entrusted his gun to her? Would he have understood her decision if she had told him about the last notation Christine made in her notebook? *Her name is Lisa. I've seen her birth certificate. Her mother died from a surfeit of love. Grace Cooper would never have allowed Dougie Barnes to take her daughter from her. That was why she had to die. Like Margaret... she stood in his way.*

Christine knelt beside her and took her bloodied hands in hers. 'Ryan has called an ambulance,' she said. 'It's on its way. So are the police.'

'I had to end it.' Jessica sounded disconnected, as if she was speaking through crossed wires. 'He killed my mothers.'

'I know... I know... shush... *shush*.' Christine was crying silently as she prised Jessica loose from her father and seated her on the edge of the bed.

The gun lay where she had dropped it. Neither of them picked it up. This was a crime scene. Everything would remain in place until the police arrived.

FIFTY-FOUR

'You're in deep shock,' Anna Leeson said, when she heard that Jessica intended to enter a guilty plea. Christine had phoned the solicitor as soon as Jessica had been led in handcuffs towards a squad car. 'You cannot possibly make such a momentous decision in the aftermath of this tragedy.'

'You mean in the aftermath of murdering my father.' The whys and wherefores were not important. Anna's cautions, her advice to make no comment to questions Jessica was unable or unwilling to answer, went unheeded during her interrogation at the garda station.

Without hesitation, she signed a statement claiming her guilt. The two detectives who interviewed her were impassive, a professional mask that never quite managed to hide their shock that she would admit to such a cold-blooded crime. In this new reality there was no room for doubt. She had his blood on her hands. His blood ran through her veins. It was time to atone.

At an emergency court hearing, a judge decided that her criminal connections made her a flight risk. She was a chameleon, capable of changing colour when the occasion demanded, he claimed. The SFDN group had imploded by then, and Jessica would be kept on remand until her case was heard.

Christine wanted to give evidence in court. To make a jury experience her terror, the drowning sensation that banished all rational thought when she opened her eyes and saw Samuel Newman standing before her. To describe the chill of steel against her temple, the belief that a bullet was about to spin her into an abyss. She would tell them that Jessica struggled to take the gun from him and how, in their struggle, he accidentally fired on himself.

She would not have faltered when she committed perjury. When it came to Jessica, right and wrong had overlapped.

'I would be dead if you hadn't intervened,' she said, when she visited Jessica at Long Acre where she had been placed on remand.

'No, you wouldn't,' Jessica replied. 'I knew exactly what I was doing.'

'Do you know what you're doing now?'

'I'm taking responsibility for my actions.'

'You have to listen to Anna and change your plea before you go to trial,' said Christine. 'She believes your defence team has an excellent chance of persuading a jury that when you discovered the enormity of your father's crimes, you were unable to cope with that information and it snapped something in you.'

'I've been psychiatrically assessed,' Jessica replied. 'I'm mentally accountable for what I did. As for his crimes, I discovered *nothing*. It was you who lifted the rock. He killed a woman I never had a chance to love. And Margaret...' The pummel of elbows, or, maybe, heels against her abdomen made her pause. She welcomed every movement, no matter how slight, and worried constantly that her stress was having an impact on her baby. 'I ran away from Siobhán Doolin in case I heard something I could no longer ignore. And Bessie, also – but it was impossible to keep running. I don't know if he drove the car that killed my mother, or pushed Margaret from Devil's Reach. But I know without a doubt that he organised their deaths, just as he organised the men who tried to kill you. He's the reason Richard almost died – but without proof, he would never have been brought to justice. All I had was my own conviction... in *here*.' She fisted her chest fiercely then forced herself to stop as Christine's eyes widened. Her mental state was constantly being evaluated. She was a puzzle to everyone except herself.

'What about your baby?' Christine asked. 'Are you willing to give birth in prison?'

'Yes, I am.' She saw with clarity; everything in the narrow confines of this new world was outlined sharply enough to hurt her eyes. 'I don't deserve to be a mother.'

'That's nonsense, Jessica. You can't honestly believe that.'

'I ruined your marriage and never gave a thought to the consequences.'

'If my marriage had been secure, you'd never have ruined it.' Christine spoke with some of her old authority. 'There's no going back for either of us now. And Richard, also. You're the mother of his child. He'll want you both with him when he leaves hospital.'

'I'm guilty, Christine. I carried out an execution. It seems I'm not so very different from my father, after all. I'm not going to change my plea.'

Patricide. The word horrified her but that was her crime. What would have happened if he had refused to hand over his gun? Such a risk to take... but she had gambled on his willingness to have control over her and, in doing so, he had signed his death warrant.

She would not waste the court's time with a drawn-out trial. No examination of witnesses, no jury to convince.

. . .

Jessica's trial was a formality where justice was swiftly administered. She caught a glimpse of her reflection as she was led from the prison van into the court and noticed a subtle difference to her shape. Her baby's head had dropped. She had been told that when this occurred, her breathing would become easier. It was impossible to imagine ever being able to breathe normally again.

When the judge passed down his judgement and decreed that she should serve life imprisonment, with her sentence to be reviewed after seven years, she managed to stay standing. She found the strength to turn away from the eyes that watched her from the gallery. Christine, sitting between Ryan and Richard, and Bessie Cooper, thin and taut as a bow, her hand raised in a gesture of gratitude.

A week after her trial, Jessica gave birth to Grace Margaret Stone. She welcomed the pain of labour. No epidural or any other relief options. Pain could have allowed her to scream and Richard begged her to do so. She gritted her teeth and held back an ocean, knowing that to release even a whimper would undo her. The midwife, a soft-voiced woman who had tended to other imprisoned mothers, tried to make the occasion as normal as possible when she laid the new-born baby on Jessica's chest.

The ocean broke then, a storm of tears washing over the head of her daughter. Richard enveloped them both in his arms. She had to hold on to this moment. It would be her comfort during the long nights, when every fibre of her body ached for the clutch of those soft baby fingers.

Grace could have stayed with her for a year at Long Acre. Facilities were provided for new mothers, but how could Jessica inflict the separation on Grace when their time together was over? As for herself, it would be enough to break her in two. Far better to cauterise that wound at source and return alone to prison from the hospital.

FIFTY-FIVE

LONG ACRE PRISON

Tonight, Jessica's mouth is dry, her heart palpitating unpleasantly. Somewhere along the corridor, a woman is screaming. She tries to identify the screamer but there is no discernible clue. The pitch is always the same. What must it be like to empty her diaphragm with such force? The unrestrained emotions at Long Acre run over her like stampeding hooves. The incense of desire is torrid. Cloying and inescapable, it blends with other scents that Jessica sometimes identifies but, often, is too fused with desperation to separate it from loneliness, lost hope, the heat of fury or the dreary rhythm of boredom and depression.

One miasma rises above the rest. It emanates from the mothers who have been separated from their children and is a closely guarded passion that they release into the quietness of the early hours. That is when grief and loss, the fear that they will be forgotten, grabs them by the throat and, sometimes, unable to control this storm of fear, they rail and rattle their cages.

. . .

In the therapy session, the circle of nine watches Jessica, their eyes filled with knowledge and an awareness of what she experiences each time she instinctively touches her stomach. Flat again, so trim and muscular ever since she started using the gym: spinning, lunges, squat presses, sweat and mindless counting, it stuns her mind and, marginally, tones down the voices in her head.

Six months have passed since she handed Grace over to Richard and Bessie Cooper. On visiting days, Richard carries their baby into the visiting room in a sling. He handles it with dexterity but to Jessica, it remains a mysterious tangle of straps and buckles. For thirty minutes, she can hold Grace and marvel at her skin, so downy; and those long, slender fingers, perfectly formed. Sometimes, she silently counts down the seconds so that time, a merciless thief, will not take her by surprise when it is time for them to leave.

They are precious visits that keep her sane until they come again.

Margaret continues to haunt Jessica's dreams. She stands in the doorway of the cottage. Her cries are drowned out by the ocean that will take her life a week later. Jessica forces the ocean into silence. This is her dream and her time to listen to Margaret.

She is covered in a film of sweat when she awakens. Always, when remembering their departure from Cullain, she heard only the promise made by Margaret to search the world for her.

Instead of recalling those whispered endearments, she listens to the threats that Margaret uttered, unaware that they would lead to her death. Crypts, she had said to the man she loved, her voice as raw as it was on the night he was stabbed. She had secrets to tell and she would shout them to the world if he left her behind. Deep in the realm of dreams, Jessica hears those same threats repeated and when she awakens, she struggles to cling on to what they revealed. A forgotten crypt once covered by the mulch of centuries is exposed by a lighter layer of time. And the bones hidden within it are young, so very young, and much loved.

Information. Such a powerful, dangerous tool.

Christine shaped the beginnings of a circle when she wandered from a wedding and lost herself in the life of Dougie Barnes and the death of Paul Niels. That night at Rosswall Heights, Jessica joined the bloodied edge of that circle. What goes around comes around.

EPILOGUE

The sun splinters on the iridescent glass that forms a curvature of justice around the courthouse. Journalists jockey for position on the pavement and the eye of a television camera probes Christine's expression as she approaches the Criminal Appeals Court; photographers also, their crablike sideways run, poised to grab that perfect shot. She ignores the shouted questions, allows the relentless click of cameras to merge with the passing traffic. She holds firmly to Richard's arm as they ascend the steps. The Foundation Stone partnership now sundered, yet still together.

The weight that has fallen from Richard since the shooting is still evident. His suit hangs badly on him and there is a gauntness about his face that speaks of sleepless nights. Today, a judgement will be read. They will discover what the future holds for Jessica. The person at the centre of the appeal remains behind bars at Long Acre.

In Rillingham-on-the-Weir, a massive police operation has drawn to a close. Thanks to Jessica, who had been enabled through therapy – and the circle of women who helped her – to recall the threats Margaret made on the night Samuel Newman and his daughter left Cullain, the remains of four young men were formally identified and their bodies removed from the old castle graveyard. Nature will once again lay claim to the crypt that remained hidden and forgotten until Dougie Barnes turned it into a burial chamber for his victims. But it was the evidence of Billy Macken, turned state witness, that shone a light on the activities of Samuel Newman and encouraged Jessica's defence team to launch an appeal against the severity of her sentence.

In a rare move away from the usual appeals procedure, Christine had been allowed to be a witness on Jessica's behalf. She described how the void she faced exploded into a million lights when Samuel Newman dropped to the floor. She hoped the judges would understand that his daughter – reared to believe in imaginary evils that hid the true depths of corruption – had saved two lives that night.

Anna tries to hide her nervousness behind a too-bright smile. Her voice is brisk with confidence but Richard is unable to pretend. His foot taps nervously on the floor as the judgement is read. His grip on Christine's hand is painful when they hear that Jessica's life sentence has been reduced. Taking into consideration the time she has served already, and in recognition of her good conduct record, along with her involvement in therapeutic activities, she will be granted periods of temporary release, beginning now, and continuing until her sentence comes to an end in another two years.

They leave the court together. The media clamour for attention. They demand a comment, words that will form a headline, a photograph that will tell a story. Is there a force that is mightier than the sum of all our parts? Christine wonders. A force that works in strange and mysterious ways to punish evil? Or does truth come about through the randomness of fate, the chaos of memory and the whim of unanticipated consequences?

At the bottom of the steps, a taxi waits to take her to the airport. Ryan will be waiting for her when her flight lands. Already, she feels the distance widening between her and

Richard. When he smiles at her, he looks like the man she once loved. She loves him still, but it is purely an echo that celebrates the happiness they shared for eleven years.

Bessie Cooper waits beyond the huddle of press and media. She holds a small child by the hand. Grace Margaret Stone has her father's dark hair and her mother's stunning green eyes. Her jawline is soft and unformed, her mouth a pout of love.

A LETTER FROM LAURA

Dear Reader,

Thank you for choosing to read *After the Wedding*. If you enjoyed it and would like to hear about when my next book is out, sign up below:

www.bookouture.com/laura-elliot

I hope you enjoyed the story and became engrossed in the lives of my two main characters, Christine and Jessica. For fifteen months I engaged with them on a daily basis. Whether I was at my writing desk or dealing with them in my head, they were my constant companions. We even holidayed together and, as the three short breaks I took during our Covid-dominated 2021 all had one thing in common – rain – I found it impossible to silence them.

I'm often asked where the idea for a new book originates. It's a hard question to answer. Usually, by the time a story is told, the idea that acted as a launch pad is so degraded that it has turned to dust. Particles may remain but the great thrust-off that began it all has been absorbed into the writing process, distilled into the development of plot and character, and the passage of time it takes to bring a book to its conclusion. *After the Wedding* followed the same path. I know that there were real-life incidents that planted seeds in my imagination; anecdotes that made me pause and wonder if they could be fictionalised; books and dramas that inspired me; yet they have all blended together into a mulching stew.

The only clear recollection I have of that 'juggling possibilities' phase is a memory from my very early years. I'm about three years old and walking with my father along the bank of the Grand Canal in Dublin. I remember everything with cut-glass precision: the black barges, the blue sky, the wending canal path. I feel the warmth of my father's hand, the sense that I am doing something that is grown-up and important. This cherished memory sums up those safe, contented early years, but I've been told many times about another incident that occurred around the same time.

My parents had a flat on the top storey of an old Georgian house. Somehow, I managed to climb out onto the window ledge and was sitting there, legs dangling, when my terrified mother crept up behind me and drew me back to safety. I'm sure she carried that memory to her grave yet I've no recollection of that incident. None whatsoever, despite my efforts to recall those trembling moments. Instead, my enduring memory is that serene canal walk I took with my father. Why one and not the other? Is that dangerous experience so deeply embedded in my unconscious mind that it is ordained never to rise to the surface?

The enduring dominance of memory intrigues me, as does its sleight-of-hand trickery, rose-tinted glasses and haunting resonances. And by the way it comes upon me, sometimes gently, sometimes slyly, sometimes with the force of a drum beat. Its power can bring me to a standstill, give me comfort, make me cringe, sob, laugh, yearn.

Usually, such deeply forgotten memories don't appear to have a trigger, though I suspect they must: something so transient that it flitted unnoticed past me. I imagine that state of unconsciousness as a place of stillness where all my memories are contained in separate, honeycombed cells. A fanciful image,

I admit, but I am an amateur when it comes to exploring the vast, fearsome sphere that contains all we have forgotten, and that waits to gather all we will forget.

If you enjoyed *After the Wedding* and would like to leave a short review on Amazon or a site of your choosing, I'd appreciate that very much. Also, if you would like to contact me, I'd be delighted to hear from you.

With warmest regards,

Laura Elliot

www.lauraelliotauthor.com

ACKNOWLEDGEMENTS

As always, I would like to thank my husband, Sean Considine, for his support throughout the writing of *After the Wedding*. He prises me loose from my writing desk and reminds me that the real world is just a step beyond our front door.

My adult children have flown the nest yet they are always only a visit or a phone call away. To Tony, Ciara and Michelle, and their spouses, Louise, Roddy and Harry, and my beloved grandchildren, Romy, Ava, Nina and Seán – thank you for being a constant presence in my life.

A special word of thanks must go to hypnotherapist, Helen Bradley. She generously gave her time to me as she guided me through the hypnotherapy scenes with sensitivity and insightfulness.

Thank you to my editor, Claire Bord, for her commitment, her rigorous and sensitive editing, her support and willingness to discuss all elements of my work.

Thank you to Belinda Jones and Claire Rushbrook for their diligent scrutiny of my manuscript, and to Lisa Horton for a delightful cover.

Promotion and marketing are key elements when it comes to sending a book into the great outdoors, and I'm grateful to Kim Nash, Noelle Holten, Sarah Hardy, Jess Readett, Alex Crow, Melanie Price, Occy Car and Ciara Rosney.

Lastly, but definitely not least, I'd like to thank my readers. You are the most important link on the chain. I appreciate your support, your reviews, your emails and messages of goodwill. I thank you from the bottom of my heart.

Printed in the USA
CPSIA information can be obtained
at www.ICGtesting.com
LVHW041514050524
779418LV00008B/223